One INDECENT NIGHT

A.M. HARGROVE

Cover Design by Maria @ Steamy Designs

Cover Photo by Eric McKinney Photography

Cover Model: Michael Scanlon

Editing: My Brother's Editor

Proofreading: Rosa @I Scream Proofreading Services

For the lovers of The West Brothers Novels

You don't love someone for their looks, or their clothes, or for their fancy car, but because they sing a song only you can hear.

— OSCAR WILDE

CONTENTS

Stalk Me	1
Prologue	6
One	10
Two	15
Three	21
Four	27
Five	32
Six	37
Seven	41
Eight	46
Nine	53
Ten	59
Eleven	64
Twelve	70
Thirteen	76
Fourteen	82
Fifteen	88
Sixteen	94
Seventeen	100
Eighteen	106
Nineteen	112
Twenty	119
Twenty-One	126
Twenty-Two	132
Twenty-Three	139
Twenty-Four	148
Twenty-Five	155
Twenty-Six	159
Twenty-Seven	166
Twenty-Eight	173
Twenty-Nine	182
Thirty	188

Thirty-One	195
Thirty-Two	200
Thirty-Three	205
Thirty-Four	212
Thirty-Five	218
Thirty-Six	224
Thirty-Seven	232
Thirty-Eight	237
Thirty-Nine	243
Forty	249
Forty-One	255
Forty-Two	262
Forty-Three	267
Forty-Four	272
Forty-Five	276
Forty-Six	282
Forty-Seven	286
Forty-Eight	291
Forty-Nine	299
Fifty	305
Fifty-One	311
Fifty-Two	318
Fifty-Three	323
Fifty-Four	329
Fifty-Five	334
Fifty-Six	340
Fifty-Seven	349
Fifty-Eight	356
Fifty-Nine	363
Epilogue	370
Follow Me	379
Acknowledgments	382
About The Author	384

STALK ME

If you would like to hear more about what's going on in my world, please subscribe to my mailing list on my website at
http://bit.ly/AMNLWP
You can also join my private group—Hargrove's Hangout & Hellions— on Facebook if you're up to some crazy shenanigans! Please stalk me. I'll love you forever if you do. Seriously.

www.amhargrove.com
Twitter @amhargrove1
www.facebook.com/amhargroveauthor
www.facebook.com/anne.m.hargrove
www.goodreads.com/amhargrove1
Instagram: amhargroveauthor
Pinterest: amhargrove1
annie@amhargrove.com

For Other Books by A.M. Hargrove visit www.amhargrove.com/book/

The West Sisters Novels:
One Indecent Night

One Shameless Night (TBD)
One Blissful Night (TBD)

The West Brothers Novels:
From Ashes to Flames
From Ice to Flames
From Smoke to Flames

For The Love of English
For The Love of My Sexy Geek (The Vault)
I'll Be Waiting (The Vault)

The Men of Crestview:
A Special Obsession
Chasing Vivi
Craving Midnight

Cruel and Beautiful
A Mess of a Man
One Wrong Choice
A Beautiful Sin

The Wilde Players Dirty Romance Series:
Sidelined
Fastball
Hooked

Worth Every Risk

The Edge Series:
Edge of Disaster
Shattered Edge
Kissing Fire

The Tragic Duet:

Tragically Flawed, Tragic 1
Tragic Desires, Tragic 2

The Hart Brothers Series:
Freeing Her, Book 1
Freeing Him, Book 2
Kestrel, Book 3
The Fall and Rise of Kade Hart

Sabin, A Seven Novel

The Guardians of Vesturon Series

One INDECENT NIGHT

PROLOGUE

SYLVIE

Groaning, I rolled over, or tried to anyway. My head clanged like the Liberty Bell—that is if it could still actually clang—and my mouth felt like a hundred possums had died in it. What the hell had happened? "Ugh, water. I need water."

"Hang on a sec, sweets. I'll get you some," a deep, sexy voice said.

Wait a second. I had my own hotel room. Who the hell was that? I opened one eye and saw a man's naked ass climbing out of bed and walking to the small fridge. I might add, said ass was perfectly formed and sculpted with those hot indentations on the sides that flawless muscular men had. He bent down, grabbed two waters, and turned back toward the bed.

Oh, fuck no. Please, God tell me I didn't sleep with Evan Thomas, my cousin's best friend.

I lifted the covers ever so slightly and yep, I was bare-assed naked too.

Ahh, double fuck. I was so screwed.

Mr. Hot and Sexy Muscular Ass and Perfect Face and Body, Evan, slid back into bed and handed me a water after he opened the bottle. "Here ya go, sweets. How ya feeling?"

I swallowed. "Uh, er, not too good."

"Yeah, I kept telling you last night to take it easy on the Reposado, but you kept telling me it was fine."

"I did?" I mumbled into the sheets.

"Uh huh. Your exact words were, 'I'm a tequila expert, slick. Pass me that bottle.'"

"I did?" I actually squeaked the words out that time.

"Yep, and that was after you kicked your shoes off dancing on the table. Then we never could find them. You jumped on my back, begging for a piggyback ride, slapping my ass the whole time, yelling, 'Yeehaw. Giddy-up, slick.'"

"Oh, God." I buried my face in the pillow.

"Hey, you were positively adorable. Pearson never told me how much fun his cousin was."

Suddenly, the pillow I was hiding behind vanished, and he was hovering over me. "Sylvie, you can't hide from me." Then his mouth dipped to kiss me.

"No!"

He backed away and asked, "What's wrong, sweets?"

"You can't kiss me!"

"Why not. After what we did last night, I wouldn't think you'd be opposed to a little kiss."

Oh, God, what the hell did we do last night?

"My breath smells," I yelled, "like a bunch of dead possums."

He stared at me a second, then said, "I love dead possums," right before he kissed me. This was no casual peck on the lips. This was the real deal—he even gave me tongue. Jesus, I needed to get him the hell out of here. Wait. What if I was in *his* room? Fuck, fuckery, fuck. How did I let myself end up in this situation? Oh, right. I was drunk off my ass.

"Hey, sweets. Let's get dressed and go eat. I'm starved. But how about a little shower action first?" He took my hand and pulled.

"W-wait. You have to fill in the blanks."

"Huh?"

7

"I'm sorry, but my memory is a bit fuzzy." I finally confessed to him.

Why, oh why did I do that? It was the worst thing I could've done. Instead of insulting him, he treated me to his woman-killer smile. It always had melted me. This time, my heart nearly combusted. Perfect teeth, lips, and a face to match, he was every woman's dream. Dark hair, all tousled from a night's sleep—or maybe rough sex—bright green eyes and that damn sexy body, made my vagina clench.

"Sweets, you were *crazy wild* in bed." He winked. "I'm talking my kind of woman."

What the hell did I do? I always considered myself tame between the sheets.

"Um, would you care to explain?"

His cheeks turned positively pink! Oh shit. That spelled huge trouble.

"Yeah, well, first you jumped on the bed like a five-year-old. Then you stripped and jumped on the bed, and sweets, it was fabulous. Then you undressed me and made me jump on the bed, but you got worried my head would hit the ceiling, even though I tried to tell you it wouldn't. And then ..." He rubbed his face and looked very sheepish. What could I possibly have done that embarrassed him so?

"What? Tell me!"

"Yeah, okay, you went down on me like a Dyson, and then asked me if I owned a butt plug."

"I what?" I choked on the words.

"Uh huh. And you wanted to know if I had any handcuffs to which I said no. Then you asked if I would spank you, which I did. Your ass was a lovely shade of pink. You wanted to know how good of a flogger I was. I admitted not good at all, seeing as I'd never flogged anyone."

"Flogger?"

"Yep. Said you'd always wanted your clit flogged."

"My cl...oh, my God. Stop. I don't want to know anymore." I

wanted to crawl into the deepest hole and die. Clit flogging? Where the hell did that come from?

"Out of curiosity, is that a real thing? Clit flogging?"

"How would I know? I've never heard of it until now."

"Weird. Ever since you mentioned it, it's made me wonder."

My hand unconsciously reached for said clit. "Wouldn't that hurt?" I asked, cringing.

"No clue, seeing as I don't have one. A clit that is."

"I have to go." I tried to get up.

"Sweets, we need to shower first. All that sex we had last night, we sort of reek."

Sniff, sniff. The entire room smelled of sex now that he mentioned it. "Whose room is this?"

"It's yours."

Thank fuck. "Evan, what time is it?"

"Nine thirty, why?"

"Oh, shit. Oh fuck. Evan, I'm happy we had a great time last night and all, but I have an eleven o'clock plane to catch so you need to leave. Now."

"Wow. I've never had to do the walk of shame before."

"Sorry, but I have to hurry. So, if you can hurry up and get dressed and go, I'd really appreciate it."

"No problem. But Sylvie, one thing first. This thing between us. It's far from over." He dropped another kiss on my lips, flashed me a sexy grin and got out of bed. Damn, the guy was one sexy dude.

But he was completely wrong. This thing between us was dead and buried. I would never show my face to him again, under any circumstances.

He dressed and left. After he was gone, I wondered a lot of things. Did he use a condom? Was he clean? How many times did we do it? From the feel of things between my thighs, it was a lot. Damn, why did I get myself into this mess?

ONE

SYLVIE

MONDAY MORNING, I DRAGGED MY TIRED BUTT INTO THE office. Starr greeted me with a huge smile filled with questions. Everyone would want to know how the wedding was. After all, one of our counselors, Rose, had married my cousin, Pearson, who happened to have been one of our patients here. It wasn't every day something like that occurred. Actually, it never had happened before. Theirs had been under very unusual circumstances, to say the least, and was a long, complicated story, best told by them, as it wasn't mine to tell.

"So? How was it?" Starr asked.

"Ugh."

"Is that a good ugh or a bad ugh?"

"Both," I answered.

Starr clapped her hands and followed me down to my office. "I can't wait to hear all the details. How did she look? And Pearson? What about him?" she asked the questions in a dreamy tone. Pearson was one of the best looking guys ever, and all the women here talked about him when he was an in-patient. Honestly, it was hard not to. Even I noticed and I was his cousin.

"Give me a minute. I need more coffee."

"Oh, I can get that."

Before she even got out of my office, Leeanne, the director of Flower Power Serenity Center, stuck her head in and said, "Well? Was it absolutely fabulous?"

"Grrrr."

"Wow, someone's in a bad mood today," she said with a grin.

"Here," Starr said, handing me a huge mug of my favorite brew. "This should help."

Leeanne took a seat across from my desk as I plopped into the chair and tossed my bag down. "I guess you can tell I had way too much fun. The fact is, I haven't had that much fun since college," I groaned, putting my head in my hand.

"That bad? You need some essential oils." She jumped to her feet, took my diffuser out, and a few minutes later, the oils were permeating the air. "This will make you feel better in no time." Leeanne was a huge believer in oils and we had them everywhere in the center. Then she stuck a floral wreath on my head for some extra help.

"Thanks."

"Now can we have all the juicy details?" Starr asked.

"All right. The wedding was gorgeous, along with the bride and her little flower girl." I was referring to Montana, the bride, Sylvie's, daughter. She was precious. "They both wore similar dresses, carried similar bouquets, and wore similar floral head wreaths. Here, let me show you." I pulled out my phone and showed them pictures my sisters had taken.

They both oohed and ahhed over them, along with the pictures of Pearson.

"Who are they?" they asked about the men with Pearson.

Those are Pearson's brothers, Grey and Hudson, and that one is his best friend.

Leeanne asked, "Are you serious? Does he know any normal looking people?"

"Right? It was a den of hot men."

"Are they married?" Starr asked.

"Yes, but the best friend is single."

We were interrupted then by one of the front desk admins. "Sylvie, I have a delivery for you." She came in with a huge bouquet of red and white roses and set them on my desk.

"My, oh, my. Someone has an admirer," Leeanne said.

I frowned as I took the small card out. My frown deepened as I read it.

I MISS YOU ALREADY, sweets, and can't wait to see you again.
Evan

"OH NO."

"What?" Starr asked.

I crumpled the note and tossed it into the trash, jumped to my feet, and chased down the admin. When I caught her, I said, "Lisa, if anyone named Evan calls for me, tell him I'm not in and whatever you do, don't give him my number. Cell or office line."

"Sure, Sylvie."

"Thanks."

By the time I got back to my office, Leeanne and Starr were practically drooling for information.

"What was that all about?" Leeanne asked.

I sighed and stared at the beautiful flowers. Then I suggested she take them.

"You can't be serious."

"Yes, I am."

"Who're they from?" Starr asked.

"No one."

Leeanne was too perceptive to buy this. "Sylvie, why are you acting so strange?"

"I really screwed up," I groaned. Then I gave them sketchy details of what happened at the wedding with Evan. Of course, I left out the part where he fucked my brains out.

"And you don't want to see that hot hunk of muscular love

again?" Leeanne asked. Leave it to her to come up with a phrase like that. If she only knew what had really happened, she'd understand why I was running scared with my tail tucked between my thighs.

"No! Pearson said if I ever so much as got near him, he'd personally kill me. Apparently, Evan is the worst kind of womanizer. And if Pearson said that, he must be the man-whore to end all man-whores because Pearson was one himself."

Leeanne gave me a pointed look. "Just because you go out with him doesn't mean you have to sleep with him."

It took every ounce of control I had not to squirm under her gaze. "I do realize that, but it's best to stay away." My hands suddenly became an item of interest to me.

"Hmm, I think you're crazy. I would hop on that pony and say giddy-up in a heartbeat."

My head jerked up so fast, I almost pulled a muscle in my neck. Could she possibly know? There's no way.

"You'd what?" Starr asked, laughing.

"Hell yeah. Did you take a close look at him? Womanizer or not, I wouldn't pass up that opportunity for anything. As they said in my day, I'd let that man eat crackers in my bed any time."

"I don't get it," Starr said.

Leeanne rolled her eyes, which made me snort. I was the biggest snorter around when I laughed. Leeanne was the last person you'd ever expect to give an eye roll.

"It means that I wouldn't mind if he left crumbs in my bed. You know, eating crackers, and leaving the messy crumbs on your sheets?"

Starr stared at her with a lost expression.

"Oh, never mind," Leeanne said. "Anyway, Sylvie, I think you're crazy. Grab that man, latch on with both hands, and take that thing for a spin. He's the absolute Lamborghini of men. That's my advice and that's all I'm going to say."

If only she knew I'd taken that thing for a spin, and worn out the tires, she'd be shocked. Maybe I should ask her about clit flogging. No, I'd best keep my mouth shut on that one.

My phone rang, interrupting us. "Sylvie West." It was Lisa, the admin. After I hung up, I wanted to die.

"What now?" Leeanne asked.

"He called."

"And?" Her eyes lit up like sparklers.

"I told Lisa to tell him I wasn't in. He said he'd call back later."

"Well, Ms. West, what are you going to do? The man sounds persistent."

"I don't know."

"Ride that pony," Starr said. "I'm on his side. He can't be that bad if he's your cousin's bestie."

Why can't Rose be here when I needed her the most? And there was no way I would call and interrupt their honeymoon. I was a big girl and could take care of my own problems.

Oh, yeah, I sure did a great job of demonstrating that at their reception.

TWO

EVAN

Sylvie West. Her name rolled off my tongue like velvet, exactly like her pussy had. I could not stop thinking about her. This was the first time a woman had affected me so. And to think she had forced me to do the walk of shame. Every time I thought about it, my mouth curved into a smile. But what did me in the most was her lack of inhibitions between the sheets. I adored how free and easy she was. Why couldn't every woman be that way? I couldn't stand when they played shy until you coaxed them out of their shell and all of a sudden, they became insatiable.

The flight home from St. Lucia had been unbearable. I kept thinking about how it would've been great if we could've become members of the mile high club. That was the wrong thing to think of too, because I ended up with the worst erection the entire flight.

Even now, I kept replaying Saturday night in my head, seeing her jumping on the bed, naked, and how she sucked me off. She was fabulous. If I didn't pull my head out of this scene, I'd be in huge trouble. But, if I didn't see her again soon, I didn't know how I would cope. I sounded like a teenager in puppy love. What the fuck. *Think with your brain and not your dick, Evan.*

I was in the elevator, on my way up to StarWorks Financial when an idea struck. I would hit her up with some flowers this morning. I knew she worked in the rehab center Pearson had gone to. I had been there the day he checked out, but couldn't remember the name of the place. I could always call my mom. She never forgot those kinds of things.

My feet chewed up the floor as I didn't waste time getting to my office. The receptionist greeted me as I walked in.

"Good morning, Mr. Thomas."

"Morning, Sharon."

"Can I send coffee down?"

I called back, "Yes, thanks," and kept moving.

My assistant, Cole, was already at his desk when I rounded the corner. He rose when he saw me.

"Mr. Thomas. How are you this morning?"

"Just fine, Cole. And you?"

"Fine, sir."

I was the CEO of a hedge fund I'd started. Cole was a great assistant. I was grooming him to become a compliance officer.

"What's on the agenda for today?" I asked.

"The Director of Compliance sent up the reports you requested on the acquisition you're looking into. I've reviewed them and everything looked good to me. They're on your desk, sir. You have an appointment with Brightwater today. Mr. O'Quinn will be joining you, of course." Tom O'Quinn was the CFO.

"What time is the meeting?"

"Eleven in the conference room and then lunch afterward."

"Good. Plan to be there. I want you to sit in and take notes for me."

"Mr. Thomas, are you sure?"

I frowned. "Have I ever asked you to do anything I wasn't sure of?"

"No, sir."

"Be prepared. I want you to know all the facts and figures for

Brightwater. Can you tell me right now what your opinion of them is?"

"Yes, sir. I think they would be a good addition to our portfolio."

This was a test I hadn't let him prepare for. "Why?"

"They are above board in everything. No violations of any kind regarding compliance. Their returns are solid. Nothing to indicate anything out of order. I like where they are going with some of their investments. They're looking at things that some of our other accounts are avoiding, such as some of the tech investments others seem to be missing."

"Tell me more."

"Mr. Thomas, I'm heavily involved in the video gaming industry."

"Go on."

"I actually compete, for fun and for money."

My brows rose. He flushed when he noticed. "Is that a fact? And just so you know, I'm not judging you. I'm only interested."

"Yes, I'm actually on a team where we compete nationally. This is why my interest is so keen. Some of these smaller stocks yield excellent returns, such as AVID. You may want to check them out. But Brightwater invests in these and that's one of the reasons I'm a fan."

"Good to know. I'll dig in a little deeper then."

My coffee arrived and after my second cup, I was finished with my review of the compliance reports. The team had done an excellent job of vetting Brightwater. I went on to investigate some of the tech stocks that Cole had mentioned, and again, I was impressed. It would be good to have these on board for more diversification. This fund seemed to be something Star-Works could certainly benefit from.

First, I sent a congratulatory email to the Director of Compliance and her team on doing such a thorough job. Then I called Cole in.

"You wanted to see me, sir?"

"Yes. Good job on this. I'm curious. On all these tech stocks, a few of them are traded under different names, and in the Chinese market. I want more information on the solidarity of the Chinese gaming industry. I don't want to jump in feet first and have the whole dam thing collapse. Understand?"

"Absolutely. But the industry is so huge and even part of Vegas now, I hardly think that's an issue."

"Which of them do you recommend over the others?" I asked.

"The Chinese actually own several of the gaming stocks. One of them, Ace High, has produced the most. It's traded under the name Trevor. They developed the number one game in the industry. I'm sure you've heard of it—Day Light?"

I chuckled. "This is completely out of my league. I played Game Boy when I was ten."

"Game Boy? Like Mario?"

"Yeah. I loved Super Mario."

"Well, you need to get up to date, sir. The gaming industry is nothing like that now."

"I don't imagine it is. Don't you compete with people online?"

"Exactly."

"To be honest, I don't have much time for that."

"I'm not a huge sleeper so I do it during the night."

"You're still young, Cole. Wait until you're my age."

He laughed. "Mr. Thomas, you're what? Thirty-five?"

"On the nose."

"I'm not that far behind you at twenty-seven."

"Just wait." I remembered thinking that when I was his age. "Thanks for the information. Be ready to head to the conference room at ten forty-five."

"Yes, sir."

After closing the door, I ran a quick search on rehab centers in Westchester County and ironically, there were over a dozen. That left me with looking at each one of them. It didn't take long for me to locate Flower Power Serenity Center. The pictures of the place were the giveaway, especially when I saw the VW van decorated with all the flowers and peace symbols. I called the number listed and asked if a Sylvie West worked there. The woman who answered wasn't very open to my question, so I told her it was only because I wanted to send flowers. She immediately answered. My next call was to place the order and send the message. I hoped Sylvie was impressed, because the bouquet she was about to receive was going to be quite large.

After waiting for about an hour, I called the center back and asked to speak to Sylvie. I was put on hold, but when the receptionist came, she told me Sylvie wasn't in. I asked for her cell phone number, but she wouldn't give it to me.

I went back to work and in no time, Cole reminded me of our appointment. Grabbing all the reports I'd need, I placed them in my bag and met him outside my office. We proceeded to the conference room and took our seats as we waited for the others.

Cole was nervous, but I reassured him. "You'll be fine. I'm not going to put you on the spot or anything. All you have to do is take notes and remember their names."

He visibly relaxed. "Thank you, sir."

Everyone trickled in and the meeting began with introductions. It ran very smoothly and at the end, the officers of our company excused ourselves in order to discuss things. We all voted unanimously to make the offer. Brightwater accepted, and we went to lunch to celebrate. I was excited to get them added to our portfolio.

When we returned to the office, Cole emailed me his notes an hour later. That's when I decided to try Sylvie again. This time, she told me Sylvie was gone for the day. It wasn't even three yet. Was she ill? I asked, but the receptionist wouldn't tell me.

"Are you sure you can't give me her cell phone. I'm her

cousin, Pearson's, best friend. You must remember him. He married Rose, one of your employees."

"Yes, I remember him, but we're not allowed to give out anyone's number without their permission."

"I understand. I'll call back tomorrow. Thank you."

I'd never felt such great disappointment as I had then. Talking to Sylvie was going to have to wait another day.

THREE

SYLVIE

D URING THE PAST FIVE DAYS, EVAN HAD CALLED THE CENTER at least a dozen times. I couldn't keep asking the front desk to tell him I wasn't here. Eventually I'd have to talk to him, but that was the last thing I wanted.

Rose wouldn't be back until next Wednesday and I couldn't wait. She was the only one I'd spill my guts to. I hadn't even told my sisters what had happened. On the flight home from St. Lucia, they'd tried their best to wheedle the information out of me, but all I said was, he'd escorted me to my room and that was it. Only every time his name was mentioned, my face turned an unsightly shade of red, and Piper would elbow me in the ribs. They knew something had happened between us. I just refused to confess to it.

At work, Lisa told me she would not keep fielding my calls anymore. The man had been nothing but polite. He not only sent me flowers but every day something wonderful had arrived. On Tuesday, a delicious breakfast of cinnamon pancakes, a large coffee latte, and a chocolate chip cookie with a lovely note was delivered to me. The note said:

. . .

GOOD MORNING SWEETS,
   Something delicious and sweet for my girl.
Evan

EVEN I HAD TO ADMIT, it caused my belly to flutter—not a little but a lot. I devoured those pancakes and they were the best I'd ever eaten. I'd never tell Rose though, because I'd always thought hers were until now.

I thought that would be it because I still wasn't taking his calls, but no. On Wednesday, at eleven forty-five, a scrumptious lunch of a lobster salad showed up. How did he know lobster was my favorite? It was served with a light champagne dressing, a small crusty loaf of bread, butter, and for dessert, a creme brûlée. Oh, man, he was killing me. Whoever said the way to a man's heart is through his stomach had it wrong. It was the way to a woman's heart. This time, his note said:

MY SWEETS:
   I hope your day is as wonderful as you are.
Yours,
Evan

SURELY, this would be the last if I didn't pick up the phone and thank him. But no. On Thursday, a huge box arrived. Inside was a perfectly naughty thong and matching bra, along with a flogger. I slammed the lid back on the box and stuffed it under my desk. Holy shit, what in the hell was he thinking? My hands trembled as I opened his note.

SWEETS:
   My curiosity is still piqued. What about yours?

Yours,
Evan

MY CORE TIGHTENED and I rubbed my flaming cheeks. Jesus, there was sweat on my upper lip. How could he do this to me? I hadn't seen him in what? A week? Almost. It seemed like a century. What was wrong with me? He should be out of my system by now.

That night when I got home, I opened the box, which hadn't been easy to sneak out of the building. I worked with some nosey fuckers. I had to stay late and then wrap a sweater around it so no one would ask any questions. Luckily, most of them had already left for the day and the evening shift had arrived.

When I checked out the flogger, I was fascinated. The handle was purple and black braided leather while the strands were black. My fingers touched the long, soft lengths of suede, wondering how it would feel to have him use it on me. I was instantly aroused. Maybe there was a hidden side of kinkiness to me I didn't realize was there. I put the flogger away and picked up the thong. But when I inspected it, it wasn't a thong at all. It was a pair of crotchless panties. Good Lord, the man was bold. I stuffed them in the same drawer with the flogger and tried to forget about them. Only it was impossible. I ended up using my vibe to get rid of the wicked feelings they evoked.

On Friday, I dragged myself into the center. Lisa stopped me and said, "I'm done. If he calls today, I'm sending it through."

"Fine." I was done holding him off too. If the man couldn't take a hint, I would have to pull up the big girl pants and tell him. I was too tired to argue with her anyway. That stupid flogger had kept me up all night. All I could do was think about what it would actually feel like if he used it between my thighs.

I opened my office door and practically threw my crap on the desk. Coffee was an urgent necessity, so I marched to the cafeteria and grabbed two huge mugs worth. On my way back, I bumped into Leeanne, literally, and spilled one of them down my white shirt.

"Shit."

"Sorry, Sylvie. I wasn't looking."

"Same. And I didn't bring an extra shirt today."

"I don't have one either. Maybe someone up front does."

"I'll check." I cursed myself for taking my sweater home last night, and then I cursed Evan for sending me that flogger, which in turn, forced me to use the sweater to hide the box, and which also had made me tired. Dammit.

I went to my office and called Lisa. "Hey, you don't by any chance have an extra shirt here, do you?"

"No, sorry, but I was just getting ready to call you. You have a visitor."

"I do? Who is it?"

"Says he's your cousin. Tall, dark, and super sexy," she whispered into the phone.

Chuckling, I said, "Yeah, that must be Grey. Send him back."

"Is he Pearson's brother?"

"Yeah."

"Gah, he's dreamy."

"They all are."

"I'll tell him to come now."

I was dabbing at my coffee stain when a knock sounded on the door. "Come on in, Grey."

The door opened, and he walked in. "It's not Grey."

My head jerked up to see Evan standing there. "What are you doing here?"

"Sorry for the subterfuge, but I had to find a way to see you. You're quite stubborn, you know."

"So you lied?"

He shrugged. "With permission."

I gawked at him. "What does that mean?"

"It means I spoke to Grey first. He said it was okay."

"Oh, my God. You're both conspiring against me."

"Sweets, I only wanted to return something of yours and you gave me such a hard time of it, this was the only way I knew how."

"What are you talking about?"

He reached into his pocket and pulled out a thong. Then the bastard dangled it in front of me. "Recognize this?"

Shit. It was mine. I went to snatch it, but he pulled it out of my reach. "Oh, no. It won't be that easy. In order to get it back, you have to go to dinner with me."

"What? That's blackmail."

"Not really. What will I do to you if you don't go?"

He really couldn't do anything.

"See, you get my point. We can go anywhere you'd like, as long as it's a sit down dinner where they have a great wine list."

"And if I choose not to go?"

He smirked. "That's easy. I get to keep this." Then the asshole put it up to his nose and inhaled. "Ahh, my favorite scent."

Fuck! My face heated to a million degrees. Why me?

"You know, that flush quite suits you."

"Shut up."

"Such an angry pussycat."

I wished I had pussycat claws right now. He'd be feeling the brunt of them. "When would this dinner take place?"

"Tomorrow."

"Yes. What time?"

"My driver will pick you up at six."

"Your driver?" He had a driver?

"Yes. See you then."

"Um, Evan, how shall I dress?"

"I prefer you *undressed*, but cocktail attire is fine. Oh, and here." He dug into his pocket again and handed me an envelope. "Enjoy."

I stared at the envelope briefly and when I glanced up, he was gone. The envelope was thick and fancy. I tore it open and inside was a gift certificate for an undetermined amount to a local spa for tomorrow morning. Jeez. This guy was full of surprises. I called the number and they had me scheduled for a full-body massage, facial, manicure, pedicure, and Brazilian. I'd be getting the royal treatment.

Then I thought about the waxing. Well, he'd already seen me down there so I guess he knew I was bare. What was the big deal? Did he have plans or something? If he did, he'd be in for a big surprise. That part of *us* was over and he'd just have to take it like a big boy.

FOUR
EVAN

I MADE A RESERVATION AT ONE OF THE MOST EXCLUSIVE restaurants in the city. We were going to have our meal prepared tableside by one of the best chefs in town. Sylvie had no idea of my financial worth or the strings I could pull to get what I wanted, and I planned to keep it that way. She probably didn't even know where I worked or lived, for that matter, and that was fine by me.

We hadn't kept up much after Pearson and I went to college. The only thing I remembered about her was that she tried to follow us around when she was twelve or thirteen. Pearson had always been kind to her, but I thought she'd been annoying as hell. She was lanky, wore braces, and was in that awkward stage everyone went through. He'd stick up for her telling me I had to be nice to her. I'd never had any siblings, being an only child, so I was a spoiled brat. Of course, being an older teenager who'd thought I was cool as hell, didn't help either. I did as he asked, never knowing what a beauty she'd grow up to be. Then the few times I'd pop over to the West's when I was home on break, I recalled seeing her a time or two but never paid her much attention. Pearson told me if I ever so much as touched her, I was a dead man. Not that I was interested, but by then, I had quite a reputation with the ladies, and he wanted to protect his cousin. Too bad I hadn't bothered to check out what was right under my nose.

Tonight I would take the time to really get to know Sylvie. That was, if I didn't make a fool out of myself and ogle the poor woman to death. She had sailed through her awkward stage with flying colors and it was baffling as to how she hadn't been swept away by some lucky bastard. Maybe if I played my hand right, I'd be that lucky bastard and she'd end up as mine. So far, my plan hadn't worked too well. After she slapped me on the ass at the reception, my mind was made up. She was the one for me. No other woman had attracted me like she had. She was the honey and I was the bee. If only she realized when I had.

I hoped she enjoyed her day at the spa. I had tipped them very nicely to ensure she was pampered and given the royal treat-ment. Hopefully, it would help her relax for tonight. Those claws of hers needed to stay retracted because if I had my way, we were going to have a repeat of last Saturday night, which would include the use of the flogger I gave her. It looked so enticing, I'd bought one for myself.

I checked the time and noted my driver should be here any time. I gave myself one last glance in the mirror and headed to the kitchen. I'd given the housekeeper the rest of the weekend off. If we came back here, I wouldn't risk any interruptions. I grabbed the chilled bottle of Cristal in the refrigerator, along with a bucket, and two champagne glasses. By the time I'd place the bottle in the bucket and filled it with ice, my driver, Robert arrived.

"Let me take care of that for you, sir."

"Thank you, Robert. And how are you this evening?"

"Fine, sir. And you?"

"I'll know more after we pick up Ms. West."

Robert finished with the champagne, grabbed a linen towel from the kitchen, along with some cocktail napkins, something I wouldn't have thought to bring.

"Excellent idea, Robert. You always remind me of why I hired you."

"I try, sir."

"You do more than try. You accomplish."

"Thank you, sir. Shall we?"

"We shall." We took the elevator from the penthouse directly to the parking garage, where the limo awaited.

"May I speak freely, sir?"

"Of course."

"I don't remember during my time with you ever taking you out on a date."

"There's a reason for that. You haven't."

"The lady must be important, sir."

"She is, only she doesn't realize it yet."

"I see, sir."

"Robert, I hope she does."

He chuckled. "You never seem to have issues in that department, according to the news."

"This one is different. She has taken a lot of persuading."

"Sir, if anyone can do it, you can."

"I appreciate your vote of confidence. You have her address?"

"I do, sir."

"Excellent." I raised the glass partition in order to get some work done on the way. Robert had been with me several years and didn't think this rude. He understood I used every spare minute I had in order to enjoy the rest of my free time when possible.

It wasn't long before his voice came over the speakers. "Sir, we're here."

Shutting my phone off, I glanced up to see we were parked in front of a small brick townhouse. I exited the limo and walked to her door. There was a sign on it that said, "Enter At Your Own Risk." Her sense of humor shone again, as it did at the reception. I was determined to see that side of her again tonight.

I pushed the buzzer and a long minute later, the door swung open. My mouth watered at the sight of her.

"Sylvie," I breathed.

"Evan."

"Are you ready?"

"Don't I look it?"

I offered her my arm with a smile. "Sweets, you would look ready if you had nothing on."

"Don't get smart with me, Evan."

"Never. I'm only being honest."

As she gazed at me, I gave her my best innocent look. She harrumphed, then checked out where we were headed.

"You rented a limo for the night?"

"Something like that."

"Wow, you really are trying to impress me."

"Babe, you ain't seen nothin' yet."

She took in the interior and then responded, "Just so you know, I'm not easily impressed."

"Fair enough."

I reached for the bottle of champagne and popped the cork. After pouring the first glass, I handed it to her. Then I poured one for me."

"Cheers," I said as we clinked glasses.

"Yum, this is delicious," she said, licking her lips, the very ones I was dying to kiss.

"It is."

"What is this?"

I lifted the bottle so she could read the label.

"Wow. You are going all out, aren't you?"

"As I said, I aim to please. Tell me, Sylvie, how was your day at the spa?"

"Oh. I didn't go."

As usual, the woman stunned me. "Why's that?"

"I had other plans for today, so I changed my appointment for next weekend."

"I see." She had the most unusual way of thwarting everything I tried to do. No one ever did that to me.

"You're angry."

"No, I'm not."

"Evan, I'm a psychologist and trained to read people. Why are your hands clenched and your knuckles white?"

"Why do you thwart me in every possible way?"

"I don't."

I chuckled. "Then what do you call it? I'm only trying to be nice."

"You didn't take the hint."

"The hint?"

"That I didn't want to see you."

"You wouldn't even give me a chance."

"The reason for that is I didn't want to."

"Why is that? We had such a great time together. What are you afraid of?"

"I'm not afraid."

Now it was my turn. "Sylvie, I'm a businessman and I'm trained to close deals. Why are you lying to me?"

Her gray eyes landed on mine and I'd definitely hit on something. Whether or not she'd actually explain it to me would remain to be seen.

FIVE
SYLVIE

A MORE THAN HANDSOME EVAN DRESSED IN A CRISP WHITE
shirt, opened at the neck, a navy jacket and matching pants, a
limo, and Cristal champagne. What next? I should've expected
the question but was unprepared for it when it came.

"You're my cousin's best friend. He'll kill us both."

"Maybe, maybe not. We're two adults who should be able to
date who we want."

I had crushed on this man like crazy when I was a kid, but he
had ignored me. Was that a reason to play this hard to get? No,
but a seriously broken heart was, and he was the man who could
break this barely mended one of mine again.

"The truth then. I was in a serious relationship with someone
and it went very badly in the end. I have sworn off men because
of that."

"I see. Why didn't you tell me you were into women?"

I smacked his arm. "You know damn well that's not the case."

"I was kidding. Not every man out there is going to break
your heart, Sylvie."

"True, but my heart can't afford to be shattered again. And
honestly, Evan, I imagine you're fairly good at leaving a trail of
them behind you."

"Why would you say that?"

I didn't answer him immediately. Taking in my surroundings, and then him again, I carefully formulated my response. "First, you obviously know how to sway a woman. Look at this." I gestured with my hand, indicating the limo and champagne. "Then there were all the gifts, not to mention you."

"Me? What about me?"

"Have you looked in the mirror? I'm sure women fall at your feet with the snap of your fingers."

He frowned. "That's not very fair. I can't help the way I look."

"You're like my cousins. They all were gifted too."

"Oh, and you weren't? Have *you* looked in the mirror, Sylvie? I'm sure when you walk into a room, all the men's eyes are glued to you."

I knew men were attracted to me. I wasn't blind. But I wasn't close to the level of Evan Thomas.

"Nothing to say to that?"

Suddenly, my chin was between his thumb and index finger and I could do nothing but stare into his mesmerizing green eyes. "I can promise you something. You and I can have a very interesting relationship, not to mention a very satisfying one too, if you give us a chance. That's all I'm asking."

I whispered back, "But what about my heart?"

"What about mine? Have you stopped to think about that?"

I hadn't. It never crossed my mind. He released my chin and took a hefty drink of his champagne. I did the same as I pondered his words. What did I have to lose? I could think of a few things. My cousin, my heart, my sanity. I burst out in laughter.

"What's so humorous?"

"You wouldn't appreciate it."

"Sylvie, give me one night. This night. Can you do that? If after tonight you don't enjoy yourself, and not under the influence of tequila, I'll never call or bother you again. How does that sound?"

"I can agree to that." Only I had a feeling this night would be the best date I'd ever had.

We pulled up in front of Bon Appetit, one of the most famous restaurants in the city. I eyed him as the driver opened the door.

Evan got out first and then extended his hand toward me. I took it and felt its warmth all the way down to my toes.

"Thank you, Robert. I'll text you when we're ready."

"Yes, sir. Enjoy your dinner."

Robert got back into the limo and drove off.

We entered the restaurant, my hand on his arm, and they greeted him as though he was their best friend. Evan must have some kind of clout. I was beginning to wonder about this.

"Mr. Thomas, so wonderful to have you here."

"Thank you, Gerard. This is Ms. West. She's my guest for the evening."

"My pleasure, Mademoiselle."

"Merci," I said.

"Ah, Mademoiselle, parle français?"

"Oui, Monsieur."

He bobbed his head, smiling and said, "Suivez moi, s'il vous plaît?" We followed him to our table. It was located in a private room where he explained that chef would be cooking us our dinner tableside.

"How wonderful!" I clapped my hands. After we were seated and Gerard explained that our waiter, Phillipe, would be here momentarily, I inspected our little room.

"This is quite the score here, Evan. Exactly how connected are you?"

He played innocent. "I don't know what you mean."

"Don't play dumb. You can't get a reservation—especially one where the chef, one of the best in the city, comes to your table and cooks—at a moment's notice. Give it up, Evan."

"I happen to know someone."

"Just someone? Or lots of someones?"

He reached for my hand and took it in his. "Does it matter?"

"Not really. I'm just a bit curious about who I'm out on a date with."

"If I told you, would it make a difference if you'd go out with me again."

"Not in the least. You could be the wealthiest man in the world and I wouldn't care."

"I entertain clients here. Jean, the chef, appreciates my business because I've been coming here for a while."

He hesitated a bit when he said the words, so I suspected there was more to it, but let it go.

Phillipe walked in and Evan ordered a bottle of wine. Phillipe handed us the menu choices for this evening.

"This looks delicious. I've never eaten anywhere where the chef cooks at the table."

Evan said, "You're going to love this. Do you mind if I order, that is if you approve of everything?"

"There are some things I've never had."

He went over what he intended to order and it sounded amazing so I agreed. When Phillipe returned, Evan gave him our selections. He said he'd return with our amuse bouches.

"Jean loves to surprise his guests with these. I'm sure they'll be excellent."

He was right. Phillipe returned with our wine and a plate of single bite puffs filled with God knew what. All I knew was they melted in my mouth and tasted heavenly.

"Mmm, if dinner tastes like these, I'll be the happiest woman on Earth."

"You will. I guarantee."

"This wine is delicious too."

"Jean has an excellent cellar. It's one of the best in the city."

I smirked. "And you know that how?"

"One of my friends told me." He returned my smirk.

"Hmm, I'm sure. I may start calling you, Evan Thomas, international man of mystery." His brow creased. "You don't have to get so serious, you know."

The crease disappeared and he smiled. "I'm not serious. I was only thinking. Have you ever been to Paris?"

"When I was in college. I studied abroad for the summer. I was enchanted with that city. Then I came home and reality hit. My parents made me realize I had to earn a living and it wouldn't be romanticizing by the Seine. How dare they!" His deep chuckle sent a tingle down my spine.

"Is that how you became interested in psychology?"

"Sort of. I'd always been interested in it. It really blossomed when a close friend of mine got into drugs. I tried to help her and she spiraled. Nothing I said or did was good enough. That was my trigger. I didn't want what happened to her, to happen to any of my other friends or family. That's how I made the decision to get my master's in it and train in abuse counseling. Little did I know that I would actually end up helping a family member at the time."

"Isn't it strange how life can be so weird at times? Like maybe it was destiny."

"The weird thing is, our families had drifted apart. My mom and Pearson's mom had a ridiculous falling out. I'm not even sure what it was over. But the wedding pulled them back together. Pearson and I had planned to have a family reunion. We didn't realize at the time that he and Rose would end up getting married. I love their story. I only wish the last part hadn't happened to him."

"Don't we all. But he's a persistent bastard and if anyone could've survived it, it was Pearson. He proved that to us, too."

"He sure did. I am so proud of that man," I said.

"You and me both. I'm also happy about something else. He brought us together." His green eyes sparkled and I knew then they spelled trouble. Either I needed to end this tonight or I would be in this man's bed before I could stop it.

SIX
EVAN

THE DINNER WAS PERFECT. JEAN WAS AT HIS BEST AND I DON'T think I'd ever eaten better food. Sylvie was smitten with him and he with her, as they conversed in French. She didn't think I understood, but I was fluent in the language too. I smiled as they chatted about Paris, wine, bread, and the wonderful cafes she loved so dearly. And then as she moaned when she tasted each bite, I found myself in need of adjusting my hardened cock. Her mouth, her lips, the way she wrapped them around her fork, reminded me of the way she'd sucked me off and it was difficult not to imagine her doing it again. And again. And again.

"Evan, don't you agree?"

"Hmm?"

"You're a million miles away. I was telling Jean that this is the best meal I've ever eaten. Don't you agree?"

"Absolutely. Jean, c'était excellent." I patted my stomach for emphasis.

"Ah, merci, monsieur. For you, anything."

He finished up and left us.

"Jean is very infatuated with you, Sylvie."

"Stop. We were only talking."

"Of course, but his eyes lit up when you did. That's great

though. A chef like Jean needs to hear from his customers how wonderful he is. I'm happy he liked you. Someone else likes you too."

"Oh, and who might that be?" She teased me.

"I don't know. Care to take a guess?"

"You are a very nice dinner companion and know how to spoil a woman."

"Sylvie, I don't do this with every woman."

Her brows knitted. "Why not?"

"Because there are few if any I care to date."

"I find that difficult to believe."

"There are many who'd like to date me, but they're usually after something other than me."

"I don't understand."

He leaned back in the chair and crossed his legs. "You wouldn't because you're not an opportunist. That's what I like about you."

"And here I thought it was all about that one night. You surprise me, Mr. Thomas." Her gray eyes sparkled with mirth. She had a way about her that made me laugh.

"Sylvie, would you like to go somewhere and dance?"

"Dance? I ... sure. Let's go dance."

"I know a place a few blocks from here, would you rather walk or ride?"

"If we go slow, I'd prefer to walk." She aimed her thumb at her scrappy, and sexy-as-hell, sandals.

"I get it. You can hang on to me, and if your feet hurt, I'll carry you."

"Not on your back, I hope. There'll be no ass slapping tonight."

"I was rather hoping there would be," I said in a disappointed tone.

"Sorry to burst your bubble, cowboy. No giddy-upping for you."

ONE INDECENT NIGHT

I chuckled and the check arrived. Her head popped up as she tried to see the bill.

"What are you doing, nosey?"

"Just curious. Never saw any prices."

"In a restaurant such as this, they never post any. And, cherie, it's none of your business." I dropped my Centurion Card down and handed the portfolio to Phillipe when he arrived.

"Thank you, sir."

He returned quickly and I left both him and Jean sizable tips. Then Sylvie and I left for the dance club I was known to frequent on occasion, but only because I owned it. I would keep that little secret to myself. It was exclusive and for the elite, and I made sure it stayed that way. When we got to the door, the bouncer recognized me and allowed us to pass through. There was a cordoned off section that we entered and the waiter immediately came to take our drink order.

"Good evening, Mr. Thomas. Will it be the Glenfiddich 30 tonight, sir?"

"Yes, Joey, and the lady will have ..." I waited for Sylvie to fill in the blank.

"I'll take a club soda with a twist of lime."

"Thank you, ma'am."

"No alcohol?"

"I believe I've reached my limit."

"Fair enough." She was being careful tonight, which I respected. We'd had a glass of champagne, and two glasses of wine already. But there had been several hours in between, with lots of food, so she'd had plenty of time to metabolize it.

"I'm nowhere near drunk if you're concerned about that," she said. "I work at a rehab center and it isn't often that I have more than a couple of drinks in one night."

"I understand completely and you don't owe me an explanation for how much you drink. Ever."

"I was only thinking about that first time we were together. I downed that Reposado, as you told me, like it was water. That is totally uncharacteristic of me."

"Sylvie, you were at a wedding reception, celebrating. You just got carried away."

"Boy, did I ever. And I sure paid for it. It took me a few days to get over that hangover."

I took her hand and said, "I should've tried harder to stop you, but you were so convincing."

A snappy dance tune started playing so I asked, "Shall we?"

"Sure."

I guided her to the floor, and we began moving to the beat. The woman had game when it came to dancing. I remembered that from the reception. She was all over the music. Hips, feet, arms, coordinated together, and all I wanted to do was watch. Too bad she couldn't perform just for me. Naked. Fuck, why did I have to go there? My dick responded and that was the last thing I needed.

Holding out my hand, she took it and I pulled her against me as we moved to the beat. It was impossible for her to ignore my erection as it pressed against her. But there wasn't a damn thing I could do about it. The woman aroused me. End of story. The song ended and the music changed to a slow beat. I kept my arms around her as we continued to dance. Her arms crept around my neck and she looked into my eyes.

"This is very nice," I said.

"Yes, it is." She rested her cheek on my chest, and we swayed in sync to the song. I didn't want to release her when it ended, only I had no choice. Hand in hand, we walked back to the table.

After we finished our drinks, I asked her the million dollar question.

"Sylvie, would you be interested in seeing my place or are you ready to go home now?"

SEVEN
SYLVIE

As much as he tempted me, I knew if I went home with him, I would end up spending the night. That was the last thing on my agenda.

"I'd prefer to go home. But this has been such a lovely evening."

His expression caved. "And you're sure I can't talk you into it?"

"You probably could, but then I'd hate myself in the morning."

"I see."

He took my hand and escorted me out of the club where a long line of limos waited. His was the fifth one down. "Then shall we?"

Robert opened the door and Evan gave him the instructions. We were quiet the entire ride home. I couldn't decide if I'd made the right choice or not. My body definitely said no, but the angel on my shoulder was high-fiving me.

When we pulled in front of my building, he opened the door and offered me his hand. We walked side by side to my front door.

"Is it really that bad?"

"What?" I wasn't following.

He pointed to the sign on my door. Chuckling, I said, "Depends on the day."

"And what about now?"

"Tonight it's a happy home."

"That's nice to hear."

"Evan, I had a really great time."

"So did I. I wished it had ended differently, but I'll take what I can get."

"Don't sound so desperate."

"It's not desperation. I just know what I want." He ran his index finger down my cheek and I shivered.

"Oh? And what's that?" I asked, playing it off.

"Sylvie, do you even have to ask?"

"Maybe I just want to hear you say it."

"You." He leaned close and I was ready for his kiss. Only I was disappointed when he pressed his lips to my cheek and left. I watched him walk to the limo, get in, and then it drove off. It was only after that I remembered I'd never gotten my thong back. That was the reason I'd agreed to the date in the first play. That sneaky bastard! He'd tricked me after all.

I went inside and thought about the evening. It was by far, the best date I'd ever had. There was no doubt the man had money. I'd never thought about it before. But then, why should I have? He was Pearson's friend and had never given a rat's ass about me. True, I'd only been a kid, and then in high school, while he was already in college. Why should he have cared about me? He'd been a jerk and Pearson had always come to my rescue. When I went to college, Pearson told me to stay away from him because he wasn't my kind of guy. I asked him about it and he just said he was a big player. So that was that. Whenever he was around the family, he'd never brought a date, so I assumed he still was, since he was single.

My current dilemma was, should I tell Pearson about this? Would Evan tell him? I needed advice. I would talk to Rose, but

I doubted she would keep it from Pearson. How could she? They were married now. Only a few more days until they were back from their honeymoon, thank God.

After I finished my usual nighttime routine of washing my face and brushing my teeth, I crawled into bed and tried to read. There was a slight problem. All I thought about was Evan and his sexy face and body. Why did this man want me? He could have his pick of any number of women. Why me? That kept bothering me. I didn't run in his circles. I didn't even live in Manhattan, for Pete's sake. That was why I needed Rose's advice.

Sleep eventually came, but it was after two when it hit. Then at nine, my doorbell rang.

"Who in the hell would dare wake me up on a Sunday morning?" I growled to myself. Maybe they'd go away. It rang again. And again. Throwing the covers off, I stomped to the door, expecting to see my mom. Instead there was a delivery man, holding a box, a large bag, and a giant cup.

"Morning miss. I was told to deliver these to you in person. You are Sylvie West, right?"

"Uh, yeah."

"Great. Can you sign here?"

He pulled out a piece of paper with City Express on top. I signed and he left after he handed me the goods. I juggled them, kicking the door closed. There was no question who these were from. Dragging myself back to bed, I pulled the covers up and sipped the coffee. Mmm, it was good. Then I opened the bag. Inside was a warm cinnamon scone. How did he know I liked these? Taking a bite, the thing melted in my mouth. Now, the box. I untied the fancy red ribbon around it. When I lifted the lid, there was lots of tissue paper with a gold sticker holding it together. Hmm. My curiosity was getting the better of me. Inspecting the sticker, I saw three initials. Oh my god. EMT. Was that supposed to mean emergency medical technician? I laughed at my little joke. Of course they were his initials, but who in the hell had gold stickers made with their initials? Then I wondered what the M stood for.

Unwilling to ponder that any longer, I ripped into the layers of tissue paper, and gasped. On display in the box were at least a dozen or more lacy thongs, mine sitting on top. There were all sorts of colors, some with pearls, bows, and some even plain. At the bottom was one pair in plain white cotton. It made me giggle. That's when I found his note.

SYLVIE,

You thought I'd forgotten, didn't you? How could I possibly do that? It's all I've been thinking of. Here's a new supply to add to your current one. I hope they please you. Last night was much more than I expected. I hope you want to do it again soon. I know I do.

Yours,

Evan

MY HEART RACED as I read the note. How could a simple note have that effect on me? I knew the answer to that. Evan was every woman's dream. What was my problem? Why didn't I roll with it?

My phone rang and I knew it was him. I decided to have a little fun.

I answered in the sultriest voice I could conjure up. "Good morning. Thank you for my gifts. I have to say my favorite is the lacy black one with the bows on the front and back right where my—"

"Sylvie, what in the world are you talking about?"

"Mom!" Oh shit, did I ever screw up!

"Yes, this is your mother. Do you care to explain what all that was about?"

"Er, no, Mom, I don't."

"Who is giving you black lacy gifts with bows on them?"

"Never mind, Mom. What's going on?"

"You need to go to church, that's what's going on. When was the last time you went?"

"Uh, I can't say." I cringed inside, knowing what was coming next.

"Get dressed right now. Your father and I will pick you up in forty minutes."

"Mom! You can't be serious."

"I'm completely serious, Sylvie West. Good Lord above. What kind of daughter did I raise? And that tone of voice you used. After your behavior at your cousin's wedding reception, I thought you'd gotten over your wild ways. Apparently, I was wrong."

"Mom, I was only joking around."

"Didn't sound like any kind of joke to me. Now you'd better be ready. The service starts at eleven and you're going to be there. It's obvious you need more prayer in your life."

"Mom. I'm thirty years old. I'm old enough to decide if I need to go to church or not."

"Evidently, you're not. Forty minutes, Sylvie." And she hung up.

Shit. I clambered out of bed and hit the shower. Damn you, Evan, for getting me into trouble. I felt like a twelve-year-old again and all because of a box full of sexy thongs.

EIGHT

EVAN

SYLVIE SHOULD'VE OPENED HER GIFT BY NOW. I'D RECEIVED confirmation from the delivery service by text that she'd signed for it. Around eleven, I called her, but it went to voicemail. I tried again thirty minutes later, and the same thing happened. I waited an hour this time and again got her voicemail. Either she was avoiding me, or she was away. I gave up. If she wanted to talk to me, she'd have to call me back. I was already sounding desperate and needy. Any more and I'd sound like a stalker.

Around two, my phone rang. When I checked to see who was calling, I was happy to see Sylvie's name.

"Well, hello there."

"I'm going to murder you when I see you again."

Laughing, I said, "I take it you didn't like the scone."

"Wh-what?"

"The cinnamon scone. You didn't like it?"

That did bring a chuckle out of her. "No, you ... ugh. You won't believe what happened."

"I'm all ears, sweets."

She told me about her mom calling. My first inclination was not to laugh, but it was impossible. "Did you repent in church? I mean, after all, you are a naughty girl."

I heard her suck in her breath. "Me? You're the naughty one sending me all those thongs."

"But I was only returning yours and it wasn't exactly saintly as I recall."

"Yeah, well."

"And there was a plain white cotton one in the box. Did you notice that?"

"I did."

"That was my favorite," I confessed. When I picked it out, the idea of white cotton against her creamy skin heightened my lust for her.

"It was?"

"Uh huh. I sent the others because they resembled yours."

Silence greeted me at first, and then she said, "Oh."

"You still haven't answered my question, Sylvie."

"What question?"

"Did you repent?"

"Yes, I did."

"And what did you repent for?"

"I'm not telling you, Evan. What does the M stand for?"

"The M?"

"The gold sticker on the box had EMT on it. I know it wasn't for emergency medical technician."

"Very funny."

"The E is Evan and the T is Thomas so the M?"

"Wait. You thought the sticker was my initials?"

"Yeah."

That's when I lost it. Completely. It took at least a minute for me to stop laughing.

"Are you finished?" she asked.

Clearing my throat, I said, "I think so. Sylvie, those initials are the store's, not mine, although I didn't even give that a thought when I sent the box."

"You're joking."

"Why would I have gold stickers with my initials on them?"

"Yeah, I wondered that myself." Then she snorted. God, that snort always got me.

"The store is Erotic, Magnificent, and Tasteful. It's a lingerie shop that caters to everyone, from the chaste to the very bold, hence the name."

"I see," she squeaked.

"Did you like them?"

"Yes, thank you, but you didn't have to be so generous."

"Sylvie, do you have plans for next Saturday night?"

"Um..."

"Excellent. Be ready at six. Casual. Jeans this time. See you then." I ended the call quickly, not giving her time to back out. I'd have to figure out something to do, but that shouldn't be a problem.

I had work to do today and planned to get a lot done. EMT. I laughed again. My initials. To be a fly on her wall when she'd seen that.

Grabbing a cup of coffee, I walked into my office and flipped on the computer. In truth, I could work from home every day unless I had client meetings, but I didn't like the image that set. All four monitors jumped to life as I went to work on projects I'd been researching for future additions to the firm. Cole had sent me the information he'd found and afterwards I'd thoroughly investigated the ones I thought might be moneymakers. I created files on each of them and forwarded them to Cole. I was testing him to see if he would turn anything up. If he did, then whichever one didn't hold up would be trashed. If they were clean, they'd be sent to compliance for further analysis.

By the time I finished, it was after eight, so I called it a day and went to search the refrigerator for dinner. Rita, my housekeeper, usually left something for me when she wasn't here. Sure enough, there were salads and some other things to heat up. I hated eating this late, but I'd lost track of time when I was working.

My phone rang and I hoped it was Sylvie. It wasn't.

"Cole."

"Sir, I received the files. I'll get on it first thing in the morning."

"Great. There are some promising ones there. I'll see you tomorrow. And Cole?"

"Sir?"

"I'm very impressed with your work."

"Thank you, sir. Have a good rest of the night."

The next morning, my alarm went off at five. I dressed and went out for my run, then came in and worked out in my gym, lifting weights. I was at work by seven. I liked to start Mondays off, arriving before everyone. Except Cole was already at his desk.

"Good morning, Mr. Thomas. May I get you some coffee?"

"No need. I can get it. What about you? Need a refill?"

"That would be great, sir."

I grabbed the mug on his desk and went to the kitchen. We were the only two there, so the place was nice and quiet. When I got back, his nose was stuck to his computer.

"Careful there, you're going to ruin your eyes."

"They're already ruined." He aimed a thumb at them. "Contacts."

"If you keep your nose smashed into that screen, you'll end up needing bifocals too. Cole, how long have you worked here?"

"Close to two years, sir."

"And how long have you been my assistant?"

"Fourteen months, sir."

"When do you think you'll start calling me by my first name?"

"Um, I didn't think it was appropriate."

"Maybe not at a business meeting or in front of other employees, but when we're here, working together, I'd prefer you'd drop the sir, and call me Evan."

"Yes, sir. I mean Evan."

"Thanks."

I went into my office and got to work. My phone began ringing at eight. After that, it was difficult to get much done, which was why I needed Cole. The bad thing was, if I promoted him, then I'd need a replacement and he was the best. But I'd never hold him back because of that.

At six thirty, the receptionist called. Cole had already left so he wasn't there to field my calls.

"Sir, I'm sorry to disturb you, but there's a Miss Jessica McCray here and she insists on seeing you. I told her she couldn't without an appointment, but she refuses to leave."

Fuck. What does she want?

"It's fine. Escort her back, please."

Several minutes later, Jessica, dressed as though she were going to a fancy cocktail party, showed up at my door.

"Evan, why aren't you ready?"

"Ready?"

"Yes! You promised you'd take me to my art event. The one my company is hosting. Remember?"

Oh, shit. I totally forgot about that.

"Right. What time does it start?"

"Now!"

"Okay, give me a minute."

I hurried into my private bathroom, brushed my teeth, checked my appearance, changed my tie, and figured it would have to do.

"Let's go."

We took the elevator down and walked out when I started to hail a cab. She said, "You mean we aren't taking your limo?"

"It would take Robert too long to get here."

She huffed out a breath. This is why I hated doing her favors. She was the most spoiled little rich brat I knew.

"Whatever. You know how I hate cabs. They're so filthy. You have no idea of the germs inside."

"Didn't you take one here?" I asked.

"Yes, and it was dreadful, I tell you."

"Would you rather walk?"

"I can't walk in these," she screeched, pointing to the stilettos she wore.

"Then, Jessica, I'd suggest you forget about the germs and let's go."

We climbed into the cab and left. When we arrived, the line was non-existent, so I wasn't sure why she was pouting. It wasn't like we were making a grand entrance or anything. The gallery was a bit crowded, but not to the point where you couldn't move around. I wasn't even sure who the artist was, so I inspected the paintings. They were all right, but not to my taste.

"Evan, you have to buy one," Jessica said.

"Why?"

"To support me, that's why."

"I don't even like them."

"Hush. We can't let anyone hear."

"Jessica, I agreed to escort you here, not to buy any paintings."

"Come on, it's not like you can't afford it."

"That's not the point. I'd buy every fucking one if I liked them, but I don't."

"Jesus, you don't have to be like that," she said.

"Like what?"

"An ass."

Instead of standing there and arguing, I walked away and hunted the bar. Then I realized there wasn't one. There were only waiters wandering about with wine on trays. Fine, I'd have one of those. But when I took a sip, it was the worse tasting wine I'd ever had. Then I realized this was an artist on a pauper's budget. I wish Jessica had told me. I'd buy a painting to help the guy out. I wandered around, checking them all out so I could purchase the one I like the best. They were actually cheap, so maybe I'd buy two. There were a couple of colorful abstracts that were okay, so I went to the cashier to make the purchase. Jessica spied me there and came over.

"You changed your mind?"

"Why didn't you tell me he was a struggling artist?"

She shrugged. "How could you tell?"

"From the awful wine you served. Who is it anyway?"

"It's a she not a he and she goes by Zada."

"Is she here?" I asked.

"No, she's super shy and was afraid to come."

"Tell her that won't help her business."

"Evan, I tried. She won't listen."

"Also tell her to do more of those. They're better than her other stuff."

"Thanks for buying them."

A photographer was going around taking pictures and snapped a few of us. Afterward, I asked, "Do you mind if I leave? It's been a long day."

"Not at all. Thanks for coming. I'll have those delivered to your office."

"No, send them to my home."

"Will do."

"See ya, Jessica." I bent to kiss her cheek, and the photographer snapped another photo.

They always did that when I went out anywhere. It was so annoying how they got into your face.

NINE

SYLVIE

Two days ... Rose would be back in two days. Starr skipped into my office to remind me. "Can you believe it. I can't wait to hear about her honeymoon. I wonder if she has any pictures of Pearson in a bathing suit." She snickered.

"You're terrible, lusting after my cousin and Rose's hubs."

"I'm not lusting after *him*, only his sexy bod." She waggled her brows.

"Stop. You're embarrassing me."

"I am not. You're just as bad."

"Me? How so?"

She shrugged and said, "I see how you ogle those pics of hot guys on the internet. Don't you dare deny it." Busted.

"True, but Pearson? That hits too close to home."

"Not for me." She left and I thought of Evan. I knew what she was talking about. Good looking, sexy bod, and ... stop it, Sylvie.

I turned on the computer to catch up on the news before work and there on the front page was a picture of the man himself, kissing some gorgeous blond on the cheek. The caption read, Evan Thomas, CEO of StarWorks Financial, seen with heiress Jessica McCray, at a gallery showing last night.

What the hell! He said he wasn't seeing anyone so what was this all about? That was it. I would text him and tell him to forget about Saturday. No way would I go out with a liar. He could have his heiress. Clearly, I wasn't up to par.

I fumed as I shut the computer down. The rest of the daily news held no interest for me. My first client was due in twenty minutes, so I needed to cleanse myself of this anger. I turned on my essential oil diffuser, though today I probably needed a Xanax.

Leeanne walked in and wanted to know how I felt about adding an additional yoga class to our agenda. One look at me had her plopping down in a chair. "What happened?"

"Nothing. I just read something that pissed me off."

"Where's your medallion?"

She was referring to the oil diffusing medallion I wore around my neck. I opened the top desk drawer and grabbed it. Then I placed several drops of lavender in it before I put it on.

"That should help. Other than this, how's it going?"

"Well, my mom thinks I'm a ho."

Leeanne cackled. "A ho? Would you mind giving me a few more details?"

"I can't, really. But it was all in jest, only she thought I was serious. She actually made me go to church yesterday."

"Sylvie, that's hilarious, but I wish I knew the whole story."

"Yeah, well, it was funny yesterday. Today it pisses me off."

"Keep breathing in the lavender. I have to go. Lunch?"

"That depends on my schedule. Check back?"

"Okay."

Leanne and I were friends, but that kind of information I'd only share with Rose. Something tickled my mind, and it suddenly plowed into me like an eighteen wheeler. Evan was CEO of a company. Damn, no wonder he had all that money. Turning my computer back on, I googled him.

What came up shocked me. Why hadn't Pearson shared this

with me? Oh, because I wasn't supposed to get close to him, that's why.

Evan Thomas was CEO of StarWorks, a hedge fund that he'd created. He earned both his MBA and Master of Entrepreneurship from Wharton's. Wall Street had predicted StarWorks would be one of the higher income producing hedge funds of the decade and they were right. Evan was loaded. He was currently the owner of multiple businesses he'd invested in, and then bought out, but he also held controlling interest in stock in several other corporations.

Not being very business oriented, I didn't know the intricacies of what this meant, other than Evan was a powerhouse in the financial world. Now it made sense—the reservations, the limo, and so on. When you had clout like that, you could get anything you wanted, including women. He didn't need me. I would only be another tick mark on his bedpost. No wonder Pearson had warned me about him.

It was time for my first client, so thoughts of Evan were shoved aside. As usual, the rest of the day sped by.

That night, my phone rang. It wasn't a number I recognized and I almost didn't answer it, but something made me at the last minute.

"Hello."

"Aunt Sylvie!" a tiny voice said.

"Is this who I think it is?"

"It's me, Montana."

"That's what I thought. How's the mighty Montana doing?" Montana was my friend, Rose's, five-year-old daughter.

"I'm sad."

"Sad? Why are you sad?"

"I miss Mommy and MisterDaddy."

"I see. But guess what?"

"What?"

"They're coming home tomorrow night."

"I know. Aunt Marin said so, but I want my mommy now. She reads me books and MisterDaddy does too."

"I bet Aunt Marin would read to you."

"She does and she's real nice. But not like Mommy."

"Is Aunt Marin there?"

"Yeah."

"Can I talk to her?"

"Uh huh."

Marin, my cousin, Grey's wife, got on the phone. "Looks like you have a case of a homesick girl on your hands," I said.

"I sure do. She's pitiful. We've tried everything. Even Kinsley can't cheer her up."

"Want me to bring her to my place? Maybe a change of scenery will do her some good."

"You don't mind?"

"Of course not. She's stayed here plenty of times."

"Thanks, I owe you one."

"Hey, Marin, don't tell her. Just say you have a surprise for her."

"Ooh, I like the sound of that."

They only lived about ten minutes from me, but their house was a lot fancier than mine. My cousin, Grey, was a cardiologist, so he made a lot more money than me. I didn't begrudge him, though. He worked hard and had been through hell when his first wife died. Marin was the blessing he really needed.

I rang the front bell, not using the back door as I usually did. Of course, that brought the sound of kids yelling, the dog barking, and Grey shouting over all the mayhem, telling everyone to hush. When he opened the door, three faces stared blankly at me, namely Kinsley, her little brother Aaron, and Montana. Then she shouted, "Aunt Sylvie," and threw herself at me.

She wrapped herself around me like a soft taco shell, so I walked inside, still holding her.

"Guess it's obvious what she needed," Grey said. Marin walked into the room, smiling. She had Montana's bag packed.

"I figured we'd call Petey and let him pick her up at your place in the morning, if that's okay."

Petey was the driver that took Montana to school and back every day. "Fine with me."

Then I asked Montana, "You ready to spend the night with me?"

"Yeah!"

Both Marin and Grey mouthed their thanks as I exited with the little one still clinging to me. But then I remembered I didn't have a car seat.

Marin was standing there, knowing exactly what was running through my mind. I guess that's what moms do. "Hang on. I'll grab you the one Rose left here. I never used it because we have so many."

Grey came back carrying it. "I'll put it in for you."

"Good, and can you show me how to use it?"

"This one's a breeze."

After Montana was latched in, we waved goodbye and off we went. When we got home, and I unbuckled her and took her bag out, I asked, "Didn't you have fun there?"

"Yeah, but I want Mommy and Mister."

She called Pearson, Mister. When she first met him, Rose told her he was Mister Pearson. She said that was too long so she shortened it to Mister and it stuck.

"Only one more day and they'll be back."

"How come they stayed so long?"

"Because it was their honeymoon."

"What does that mean?"

"It means when you get married, afterward you go on a vacation called a honeymoon."

"How come I couldn't go?"

"Because that's a special time just for the bride and groom."

"Oh. Can I go next time?"

"You'll have to ask them."

It was already late, and her bedtime, so I asked, "You want to sleep in the guest room, or with me?"

"With you!" She clapped her hands.

"Okie dokie. Time to brush your teeth and wash your face."

"Is my face dirty?"

"Yep. I see dirt here, there, and right here." I pinched her nose and she giggled.

We went into my bathroom and she did as I asked. When she was finished, it was my turn. She sat and watched me go through my routine and asked all kinds of questions. How come you do this? Why do you use that? What's that? And so on.

When I was done, we changed into our PJs. I nearly died when she eyed me and said, "Aunt Sylvie, your boobies are bigger than my mommies."

"Good to know, honey. Hop in that big bed over there." She scrambled over to get in it, but it was a bit high, so I had to give her a boost. Then we both cracked up.

"Good night, daisy face," I said.

"Good night, daffodil."

"Montana, I'm glad you're spending the night and you know something?"

"What?"

"I miss your mommy too. Now go to sleep."

She curled up next to me and closed her eyes. I couldn't help thinking how precious she was.

TEN
EVAN

WEDNESDAY STARTED OUT LIKE SHIT. I WOKE UP TO A TEXT from Sylvie.

Sorry, I won't be able to make it on Saturday.

That's all she said. Nothing else. I texted her back but got no response. I texted her three more times and not a single word. What the hell happened between Sunday and now? I waited until the evening to call, but it went to voicemail. I left a message, but she didn't return my call. I called two more times and nothing. I almost got in my car and drove to her house. If she didn't answer my calls or texts by tomorrow, that's probably what I'd do.

The next morning I went back to wooing her. This time the floral arrangement I sent to her was twice as big as the last. The scent should fill up the entire building. Then I called Cole in.

"Did you need me, Evan?"

"Yes. You're married and I need a bit of advice because I want to send a nice gift to someone."

"Let me call my wife."

He was on the phone for a couple of minutes, then asked, "How well do you know her?"

"Not well, but I'm trying to get to know her better."

He relayed this to his wife. Then he said, "Something low key. She said you don't want to overpower her. It may run her off."

Great. "Any ideas?"

"Chocolates. Wine."

"What about jewelry?"

He held the phone away from his ear, laughing. "She's yelling at me because she heard you. Definitely not jewelry. That will have her hitting the ground running for sure."

"I think I have it. Tell your wife, thanks."

I'd send her the best bottle of Reposado, even though she drank enough of it to get the entire city smashed, and a T-shirt that said St. Lucia. That was a fun kind of gift. What really made my decision was I intended to hand deliver them too. If she didn't want to see me again, I was going to find out why.

I was worthless the remainder of the day and if I knew I wouldn't be intruding on hers, I would've driven up there earlier. But I waited until after four. I figured traffic would be hell, with rush hour. Robert was great at navigating through it, so I attempted to get some work done, but failed.

"How's the family?" I asked him.

"Very well, sir. I take it you had success with your lady friend."

A rueful laugh escaped me. "Hardly. I'm still trying to woo her."

"I see. Might I make a suggestion?"

"I'm all ears, Robert."

"Ease off a bit. You may be trying too hard."

He gave me something to think about. "I never had to work this hard before."

"No, sir. And she may be a frightened filly."

"What do you mean?"

"As with a filly, you approach gently and with ease. If you go in boldly, you'd never befriend one or get her used to you. Treat your lady the same. Let her get used to you. Back off some.

Women like to be courted gently, sir. You're used to holding the reins and giving orders. You understand the business world. Start noticing her cues."

"You know something? You're right. Turn the car around. If I show up like this, she'll never want to see me again."

"Yes, sir."

Why hadn't I thought of that? I was overpowering her, and she was probably freaking out. But something else had happened. I had to get to the bottom of it. Perhaps she'd eventually tell me, but for now, I'd back off and give her some space. We hadn't got too far out of the city, so we were home before five. Robert pulled into the underground garage and I thanked him for his advice.

"Enjoy the rest of the night off."

"Thank you, sir. Have a nice evening yourself."

I rode the elevator up to my home and when the doors opened, I stepped out and immediately smelled the dinner Rita was cooking.

"Mmm. What's that?" I asked.

"Chicken Cacciatore."

"You haven't fixed that in a while."

"I know and it's one of your favorites. I thought you'd be out tonight."

Smiling, I said, "A change of plans."

"This should be ready in about forty-five minutes. Are you hungry?"

"Yes and your timing is perfect. I'll be back." I grabbed a beer out of the fridge and went to change clothes and on to my office. Cole had sent his final report on the four corporations I'd looked into over to the compliance group and they sent their report back on the first company. I read through it and saw they gave it the green flag. Cole had red-flagged one of them and I was anxious to see if compliance agreed. When I finished, I went to grab dinner.

"I have you all set here, Mr. Thomas."

A.M. HARGROVE

"Thank you, Rita. It looks delicious." And it was. Her chicken was restaurant-worthy and I devoured every morsel. Then I attacked the salad she'd set before me. That left the piece of cake. It was chocolate with chocolate icing. I bit into it and it was perfection. I did love sweets. Good thing I worked out almost every day.

Rita came to clear the plates and I said, "That was excellent, especially the cake."

"I had a feeling it would be your favorite."

"You spoil me too much."

I grabbed a second beer and went to watch TV. I rarely did that, but getting home early tonight had been an unforeseen event. There was a stack of newspapers on the coffee table from the week I hadn't gone through yet either. Rita kept them for me until I put them on the kitchen counter, my cue for her to throw them away.

I started with Monday's, then got to Tuesday's and that's when I saw it—the picture of Jessica and me. I was kissing her cheek at the gallery event. I read the caption and shook my head. Why did they always have to put this crap in the news? *Evan Thomas, CEO of StarWorks Financial, seen with heiress Jessica McCray, at a gallery showing last night.*

It was difficult going anywhere without my picture showing up. I needed to get on this and stop this shit from happening. Jessica was only a friend. She was the last person I'd date, but this picture made it look like we were lovers. Moving onto the next section, I started to scan through it when suddenly, something struck me. The timing of when Sylvie texted me on Tuesday morning coincided with this picture. Could she have possibly seen it and ... no, she would've asked me first. Or would she?

The more I thought about it, the more I wondered.

My phone rang and it startled me. But then my mouth curved into a grin. "Pearson? How's the newlywed doing?"

His deep voice blasted me through the phone. "What the

fuck, Evan? What are you doing with my cousin? I told you to stay away from her, how many times? I turn my back for a minute and you launch yourself at her like ..."

"Wait a minute. I didn't launch myself at her. It was the other way around. She's the one who made the first move."

"You expect me to believe that?"

"I don't expect anything. It's the truth. It happened at your reception. I'm your best friend and have been for ages. I wouldn't lie to you."

"Then how about this. Stay. Away. From. Her."

The call ended. This was something I never expected. He'd always told me she was off limits, but that had been when we were younger. I thought if I explained things, he'd be cool with it. Man, was I ever wrong.

ELEVEN

SYLVIE

WHEN ROSE CAME IN ON FRIDAY, SHE CAME DIRECTLY TO MY office. The expression on her face let me know something was up.

"What is it?"

She started to squirm.

"Rose, what happened? Everything was fine yesterday." It was true. I'd shared with her what had occurred between Evan and me, and I begged her not to tell Pearson. We didn't have time to talk privately on Wednesday night when they stopped by to pick up Montana. Besides, they were all so excited to see each other, it hadn't been the appropriate time.

She fidgeted before she sat down. "Please tell me you won't hate me."

"You told him, didn't you?"

"It's not what you think. I went home and was so distracted, he coaxed it out of me."

This made me furious. "How the hell did he manage that?"

"He said as husband and wife, there should be no secrets between us and that it would put a wedge in the middle of us. I tried to explain it had nothing to do with him, but he wouldn't let it go. He can be very persuasive, you know."

I knew that. He hadn't become one of Manhattan's best attorneys by chance. "Yes, you're right. So then what?"

"I caved. But that's not the worst." She eyed me and said, "Oh, Sylvie, I'm so sorry."

"What? What are you sorry for?"

"He called Evan."

"He what?" I shouted.

"I knowwww. I begged him not to, but it was all I could do to stop him from driving into the city and punching the man in the face." Rose pushed to her feet and paced, wringing her hands.

"I'm calling him."

"Who, Pearson?"

"Yes. He had no right."

"Sylvie, stop. He's calmed down now, but if you call him, it'll rile him back up and I can't promise anything then."

"Rose, I'm an adult and can choose who I go out with. It's not Pearson's or anyone else's place to interfere."

"But I thought you said it was over."

"W-well, y-yes, it is," I stuttered, "but still. He can't treat me like a child."

Rose took my hand and said, "He doesn't see it as that. He sees it as protecting you."

"Protection my ass. He'll run every man off in my life."

Rose chuckled. "You're acting as though you want to see Evan again."

"It's not that. It's that I want to make my own decisions on who I date."

Rose sat down again. "I understand. Promise me something. Don't call Pearson until tonight. That way I can calm him down and talk some sense into him when he goes ballistic, like I know he'll do."

"Fine. I'm still a bit pissed at you though. I know you're supposed to share everything in marriage, but now I'm not sure I can trust you, Rose."

"I'm really sorry. I didn't mean to hurt you, Sylvie."

"Guess I'm gonna have to find a new friend to confide in."

"Ouch. That really hurt." She came over and hugged me. "You can't really mean that."

"Of course not. But I learned my lesson. If I ever date anyone who remotely knows Pearson, my lips are sealed where you're concerned."

My day had been ruined. The only thing that got my full attention was how angry I was at my cousin. I apologized time after time to each of my patients, making up one excuse after another. It seemed ever since Pearson and Rose got married, my life had turned to hell and it was all because of that one crazy night with Evan. Why the hell did I have to get so smashed?

I thanked God when the day finally ended. The way I felt right now, I could use a bottle of tequila. Gathering up my things, I headed to the car. I was going to give Pearson a piece of my mind and then enjoy my Friday evening ... alone. How pitiful was that?

I pulled into a parking space and sighed. I loved my little townhouse. It represented everything I loved in a home ... it was cozy, cute, and every time I entered it, I instantly relaxed. On my porch sat a box. Looked like the UPS guy left me something. After I dumped my load inside, I came back out to collect it, then went to change my clothes. All I wanted right now was to get into my stretch yoga pants and a soft T-shirt. Then I padded into the kitchen to make a cup of herbal tea and open the box.

Inside was a bottle of extra Añejo tequila, which I had never tasted before, along with a cozy T-shirt that had St. Lucia written on it. There was a note in the box that instructed me to sip the tequila slowly, neat. And that was all. I knew who it was from, but I was a little sad he hadn't signed it.

I was a little fearful of the tequila because the last time I'd had any, it left me with a hangover that lasted a couple of days. But then again, I drank it like it had been water—or so I'd been told. Tearing off the plastic and twisting off the cork, I inhaled and it didn't smell at all like tequila. A spicy aroma with a hint of cinnamon invaded my senses. Hmm, I might give this a try after I meditate.

As I sat on the floor, getting ready to do just that, someone pounded on my door. Not softly either. It was an incessant banging, like they wanted to break the door down. Who in the heck was that? I stared out the peephole to see Pearson standing there. Great. He's exactly the person I wanted to talk to.

I swung the door open and said, "You ass—" just as he raised his fist to knock again and instead of hitting the door, he pounded me dead center on the nose.

"Owww!" I staggered backward as my ass hit the floor. Stars swam before my eyes for a second.

Pearson was by my side, saying, "Shit. I didn't expect you to be standing there."

My hand reached for my nose, which dribbled blood, and I got up and staggered to the kitchen. Leaning over the sink, blood trailed down to the drain.

"Let me have a look."

"No, get me some ice first," I said, my tone nasally.

He grabbed a towel, put some ice in it, and handed it to me. "Here."

My nose throbbed as I placed the pack on it. "Shit, this hurts like a mother. I wonder if it's broken."

"If you let me look, I might be able to tell you."

"How would you know?"

"Sylvie, I've been in plenty of fights to know what a broken nose looks like."

"Okay."

He lifted the pack off and said, "We're going to the hospital."

"Can't Grey fix it?" Grey was his brother.

"Grey's a cardiologist. He fixes hearts, not noses. Let's go."

We got into his fancy car and on the way, he called Rose. She bit his head off when he told her what happened. It was an accident, but I was going to make him feel terrible about this.

"You need to stay out of my life, Pearson. I'm not eighteen."
I sounded like a high-pitched bird.

"You can't date Evan."

"I can date whomever I want."

He growled something unintelligible and then was quiet. We
pulled into the parking lot and walked inside. By the time they
finished checking me in, Grey showed up. Evidently Pearson had
called him and he hadn't left the hospital yet.

"I can't believe you punched her, Pearson. Let me take a look
at this." I pulled the ice pack away, while he checked my nose
out. "Follow me."

We followed him through the automatic door. It was nice to
know someone who had connections. He spoke to the nurses at
the station and they put me in one of those curtained off rooms.

Grey said, "They're paging an ENT now. It definitely looks
broken to me. But let the specialist be the judge. I hope you
don't need surgery."

"Surgery? What the heck. Can't they just bend it back?"

"Sylvie, that's not how it works," Grey said.

I punched Pearson's arm. "If you would just mind your own
business, this wouldn't have happened."

"What's going on between you two?" Grey asked.

"He's trying to boss me around."

"She wants to date Evan."

Grey laughed. "You two need to settle this. Pearson, Sylvie is
thirty and can decide who she wants to date. Besides, isn't Evan
your best friend?"

"Yeah, that's the problem. I know too much about him."

"Whoa. You didn't hear Sylvie warning Rose away from you,
did you? And she knew a hell of a lot about you too."

Pearson shifted from one foot to the other. "That was
different."

"How?" Grey asked.

"Rose knew all about me too."

"Take my advice—both of you. Everyone has to figure out

68

their own shit. You can't boss her around anymore. She's an adult, Pearson. And on that note, here comes Will."

Another doctor walked in and Grey said, "Will James, meet my cousin, Sylvie West, who my brother, Pearson, cold-cocked in the nose."

The day couldn't possibly have been worse.

TWELVE

EVAN

ROBERT DROPPED OFF THE GIFT TO SYLVIE LATE THIS afternoon. I'd bought it for her so I figured she may as well have it. Hoping against hope, I thought I might receive a thank you, but one never came. I suppose I should get used to the fact that I'd been dumped, plain and simple. I was slightly crushed. Not so much by the fact she'd dumped me, but because she'd never given me any sort of explanation. I'd expected more out of her after our conversations and how I thought she wasn't that kind of person. I'd always prided myself on being a great judge of character too, and believed she'd had it in spades. Guess she fooled me.

Even after Pearson's call and listening to him rant, I figured I'd give him lip service and then do whatever the hell I wanted. I was a grown man and sure, he was my best friend, but I was past taking orders from him. Sylvie was an adult and it was time he treated her as one. I hope his tirade wasn't the reason she hadn't responded to me or texted me a thanks. If so, I had to let it go. I didn't want or need someone who couldn't think for themselves.

Saturday morning, I woke clearheaded, so I went out for a run. It was a beautiful day, which made my run more enjoyable. When I finished, I stopped off for some breakfast, then went home. At noon, I had planned to meet some friends to shoot some hoops at the club I belonged to. After two hours, we wrapped it up.

One of the guys, Bradley, asked if I had plans that night.

A bitter reply hovered on my lips, but instead, I said, "Not tonight."

"What? Mr. Man About Town lost his charm?"

"Funny. No, as a matter of fact, I just happen to enjoy lying low every now and then."

"Why don't you come out with us?" he asked.

"Explain who us is."

"A friend of mine from the U.K. is in town for business and he wants to go out. Mitchell, Kent, and I thought we'd take Colin out. Come join us. Have a guy's night out."

"Sounds good. Where to?"

"Club SoHo. You know it?"

"Yeah, I think so. What time?"

"We're getting dinner first. Wanna go?"

"Nah, I'll meet you afterward. Text me when you're done, and I'll meet you in SoHo."

Bradley asked, "You sure?"

"I don't think I can handle eight hours of you guys."

"Ha. Make sure you have a couple of drinks then because you don't want to be completely sober around a bunch of drunk dudes."

"True. See you tonight."

After I ate some of that chicken cacciatore that Rita made, I had a couple of drinks and waited for Bradley's text. I hoped it didn't come at midnight. I was past staying out until the sun rose. My life was better than that. It finally came around nine forty-five. I'd given Robert the night off, so I hailed a cab and headed to SoHo.

By the time I got there, the place was packed. Music blared and the line at the bar was hideous. A woman a couple of people ahead of me eyed me and said, "I'll get yours. What're you drinking?"

"Grey Goose, soda, extra lime."

A few minutes later, she handed me the drink and I passed her a twenty.

"No need. You can get me next time."

"What if I can't find you," I said.

"Don't worry, I'll find you." She winked and walked away.

Checking out the crowd, I figured it best if I texted Bradley. He answered immediately, which surprised me. They were toward the back, near the dance floor. Pushing my way through the crowd, I found them standing near a group of women.

As soon as I walked up, all eyes focused on me.

"Hey, man, you missed a great dinner," Bradley said. Then he introduced me to Colin, because I knew everyone else. The women were eyeing all of us and it was awkward because this was when we should all be exchanging names. I never used my real name in a club. I couldn't remember if Bradley knew that. Evan was fine, but not Thomas.

One of the women approached me and said, "Hi Erwin, I'm Emily." She must've heard Bradley introduce me to Colin, but I didn't bother to correct her. "Hi Emily. Hope you're having a good time tonight."

"I wasn't until I saw you."

"Really?"

"Yeah, there's nothing like a six plus feet of hot and hunky man."

Fuck. Why did I always get the drunk ones?

"Hey, Lydia, don't you think Erwin is hot and horny?"

The guys laughed

"Emily, how would you know I was horny?"

"Aren't guys always horny?"

"No."

"Hey, Lydia, did you know guys aren't always horny?"

Christ.

"Emily, will you excuse me for a minute?"

I turned to the guys and said, "I have to get away from them."

We went back toward the front, but the female trio followed us.

Bradley elbowed me and said, "Looks like your admirer is bedazzled."

"Excellent." I scoped out the place, searching for the woman who bought my drink and she magically appeared by my side.

"Looking for me?"

"Yes, I need your help. See those three women tailing us?"

"Yeah. Do you want me to scare them away?"

I grinned. "Not exactly. Can you pretend to be my date for a while? One is sort of stalking me."

"Sure. But how do you know I won't really want to be your date?"

"I don't. I'm taking a chance."

"Brave of you. I'm Kristen, by the way."

"Pleased to meet you. I'm Evan."

Then I turned around and said, "Hey guys, you remember my date, Kristen?" And I introduced her to the rest of the group. Eventually the trio disappeared, only now Kristen was hanging out with us. That wasn't bad, but I didn't want to give her any ideas either.

It wasn't long before I became aware that Kristen's attention was solely focused on Colin. The good news was he was returning it. I whispered, or rather yelled into her ear since the music was blaring in here, "Why don't you go and talk to him? "

"Oh, I don't know."

Taking her wrist, I maneuvered her next to Colin. "You two seem like a good match," I said.

Colin gave me a weird look. "Isn't she your date, mate?"

"She was my fake date to get that lunatic away from me."

He instantly brightened. "In that case, Kristen, would you care to dance?"

"Thought you'd never ask." She gave me a thumbs up as they headed toward the dance floor.

Bradley said, "Since when did you become a matchmaker?"

"Since about one minute ago. Apparently, Colin thought she was my real date."

"She's smokin'. I'm surprised you passed her off. What's happened to the Evan I know?"

He's right. Ordinarily, I would've ended up in either her bed or a hotel room. I never took women to my place. That was completely out of the question. No one knew where I lived and it would remain that way. Only a few people were allowed into that inner sanctum. I didn't want the press getting wind of that. My address wasn't even linked to the business. I had another apartment in Manhattan that I used as a dummy address, when necessary, but I never went there, never even took women there. If we couldn't go to their place, then it was a hotel.

"Not really my type," was my only reply. He shrugged to that. The real reason was she didn't come close to Sylvie, who still occupied my brain and I realized another woman wouldn't fill her place for quite some time.

It was just past midnight when I told my friends good night. I was ready to ditch this scene. The loud music had given me a slight headache and I was tired of shouting to my friends in order to have some sort of conversation.

When I got into the cab, I pulled out my phone and saw a text from Pearson, which was a surprise. I figured that wouldn't happen for quite some time. It was even a bigger shock when I read it.

Come to our family dinner tomorrow at my parents. I owe you a huge apology. Sorry for the way I reacted.

I texted him back immediately.

Sorry it's so late but I just got this. Apology accepted. I'd love to come. What time?

Not expecting to hear back until the morning, the three flashing dots were a surprise.

Be there at one with an empty stomach. You know how Mom loves to feed us.

I laughed because he was right. Paige West was one of the best cooks and when you went there to eat, she stuffed you until you could barely move.

Will do and see you then. Thanks.

When was the last time I'd eaten Sunday dinner with the Wests? Was it when Pearson was in law school and I was in grad school? I couldn't remember, but my mouth was already watering in anticipation.

THIRTEEN
SYLVIE

THEY DID THE SURGERY THAT SAME NIGHT. LUCKY FOR ME, IT was because of Grey's connections. Otherwise, I would've had to wait until Monday. A plastic surgeon, along with Dr. James did the procedure. I was left with a giant bandage across my nose and one underneath it. It looked ridiculous. My eyes were nearly swollen shut and they had purple bruises underneath.

They released me that night, but Pearson drove me directly to his house. Rose refused to let me stay alone, since I was on pain medication. I went straight to bed and didn't wake up until almost noon. It was the throbbing pain that did it.

I stumbled out of bed and went to the bathroom to pee. Montana was asleep when I arrived, and when she saw me, she laughed.

"Why do you got that white thing on your face, Aunt Sylvie?"

I mumbled something and hit the john. It seemed like I peed for an hour. When was the last time I went? As I washed my hands, I looked in the mirror and moaned.

Montana waited for me right outside, with her hand held out.

"Mommy said I'm sposed to help you to the kitchen. She has pancakes."

"That's nice." I wasn't hungry in the least. All I wanted was an Advil for the pain.

Montana pulled out a chair for me and Rose handed me a pill along with a glass of water.

"What's this?"

"It's a Lortab. I have to keep it under lock and key, Pearson's orders. You know why."

Former addicts can't take a chance.

"Can't I take Advil or something less strong? These things knock me out and I don't like that."

"Sure," Rose said. "We can try it to see if it works. I just don't want you in pain. He really did a number on you. Sylvie, he feels terrible about this."

"I can see why. His fist really packed a punch."

"Will you ever forgive him?" she asked.

"For this? It was an accident. If he meant to punch me, I'd kick his ass."

Rose only shook her head.

"Seriously, Rose, there's nothing to forgive. But I am still pissed off about what he did with Evan."

"He knows and he's going to apologize to you both." She pointed to the breakfast on the table. "You should eat."

"I'm not hungry."

"Maybe a bite?"

Not wanting to hurt her feelings, I did as she asked. My nose was crammed so full of stuff, I couldn't taste a thing. "I'm sure these are wonderful, but my taste buds are shot."

"You poor thing. Is there anything I can do for you?"

Montana ran into the kitchen and handed me a picture. "Here, Aunt Sylvie. This is for you."

I covered my mouth when I saw it. "It's perfect."

I tried to put a princess band-aid on your nose, but it was kinda hard.

"It's perfect," I said, handing it over to Rose.

I heard her suppressed giggle as she coughed. "Pop Tart, I love this. How about watching a video?"

"Sure." She ran back out and I snorted or did my best imitation. It wasn't the same with this nose situation going on.

"It looks like I have a giant marshmallow on my face."

"I was thinking a doughnut."

Then we both cackled. Pearson walked in through the back door then.

"What's so funny?"

Rose handed him the picture and he sighed. "This is my fault."

"Now you can add to your list of misdeeds that you broke your cousin's nose when you were sober." I snorted at my little joke, but it sounded more like I was choking. Pearson ran over and pounded my back.

"What are you doing?"

"Saving you from choking."

"I was snorting. It sounds different with all this crap jammed up my nose."

"Jesus, I'm worthless."

"Shut up. Listen, you idiot, it was an accident, but I'm still pissed at you. When are you going to start treating me like an adult?"

"Yesterday," he said, with a grin. "I've learned my lesson the hard way and I'm sorry. You're right, Sylvie. You're old enough to make your own decisions on who you want to date and if it's Evan, then you have my blessing. I had no right to butt into your life. Will you forgive me?"

"Wow. I wasn't expecting this. But there's nothing to forgive. And thank you."

"You're welcome. And so you know, I'm going to apologize to Evan too. He's been my best friend for as long as I can remember and it was stupid of me to overreact that way."

"That's very noble of you, Pearson."

"I'm pretty good at apologizing. It's one thing I learned to do quite well at rehab. So how are you feeling?"

"Ugh. Like I have a broken nose."

"You probably don't remember, but both doctors said today would be the worst. Tomorrow you'll feel much better. I'll take you in on Monday for them to remove the packing and you'll feel even better after that."

"Yeah, I think so. This stuff is annoying."

Rose said, "You should rest today. Sleep is your friend."

"That was my intention," I said, rising from the chair. "I'm going to take a nap." That was funny since I had just woken up. I didn't think I'd sleep, but when my head hit the pillow, I was out.

It was getting dark when I woke up. Jeez, I must've been tired. I went to the bathroom and then the kitchen for something to drink for my parched throat.

No one was around, but there was a note on the counter saying they'd be back before dinner. I guzzled some orange juice followed by some water. There was a bottle of Advil on the counter, so I took some more, since that seemed to do the trick, and went to watch TV.

I must've dozed off, because I heard the front door open and the group of them walked in with Montana chatting excitedly about the fun she had at the zoo. She loved the monkeys and the rabbits there.

"We're gettin' pizza tonight, Aunt Sylvie. Want some?" Montana asked.

"Yum. Sounds good," I said.

Pearson ordered it and when it arrived, I was able to eat one slice.

"Did you like it?" Montana asked.

"I sure did," I said.

"Mommy has ice cream for dessert too."

"My favorite." My taste buds were still blunted, and I had a feeling they wouldn't return until this mess was removed from my nose, but I bet the cold would feel good in my mouth.

After we finished our desserts, I announced I was hitting the sack. Before I left the room, Pearson said, "Oh, tomorrow is Sunday dinner at Mom's. If you're feeling up to it, do you want to go?"

"I'd love to, but did the doctor say if I could shower?"

"Yes, you can but don't get the bandage wet. It might be best if you take a bath and wash your hair separately."

"I can help with your hair," Rose offered.

"That would be great. Good night everyone."

"Can I tuck you in, Aunt Sylvie?" Who could deny that sweet little girl anything?

"Sure thing."

Montana waited for me while I brushed my teeth and washed my face around the massive bandage. Then she pulled the covers up over me. "I guess you say your prayers laying down, huh?"

"Oh, yeah, that's what I do." The guilt that conjured up had me instantly reciting prayers. Then she kissed me on my forehead.

"I love you. Sleep tight and don't let any mosquitos bite." That was a new one on me.

"Good night."

She flipped off the light and I dropped off to sleep.

When morning came, I felt so much better. It was as though someone gave me my energy back. I went to the bathroom and filled up the tub. I couldn't wait to take a bath. Afterward, I changed into fresh clothes that Rose had picked up for me. A pair of jeans, a black sweater, and some black booties did the trick.

Rose would have to help me with my hair. I went to the kitchen for some coffee and everyone was already up.

"Good morning everyone," I said.

"You look great today," Rose said.

"I feel so much better," I answered, heading to the coffee pot. "A day of sleep did wonders. All I need now is clean hair."

"We can do that," she said.

"I'm happy you're better. You didn't look so hot yesterday," Pearson said.

Aiming my thumb at my face, I said, "Oh, and this is the picture of hot?"

Montana giggled. "You look funny, Aunt Sylvie. How long you gotta wear that thing on your face?"

"I don't know, goofball." I tickled her belly.

Everyone ate breakfast, and then Rose helped me with my hair. It wasn't bad, since we played beauty salon in the kitchen, with Montana standing on a chair as assistant. Close to one, we all hopped into Pearson's car and drove over to his parents. Everyone was already there, with the exception of Hudson, who couldn't make it because all of his in-laws were in town visiting.

When we walked in, Aunt Paige and Uncle Rick hugged me and made a huge deal over the nose, then came Grey, who had seen me on Friday night.

"You look much better already," he said.

"I can't wait to get this thing off."

"Oh, Sylvie," Marin exclaimed. "It must've been awful. I'm going to teach my brother-in-law some manners."

"Not to worry. Rose and I have already handled that."

We finally made it to the den where I got the surprise of my life. Evan stood there and I wasn't sure who was more stunned, him or me.

He was at my side in an instant asking, "What in the world happened to you?"

FOURTEEN

EVAN

When she walked in with her nose bandaged up, I had to look twice. I almost didn't recognize her.

"You might want to ask Pearson. But before you get all wound up, it was an accident." What the hell did that mean?

My head swiveled to Pearson, who had guilt written all over him, and I asked, "Well?"

"I punched her."

"You what?"

Before he could say another word, Paige said, "Everyone, let's give these people a bit of privacy."

Rick agreed and shuffled everyone out of the room except for Sylvie, Pearson, Rose, and me.

"You were saying," I prodded.

"Pearson, maybe I should handle this."

At Pearson's nod, Sylvie said, "He came over while I was meditating, so he pounded really hard on the door because at first I didn't answer. He didn't expect me to open the door when I did, so suddenly it was me standing there, and not the metal door, and he pounded my nose instead. You can probably use your imagination for the rest. I had surgery on Friday night for a broken nose, but everything is fine."

"You broke her nose?" I asked him, anger riding me.

"Yeah, and it was the most awful thing ever."

I wanted to grab him around the neck and squeeze it until he couldn't breathe.

"Evan, like I said, it was an accident," Sylvie reiterated.

"Why did you go over there in the first place?" I asked.

"Honestly, I was still pissed. After the conversation you and I had, I was going to have it out with her." I opened my mouth to berate him, but he held up his hand, palm toward me. "Let me finish. Then this happened. She let me have it on the way to the hospital. When we got there, Grey handed it to me as well. I realized I was being foolish, not to mention an ass and an idiot. I was intruding where I shouldn't have been. She's an adult and old enough to make up her own mind. So I apologized to her, and then to you. This was all a huge accident, but it made me see my errors and if I've learned one thing, it's humility. I was wrong and admitted it."

The anger fled out of me when he said those words. How could I still be pissed or even hold a grudge when he recognized he'd been wrong? I wasn't that small minded.

"At least something good came out of this," I said.

Pearson nodded and added, "This is why I wanted you both here today. I'm not sure where you two are, or if you're even seeing each other. But if so, you have my blessing, not that you needed it, to see each other." When he finished speaking, he and Rose left the room.

Sylvie frowned. I wanted to reach out and smooth it away.

"I'm sorry about your nose."

"Me too, but at least it resulted in Pearson finally treating me like an adult. It hurt like a mother though."

"I bet. I wish I had known. I would've come over and given you a back rub."

"By the way, thank you for the tequila and shirt. I've been staying at Rose's since Friday and didn't have a chance to text you when all this happened. Today is the first day I've felt like a human."

I stepped closer to her and touched her cheek. "Can I ask you something?"

Her eyes took on a wary appearance. "What?"

"We were set to go to dinner and you canceled. Why? And please be honest."

"I saw you in the paper with another woman."

"At the art show?"

"That's right."

"She's a friend and I was doing her a favor. The events company she owns was putting on the show and I promised her a while ago I'd go. I'd actually forgotten and was still at work when she showed up and cursed me out for it. We met in college and have been friends since. We've never slept together, and neither of us have wanted to. In fact, she annoys me if I spend too much time with her. I'd be happy to introduce you to her if you'd like."

"A friend?"

The corners of my mouth lifted. "Definitely a friend. Nothing more."

"I see."

"Does that mean you'd be willing to go out with me again?"

She smiled, I think. It was sort of difficult to tell with that humongous bandage on her face. "Maybe."

"Maybe?"

"What did you have in mind?"

"You name it and we'll do it."

"I want to go to the top of the Empire State Building."

"I'll pick you up on Saturday at ten. Plan for a fun day. We'll go to the top of the Empire State Building and then spend the day in the city."

Paige came in and told us dinner was ready. I took Sylvie's hand and we walked into the dining room.

"Aunt Sylvie, you gonna eat the chicken?" Montana asked.

"Sure am."

Montana eyed me for a second and asked, "You gonna eat it too?"

"Only if you do."

"Everybody eats it. G-mamma's chicken's the best."

"Guess what?" I asked.

"What?"

"I used to come here with your Daddy when I was a kid and eat it all the time."

She turned to Pearson and asked, "He did?" Her big round eyes were cute as hell.

"He sure did. G-mamma would get mad at us because our hands would be filthy. She'd make us get up and go scrub them."

"Did you get all the germs off?"

"We did," Pearson said. What he didn't add was we had to or Paige would beat us with her flyswatter. She never took any crap off of us. She was used to boys, having raised three of them.

Paige chuckled. I asked her, "Are you thinking what I am?"

"If it has to do with a flyswatter I am." The other guys joined in. The women only stared because they didn't have a clue. We'd best keep it that way.

The food, as usual, was delicious. Sylvie only picked at hers, so I asked, "Is everything okay?"

"I still can't taste, which is driving me crazy. All this good food for nothing."

Grey said, "It'll be better after tomorrow."

"I'll probably go crazy then, eating everything in sight."

Paige came out with some apple cobbler and vanilla ice cream. I smelled the aroma wafting off it. "This reminds me of when I used to come here during our college breaks."

"You were skinny as a rail and I needed to put some fat on you back then."

"You and my mom. I couldn't eat enough to put any fat on."

"I wish that had been my problem," Sylvie.

"Me too," Rose said. "It's never fair. Men never have to worry about weight like women do."

"Babe, your weight is perfect," Pearson said.

"So is yours," I told Sylvie. "I don't know what you're complaining about."

"I watch what I eat," I said.

"So do I," Pearson said.

"You what?" Rose asked. "You watch how much you *can* eat." Then she looked at the number of chicken bones piled on his plate. "See what I mean."

"Babe, you can't expect me to hold back. This is Mom's famous chicken."

Rose rubbed his stomach and grinned. "I know."

"I'm sending some home with you, Rose," Paige said.

Pearson looked like he was ready to clap his hands. I laughed at him. "You look about five right now."

"Yeah, you do," Sylvie agreed.

The kids wanted to go out and play, so Rick went with them. The women got up to clean, but when Sylvie tried to stand, I stopped her. "You sit. I'll help."

"Don't worry, we've got it. Besides, the two of us can handle it," Marin said.

Paige went into the kitchen, but they ordered her back out. Pearson and Grey cleared the table and came back to suggest we move to the den.

I pulled Sylvie next to me on the couch. I wasn't taking any chances of her being away from me.

"How's the company doing, Evan? Rick keeps up with it better than me," Paige asked.

"He's killing it, Mom," Pearson said. "He's also bought out a few more and is really doing well."

Paige laughed and said to Pearson, "Thank you, Evan."

I got a laugh out of that too, but added, "It's true. It's surpassed my expectations, for sure. But it does keep me busy."

"Then my question is, do you still love it?"

"Most definitely. I'm always looking for new companies to add to the business, too."

"That's great. I couldn't be happier for you."

Then it happened. "What business are you in?" Sylvie asked.

I took a deep breath and began the plunge, but before I got the chance, Pearson asked, "You haven't told her?"

"Told me what?" she asked.

"Evan is probably Manhattan's most eligible and wealthiest bachelor."

I mouthed the words, "Thanks a lot, bro."

FIFTEEN
SYLVIE

Speechless didn't come close to describing how I felt. I knew he had money and lots of it. I knew he was bright by his degrees I'd discovered through googling him. But the wealthiest and most eligible bachelor? Um, no. I was so out of my league.

Yes, I was smart enough to hold a master's in psych, but not close to what he had. Uneasiness settled over me as I sat there. Obligated to say something since everyone was eyeing me, I said, "Wow, that's quite an accomplishment. What kind of company?"

"It's a hedge fund."

Pearson chuckled. "Don't let him off so easy. It's not just a hedge fund. It's one of Wall Street's darlings. He's the golden boy, if you will. Evan has the Midas touch."

"Now you're embarrassing me," he said.

He really did look uncomfortable with the accolades.

"You should be proud. If you built all that on your own through hard work, I think that's amazing." It was true. I admired anyone who could achieve those lofty goals.

"I appreciate that. It wasn't easy, but it was something I enjoyed along the way."

"It's great you found something you love to do."

Pearson piped in. "Kind of like you and Rose. Both of you

love what you do. And you with helping others get back on their feet after addiction."

"True, it is fulfilling."

The kids ran back inside, with Kinsley yelling something about a tummy ache to Grey. "You probably ate too much," he said. She kept whining, so he took her into the kitchen where Marin was.

Rose came into the room and Montana said she wanted to watch a movie. It was getting close to five, so Pearson decided it was time to leave.

Evan pulled me to the side and said, "Don't forget, next Saturday at ten. I'll pick you up."

"I won't. Hopefully, this massive thing will be gone by then." My hand covered the bandage.

"You still look adorable with it on." He kissed my cheek and after I hugged and thanked my aunt and uncle, and he did the same, we walked out together.

On the way home, Montana asked, "Aunt Sylvie, do you like that other man?"

"I guess so. Why?"

"Cuz he kissed you." She giggled.

"Yes, he did."

"Do you like when he kisses you?"

Pearson caught my eyes in the rearview mirror and waggled his brows.

"He only kissed my cheek, mighty mite."

"Do you want him to kissy face you like MisterDaddy does to Mommy."

"Hmm. I'll have to think about that. Does MisterDaddy do that to Mommy a lot?"

"All the time. 'Specially when they think I'm not watching."

Suddenly, a coughing spell hit Rose. I tried my best not to snort, but it didn't work.

"What was that?" Montana asked.

"I had a tickle in my throat. These bandages make my nose and throat itch."

"Oh. Can't you take it off?"

"The doctor will tomorrow."

"That's good then you won't look funny no more."

We got back to the house and I asked Pearson if he would take me home. Rose put up a fight, but after I insisted that I was fine, she backed down.

"I'm only taking Advil and I'm not feeling dizzy or faint in the least. There's no reason why I can't stay in my own place tonight."

"She's right, Rose. I'll pick you up for your appointment tomorrow and drive you. You don't know how you'll feel afterward."

That much was true, so I agreed.

It was great to be back home and sleeping in my own bed. Rose was the perfect host, but there's no place like home. I snuggled in my bed and read for a while. Around nine, my phone rang. A smile spread across my face when I saw Evan's name.

"Hi."

"What are you doing?"

"Reading. You?"

"The same. I'm reading Financial Times. You?"

"The Raunchy Duke."

"Repeat that."

"Do I have to?" I snorted.

"Yes, Sylvie, you do."

"The Raunchy Duke."

"Is it good?"

"That depends on what you consider good."

"That's not an answer. Do you consider it good?"

"Very."

"Why?"

Jesus, was this the inquisition? He asked, I'd tell. "Because it's about a swoon-worthy Dom who uses all his sexuality to seduce an innocent young woman who ends up falling in love with him. But the unexpected happens when he falls in love with her. He's sworn he'll never love anyone, but she brings him to his knees."

"I'm still stuck on swoon-worthy Dom." A soft chuckle reached my ear and shivers raced up my spine.

"What about that intrigued you?"

"I'm intrigued because you are."

"Evan, I read this stuff all the time. It's no novelty for me. You should try it."

"Maybe I will."

"Let me know how you like it. I'm sure it's much more entertaining than Financial Times."

Now he really let out a hearty laugh.

"I can't wait until tomorrow," I said.

"Why?"

"I'll be able to breathe again."

"Oh, right. Do you want some company when you go?"

"Pearson is doing that. He's been very accommodating throughout this. He really feels bad."

"I'm sure. God, I would too."

"I know, but he thought he'd be pounding on the door, and that door is steel so if you knock, you really have to hit it hard."

"He did that all right."

"I hope I don't end up with a ghastly hump."

"Didn't a plastic surgeon do it?"

"Yeah, but still."

"You'll be as gorgeous as ever."

"Aww, that's so sweet."

"I mean it, Sylvie. Now go to sleep. You need your rest. I'll be thinking of you and I'll call tomorrow."

"Okay."

"Can't wait until Saturday." His voice sent shivers all over me.

"Same here."

When we ended the call, I thought again how sweet he was.

Was I crazy to be going out with him again? He could have any woman he wanted, but he seemed intent on me.

I refused to dwell on it. Second guessing this was stupid. If it worked fine; if not, then I'd move on.

I fell asleep with the Raunchy Duke paddling his innocent lady's ass. Unfortunately, in the morning, I woke up all bothered, because I dreamed I was the woman, and Evan was the duke.

Pearson picked me up at ten thirty for my appointment. When they called me back, I grabbed his hand and made him go with me. A case of the nerves hit.

"What if this hurts?" I asked him.

"I don't think it will or they would've told you to take something."

The nurse showed us into a room and told us the doctor would be in momentarily.

He showed up with his pearly whites glowing. Plastic surgeons had an image to keep up, I guess.

"How are you doing?" he asked.

"Other than this bandage driving me crazy, I'm good."

"Let's take care of that."

The nurse had left a tray with all kinds of things in those sterile paper bags. She came in while he gloved up. He ripped open one of the bags as she put a gigantic napkin thingy around me, covering me from my neck to my waist. Then the doctor pushed something with his foot and the seat moved into a flat position.

The nurse held the tray as the doctor took the bandage off under my nose.

"Is this going to hurt?" I asked.

"Not pain, though it will feel weird."

Then he began pulling stuff out. I thought he was done, but no. He kept pulling. And pulling. How much shit was in there? Was it crammed all the way to my brain? My God, was he ever going to finish? Finally, he was done. I was waiting for him to pull a rabbit out of there too.

"I bet you thought that was never going to end."

"Yeah."

He chuckled and said, "That was only one side."

The fuck! "Are you kidding?"

"Sorry."

"Is my nose that big?"

Then he and the nurse laughed. "Your nose is actually small. It's amazing what you can fit in there."

This time I knew what to expect. When he was finished, it was such a relief. Then he took the rest of the bandage off that went over the bridge of my nose.

He pressed around a bit and said, "Hmm, this looks really nice. Do you want to see?"

"Yes!"

"Don't be alarmed by the bruising because all that will fade away." He handed me a mirror and my nose looked like a cross between a green and purple grape. He took some gauze and cleaned me up, which made it look better, but it was still purple-green. My eyes looked awful too. They were swollen and bruised.

"In about four weeks, you'll look back to normal. It takes four to six weeks for the swelling to go down. I want to see you in a week. I want this to stay in place. It's kind of a splint, but it's there more for protection than anything else."

It took him a couple of minutes to place it on. He gave me my care instructions and we left. Pearson offered to take me to lunch, which I accepted. I was starving. Maybe I could taste again. I also wanted to pick his brain about Evan.

When we were seated, I aimed my gaze at him and said, "Ok, cousin, I want all the juicy details on your friend. Everything. Now give it up."

He looked at me like a deer in the headlights.

SIXTEEN

SYLVIE

"WHAT DO YOU WANT TO KNOW?" PEARSON ASKED. HIS wariness almost made me laugh.

"I'm not going to bite, you know."

"Funny, Sylvie. Here's the thing. I'm stuck in the middle and it's a bad place to be."

I patted his hand. "Tell me about it."

"I understand you get it. You were there with Rose and me. But Evan and I go way back. And I've always had his back."

"There was a time you always had mine too."

"I've never stopped having yours. Why do you think I stormed over to your place the way I did?"

My throat was suddenly like cotton, so I picked up the glass of ice water sitting in front of me and drank half of it down. "Is he that bad?"

"No, he's the best. However, with that being said, a guy with his kind of lifestyle has so many opportunities to ..."

"To what?"

"Sylvie, women throw themselves at him."

We were interrupted by the waitress and gave her our order. After she left, I thought for a second. "Kind of like they do to you?" I asked him.

"Yes, no. I wasn't sober most of the time."

"Pearson, that was only in recent years. I remember way back, even when you would come home from law school, women were doing that to you."

Our beverages were delivered—iced tea for me and water for Pearson—and he said, "You're right."

"So what? I'm supposed to avoid him because other women want him?"

He blew out a sigh. "I guess not."

"Have you seen the way other women look at you?"

He shrugged. "I don't pay attention to that."

"Why?"

"I'm not interested. I love my wife more than anything."

"But you don't think Evan is capable of being monogamous?"

"I never said that!"

"Pearson, you didn't have to. You implied it."

He scrubbed his face for a second and said, "I guess I'm projecting my old self onto him."

"Now that we have that taken care of, I want to know about him."

"In which way?"

"I had no idea about his business," I confess.

"I'm not sure how much I should divulge because that's his deal to share with you, but he's extremely successful and very modest about it."

"Ooh, I like that. He doesn't brag about his success." That impressed me. I wasn't fond of people who flaunted their wealth. It was so obnoxious.

"He'd never do that. Sometimes I think it embarrasses him. That's not to say he isn't proud of his accomplishments, but you'll never hear him say things like—oh, you won't believe my portfolio these days. Or you won't believe the accounts I've added. He just isn't that kind of guy. He never even talks about all the houses he—" Pearson abruptly stopped.

"All the houses he what?"

"Again, I don't need to be running my mouth. That's his business, not mine."

"When he was growing his business, did you know about it?"

"Well yeah, because initially, I helped him with some of the legal documents until he became too large and had to hire a firm that specialized in corporate law. But he still keeps me apprised of things. Sometimes, he runs ideas by me and bounces them off me too."

It was obvious Pearson was in Evan's inner circle. "What kind of ideas?"

"Sylvie, I can't tell you everything. If you want to know, ask Evan. In fact, I feel as though I'm betraying him."

"Betraying him? How?"

"I can't explain. But if you want to know anything else, you'll have to ask him."

I traced my finger along the edge of the table, wondering if he'd answer my next question. "Can you at least tell me this? Has he ever been in a serious relationship?"

Pearson groaned. "Sylvie."

"Come on, Pearson, that's something I should know, don't you think? I mean, look what Rose knew about you. I told her all sorts of stuff, building you up."

"Yeah, but she had a fucking file on me too."

I wanted to shrivel in my chair because he was right, but still. I had rooted for him in that relationship and did my best to encourage it.

"True, but I didn't have to say all the positive things about you that I did. If it hadn't been for me, you two would still hate each other."

That grabbed his attention, because he knew I was probably right. Rose and Pearson had an interesting story, one that was best told by them. I was sounding like Pearson now.

"Okay. Yes, he was in one serious relationship and it ended very badly. It nearly ruined him."

My hands went straight to my chest, overlapping each other. "Oh, that's awful."

"It was. I didn't think he'd ever have anything to do with another woman again. That's when he went on his spree of, well, one and dones. Ever since, he's wanted nothing to do with women long term. That's why I went crazy when I heard you'd been seeing him."

Now it makes so much more sense. "Why didn't you explain this in the first place?" I ask, leaning back in the chair. It makes me think about some of the things he's said. The times we were together, he acted so sincere, and I believed him. If Pearson hadn't been his best friend, I would have more doubts, but I knew he was being honest. He wouldn't go to those extremes if he'd wanted a one-nighter. He'd had his chance to walk away after St. Lucia and hadn't.

"Why are you frowning? Those creases in your brow are so deep someone could hide in them," Pearson said, breaking into my thoughts.

"Nothing."

"Nothing my ass."

Thank God, the waiter arrived at that moment with our food. At least I could conjure up something to tell Pearson. But what?

As soon as he left, I dug in, saying, "I'm starving."

Pearson's expression screamed *bullshit*. Then he said, "Don't worry, Sylvie, I'll wait for your answer until after we eat."

I about choked on my salad. When he started to get out of his chair to maybe do the Heimlich, I held out my hand and grabbed my water. After a healthy gulp or two, I said, "Just went down wrong. I'm fine."

"Uh huh. And why is your face so red?"

"Coughing. Doesn't it make your face red?" I answered, and then continued eating.

As promised, when we were finished, he said, "So, why the frown?"

There was no use keeping it from him. "Evan has not been treating me as a one nighter, even though I've given him every opportunity to do so. In fact, he's the absolute opposite. The night of your reception, I was completely out of my mind drunk."

"I seem to remember that," he said wryly. "You were yelling at everyone to do those silly chain dances."

"Yeah, that and other things too, apparently. Evan said I jumped on his back and slapped his ass and yelled *giddy-up*."

"Damn, I'm actually a little sorry I missed that."

"Don't be. I lost an expensive pair of shoes too. But you know we spent the night together, right?"

"Yes." He didn't sound too happy about it.

"Look, I wasn't happy about it either. In fact, I'd made up my mind not to see him again. But he was so persistent, he broke me."

"Broke you?"

"Yeah. He made me cave."

Pearson didn't say anything.

"Well?"

"I'm speechless. This is not the Evan I know."

"After what you told me, that's what I was thinking. Have you talked to him?"

"Yeah. I apologized. But I'm not getting into what else we discussed."

I raised both my hands and almost laughed because I sort of looked like he was arresting me. "That's fine. I don't want to know. But maybe he's changed."

"Sylvie, go easy on him."

"What do you mean?"

"He was totally destroyed in his last relationship. He's fragile where his heart is concerned. On the outside, he appears strong and hardened, but that's only a facade. If you break through his walls, and I think you already have, you need to go easy with him."

Pearson scared me. What if I wasn't strong enough, or what if I wasn't good enough for him? And what about my heart? What if I let him in and he broke *me*? There was only one way to find out.

SEVENTEEN

EVAN

AT TEN IN THE MORNING ON THE DOT, I ARRIVED AT SYLVIE'S. When I knocked on the door, she was waiting for me.

"This seems a bit silly, you driving out here to pick me up. I could've easily taken the train in and met you," she said.

"Not a chance. By the way, let me check out your nose." I tipped her chin up with my index finger and took a long look at her.

"Pretty bad, isn't it?"

"Not at all. Other than the bruising, which is fading fast, I was going to say it looks much better. Especially now the huge bandage is gone."

She opened up her bag and pulled out a large pair of sunglasses. "I have the perfect disguise." She put them on, and they hid a lot of the purplish discoloring around her eyes. "See?"

"Don't those hurt your nose?"

"Not at all, and the splint helps. I get it off this week".

"Well, you don't need to hide behind those, but I understand if it makes you feel better. You ready?" I held my hand out and she put hers in mine. Admittedly, I adored this simple gesture.

We walked out to the limo where Robert waited. He opened

the door for us as we slid inside. I didn't have to tell him where to take us.

Along the way, we talked about our busy week. It was funny how even though we'd spoken every night, there were things we found to talk about that were unimportant, but interesting nevertheless.

We arrived at the Empire State Building and she made sure her phone was ready for photos. Once at the top, she took tons of pictures and then selfies of the two of us.

"I can't believe you've never been here," I said.

She frowned. "I've been here plenty of times."

"Then why was it so important to come?"

A perfect smile spread across her gorgeous face. "Because I've always thought this is one of the most romantic places in New York."

My heart stuttered in my chest. "Right here?"

"Why, yes. Take a look. The view is magnificent. Even though there are crowds of people, it still seems so intimate somehow."

Glancing around, I absorbed the view. I'd been here before but had taken it for granted. Sylvie was right. It was magnificent. You could see for miles in every direction and it was breathtaking. Until I lasered in on the one thing that was even more important—Sylvie. I leaned down and brushed my lips over hers, surprising her a bit.

"You're right. This is romantic, but the view is paled by you."

She gaped. I didn't wait for an argument, because I had a feeling one would come. Instead, I took her hand and moved toward the elevators. We waited in line and her eyes singed me. I grinned, not because I'd shocked or surprised her, but because I'd hopefully made this even more romantic for her.

When we walked outside into the cool November air, I put my arm around her, holding her close. We only had to wait a couple of minutes before Robert showed up. Our next stop was the Statue of Liberty. It wasn't the actual tour though. My boat would take us out and circle it so we would be as close as possible.

Robert drove us to Battery Park where the marina was, and we exited the car.

"I'll text you in a few hours."

"Yes, sir." He drove off.

A confused Sylvie asked, "What are we doing here?"

"You'll see."

I escorted her to my boat. Well, that wasn't quite what it was. It was a yacht. We walked down the dock and there she sat. The StarLady. I'm not sure if Sylvie noticed the name, but I didn't say a word.

She did act surprised when we walked aboard and I introduced her to the captain and four-man crew, who would be serving us today. We'd be having lunch aboard.

Then we went on a tour, and she asked, "Do you own this?"

"I do."

We heard the sounds of the engines rumble to life and she inquired, "Where are we going?"

"To Bermuda, of course."

A look of panic settled over her. "I can't go to Bermuda! I have to work on Monday."

I laughed. "Sylvie, I was joking. We're going on a tour around the Statue of Liberty."

She playfully punched my arm. "I'm gonna kill you. You sounded so serious."

"We could do the islands sometime. Or the Mediterranean. I have another yacht that's anchored elsewhere."

"You're just full of surprises, aren't you? What else do you have hidden in your back pocket? A Harry Potter magic wand?" She leaned around me, trying to see behind me.

I held up both hands. "No wand, I promise." We continued with the tour and I showed her the main stateroom, which was fairly plush, having a king bed with an ensuite. I'd made sure when the yacht was designed that the bathroom was spacious. I wasn't going to pay the price if I didn't have a decent bathroom. There were several other staterooms, but they weren't as elegant or spacious as mine, but they were very nice. There was a dining room, a couple of living areas, viewing area top deck, and an office for me to conduct business in, if necessary. There were outside gathering areas as well, but we'd be mostly inside today, as it was November and too chilly to stay out too long. There was also a kitchen and rooms for the crew.

"This is amazing," she said.

One of the crew appeared and asked if we wanted something to drink. We both requested coffee and went to one of the living areas where it was served.

"So, Evan, exactly how many homes and yachts do you own? I'm not asking because I'm into all that, I just don't want to get blindsided again."

"I thought of it more as a surprise."

"A surprise is when you give someone a cake or a party. Showing someone your yacht is a little more than that."

"I suppose you're right."

"It kind of makes me feel uncomfortable."

"Uncomfortable? How?"

"Because it's way out of my league."

I took both of her hands in mine. "This is exactly what I adore about you. You don't care about these things. Every other woman I've been with only wants this. You are the only woman I've ever considered taking home. No one, and I mean no one, except for Pearson, my parents, Robert, my housekeeper, and the head of security at my company knows where I live. I keep a dummy apartment in the city as a decoy."

She looked horrified. "Why would you do that?"

"To keep the wolves at bay. The paparazzi are often in my face when I go out. You saw it when I went to that gallery showing. They had Jessica and me married off years ago. They hang outside that apartment building to catch me."

Her expression was telling me to stop talking, but since I started, I might as well tell her everything.

"When you're famous on Wall Street, everyone wants a piece of you. The vultures come out, trying to eat you alive. I've set things up to guard against that. What you see on the internet is what I want people to see. It's basically my CV. If someone is looking for me to buy out their organization, they need my information. Of course they'll run financials and other things, but their initial search will come from the internet. I want them to see I'm a viable businessman. Other than that, and what the paparazzi has, there is no personal information available. I have someone constantly sweeping it to keep my data clean. If I go out, I never use my real name either."

"But you did when we went to dinner the other night and to the nightclub. Or I think you did."

"Sylvie, I own both of those places."

"I see."

She was very quiet.

"Are you angry?"

"No." She squeezed my hand. "I actually kind of feel sorry for you."

I chuckled. "I expected a lot, but not that."

"It would be awful hiding all the time."

"The way it's set now, I'm not really hiding anymore. I'm free to go and do as I please."

She sighed. "That's good. For a minute, I was worried about you."

I told her the story of my business, how I never expected it to grow to this level. It surprised me, but then again, I worked my ass off for it too. Things fell into place, year after year. I was demanding, but fair, to my employees, and I never expected more out of them than I expected out of myself. They were told up front, and still are, and if they couldn't handle it, they were sent on their way with a hefty severance package. Everyone signed a no-compete clause when they came to work with me, because we did things differently at StarWorks. We worked harder and smarter than most organizations and I wanted to keep that in house. I'd only lost a few people over the years, and they ended up leaving the business entirely.

"You're remarkable, Evan."

"No, just a hard worker. I'm telling you this for a reason. Full disclosure, you might say. I want us to be together. I'd like for us to see each other consistently, as in more than the occasional date. I haven't felt like this about someone in a very long time and I'd love to explore these feelings with you."

"I would too. I confess it's a little daunting, being with you though."

"Why?"

"You're so huge."

"Excuse me?"

Her face turned bright pink and it was so adorable I wanted to kiss her right then.

"Not that! Your persona."

"I rather liked the idea of the other," I said with mirth.

"Stop! Be serious for a moment."

"All right."

"I'm very much afraid of getting hurt," she said.

I glanced at my shoes. If she only knew. "You're not the only one. But how will we ever know if we don't try?"

"We won't." She circled a finger over the knee of her jeans.

"And what if we miss the greatest chance at love?"

"We'd both regret it forever?"

"I think so." I picked up my coffee mug and handed hers to her. "Here's to not regretting anything."

We clinked our mugs together and I prayed this would go better than my last relationship. It had to or I wouldn't survive.

EIGHTEEN

SYLVIE

WHEN OUR MUGS CLINKED TOGETHER, SOMETHING CLICKED into place. I wanted this relationship to work. I hoped what was between us would blossom into something greater. Even though his wealth and lifestyle freaked me out, maybe I could get used to it after a while.

"Do you mind telling me where your other houses are? At least I can get all of this over in one session."

"Spoken like a psychologist."

"Oh, God. That did sound bad."

"Not really."

"Evan, I was raised totally middle class, so all of this is terribly intimidating," I said, extending an arm out.

He took my arm, pulled it in and then folded his hand so he could press a kiss onto it.

"I understand, because I was raised the same way. I never intended to be this wealthy. It just happened. But I'll tell you about my homes. I love to ski, so I have a place in Vail, but I've been thinking about selling it to buy something else."

"Where?" I asked.

He shrugged. "I'm not sure yet. I've been skiing at Vail for so many years now, I think it's time to go somewhere else. Maybe Utah. I'm still trying to figure it out. Do you ski?"

"A little, if you can call it that."

He grinned. "Can you explain?"

"I used to go in college to those small ski places near Syracuse. I was sort of a bunny hiller."

"And I bet you had a lot of guys chasing you down the bunny hills."

"I had a steady boyfriend back then, so no."

"Have you ever been out west skiing?"

"No, but I've always wanted to."

"Then we'll go. Maybe over Thanksgiving, if your family will approve."

"My family. It's more my mom. She'll throw a fit, then say it's okay. And to that, I can't believe Thanksgiving is next Thursday. What about your other homes? Where are they?"

"There's one other in the Caribbean. On Canouan."

"I've never heard of it."

"It's small, part of the Windward Islands, past St. Lucia. I offered it to Pearson and Rose when they got married, but the house wasn't big enough for their reception and the island is pretty exclusive and difficult to get to, so they decided on St. Lucia instead."

"I bet it's gorgeous."

"We can go there instead of Vail if you'd like."

I'd never been in this position before, choosing one fancy trip over the other.

Before I could answer, he said, "I have an idea. Since November can be iffy for snow, why don't we go to Canouan first and then maybe head to Vail after Christmas?"

"Sounds great to me." Who was I to complain? A free vacation anywhere sounded awesome. "I'll let my family know I won't be home for Thanksgiving. Would you mind doing me a favor?"

"Sure, what is it?"

"Can you come to my house for dinner beforehand so they can meet you?"

"I'd be happy to."

One of the crew came in to let us know we were getting close to the Statue of Liberty.

Evan said, "Come on. Let's go up top where the view is better."

Once there, we saw the statue in the distance. I'd seen it before and toured it several times, but this was much more special.

"Isn't she magnificent?" he asked.

"That she is," I agreed. "I love the view from the crown too."

"Yeah, it's pretty amazing to think about when you're inside."

"Bartholdi was a genius to design it so you could climb up to it."

He took my hand in his and said, "Like so many ancient buildings in Rome, I am amazed by the architecture when I'm there."

"I've only been once and for a few days, but yes, when I did go, I wondered about how they did it without modern day equipment."

"Yes. And after thousands of years, those buildings are still standing. It's a testament to what they did, versus what we do."

"Planned obsolescence," I said.

"Yes. That's why after a couple of years, you need a new phone or computer, or washer and dryer. I want a company that doesn't do that to the consumer."

"There are a few out there that don't. But the technology evolves and then your computer becomes worthless and you end up having to get a new one anyway."

"Exactly." He laughed. "How in the hell did we get on this discussion?"

"No idea," I answered and then I cracked up too.

After our third pass around the statue, a crew member came to let us know lunch was ready. Evan took my hand and we moved to the dining room, where it was set up to eat. This wasn't just some picnic of peanut butter and jelly sandwiches. No, we were having lobster, tomato bisque, salad, and a vegetable medley. For dessert, we would be having molten chocolate lava cake. How did I know? There was a card on the table with the menu on it. Fancy schmancy.

"This sounds amazing," I said as the tomato bisque appeared in front of me, as if by magic."

"I hope you like it," Evan said.

"How can I not? Lobster is my favorite." I tasted the bisque and hummed my pleasure. "It's delicious."

He smiled and tried his. "It is good."

Soon our salads were served, along with bread that was warm and crusty, with butter. I was in food heaven. I polished off my soup, and salad, but left most of the bread. I was saving myself for the lobster.

The waiter came back with all the equipment—a cracking tool, lobster fork, bib, and gloves. But then he wanted to know if I preferred for him to do it.

"No, this is the fun part, but thank you."

After he vanished, Evan said, "This is another thing I love about you."

"What? That I like to get my hands dirty?" I grinned.

"Yes, and that you actually enjoy it."

"Is that a compliment?"

"You bet it is."

"Then, thank you." I picked up my water glass and said, "Happy lobster cracking." He rumbled with laughter.

It took me no time at all breaking up my crustacean. I was a master cracker. I expertly de-shelled the tail, even removing the vein that ran along the back. When I cut into the tender meat and dipped it into the butter, it melted in my mouth.

"Mmm, delicious."

Evan glanced up from his and said, "Damn, you're really good at that."

"Uh huh." I continued on with eating the tail until it was gone. Next, onto the claws. I pulled them off the body, grabbing the knuckles. Then I pushed the meat out of the knuckles using the end of my tiny fork. Evan watched me in fascination. I dipped that meat in the butter, and said, "You'd better eat or it's going to get cold."

"Yeah, sure."

When it came to the claws, I broke those up by spreading them apart by the claw itself. Using the cracker, I split the small part and got the meat out. Then onto the chunky side. In no time at all, the meat was freed and I was a happy woman. The only things I had left were the legs and I'd need a rolling pin to get that meat out, so sadly, I'd have to let those go.

"How did you ever learn to disassemble a lobster like that?" Evan asked. "It was almost surgical."

Chuckling, I said, "We used to go to Maine every summer for our family vacation. We all had to learn how to eat lobster in order to survive. I remember hating it at first. But obviously I grew to love it." I looked at his plate and he'd barely touched his. "Would you care for some assistance?"

"You don't mind?"

"No. I'd love to."

"Be my guest."

It only took me a couple of minutes to have the lobster ready to eat and he was one giant grin. Then he scarfed it down faster than I did mine.

"See, I told you it was delicious."

He reached across and swept his thumb across my chin. "You had some butter there."

"Thanks. I hate when you have something like that and people don't tell you. Or if you have pepper stuck between your teeth and they let you run around all day with a giant hunk of something in your teeth. By the way, do I have anything in my teeth now?" I showed him all of them and he only laughed.

"All clear."

"Hey, it's important. I'd tell you, you know."

"I'm sure you would."

The waiter appeared again on silent feet to clear our plates. I nearly jumped this time when he asked, "Are you finished, ma'am?"

"Yes, thank you."

When he was gone, I asked Evan, "Does he even walk? I never heard him come in. He's like a vampire."

"A vampire?"

"Yeah, you know how they can just appear anywhere and are super fast. Well, maybe not him, since it's in the middle of the day and he'd burst into flames, but you know."

"Did you learn this from one of your books?" I could tell he was trying not to laugh.

"Oh, yeah. Paranormal romances are awesome."

"I thought you were reading The Raunchy Duke."

"I am."

"Isn't that a historical romance?"

"Yeah. I read anything with romance in it. I'm flexible like that. For instance, if your Financial Times had romance in it, I'd probably read it too. I wish my psychology journals had romance in them."

"You really are a romantic."

I had a sudden image of that dream I'd had, where Evan was the raunchy duke and I was the virgin getting my ass spanked. "You have no idea."

NINETEEN

EVAN

THE CAPTAIN ANCHORED THE BOAT AT THE MARINA AND Robert was waiting to whisk us off to our next destination. When we got to the car, Robert handed me the tickets after Sylvie had gotten in, so she didn't see. Then we sped off.

Robert weaved in and out through traffic, which wasn't too terrible today, and we arrived in plenty of time before the two o'clock matinee. As the car came to a stop, Sylvie looked out and asked, "Where are we?"

"You'll see in a minute." I helped her out and a grin appeared on her face.

"Oh, my gosh, you didn't! I'm so excited. I've wanted to see this."

"I'm glad. I took a chance on it and figured even if you had, since it was a romantic play, you wouldn't mind seeing it again."

She gazed at me, her face radiating joy. "That's so thoughtful of you." Her hand wrapped around my wrist and she tugged me close and rose on her toes to press her lips to my cheek. My arm automatically wrapped around her and I hugged her against me. It felt so ... right, having her this close.

"I'm glad you approve."

"I not only approve, I'm overjoyed that you took the extra

time to think about me in this way." We walked arm-in-arm inside the theater. I purchased us a couple of bottles of water and we headed toward our seats.

As we walked in on the main level, she said, "You didn't."

"What?" We continued walking down the aisle until we got to our seats.

"Seriously? Front and center? How did you manage this?"

"It's a matinee and I have connections."

She flung her arms around my neck, which took me by surprise. "I've been to plenty of shows, but never sat in these kinds of seats. Thank you!" Then she kissed me on the lips. It was a chaste kiss, but I wish it hadn't been. It was probably for the best because we were up in front of the theater, which was beginning to fill, and would've had quite an audience.

We sat down and she took my hand. "This is amazing. I can't tell you how excited I am."

"You know what they say about actions speaking louder than words."

"Yeah. Am I making a spectacle of myself?"

"Not at all, and I love it, so who cares? We have fifteen minutes before the show starts, do you want anything? Maybe use the restroom?"

"No, I'm fine. I just want to stare at the stage." She sighed.

"Okay, I'll be right back."

Since we were at a show, I thought some candy was in order, so I went to the counter and purchased some. When I came back, I watched her head as it bobbed around, studying everything. *Good call, man.*

Sliding into the seat next to her, I said, "Want some?" I shook the box of Skittles I'd bought.

"Skittles! Yes." She held out her hand like an eager kid as I sprinkled some in. I watched as she put one into her mouth and chewed. "Mmm. I love these."

"Do you like these too?" I asked, pulling the box of M&M's out that I'd bought as well.

"Oh, my God. I'm going to be as big as a house after today. Lobster with butter, molten lava cake, Skittles, and M&M's."

"And that doesn't include dinner," I said, laughing. "But believe me, you are nowhere near the size of a house."

"Um, these hips can dispute that."

"Um, I know those hips and I think they're perfect."

That was not the right thing to say because her face flushed, and she clammed up instantly.

Dammit, Thomas, why can't you learn to shut your mouth?

I had to fix this and fast, because I didn't want to put a damper on this day.

"Listen, I probably shouldn't have said that, but it's true. Besides your winning personality and your gorgeous looks, it's one of the other things that attracted me to you."

"My winning personality?"

"Yes. You were a breath of fresh air. Fun loving, didn't give a damn, and weren't out to impress anyone. You did what you wanted to do without regard to what others wanted."

"Evan, I was trashed."

"Not at first, you weren't. I was eyeing you way before then."

"Really?"

"Yes. I followed you around all night, but it took me forever to work up the courage to talk to you. You were pretty much on your way to being trashed by then."

We didn't get to say anything else, because the lights dimmed, the curtain rose, and the music began. Truth be told, I watched Sylvie more than I watched the play. I felt like the main character in the play at times when he took the prostitute places and observed her enjoying herself. At times, Sylvie wore such a complete expression of delight, it filled me with more joy than I could ever remember.

At the end, she cried. "That was amazing. I loved it. Thank you so much for bringing me."

She made me feel like a king. "You're welcome. And look." I

showed her both boxes of candy. "You hardly ate any candy at all."

"I was so engrossed in the play, I couldn't." We stood and she suddenly threw herself at me. "Thank you. No one has ever taken me to a play before. This was ... just wonderful."

Robert was waiting for us outside and we got into the car and she said, "I don't think we can top that. I'm sorry. It's just not possible."

"You're probably right, with the way you're feeling now." It was true. She was on cloud nine and I doubted it could get any better. It only took a few minutes to get to the next spot.

"Are you kidding me?" she asked as we got out of the car.

"Are you disappointed?"

"No! I've never been and always wanted to."

"I didn't know, and figured if you had, then we could check out the latest additions and leave. Although we have dinner reservations at eight thirty. I hope you like Italian."

"I love it."

"Great. Then let's explore Madame Tussaud's."

We walked inside and she went crazy with the selfies. Soon I joined in as we laughed at ourselves in some of the ridiculous poses, especially with the Hulk and other superheroes. We ended up having to leave before we finished exploring because there was so much to see and decided we'd have to come back again.

"I never imagined it would have so much," she said. "I didn't know about the 3D cinema."

"Neither did I. I have to admit, it was much more enjoyable than I'd expected."

"At first, it was a tiny bit creepy because they looked so real, but I got over that pretty fast."

"I'll say, the way you jumped in with the selfies."

She grabbed my hand. "We'll have to check those out over dinner. By the way, where are we going?"

"It's a surprise," I said as we got into the car. Robert drove off and we headed to Little Italy. I had a favorite restaurant there and I hoped she loved it as much as I did.

Our table was waiting for us when we arrived and the owner greeted me with a warm welcome. Then he saw Sylvie and immediately hugged her.

"Ah, signore, she is bellissima. Very beautiful. Signore Thomas, please follow me."

My favorite table awaited us, in the back in a private alcove. We were seated and given menus. A waiter appeared in moments, pouring our water, and taking our drink order. I ordered a bottle of wine and we checked out the menu.

"Everything here is fresh and made daily, including all the pastas."

"I'm overwhelmed."

"May I suggest something?"

"Yes."

"All of the seafood dishes will be excellent as he buys the fish each morning from the vendors. He prepares it so it will literally melt in your mouth. None of his traditional dishes are what they seem. The lasagna is prepared with béchamel sauce. It's fabulous. The Bolognese is the best I've ever had, coupled with his homemade pappardelle, makes it a wonderful dish. With any of those you can't go wrong, but honestly, anything you choose will be excellent. Oh, he'll most likely have some specials."

"You just made my decision more difficult." The twinkle in her eye lit up her face.

"Let's see what the waiter says and maybe that will help. I'm undecided too."

The waiter showed up with the wine and it was delicious. Sylvie agreed. He then read off the specials and we both chuckled, saying how confused we were over what to order. He said he'd be right back.

He returned with Flavio, the owner, and he asked us what appealed to us. I was interested in one of the seafood specials, as was Sylvie, but we were both interested in some of the pasta.

"I tell you what. We send you one of the specials, then we make up a dish of a trio of the lasagna, Bolognese, and lobster ravioli, for each of you. Then you no have to decide. How's that?"

"Wonderful," I said. "Thank you, Flavio."

"My pleasure, Signore Thomas." He bowed and left.

Sylvie asked, "Is Robert going to come in here and wheel us out in wheelbarrows? Because I've gotta tell you, there is no way I'll be able to walk if I eat all that food."

The expression on her face had me laughing. When I was able to speak, I said, "Sylvie, you don't have to eat it all."

"But I love pasta and I might not be able to control myself. If I get too bad, will you mind if I unbutton my jeans?"

"No, and again, these are the kinds of things I love about you. The fact that you'd even ask me this is hilarious."

"But my pants are already tight, even though I didn't eat that much today, but after this dinner, I might have to borrow yours."

"Now that I'd like to see."

When our food arrived, Sylvie was in heaven. Every time I tried to ask her something, her hand would come up and I'd have to wait for her answer.

"This is orgasmic. I've never eaten Italian food this good. I can't answer you when I'm in the middle of processing a bite."

"Processing a bite?"

"Yes, I'm enjoying every aspect of it."

"You're really into food, aren't you?"

"Pasta is every woman's dream, Evan."

Most women I'd ever taken to dinner had only pushed the food around on their plates and pretended to eat. Not this one. She ate with gusto and pleasure and it pleased me greatly. She didn't put up any pretenses about it.

After her plate was half empty and the one we shared was completely empty—due to me eating most of it—she leaned back and sighed. "That was a true delight."

"I agree and I'm glad you enjoyed it."

She reached for the button of her jeans and popped it open. "Ah, much better."

"You're a mess."

"No, I'm fat."

"Hardly."

The waiter showed up and asked if we'd like dessert.

Sylvie held up a hand.

"The lady says no and none for me either."

"Very good, sir."

We sat and were enjoying our wine when Flavio stopped by.

"You were happy with the choices?"

"Very," I said.

He looked at Sylvie and she said, "It was amazing. The best I've ever had."

"Grazie. Thank you." He bowed and left.

It was close to ten o'clock and I wondered if she would consider going to my place. I'd tried the last time and she'd said no. Would she say the same thing again?

The waiter brought the check and I placed my credit card on it for him to take. When he brought it back, I signed it, leaving him a huge tip. On the way out, I also gave Flavio a large cash tip as well.

Once outside, I asked, "Well, Sylvie, where shall I tell Robert to take us. My place or yours?"

TWENTY

SYLVIE

Taking Evan's hand in mine, I said, "Yours." His smile sent shivers down my spine and I knew tonight would be a repeat of what happened on St. Lucia. But this time it wouldn't be a mistake. I would be a willing partner with a full memory of everything we did.

We arrived at an underground garage and exited the car. Evan thanked Robert as we parked and they exchanged a few words. I was so nervous, I didn't pay attention. What had I gotten myself into? Was I ready to take this step or had this been a mistake?

Evan wrapped his large and warm hand around mine and we walked toward the elevators. He punched in some numbers on a keypad and up we went. I wasn't sure to which floor, since the elevator didn't have the usual numbers on it. When the doors swooshed open, we were in some sort of lobby or vestibule. There was another door in front of us and we walked up to it. I watched him enter a series of numbers onto another keypad and press his fingertips on a pad. Then I heard a click as the door unlocked.

"Is this some sort of high tech security lock or something?" I asked.

"Yeah, I don't want any snoopers entering, you might say."

"How can they even get through the elevator?"

"You'd be surprised. They've come disguised as the maintenance man, an electrician, the internet guy, you name it."

"But I thought you said nobody knew you lived here."

"I did, but that doesn't mean people aren't curious about who actually does live here. I'm not even listed on the building's tenant list. All my mail goes to the business address."

I smiled. "You really are a man of mystery."

"I suppose so. Would you like to come in?" He waved an arm and it made me laugh.

I walked through the entryway and tried hard not to suck in a breath. The room opened to an expansive living area where one entire wall was nothing but windows that looked out over the city of Manhattan. It was stunning. I found myself in front of the view and hardly remembered walking there. In the distance, I saw the Empire State Building and even the Freedom Tower.

"This is incredible," I said as I felt his presence next to me.

"It's the very reason I bought the ... place."

I glanced up at him when he said that, because I sensed there was more to the story. "The place?"

"I own the building. I'm also heavily invested in real estate."

"Out of curiosity, did you own the Italian restaurant we went to tonight?"

He shook his head. "Sylvie, I don't own everything."

To me, it seemed he did. Of course, when all I had to my name was one small townhouse and a car, anything more than that seemed like a lot.

He turned me towards him and asked, "Does it bother you that I have all this wealth?"

"In some ways, because it makes me seem insignificant." He went to say something, but I stopped him. "But in others, it doesn't because you worked hard for it and earned it."

He appeared thoughtful for a second and said, "Thank you for that. And I don't ever want you to feel insignificant because you are not that to me at all. In fact, you are quite the opposite.

The mere fact that you are standing here should tell you something."

"Oh?"

"You don't remember?"

I tried to recall what he was saying, but couldn't.

"Sylvie, you're the first and only woman I've ever brought here."

Then it hit me and a huge grin settled on my face. "Yes, and thank you for trusting me enough to do that."

"Let me show you around."

Since we were in the living room, we started here. It had a massive TV, because apparently Evan loved sports. The furniture was welcoming and not stiff and formal. I threw myself on one of the sofas and exclaimed, "Oh, I love this. It's so comfy."

"I've been known to take long naps on them."

"Can't blame you for that."

Moving on to the rest of the place, the dining room was huge, but I asked myself if he never brought anyone here, why he needed such a large one. And then the kitchen was a gourmet cook's dream. Expansive, with all the top appliances anyone could want, it also had a huge island with seating, a beverage cooler, wine cooler, and just about anything one could imagine.

"Wow, this is amazing! Do you cook?" I asked.

"I dabble, if you want to call it that. But I have a house-keeper who cooks for me during the week. She spoils me something fierce."

A wave of jealousy tore through me. I imagined this house-keeper to be young, attractive and to wear one of those French maid outfits when she worked. Oh, my God, I had it bad already.

"Why is your face red, Sylvie?"

My hands flew to my cheeks and they were hot. "I didn't realize they were." I was a terrible liar. That only made them redder.

"Sylvie, what were you thinking?"

"Nothing, really."

He'd backed me against one of the counters and now had me caged.

"Come on, I know you're hiding something. What is it?"

"Really, it's nothing."

"Then why are your shoes suddenly so interesting? You were fine until I mentioned that I had a housekeeper. Is that it? That I have a housekeeper, who happens to be in her late fifties?"

I immediately glanced up to see his eyes dancing with mirth. Dammit! I gave it away. Why was I always so stupid?

"You were jealous of Rita, weren't you?"

"Rita?"

"Rita, my fifty-eight-year-old housekeeper who spoils me like her own son."

I scrunched up my face and squeaked out, "Maybe." But I didn't dare tell him about the image of Rita in the French maid's outfit. He'd never let me live that down.

"I can't wait to introduce the two of you. She's going to love you and be so happy I finally have a girlfriend."

"Is that what I am? Your girlfriend?"

"I certainly hope so."

"Then are you my boyfriend?"

"Why do I feel like this is so cheesy and we're in junior high?"

"I don't know, but I think it's kind of cute." I bit my lower lip.

"Hmm. Wanna know what I think is much cuter?"

"What?" I asked.

Suddenly, I found myself sitting on the counter, where I was now face-to-face with him. He took my chin between his thumb and finger and said, "This." Then his lips captured mine in a heated kiss and everything else I'd been thinking of, including Rita and the French maid's outfit, was erased from my mind. All I knew from that moment on was how his lips and mouth made me feel. Hot and sexy. When his tongue slipped past the opening of my mouth and the kiss deepened even further, I was completely under his spell. I decided right then I never wanted this kiss to end.

Unfortunately, we had to breathe, which really sucked. I must've voiced that out loud, because Evan burst out laughing.

"What?"

"The things you say. Breathing sucks. You're hilarious."

"I didn't mean to say that out loud, but it's true."

He wrapped my legs around his waist, put my hands on his shoulders and said, "Hold on."

"Oh, wait, is this the reverse piggyback?"

He laughed again. "Yeah, and this time, I get to kiss you."

He finished the tour, saving the best room for last. His bedroom.

"Holy crap, my whole house could fit in here." It had a sitting area with a fireplace, the kind you turned on with a switch. The closet was larger than my bedroom, and the bathroom was like a luxury spa.

"Wanna take a bubble bath?" he asked. He set me on my feet, and I walked around, inspecting the place.

"Dude, your shower is a palace." It was true. I counted ten shower heads. "How do you ever get out of here?"

"You can turn only one on, if you want."

"I see."

The tub was gigantic. It could probably hold four adults. "You could have a party in here."

"Sylvie, the only party I'd like to have in there, would be with you." His voice gave me goosebumps. Was I ready to get naked in front of him? I knew coming here would result in this. Why was I acting like a virgin?

"Evan, I'm nervous."

"I can tell. What can I do to make it easier?"

"Turn the water on, put the bubble bath in, and dim the lights."

"Yes, ma'am."

I watched him go about it, and then he turned to me, asking, "What next?"

"Kiss me?"

"You don't have to ask."

I was in his arms and we were practically devouring each other, when I said, "Do you think we should undress?"

"That's an excellent idea."

"You first," I said.

"Fine, but Sylvie, I'm going to be the one who undresses you."

I nodded and then watched him get naked. First, he unbuttoned his shirt. Next, his jeans. He was down to his boxer briefs and I had the outlined glimpse of what lay beneath. I licked my lips. Then he slipped those off and he was exactly as I remembered. Magnificent.

He walked up to me and lifted the hem of my sweater. It whooshed over my head, leaving me in my bra. Then he unhooked it and just stared. My nipples hardened under his gaze.

"You're perfect, just as I remembered." A hand teased one nipple as the other unbuttoned my jeans. I moaned, responding to his touch. My pants fell to my ankles and I stepped out of them, leaving me in one of the thongs he'd sent me. It was the black lacy one with the bow right in front.

"You look gorgeous in this." He dropped to his knees and placed his mouth on me. When he opened it around me, I moaned again.

"Evan."

"Hmm."

Two hands gripped my hips as he tongued me over the silken fabric. The feel of his mouth and teeth was divine. If his hands hadn't been holding me, my knees would've buckled. Then he tugged the thong to the side and his tongue flicked over me repeatedly, before it circled and pressed down. I cried out his name as I came.

Afterward, he pulled the thong off and I was finally naked.

He picked me up, sat in the tub with me in his lap. I was leaning against his chest and felt his erection against my back when he lifted my hips and slid carefully inside.

"Is this okay?" he asked.

"Ahh, yes."

"Lean forward, hands on my thighs."

I did as he asked.

"You're now in control."

His legs were together, and I rose and fell on him, first slow, then faster. His hands directed me, as he filled me, stretched me. How could I have not remembered this? I rocked my hips to hit my most sensitive spots, both of them, until I was in a frenzy, and the deep sounds he made only drove me harder. The orgasm I chased was within my grasp and it plowed into me as I gasped. My inner muscles spasmed around him as he groaned loud and long, spilling himself into me. I fell back against him, panting.

He smoothed my hair back, kissing my neck. I felt slightly awkward now and didn't know what to say. I wanted to say, "Whoa, that was epic." But would that sound juvenile? He saved me by speaking first.

"The only thing missing was that I didn't get to see your beautiful face when you came."

I melted.

TWENTY-ONE

EVAN

Sylvie looked over her shoulder at me with a hint of shyness in her eyes. I wasn't having any of that. I turned her around to face me so I could kiss her plump lips. The sounds she'd made as I'd thrust into her were enough to set me off and here she was again, moaning into my mouth. I tore myself away from her saying, "You keep that up and I'm going to have to fuck you again."

"Would that be so bad?"

"Not bad at all, but we're turning into raisins." I held up her hand to show her. A bubble of laughter filled the room. "Come on." I set her aside, stood up, and her eyes circled as she ogled me. I'll admit it was a proud moment. Reaching for a couple of towels, I wrapped one around her first, and then me.

We dried off and I carried her to the bed. Moments later, I brought back two bottles of sparkling water. "I hope this is okay."

"It's great."

We drank and then climbed under the sheets.

"This bed is fantastic. It's so comfortable."

I pressed a button and the shades closed. "It's really bright in the morning and these are blackout shades."

"Evan, can I ask you something?"

"Sure."

"I noticed you didn't wear a condom."

I didn't waste one second before rolling over and looking her in the eyes. "No, I didn't. When we were in St. Lucia, I asked you about it and you told me it was okay not to because you were on the pill. I'm safe, Sylvie, if that's what you're concerned about."

"Well, that's good. I don't remember any of that. I'm glad you asked."

"I would never have done anything else. You are on the pill, aren't you?"

"Yes."

I sighed. "For a moment there, you had me scared."

She brought her hand to my face, saying, "Thanks for asking while I was drunk out of my mind. That's something I never would've thought of in that state."

"You're welcome." I kissed her. "Are you tired?"

"Yeah, I am."

I pulled her against my side. "Go to sleep, sweetheart." Her eyelids fluttered closed and I watched as she fell asleep in my arms. I had dreamed about this since I'd gotten home from St. Lucia. I'd wanted her back in my bed and now I hoped she was here to stay.

My mind leaped ahead to Thanksgiving. I had to notify my people that I would be arriving on Thursday. I also had to let my flight crew know. They probably wouldn't be happy, but they would earn double pay so that should alleviate some of their irritation over having to work on a holiday. I made mental notes of everything to be done tomorrow before sleep claimed me.

When I woke up, the room was dark, and Sylvie was wrapped around my torso, using me as a pillow. One of her hands was dangerously close to my dick, so I didn't want to move. I already had morning wood and moving would only make it worse. I was an early riser from habit, so I didn't know how long she intended to sleep. In here, it was easy to forget the day was passing on with the blackout shades. Reaching for my phone, I was surprised to see it was already eight.

I typed out a message to my staff at the house in the islands, letting them know I would be arriving Thursday afternoon. Next, I sent a message to my flight crew, telling them to be prepared to leave Thursday at ten in the morning from Westchester for Canouan and returning on Sunday morning. I would plan to stay at Sylvie's on Wednesday night since she was close to that airport.

Then I slipped out of bed, trying not to disturb her. I hoped she could sleep late. I threw on a pair of old jeans and a T-shirt and went to the kitchen to brew some coffee. After I poured a cup, I took it to the office with the intentions of getting some work done. When I turned on the computer, one of my emails had already been answered. My pilot said he'd have everything ready for wheels up at ten a.m.

There were reports to review and other things, but my mind was occupied with thoughts of the woman who was still asleep in my bed. What the hell was I doing in here working when I could still be naked next to her? Was I insane? It seemed so.

Shutting down my computer, I drank the rest of my coffee and went back to bed. Sylvie was still curled on her side, where I had been laying, so I crawled back in and curved my body around hers. She smelled of lavender and lemon, making me want her even more. I remembered how perfect she'd been last night, and the sounds she'd made as we fucked. But I frowned as I thought about it. I wanted more of her, more than once a week, only I didn't want to scare the shit out of her either. I thought back to Robert's advice about the filly. Slow and easy. It would be hard because when I wanted something, I usually went after it with everything I had. And I hadn't wanted a woman in ages. After tasting her again, the truth was, I'd never wanted anyone the way I wanted Sylvie.

The sound of her stretching pulled me out of my daydreaming. Her arms touched one if mine and she jerked awake. When she saw me, a slow, sexy smile spread across her face.

"Good morning, sweets." I leaned down to kiss her.

"Stop. I have morning breath."

I laughed and kissed her anyway. "I love your morning breath."

"Hmm. Yours tastes like coffee. Have you been up?"

"Uh huh. But then I decided I'd rather be naked with you."

I stretched her arm above her head and went for one of her nipples. Taking it into my mouth, I sucked it hard until it elongated and hardened.

"Oh, my. That's good."

Moving to her other one, I did the same. Then I crawled between her thighs and lifted them, spreading them wide. Using my tongue, I pushed inside of her, and then licked her in a long swipe.

"One or two?" I asked.

"Huh?"

"Fingers. One or two."

"One."

I used one finger to press inside of her and my tongue for the outside, concentrating on her clit. She was slick with desire and her pink folds gleamed. When she was about to come, I stopped. She let out a wail.

"Don't stop. Why'd you stop?"

"It'll make it better when you come."

I started everything over again, only this time I barely licked her clit. She tried to push her hips into me, but I held her down. She moaned and begged to come, but I stopped again. I took my finger and pressed it on her G-spot.

"How does this feel?"

"Yes. Good." She was panting.

"Do you want more?"

"Yes."

I added another finger. And then my tongue barely fluttered

across her clit. She begged some more. She was so close, so very close. I knew all I had to do was press on her clit with my tongue and she'd fall into her climax. But if I prolonged it, her orgasm would be that much stronger. So I did. Her head thrashed from side to side as she begged.

"Oh, God, please, Evan. Make me come. Please."

That was when I did. She clenched her thighs against me and gripped the sheets as her tiny muscles clamped down in pulsing waves on my fingers.

As soon as her orgasm subsided, I climbed up her body and thrust inside of her. "Oh, dear God." She gave a shuddering cry as I entered her.

She was wet, tight, and hot. "Sylvie." Her name came out in a cross between a moan and shout. I wanted to ask if she was okay, but something primal took over and I pumped inside of her with everything I had. My hips pounded against her as her fingers dug into my shoulders. Her expressions were magical as her brow creased and her mouth was slightly open. She watched me closely as I did her, and those gray eyes reached inside of me, touching a place I thought had died a long time ago. Reaching between us, I found her clit, massaged it, and soon her breathing sped up. Her inner muscles rhythmically clenched my cock, and that was all I needed to go off into my own climax. This wasn't just sex. It was an overwhelming total body experience I'd never had before.

When things calmed down, I kissed her. Really kissed her as though I never wanted to let her go. She was the brightest star in the sky and no one like Sylvie had ever impacted me like this before.

My body rested on my elbows as I stared at her gorgeous face. Her hair was tousled, and she was absolutely perfect.

"I've never seen anyone so beautiful as you, Sylvie West."

Her fingers traced the outline of my lips and she smiled. "Thank you."

"That was unbelievable."

"Yes, it was. Thank you."

I chuckled. "Are you going to keep thanking me?"

"I suppose, if you keep giving me these amazing orgasms."

"Don't forget, you gave me one too."

Her smile disappeared and she frowned. "You're a tease, Evan Thomas."

"I know, but it was worth it in the end, wasn't it?"

"Yeah, but in the meantime, I wanted to kill you."

"Just wait until I use that flogger on you." I winked at her.

"Say what?"

"Sylvie, you don't think I bought those to let them collect dust, do you?"

"Wait. What do you mean by those?"

"I bought one for you and one for me."

"You're joking?"

I rolled off her and opened the bedside table. When I showed her the flogger, she nearly died. Then I did something else. I ran the soft fringes of leather up and down her belly and breasts. Her nipples immediately pebbled.

"I think someone may really enjoy this. I cannot wait to try this out later today. But first, we have to eat breakfast."

TWENTY-TWO

SYLVIE

EVERYTHING REACTED ALL AT ONCE AND I WONDERED HOW IT was possible. I'd just had two orgasms. Nevertheless, a fire in the pit of my belly grew, spreading throughout my veins, heating me everywhere. And I don't even want to mention what happened between my thighs.

"Up you go."

"Huh?" I had flogger brain and wasn't paying attention.

"Come on. We need to eat and shower. Not in that order."

He took my hand and pulled me along into his bathroom. Gah, what a treat. This shower was to die for. After he turned it on, when all those decadent nozzles sprayed everywhere, I had another orgasm. He laughed as he soaped me from head to toe and shampooed my hair.

"Do you have any conditioner in here?"

"Shit. No, but there's some in the other bathroom. Hang on." He got out and wrapped a towel around himself. Soon he was back with the requested item.

"Thank you. If I didn't have this, getting a comb through this hair wouldn't be possible."

"Allow me." He did the rest and when we were finished, he asked if he could brush out the tangles. It was wonderful having someone spoil me. He gave me a T-shirt to wear along with some pretty white panties.

"Did you just happen to have these lying around?" Suspicion laced my question.

A smile danced on his lips as he said, "Oh, didn't I tell you? I occasionally like to dress in women's lingerie."

I snorted and then ended up bent over in a fit of laughter. The mere thought of him prancing around in that tiny cotton thong had me laughing so hard that I couldn't stop.

With a completely straight face, he said, "What's so funny?"

He nearly brought me to my knees before he joined in.

"I'd love to see you model these." I dangled them by my index finger.

When our laughter finally died down, he explained, "I actually picked these up when I bought the others. Wishful thinking, you know."

"If you'd told me then, I might've been angry, but now I'm glad you did. You really do have a thing for white cotton."

"There's a sense of innocence attached to it. And on you, they're sexy as hell."

"Thank you." Dang, he was attentive.

"Breakfast?"

"Yes, somehow, I'm starving, but I can't imagine why."

He linked our fingers together and said, "We need to keep up your strength."

"And why's that?"

"So you can withstand that flogging session later." He waggled his brows. I wasn't sure if he was serious or not, but my entire body fired up at his words. I hoped he was because I was definitely all in.

He made me sit at the island while he fixed breakfast. I envied his kitchen. There were expansive white Carrara marble countertops, a huge gas cooktop, a large refrigerator, and just about anything you could want or imagine in it.

"God, I love your kitchen."

"That's what Rita says. She uses it a lot more than me. Breakfast is the only meal I really cook."

"It's a dream come true."

He glanced up from whipping the eggs and said, "Sylvie, you're my dream come true."

I swallowed as warmth spread through me. My heart fluttered and then a team of butterflies landed in my belly. He made me feel like a teenager again, falling in love for the first time. Holy hell! Was I falling for him? As in falling in love? This was happening way too fast.

"What's that look on your face?"

"What look?"

"Like you're getting ready to bolt for the door, screaming."

Damn, he was perceptive.

"I, uh, just thought of something."

"Can you share?"

"I'd rather not."

He nodded and went back to cooking. Thankful he didn't press me for more, I went back to thinking. Maybe I was being dramatic. Surely, he didn't feel this way. He probably just said that about me to be nice.

"Evan, can I ask you something?"

"Sure."

"You said I was the only woman you've ever brought here. Why?"

"I thought I told you. Most women aren't after the real me."

"Have you ever been in a serious relationship before?"

He froze. For a long moment, he didn't so much as lift his head. Finally, he resumed what he was doing and answered me. "Yes, I have." That was it.

"I take it you don't want to talk about it."

He expelled out a long breath. Then he finished our omelets, plated them, added the toast, butter, and brought them around so he could sit and eat.

"Sylvie, it's a long and ugly story."

"I understand."

"No, you don't. It happened about eight years ago, when the business was really taking off. I thought I loved her, truly loved her."

His words pinched my heart. I didn't want him to love anyone else. A streak of jealousy tore through me. Jesus, I had it bad for him already.

"She betrayed me like I never thought possible. That's why I haven't been involved with anyone since."

"What did she do?"

"Do you mind if we eat first? Talking about this leaves a sour taste in my mouth."

"Not at all." I remembered Pearson mentioning it was bad.

I cut off a portion of the omelet and began eating. "Oh, this is delicious."

That brought a smile back to his face. "I'm glad you like it."

"I love it." I was super hungry, so it didn't take long for me to polish it off. He did the same and when we looked at each other, it was with humor.

"At least we know how to work up an appetite," I said.

"Did you know that a twenty-five-minute session of sex burns sixty-nine calories for women and a hundred calories for men?" he asked.

"Thank you for that information. Sixty-nine, huh?" I grinned.

"You can google it if you want. I'm not making it up."

I clamped my lips together, trying not to laugh. "If you say so."

"I'm totally serious. Would you like to place a bet?"

"Sure. How much?" I was positive he was joking. Who would come up with that number?

"If I win, you have to give me a blow job. If you win, you get to pick whatever you want."

I held out my hand and said, "Deal."

He grabbed his phone. When that cocky grin of his

appeared, I knew his dick would soon be in my mouth. Holding out his phone, his grin grew wider. "See?"

"This had to have been written by a man. Who else would've come up with sixty-nine?"

"Maybe, but it's in more than one article."

"I concede. But before we head off for blow job heaven, can we finish the discussion we started before we ate?"

He took in a sharp breath and nodded. "You deserve to know the entire story." His hands moved into the prayer pose and he pressed them to his lips before he spoke. "As you know, I was involved with someone a while back, someone I cared for very much, who I thought I truly loved. This person told me everything I wanted to hear, everything I wanted to believe. We were together for over two years. Long enough to know and trust her, or so I thought. I had suggested marriage several times and she'd claimed she wasn't interested in it, which was fine by me. I was much younger and building my business so that wasn't my focus at the time. Until she came to me one day and said she was pregnant. I thought it was weird because she told me she was on the pill."

He looked over at me, as I stared back at him. He seemed anxious, but I couldn't tell if it was because he hated telling me or if he still had feelings for this woman. Pushing to his feet, he paced for a second, then spun around, facing me again. "It was surreal the day she told me. I asked if she was sure, because of the pill. She became enraged and stormed out. I didn't know what to do. I called her, but she didn't answer. Pearson talked me off the ledge because I thought she was going to do something rash, like have an abortion, since she'd never wanted to get married. She was gone for several days, but eventually came back and said she couldn't be with me anymore because of what I'd asked her."

"So then what happened?" I asked.

"Yeah, that's where it got sticky. She left and later I found out she'd never been pregnant in the first place. She'd been having an affair with someone and they wanted to extort money from me. They had planned this elaborate scheme with the fake pregnancy and her leaving. Then she was going to have the fake baby. She had planned that we'd work out a settlement of some sort. But I hired a private investigator and he took tons of pictures of her with this other man. Pearson drew up a letter asking for proof of pregnancy, which of course, she couldn't provide, so her plan was thwarted."

"That's plain evil," I said.

"It was, especially after I'd lived with her for over two years and trusted her. I never imagined she could do something so awful. The whole thing was stupid because it was easy to discover it wasn't real, but it devastated me nevertheless." He ran a hand over his face. "So, when you brought up the past relationship, all those bitter thoughts plowed into me. I gave up relationships, until you. When I saw you at the reception, the way you acted, how you made me laugh, things changed. You were different...are different than anyone I've ever been around. You don't care about things other women do and you're honest about it. And I keep finding things about you that intrigue me even more."

I reached for his hand and said, "Thank you. Thank you for telling me. I know it wasn't easy revealing something like that. I'm sorry she hurt you so badly."

"I'm not. Don't get me wrong. I was for a long time afterward. But if she hadn't done those terrible things, who knows what would've happened? I may have been one of those unfortunate bastards locked in an awful marriage to a woman I didn't love."

"True."

"What about you?"

My brows snapped together as I glanced up at the ceiling. "I had two relationships that I'd consider important, but only one that crushed me. The first was my college sweetheart. I was naive to think we'd last forever, but he cheated on me our senior year. When I found out, I was the laughingstock because everyone else had known, except me. Even my friends, and they hadn't told me. I confronted him and he said that since we'd be graduating soon and going our separate ways, what was the use of monogamy anyway? What a cheat. Later, I realized he wasn't worth it in the end and that I hadn't really been in love. About a year and a half later, when I was getting my master's, I really fell hard. He was a psychology professor. We had so much in common and we lasted for almost two years. And then the unthinkable happened. I was already finished with my degree, thank God, when I saw him out with another woman who happened to be his *wife*. Unbeknown to me, he'd been engaged to someone else the entire time we were dating and had actually gotten married! I was so in love with him I'd never suspected a thing. When he wasn't available, he was at faculty meetings, conferences, you get the idea. He gave me no reason to mistrust him whatsoever. That night I saw him, at first, I thought he was with a student or perhaps another faculty member. I made such a fool out of myself. I went up to his table, excited to see him because he'd been away. Of course he had ... on his fucking honeymoon. And the wife, you should've seen her face when I told him how much I'd missed him and threw my arms around him, intending to kiss him. Now I feel sorry for her, but back then, I saw her as the enemy. She'd been as taken in as I had. He'd really broken me. It took a long time to get over him."

"Do you still love him?"

"Oh, hell no. Once I got over the anguish of betrayal and the —I can't believe he could do that to me feeling—I dealt with the broken bits of me and moved on. But I was like you. I haven't wanted to be involved with any men since. Until you. You've managed to slip through, Evan Thomas."

He smiled and when he did, the room brightened.

"It seems like we have even more in common than we thought." He pressed his lips to mine and everything faded into the background.

138

TWENTY-THREE
EVAN

Sylvie's story was much like mine, minus the extortion. She'd been through it in her relationship status with getting her heart broken. That told me if she gave me hers, she wouldn't be giving it casually. My world became an even better place, if that were possible.

"I'm sorry you fell for such a douche. You didn't deserve it." The truth was I wish I had fallen for her all those years ago. I was kicking myself in the ass for not paying closer attention back then.

"I guess we're sorry for each other, but the past is the past, and hopefully we've learned from our mistakes."

"Come with me." Taking her hand, I led her back to the bedroom.

"Are you ready to collect the bet you won?"

"Would you believe me if I said I'd forgotten about it?"

She stopped and pulled on my hand. "Are you serious? What kind of man are you?"

"The kind who wants to see your ass bright pink after being flogged."

Her jaw gaped open and I used a finger to close it.

"Are you surprised, Sylvie?"

"You might say that."

I guided her toward the bed, which was still unmade from this morning. It was a reminder of last night and I didn't need any of those. My imagination was running wild already. My hands reached for the hem of the T-shirt she wore, and I took it off. Her nipples were already hard, waiting for my mouth to suck on them. But I wanted her naked first. I took my time, building up the anticipation. Her eyes watched my every move as I undressed. She was so provocative as she ran her tongue across her lower lip. Maybe I should've had her suck my dick after all.

I bent down and put a nipple in my mouth. I sucked it hard, then grazed it with my teeth. Her sharp inhale pleased me. I did the same to the other and her fingers sunk into my shoulders. I walked her backward toward the bed until she fell upon it. Her legs opened wide for me and I licked her. She cried out for more, but I stopped.

When I went to the bedside drawer, she asked, "You're really doing this, aren't you?"

"Yes, I am. If you hate it, all you have to do is tell me to stop."

"As in a safe word?"

"Don't worry, sweets, I won't get anywhere near that rough with you."

I kissed her, long and passionately, until she was boneless in my arms. Then I put the sleep mask on her. It was soft satin and padded on the inside. I knew it blocked everything out because I had tested it to make sure.

"Are you comfortable?" I asked.

"Yes."

"I'm going to arrange you in a different position. Let me know if you're not."

"Okay."

I pulled her up a bit and then spread her legs again. "Don't move your arms or I'll have to tie you up."

"Is that a promise?"

"Do you want them tied now?"

"No, I was just kidding."

I dribbled some warming oil down her body, starting between her breasts and ending at the apex of her thighs. She murmured in pleasure. As I massaged the oil in, my fingers moved to more erotic places, such as her nipples, where I pinched and tugged, and to her clit, where I circled and teased. Soon, she was quivering under my touch.

That's when I brought out the flogger. At first, I trailed it gently across her skin, lingering on the more sensitive areas. Then I had her move to her hands and knees and did the same to her back. After she was comfortable, I started moving my wrist in a circular motion to get the flogger going, careful to not let it strike her in any danger zones. My aim was her buttocks and I lightly hit them, taking time to massage them in between each smack. Hearing her moans told me I was on target. When her cheeks were bright pink, I tossed the flogger aside and soothed the heat out of them, rubbing some cooling oil I had on hand. Then I asked how she was.

"More," she said, tearing the mask off.

"Flogging?"

"You." Her voice was breathy, and it spurred me on.

I buried my cock in her and she quivered around me. My hands dug into her hips as I pounded into her. I was hard and relentless as I fucked her. Something came over me and I couldn't slow down. She was soaked and tight as I thrust in and out, I couldn't have stopped unless she asked me to.

"Oh, God, Evan. I'm going to come."

She whimpered as her orgasm hit, and then spasmed around me. That's when I gave a hoarse moan and released myself into her. It went on until I was bone dry. This climax had rocked my sex world. I didn't know if it was the minor flogging, feeling her squeezing my dick with her pussy, or just the sex itself. But it was fucking epic.

We both collapsed and I rolled next to her so I could see her face.

"What's that lopsided grin all about?" she asked lazily.

"You really don't know?"

"Maybe." The corners of her eyes crinkled.

"Did you like the flogger?"

"Yeah. Where did you learn how to do that?" she asked curiously. Then suddenly, as an afterthought, she immediately said, "Gosh, me and my big mouth. I shouldn't have asked that."

"Why not?"

"Because. Maybe an old girlfriend taught you or something."

"Not that. But when I bought them, the sales lady told me if I used them incorrectly, I could really hurt someone. She gave me an instruction booklet and a great YouTube video link. To be honest, I practiced a lot and barely put any strength behind it. This one has the curved tails that don't sting as much. It's short and light so it doesn't pack as much of a punch. There are some pretty wicked ones that can hurt if you don't know what you're doing. I believe real lessons would be necessary with those."

"I really liked it. The sting was hugely erotic." She held the flogger and ran the strands through her fingers.

"Good. That was my intention. Just a little bit to get you going. Maybe I can practice more, and we can keep doing it. You looked very hot, by the way."

"Why didn't you use it on my ... you know?"

"Your what, Sylvie?"

"My clit." She avoided looking me in the eye.

"You can look at me when you say clit. I won't laugh at you."

"But I might." She was as pink as her ass.

"Yeah, you're right because it reminds me of our first night together. You were so damn funny."

"Stop. That's not fair since I can't remember."

A raspy chuckle left me, but I couldn't help it. "You jumping on the bed. And then telling me you wanted me to flog your clit.

You know, that's where this flogging stemmed from. I'd never thought of it before you."

"Well, I'd never thought of it before those dang raunchy duke books."

"Hey, maybe you should read some of that out loud to me."

"No way. If you want to read it, you'll have to buy it."

"Does he flog his helpless little virgin?"

"Why yes, as a matter of fact, he does."

I grabbed and kissed her. "I'm gonna send this raunchy duke a thank you note."

Her giggles echoed through the bedroom.

Monday was crazy since it was a short week due to the Thanksgiving holiday. Cole and I were having a meeting with the compliance team later that morning over the report he'd gone over regarding the four corporations we were checking out. They had green flagged all of them, but Cole hadn't. One of them had off-shore accounts that looked suspicious. When he'd dug a little deeper, there were things neither of us liked, things that didn't add up. I had a lot of questions for the team and was going to find out how they'd run their investigation and missed this when Cole hadn't.

They showed up ready to begin, with smiles on their faces. They didn't last long when I opened the meeting with, "Can you explain this?" And I passed out the pages of the corporation in question with the red flag on it.

The director of compliance, Martha, eyed it closely and said, "I don't understand."

"What don't you understand?" I asked.

"The red flag."

"Cole, would you care to explain?"

He went through everything he discovered in minute detail. I listened and watched Martha's expression the entire time. It went from surprise to stunned, to anger. She was pissed that he'd gone behind her and checked all of the team's findings. The next words out of her mouth actually stunned me.

"Cole, I find it difficult to believe that in your position, you would actually check up on my team." She was trying to upper hand him, which was a very bad thing to do.

Cole sat in silence.

That's where I stepped in. "Martha, Cole follows up on what I tell him to. He checks and reviews everything I send him, from financials to compliance reports. And it's a damn good thing, don't you agree?"

Her mouth flapped open and closed a few times before I said, "Don't bother answering that. I've made a decision. Cole will be taking over your position as of today."

Now it was Cole who gaped at me.

"But Mr. Thomas," Martha said.

"Don't worry, you're not being fired. I'm going to keep you in compliance as his assistant.

That wasn't something she was pleased with, but too bad. Had she done her job properly, we wouldn't be having this conversation.

"Haley, I'm moving you over as my assistant." A look of absolute horror came over her. "Don't worry, Haley. I don't bite. Cole will show you how I prefer to have things run. And then if you have any other questions after today, you can check with me."

I stood and walked out, knowing the rumor mill would run wild. Cole followed me to my office, and I shut the door behind me.

"Mr. Thomas—I mean Evan—"

"Cole, before you say anything, let me speak. I've been thinking of promoting you for some time now. Your work is exemplary and after what you came up with on this corporation, through your own investigation I might add, I find no reason not to put you in that position. You have uncovered things the entire team was unable to and I've been having you do the same research for over six months now. If you think you're not prepared for this, you should think again. Everything you've been doing for me has set you up for this. Only now you'll have some assistance. What I'd like for you to do is delegate it properly and then check everything they find. I have all the confidence in the world in you. If you need anything at all, you know where to find me. My door is always open for you and I sincerely mean that. I see you going places in this corporation."

"But, Evan, the people in that department are going to hate me, starting with my assistant."

"That's right, so you'll have to earn her respect and the others. I suggest you think about how to go about doing that."

"Any suggestions, sir?"

"Let me ask you one question and you don't have to answer it. How did I earn your respect? Now I would appreciate it very much if you would leave a detailed list of what Haley can expect from me. I know it'll be difficult to do in the time you have left today, but do the best you can. Is that fair?"

"Yes, sir. And Evan?"

"Yes?"

"Thank you for the opportunity."

"Don't thank me. You earned it. Your new contract will be sent to you from HR sometime this afternoon, along with your new salary. I'm fairly certain you'll be pleased."

He grinned. "I think my wife will be more pleased, sir."

Later that afternoon, Haley came into my office.

"Sir, I wanted to see if there was anything you needed."

"Have a seat."

She looked as though she was ready to run, screaming from here.

"Haley, there's no need to be frightened. I may be a demanding boss, but I'm also a fair one."

"Yes, sir. That's what Cole said."

"I hope he told you what you needed to get started."

"It was a lot. I hope I can fill his shoes. They're mighty large."

I chuckled. "That they are. I'm always here to help. But the main thing is if you don't know something, don't try to cover it up. Ask. One of the things I had Cole focusing on was reviewing the compliance reports. It worked to his advantage. That's where you were. How did you like it?"

"I liked it fine." She twisted her hands.

"Is there any other part of the business that interests you? I checked your information and saw your background was in finance. Would you like to end up in that department? And I'm curious how you landed in compliance in the first place?"

"Sir, it was because that was the only opening at the time."

"Who hired you?"

"Martha, sir. It was at a college job fair."

"I see. If you had your choice, what would you like to do at StarWorks?"

"Anything, sir?"

"Anything and speak freely."

"I'd love to work in marketing."

"To what end?"

"My areas of interest are consumer orientation and social marketing. In today's world, you have to have both. I know Star-Works is on the leading edge of both and I would love to be a part of that team."

"Excellent. That's what we'll work together toward then."

"Really?" A smile grew on her face as she shoved her glasses up her nose.

"Haley, my goal in having an assistant is to springboard his or her career. The good thing is that it usually helps them significantly. The bad thing is I'm in need of a new assistant every year and a half. I can't promise you anything, but I can promise you my help."

"This is awesome, Mr. Thomas. Thank you. And I promise to

work as hard as I can as your assistant. And if I'm not doing something the way you like it, please tell me so I can change."

"We have a deal. Go home and I'll see you in the morning."

"Yes, sir."

She left and I thought I had the beginnings of a good working relationship with her. At least I had it moving in the right direction. Then I thought about Sylvie and our upcoming vacation. I wondered what I could surprise her with that wouldn't be too overboard. Going to the islands would be great. I'd have to give it some thought.

My cell phone rang and speak of the angel.

"Hey sweets. What's up?"

"Can you come to meet my parents on Wednesday?"

"Sure. I thought I'd stay with you that night anyway. The plane will leave from Westchester, so that will make the drive easy Thursday morning."

"That sounds perfect. My mom threw a fit, like I expected, but Dad and my sisters intervened and calmed her down."

"Is she going to hate me on sight?"

"Probably. But your charm will get her on your side, I'm sure."

"I miss you already and it's only been a day."

She was silent. Was that hesitation on her end?

"I miss you too, Evan. I'll talk to you later."

"Ciao, baby." I heard her laughing as I ended the call.

TWENTY-FOUR
SYLVIE

Tuesday and Wednesday at work dragged. I was about to pee my pants when I thought about Evan coming tonight. And then we were going to Mom and Dad's for dinner. That sort of made me nervous. I packed last night so tonight after dinner I didn't have to worry about it.

By the time Evan arrived, I was riddled with anxiety. What if Mom and Dad hated him? But why would they? He was honest, sexy, caring, sexy, honorable, sexy, principled, sexy, sincere, sexy, trustworthy, and sexy. Besides that, Pearson could vouch for him.

"Hey," he said as I practically crawled over him when he came through the door.

"Hey back."

"Someone's happy to see me."

"I am." I kept kissing his face.

"Let me have a look." He tipped my face up to check out my splint-less nose. "It's perfect, just like before." Then he kissed the tip of it. "And your bruising is much better too."

"I think so. You can hardly tell I was sucker punched."

Evan grimaced. "Don't remind me of that."

"It's in the past." I kissed him on the lips.

"Can we skip dinner and leave tonight?"

I play punched his arm. "Why didn't you say something earlier?"

"I'm just kidding. Come on. Let's go see Mom and Dad."

We walked outside and I expected to see the limo, but it wasn't there. "Where's your car?"

"Over there."

He pointed to a black Mercedes that looked identical to Pearson's. "Did you borrow Pearson's?"

"No, we have the same kind of car. I took him when I bought mine and he liked it so much, he bought one too."

"That stinker. He's a copycat." Evan laughed.

We got inside and I murmured, "Boys and their toys."

"What's that?"

"You men just love your fancy cars."

"What do you mean? Women like them too."

"Oh, it's cool and all, but I love my little Toyota."

"So, if I were to buy you a really cool car, you wouldn't want it?"

"How much time do you really spend in a car?"

"You have me there. I barely drive this because I usually have Robert drive so I can get some work done."

"My commute is short so even if I could afford it, I wouldn't spend it."

"Fair enough, wise one."

I'd given him Mom and Dad's address and he'd entered it into his GPS so we arrived in no time. When we walked in, they were waiting and having a cocktail already.

Dad jumped to his feet and hugged me, saying, "Syllie, baby, how's my big girl doing?"

For heaven's sake, he did not just call me that in front of Evan, did he?

"Hey Dad," I said, hugging him back.

Mom came up and gave me one of her usual pert little kisses. "Hello, dear, how are you? You're looking lovely."

"Thanks, Mom, so are you. And I'm great. You guys, this is Evan. You remember him from the wedding?"

"Yes, you were Pearson's best man if I recall," Dad said.

"Evan, these are my parents, in case you don't remember. John and Cindy West."

"Mr. West, Mrs. West, it's great seeing you again."

"Please, you must call us John and Cindy," Mom said. She smiled and I could tell she liked him. He handed her a bouquet of flowers as we stood there. "These are for you, Mrs. West, for allowing me to intrude on your family."

"Oh, my, it's no intrusion at all."

"Would you two care for a drink? We have just about everything." Dad was such a great host.

"I'll have a glass of chardonnay, Dad, if you have it."

"I'll have the same, Mr. West."

"Please, it's John and Cindy."

We followed Mom and Dad into the kitchen where Dad poured us both some wine. Mom checked on her roast and we sat at the island chatting. Soon, dinner was ready.

As we ate, they asked Evan all kinds of questions about his life. I intervened a few times, as in when they got a bit nosy about his job.

"Mom, Evan owns his own company. He's in hedge funds."

"Oh, how nice. What kinds of hedges do you sell, Evan?"

"Honey, hedge funds are investments," Dad said.

"Well, isn't that something. I never knew people invested in hedges. John, we should look into that. I mean everyone buys hedges, don't they?"

Dad shook his head. "No, that's not it. Hedge funds are sort of like mutual funds."

"Oh. Why didn't you say so in the first place?" Mom could be totally spacey at times.

Evan was trying not to laugh and so was I.

"Mom, I barely understand it myself. All that stuff is so

complicated. Poor Evan tries to explain it to me, and I'm absolutely lost."

"Oh, dear. I don't blame you though. Your father always tried to explain the stock market to me, and I was a miserable failure at understanding it."

"Don't worry, Cindy, a lot of people don't understand it. Some of my largest investors don't grasp it," Evan said. "In its simplest terms, a hedge fund is for someone looking for above market returns. We use investment strategies designed to perform well in good and bad markets. That's where the term hedge comes from."

"I see." Clearly, she didn't. She was a deer in the headlights, though she was being kind about it. "Well, I'm happy your company is doing well. It is doing well, isn't it?"

"Yes, ma'am, it is."

"Gracious, me, why don't you tell us about this vacation you two are going on?" Mom was glowing. I was surprised because tomorrow was Thanksgiving and she'd given me such a hard time.

"We're going to Canouan in the Caribbean, Mom. Remember?"

"I do, but I've never heard of it."

"I have a place there, ma'am. It's very close to St. Lucia, where Pearson got married."

"How wonderful. Is your house like a tiki hut?"

"Mom! I'm sure he doesn't own a tiki hut."

"Actually, I do, but it's in addition to the house." He was really having a hard time not laughing at Mom. Dad was so amused, he only gawked at Mom.

"Well, you two be careful. I remember watching Gilligan's Island and there used to be headhunters on those islands."

"Oh my God, Mom! There are no headhunters on the island. We'll be safe."

Dad finally couldn't take it anymore and let out the loudest guffaw I think I'd ever heard from him. He stomped his foot a couple of times and snorted. That's where I inherited my snort from. Evan let his laughter loose. Then, so did I.

"What's so funny?" Mom asked.

I held up a hand because I couldn't talk. Tears ran down my cheeks and Dad was crying too. He finally got up to retrieve a box of tissues from one of the bathrooms. The three of us wiped our eyes and then all tried to gain control of ourselves. It was like getting the church giggles. Whenever we thought we had it, someone would start chuckling again, and we'd all lose it.

Finally, Mom cleared the dishes and served dessert. I hoped she wasn't angry, but we couldn't help it. When she sat back down, I apologized.

"I'm sorry, Mom, but that headhunter thing and Gilligan's Island was just too much."

"Yeah, that was kind of silly. That old show. I mean, I've never even heard of headhunters in real life. I have no idea why I said that."

"Cindy, I promise, I'll take great care of your daughter and there'll be no head hunting on the island. We'll call when we land, and you can call her anytime. I'll even text you my number just in case."

Mom tapped his hand. "That's very considerate of you. Thank you, Evan."

As we were leaving, I hugged both of them and told them I'd miss them. When we got into the car, I was howling all over again. "Oh, my God. My mom's a mess. The hedges—I almost lost it then."

"I didn't think I would make it through. I was so glad when your dad finally lost it."

"Poor Mom. You'd think she never left the house and was a ding-a-ling. Maybe Dad gave her too much wine."

"I hate to spring this on you, but my parents asked if we could stop by after we had dinner with your parents since we'd be gone for the holiday. Do you mind?"

"Not at all." *This was a major oh, shit moment for me.*

"You may have met them before at Pearson's or the wedding."

"Maybe, but I don't remember. Oh, God. Did they see me drunk?"

"They thought you were cute and funny."

"No, they did not." I wanted to tuck tail and run. But it was too late.

We pulled into a driveway a few doors down from my aunt and uncle's house.

"The neighborhood is familiar," I said.

"The old hang out, right?"

I smiled. "Yeah, when you didn't like my pigtails and braces."

"When I was stupid and full of myself."

We got out and walked into the house where his parents waited. They were so sweet as he introduced us.

"Mom, Dad, this is Sylvie. Sylvie, meet my parents, Anna and Greg."

Anna came forward and took my hand in both of hers. "We are delighted to meet you, Sylvie. We know you're Pearson's cousin and we've seen you around plenty of times. But it's a joy to have Evan bring you here."

"Thank you. I'm glad to have a chance to meet you again as well." *Please don't bring up the wedding.*

"What a lovely young lady you are. I can see why my son is so smitten with you."

"Dad. Really?"

"Well, she is, Evan. I'm glad you two are taking off for a little getaway. You deserve it, son. You work way too hard."

"Yes, you do," Anna said. "Come and sit. I know you can't stay but a minute, but would you care for a drink?"

"No, thank you," I said.

"None for me. I'm driving."

Evan caught them up on things and Anna asked me about my job. She remarked about how proud she was of Pearson and how happy she was that I had been instrumental in him going to Flower Power.

"Without you, he and Rose would never have gotten together."

"I'm just glad they found each other."

About thirty minutes later, we left with a promise to return for dinner sometime soon. On the way back to my place, I said, "Your parents are awesome. I really like them."

"I think they're pretty awesome myself. They spoiled the shit out of me growing up, but they're great people. Yours are too."

"Yeah, I love mine. Lately, Mom can be a bit whacky even though she's still lovable."

We were in my parking lot and he said, "And speaking of lovable." He wiggled his brows and that was all it took.

A wickedly funny thought popped into my head. "Last one in bed's a rotten egg."

TWENTY-FIVE

SYLVIE

WE ARRIVED AT THE AIRPORT A FEW MINUTES AFTER TEN. I was freaking out because we'd overslept due to our amorous adventures in the sack last night. It was all my fault, of course, since Evan had ended up being the rotten egg. I'd made him pay by doing all sorts of raunchy things based on my fictional duke.

He'd been so intrigued, we'd ended up acting out a scene with him tying me to the bed and spanking me. I wasn't the innocent virgin, but it sure had felt like it. After the spanking, he proceeded to lick, suck, and fuck me until I couldn't stand if I'd had to. Thank God there hadn't been a fire in the building. He would've had to carry me to safety, naked as the day I was born. He told me there was no way he'd let me stop reading about the duke and his lewd buddies because we would definitely be copying more of those scenes. I was afraid to explain to him that some of them were hardcore BDSM, of which I was in no way going to take part in. I was all for a little flogging and spanking, and the blindfolding and silk restraints were amazing, but that other stuff? Nope. Not for me. Reading about it was one thing. Doing it was another.

"OMG, I can't believe we forgot to set our alarms!" I crammed my makeup into a carryon as I finished getting ready.

"Hey, calm down. It's fine."

I didn't pay attention to him as I buzzed around the room, throwing on jeans and a shirt. He was packed and dressed, neither one of us taking the time to shower. He said we'd do that after we got there. After all, we weren't planning on doing anything except being lazy anyway.

A few minutes later we were in the car, on the way to the airport.

"Shit."

He reached for my hand and asked, "What now?"

"I forgot to make us coffee."

"If you can stand it for twenty minutes, you'll have all the coffee we want then."

"What if they leave without us?"

"Babe, that's not gonna happen. Now please calm down."

"Okay." I tried, but I was still worried.

We finally got there, and he drove around to the back of the airport. There was an entrance for general aviation, which included charter and private planes. We pulled in and parked. A car was waiting for us to take us onto the tarmac. I liked this kind of service.

"Good morning, Mr. Thomas, Ms. West. Happy Thanksgiving."

"Thank you, Mark. Same to you," Evan said. I smiled back at him, feeling like a bimbo as I didn't know what else to do.

We drove a short distance and there sat a white shiny jet. I expected a nice plane, but this was a lot larger than I'd anticipated. The steps were down and waiting for us.

"Have a nice trip, sir. I'll see you when you get back."

"Thank you."

"Thanks and have a great weekend." I finally found the ability to speak.

He nodded as we exited the SUV. Someone came out of the plane to retrieve our bags. He must've been the flight attendant.

"Good morning, sir. Happy Thanksgiving."

Evan shook hands with him and introduced me. "Sylvie, this is Jeffrey. He will be our flight attendant today."

"Nice to meet you, Jeffrey."

"Likewise, Ms. West."

We walked up the steps to the jet and I was mesmerized. "Evan, has Pearson ever been in here?"

"Yeah, we've taken several trips together. Why?"

"Just curious. This is amazing. I wasn't imagining anything like this."

"I'll show you around in a second. I want you to meet the pilots first." They were standing, waiting for us.

"Good morning, Mr. Thomas, Ms. West," they both greeted us simultaneously.

"Hi guys. Thanks for being here. Matthew, Tom, this is Sylvie."

"It's nice to meet both of you," I said, shaking their hands.

"Are we set to go?" Evan asked.

"As soon as Jeffrey has the luggage stowed and your coffee served, we'll be in line for takeoff, sir."

"Excellent." Evan turned to me and said, "Then let's get buckled in."

He walked me back to the main cabin area and it was super plush. There were leather captain's seats that reclined all the way with footrests next to each other with a table that faced two others. The other side of the plane had the exact same thing. Behind us was another area that resembled a small den complete with couches facing each other. There was a partition behind that, so I wondered if that was a separate room. I could smell breakfast cooking and it made my stomach grumble.

"Evan, you don't have to answer this because it really is none of my business, but how often do you use this plane? When you said you had a plane, I figured it was a small one, not anything like this."

"I use it quite often. Maybe once a week. It just so happens that ever since I met you, I haven't used it much. My schedule hasn't been travel heavy. It'll pick up after the first of the year though."

"How many people can it carry?"

"Easily twenty."

The engines roared to life. No, that's not true. They hummed to life. They were much quieter than on a commercial airliner.

"Is this as safe as a commercial jet?"

"My crew is more than competent. I've handpicked them— or I should say Matthew and Tom have—and they're paid much more than if they worked for a commercial airliner. Matthew and Tom are both former Air Force pilots who flew fighter jets. They can weather just about anything. I spoke to both of them before I even bought the jet because I wanted the best that was made. They oversee all the inspections and are also in charge of the other pilots that work for me."

"That's great. I'm not afraid to fly. I was just curious."

"The reason I bought this was because I was flying so much the cost became ridiculous, not to mention the inconvenience. Missed flights, bad connections, time wasted, you get the idea. With this, the plane is ready when I am. The only thing I'm at the mercy of is the weather.

"My team and I lose no time to any of the airline things that used to bog us down. And we conduct in-flight meetings, so our onboard time is not wasted either."

"A worthy investment then."

He nodded. Jeffrey showed up with two large mugs of coffee. "Ms. West, let me know if you need more cream. Mr. Thomas told me how you liked it, so I took the liberty of preparing it."

I tasted it and said, "It's perfect. Thank you."

One of the pilots came over the intercom and said, "Mr. Thomas, Ms. West, we're next for takeoff. Make sure you're buckled up, please."

In no time we were airborne, on the way to Canouan. I was so excited for this adventure to begin.

TWENTY-SIX
EVAN

WATCHING SYLVIE WAS ABOUT AS ENTERTAINING AS ANYTHING I'd ever done. She was so impressed with this plane. I guess I'd taken it for granted for the past couple of years that I'd owned it. She reminded me of a flower opening its petals in early spring—so fresh and new.

Once we hit thirty thousand feet, I unbuckled my seat belt and said, "Come on. I'll give you a tour." Behind the partition was an office, and then in the back was a bedroom, complete with a bathroom.

"Would you care to take that shower now?" he asked. "Or would you rather wait until after breakfast?"

"This plane really does have it all, doesn't it?"

She peeked into the bathroom and said, "Holy cow. You didn't skimp on the shower, did you?"

"No. I've been in showers where I couldn't even move. I know the headspace isn't great, but nothing could be done for that."

"I'd love a shower, but let's eat first."

We went back to our seats, and Jeffrey brought our plates of warm cinnamon scones, fruit, and cheese.

"Did you tell him?" she asked.

Playing innocent, I asked, "Tell him what?"

"That I love cinnamon scones."

I shrugged. "Maybe he's a mind reader."

She took a bite and hummed her delight. I'd have to make sure to give Jeffrey an extra tip. He was back with coffee refills for us and she told him how wonderful the scone was.

"I'm glad you like it."

Afterward, we headed for the shower. The water was nice, not as great as in a regular one, but I soaped her up and shampooed her hair, and then did my own and she conditioned hers. We didn't take as long as I'd like as we were on a limited amount of water. When we finished, I said, "I want us to become members of the mile high club."

"I'm in."

Our towels hit the floor as we hit the bed.

"I know one thing," she said.

"What's that?"

"No jumping on this bed." Her finger aimed at the low ceiling.

"Oh, I don't know. We could give knee jumping a try."

"Very funny."

I got on my knees and straddled her, then I kissed her, giving her no time to think. Pushing her knees to her chest, I dove down between her thighs and went for my irresistible dessert. It was a good thing the bedroom was in the back of the place because her lusty, shameless cries of pleasure would've certainly woken the dead.

After her first climax, my stiff cock plunged into her heat with abandon. I lost all sense of awareness when we made love. It was only Sylvie and me, together, having sex. All I knew was unimaginable desire, coupled with an obsession of her. I was a savage beast who wanted her complete surrender. And she gave it to me.

Her second orgasm came accompanied by the fluttering spasms of her inner walls, which sent me into my own. She clenched my ass, her nails scraping it, and it was a pain I'd gladly take any time. I thrust into her one final time as I emptied myself into her.

"We may need another shower after that." I was covered in a sheen of perspiration.

"Yeah, but it was worth each of those sixty-nine calories."

I shook with laughter. Then I gently bit her lower lip. "You are a sex goddess. And my sex goddess. I'm claiming you as mine." I dipped my head lower to bite her nipple.

"Keep that up, cowboy, and you'll have to finish me off."

"I can do that." I had her nipple between my teeth and I rapidly flicked my tongue over it.

She writhed beneath my grip and said, "Stop tormenting me."

"I thought you liked it."

"I do, but now I want to come again."

I went back to my nipple play and used my finger on her little bud. She moaned and grabbed my head, sliding her fingers into it, holding my head against her. Orgasm number three roared into her as she lay gasping under my ministrations.

"Are you trying to turn me into jelly?" she asked.

"You liked it."

"Yeah, but now I need a nap."

"We have time. Go to sleep."

She conked out before I could get comfortable next to her. Amazing. I wished I could sleep like that. I woke up almost three and a half hours later, surprised at what time it was. We would probably be landing soon. I shook Sylvie awake.

"If you want to rinse off in the shower, we'd better do it now. We've been asleep over three hours."

"Are you serious?"

"Yes," I answered with a chuckle. I rose from the bed and went into the bathroom, with her on my heels. We quickly rinsed off and dressed.

"My hair's a mess. I need to put it up."

She found an elastic and twisted it up into a messy bun. Then we went back out into the main cabin. Jeffrey immediately wanted to know if we wanted a snack or a beverage.

"We slept right through lunch. Sylvie."

"I'll take a snack and some water, please."

He came back with an array of things for her to choose from so she grabbed a bag of popcorn and peanuts and I took a bag of M&M's.

Thirty minutes later, we were on the ground. We had to stay on board until the customs agent arrived. That took about fifteen minutes, and after he cleared us, we deplaned, and our car was waiting to drive us to the house.

The weather was gorgeous, warm and sunny. Sylvie put her sunglasses on, and she glanced around to check out the island as we drove.

"It's perfect. It reminds me of St. Lucia with the mountains."

"Yes. The house is on the opposite end of the island from the airport, but it's only three and a half miles long. The roads aren't the best though. The house is on Shell Beach. I think you'll be pleased when you see it."

"How can I not be?" She took my hand and squeezed it. "Everything has been amazing so far."

When we arrived, the staff was there to greet us, and I introduced Sylvie to everyone. We went inside and I showed her around. The main house had three large ensuite bedrooms and there was a guest house with its own bedroom, bathroom, and small kitchenette. The pool faced the beach along with the outdoor terrace. The house sat on a small rise overlooking the beach, but in reality, it was only a few steps down to the water.

"This is fabulous."

"Do you like it?"

"I love it."

"Want to see my favorite part?"

"Yes!"

She followed me through the master bedroom to the bathroom, which was spacious, but there was a glass door, which went outside to an outdoor tub and shower.

"This is outrageous. I love it!"

"I can't wait to get you in here. You'll love it."

It had two rain showers, but they were nothing like the usual ones. These were serious ones, like standing under a waterfall. I almost never used the indoor shower when I was here.

"Do you worry about anyone seeing you out here?"

"No, it's completely private."

"Is the tub heated?"

"No, you don't need it. It would be too hot to use."

"This is absolutely decadent."

I took her into my arms. "I'm glad you think so." Then I gave her a brief kiss. "The staff has an early dinner prepared. I knew we'd be hungry when we arrived, so I told them to be ready for us."

We went to the outdoor dining area where the table was already set and I pulled her chair out. After we sat, someone immediately came to pour us water and wine. The dinner would be freshly caught fish and whatever the chef decided to serve. Usually it was a starch and a salad. Then he'd add a delicious dessert. My mind wasn't on the food. It was getting Sylvie naked in the hot tub.

"Why are you staring at me like that?" she asked.

"Do you have to ask?"

"You know me...I always ask."

"I can't wait to get you naked again."

Our salads arrived. We both devoured them. "I was really hungry," I said.

"So was I."

Our main course came soon after that and again, we didn't waste time. I was finished before she was so I enjoyed watching her eat.

"You're making me nervous."

"Why?"

"I don't know. It's the way you're staring at me, I suppose."

"I enjoy watching you eat because you don't pick at your food like a bird."

"This is entirely too good to let it go to waste. What kind of fish is this?"

"No idea. The chef always makes sure it's freshly caught though."

She swallowed her bite, set her knife and fork down, and pushed her plate back. "I can't eat another bite."

Her plate disappeared immediately. Then someone came to offer coffee and dessert. Sylvie declined so I said, "Just tell chef everything was excellent and to leave our desserts for later tonight. We'll eat them when we can. Thank him for us and thank you for your excellent service. We'll finish the wine and be done."

"Yes, sir." He bowed and left.

"Everyone is so courteous here," she remarked.

"That's what I love about this place. Would you like a tour of the grounds? We didn't get a chance earlier."

"I'd love one."

We walked the landscaped paths, which were lit as it was dark already, and I took her down to the beach. The staff always lit the torches at night. I'd never thought about it before when I was here by myself, or with my parents or Pearson, but it was really romantic as we walked hand in hand. As we got to the water, it was beautiful as the moonlight cast its path of silver over it. I turned to her and asked, "Would you care to go swimming?"

"I don't have my swimsuit on."

"This is a private beach, Sylvie. You don't ever need a bathing suit here when it's just the two of us."

"Really?"

"Uh huh." I started to undress to see if she would follow. She did. We waded into the warm Caribbean waters and swam a bit.

"I love the water here," she said. "I could stay in it forever."

"But then you'd look like a prune."

"You're not funny." She splashed me, which started a huge water fight.

We tried to outdo each other, but she was an excellent swimmer, always escaping my reach. At one point she dove underwater and didn't come up for a while. When I began to panic, her hands pushed on my shoulders and I went under. The little shit, I'd have to find a way to get her back, but how?

Before I knew it, she was wrapped around me, her body pressed to mine, and all thoughts about revenge were gone. Warm, wet lips pressed onto mine and she whispered into my mouth, "I want you."

My fingers found her entrance and she was ready for me as I was for her. "Hold on, I'm carrying you up the steps."

I went directly to the outside tub and set her on the edge. "And after we break in the tub, we can move on to the shower."

"I can hardly wait."

"You're as insatiable as me."

"You're right." Then she grabbed my head and pushed it down. "Stop talking already. You're wasting precious time."

I knew she was my kind of woman the night she slapped my ass.

TWENTY-SEVEN

SYLVIE

THE ENTIRE FLIGHT HOME, I KEPT THINKING ABOUT EVAN'S outdoor tub and shower. We'd spent the entire time there, except for meals, naked. It was glorious.

"Evan?"

"Yeah, sweets."

"It's going to be very difficult to top this vacation."

He pushed his hand through my hair and kissed me. "It was really great, wasn't it?"

"Thank you for taking me. It was perfect."

"Not as perfect as you, but I do have other tricks up my sleeve, so beware."

I was falling deeper and harder for him. How could I not? The man did everything right. He was polite, had my best interests at heart, asked me about everything before he did anything, was affectionate, trusting, warm, kind, and sexy and my God, so good in bed. There wasn't anything he did wrong. I kept looking for flaws, even tiny ones, and couldn't find any.

"Why the serious expression? If your brows were any more creased, they could hold my credit cards."

"I was just thinking how perfect you are."

"Oh. That bad then?"

"Haha. I was looking for one tiny flaw in you, but I couldn't find any."

A hearty laugh echoed through the cabin. "One tiny flaw, huh. I broke this finger when I was in high school playing football." He held up his middle finger and it was curved. "See?"

"No wonder I like it so much when you put it inside me."

"Okay, smart ass, how about this. You saw me naked. I have knobby knees."

"You do not. I know knobby knees and you don't have them."

He pursed his lips for a second, then said, "I have large feet."

"They're large and perfectly formed. Like your...never mind."

"Dirty minded girl."

My cheeks heated, so I fanned them. "Sorry, but it's true. Your ass is damned perfect too. See, I can't think of anything. Your parents taught you great manners."

"You haven't seen my temper explode. Wait until that happens. You'll change your mind."

"I have a temper too. Everyone has one. Anger, as long as it's expressed properly, isn't a bad thing."

"Yes, doctor psychologist."

"It's true. And I'm not a doctor."

"I do realize that. But I can bark awfully loud and it sounds pretty scary when it happens. I'm not above apologizing though."

"Again, good manners."

He smirked. "And what about you. I happen to think the same of you, Miss Perfect."

"Well, I never said I wasn't perfect."

He must've been ready for a comeback, but when I said that, he cracked up and so did I.

"Guess that makes us the perfect couple then," he said.

I didn't want to go home and back to reality, but it was unavoidable. Tomorrow would be here with work and everything that accompanied it. How could I go back to my mundane job after this whirlwind weekend?

The plane landed and we were whisked to Evan's car and then pulling in front of my townhouse before I knew it. I wanted to wind the clock back to Thursday and start all over. Instead, we both got out and he helped me with my bags.

"Evan, I don't know how to thank you. It was the best trip I've ever taken."

"You don't have to thank me. Just having you with me was thanks enough."

"I'll miss you. Sleeping alone won't be any fun."

"No, it won't. Do me a favor. Read more of the raunchy earl so we can continue our play." He pinched my butt.

"I think we do pretty well without him, and he's a duke. It's the Lewd Earl, by the way."

He chuckled over my choice of books.

"Hey, I distinctly remember you thanking me for reading it and asking me not to stop."

"Oh, I'm not laughing at that. I'm laughing at the title."

"They are pretty crazy."

Suddenly I was in his arms and he was kissing me like it was the last kiss we'd ever share. Blood pulsed through my veins while my heart pounded beneath my ribs. My core ached with need and I didn't want him to leave. I wanted him to stay forever. I knew one thing. I had fallen in love with Evan. Now the question was, did he feel the same?

He released me and stepped back. "If I don't leave now, I never will. Sleep tight, gorgeous. I'll miss you next to me." He turned without another word.

"Evan?"

He stopped and turned back. "Yes?"

"I, uh, I'll miss you too."

He smiled and my heart ached with the thought of not seeing him until the following weekend. How was I going to stand it?

"Don't worry, sweets, I'm a phone call away."

I bobbed my head up and down. Why did I all of a sudden

feel like crying when the door closed behind him? It had been a long time since I'd been this emotional over a man.

Tomorrow would be busy, so I unpacked and got my things ready for work. I went to the grocery store and by the time I came home, I was starved. After a quick dinner, I was ready to crash. I was half asleep when my phone rang. I would've ignored it, but it was my mom.

"Hey, Mom. Sorry I didn't call, but I'm so tired and had a million things to do."

She wanted to know all about the trip, so I gave her the details, minus the sexy scenes.

"He's certainly a dreamboat, Sylvie. I hope you reel this one in."

"Mom, I don't want to reel anyone in. I want it to be mutual."

"You're right. But he sure seemed like he adored you the way he eyed you."

"He's very nice to me, Mom."

"That's good, dear. Now get your beauty rest. You don't want any wrinkles before your time."

"Good night, Mom. I love you."

Evan called right after and I told him what Mom said. "She definitely approves of you. I'm sure she'll want to buy some hedges soon."

Laughter resounded in my ear. "I hope she can tell me what kind to deliver because I know nothing about hedges."

"Neither do I. We can ask Rose. She's the one with the green thumb."

"Sylvie, I don't want to talk about hedges or Rose. I want to talk about how much I miss you and that I don't want to miss you this much, which means I want to see you every day."

My breath hitched and I stumbled over my next words. "I, er, I want the same. I didn't want you to leave, Evan."

"How are we going to handle this?" he asked.

"Do you have any suggestions?"

"Yes, but I don't want you to run off with your hair on fire, so can you promise me you won't do that?"

"I, my hair on fire?"

"Yes, can you promise me?"

My fingers fiddled with the sheet as a smile took over my face. Was he going to ask what I thought he was?

"Okay, I promise."

"Will you move in with me."

My heart hit the floor. That was not what I was anticipating. Speech was lost and my brain turned into scrambled eggs.

"Sylvie, are you still with me?"

I cleared my throat. "Um, yeah," I whispered.

"What's wrong?"

"Nothing."

"Yes, there is. Don't shut down on me."

"You're right. I was not expecting you to ask me that."

"All right. Were you expecting something else?"

There was no way I'd confess to that. He'd be the one running with his hair on fire. I was even afraid to tell him I was in love with him.

"Evan, how do you feel about me?"

"I'm madly in love with you. I hate that I'm telling you this over the phone. This was something I wanted to share with you in a different way, in a better setting. Babe, are you opposed to living together?"

"Not exactly, although I can already hear my parents."

"I'm sure. What parent wants their daughter living in sin with her boyfriend? But this will only be temporary."

"What's that supposed to mean?" My hackles instantly rose. Was he going to kick me out after he got tired of me?

"Calm down, babe. What I meant was we'd do this until we got married."

"Married?"

"Yes. Or are you opposed to that?"

"Are you asking me to marry you?" Did my voice sound all breathy or was that my imagination?

"I can't yet. I have to speak to your father first. And seriously, Sylvie, I would never formally propose to you over the phone. But yes, I want to marry you. Not tomorrow, but soon."

Holy shit balls. He wants to marry me! Giddy up, cowboy.

"Sylvie, are you there?"

"Yes, I'm here. And about the living together. How would I get to and from work? That commute is crazy."

"I know. I've thought about that. Is there any way you could get a job in the city? Robert could drive you, but I know how old that could get."

A new job in Manhattan? Yeah, there are dozens of rehab centers. One of the psychiatrists we work with could recommend one, but leaving Flower Power would be really hard.

"I'll commute for the time being."

"You don't mind?"

"No. If I'm super tired, I'll stay here."

"Is that a yes, then?"

"I think so."

"Sylvie, I promise you won't regret it."

"Can we wait until Christmas to do this?"

Now he was silent. "I was hoping we could do it right away. You really only need your clothes and some of your favorite things. I have everything else. That way if you ever want to stay at your place, everything will be there."

He made a great point. "Okay. Let's do it then."

"Sylvie, I love you."

"Evan. I love you back." Was this crazy? It felt perfect.

The next day when I got to work, a huge bouquet of roses awaited me. The card said: I can't wait to see you tonight. Pack a bag and Robert will pick you up at six thirty. We'll get the rest of your things this weekend. Love, Evan.

My body shivered at the thought of living with him. I hoped this feeling never ended, because it was so amazing.

Rose came in and wanted to know how the trip went. When she saw the roses, she said, "It must've been great."

"You wouldn't believe his house. And the private jet...it's so luxurious. He was so attentive to all of my needs."

"I imagine he was," she said as she checked out the flowers. "This is huge."

"Isn't it? It's lovely. You and Pearson have to come with us to Canouan. It's unreal. I've never been anywhere like it."

"Pearson said it was really something. Looks like you snagged yourself the big one, Sylvie."

"I wish you wouldn't say that." I pouted.

"You mean snag, or the big one?"

"Both. We were mutually attracted to each other and I don't give a damn about his money. I didn't even know he had any." It kind of pissed me off.

"I know. But it's not a bad thing he has it either."

"No, but people automatically assume I went after him for that." I rubbed my face and shot her a stare.

"Not me. I know the real you and love is more important than anything."

"Thanks for that." Then I moaned. "Look at this stack."

"I know. Mine is the same. Everyone does interventions over the holidays it seems. Well, I'd better get moving."

"Oh, by the way, I'm moving in with Evan tonight."

I dropped that bomb when she was almost at the door. "You're what?"

"Yep. I'm going to commute in every day. If it doesn't work, I'll see about getting a position in the city. Good luck with work today, Rose." I started going through my workload, but I felt her eyes burning into me. I wanted to laugh but didn't. This would give her something to gossip with Pearson over tonight. Hell, she'd probably be calling him as soon as she got to her office. Then he'd call Evan, then Evan would call me. Oh, God. My head hit the desk as I started laughing.

TWENTY-EIGHT

EVAN

I WAS IN THE OFFICE FOR ABOUT AN HOUR WHEN MY PHONE rang. When I saw it was Pearson, I answered without hesitation because I figured he wanted to get all the details on Sylvie's and my trip.

"Hey, man, what's up?"

His roaring voice on the other end took me by surprise. "Are you out of your mind moving in with Sylvie? You two have only been together for what, a month?"

I'm sure he expected me to get pissed off, but I found it extremely humorous. "Um, isn't that the pot calling the kettle black or whatever that saying is?"

"You know damn well that was different. I moved in with Rose because I was leaving rehab."

"True, but you could've gone to your parents, or even here." That shut him up for a minute, long enough for me to add, "Pearson, Sylvie and I are two grown people who are fully capable of making sound decisions regarding our lives. Not that it's any of your business, but I am completely and totally head over heels in love with your cousin. I promise not to do anything to hurt her. Does that make you feel better?"

"Wow. I didn't expect that." I heard his fingers thrumming on his desk.

"What's your hesitation regarding us?"

"Honestly, I don't have any now. You just pulled the rug out from under me."

"Why? You of all people should've known this was coming. How many women have I brought to my real home? How many women have I taken to meet my parents? How many women have I taken to Canouan? How many women have flown on my private jet, other than my mom?"

"Damn, you're right. I wasn't looking at all those clues, stupid me."

"I'm waiting," I said.

"Waiting?"

"For your apology, dickhead."

"Right. Sorry I jumped to the wrong conclusions, man. I seem to be doing that a lot with you two."

"I must've really set a bad example for you along the way."

"It was after Tiffany when you went on your use and lose streak. I just had it in my head that...well you can figure it out."

"And you should know me better, that after your wedding if I kept trying to get her to go out with me, that use and lose streak didn't count towards Sylvie. I've already spelled it out for you and she's the real thing for me, man. I never thought it would happen, but it did. Now will you stop having all these doubts about me?"

"Done. Is Sylvie really going to give up her job?"

I blew out a breath because this was something I didn't want unless it was absolutely necessary. "That's completely up to her. I want living in the city to be easy, not difficult on her. I haven't told her this but if she doesn't like this situation, I'm not opposed to buying something between our two places of work. There are a lot of options, Pearson."

"True, or you could even buy a place out here and split your time between here and the city."

"I've thought of that too. The thing I want the most is her happiness and if that includes her staying at Flower Power, then we'll work it out. I was going to talk to her about that tonight, so I'd appreciate it if you wouldn't mention any of this to Rose. Can you do this for me?" Haley walked into my office, but I held up a hand.

"Sure thing."

"Hey, I hate to cut you off, but my admin just walked in. I have to go."

"Catch you later."

"And the next time, I hope it's not an ass chewing." I ended the call before he could respond.

"Sir, I'm sorry to interrupt, but there's someone at reception who's insisting on seeing you. She says it's urgent."

"Who is it?"

"She refuses to give her name."

"You know the policy. No name, no entry." I turned to my computer, but Haley didn't leave.

"Sir, she's, um, making quite a scene."

"A scene? How?"

Haley fidgeted and seemed unwilling to answer. She finally said, "Well, Sharon called and said she was saying all kinds of horrible things about you when Sharon refused to let her go back. Security is there now."

"Are you going to tell me what kinds of horrible things?"

"I don't want to repeat them, sir."

I picked up the phone and called Sharon. I heard someone ranting in the background.

"Sharon, what's going on?"

"Mr. Thomas," she whispered into the phone, "this woman is crazy. She says she's your ex-fiancé and is demanding to see you."

"What does she look like and please be specific."

"Bleached blond hair, um, shall I say very enhanced chest and lips, and she's wearing a dress that can hardly be called that."

That doesn't sound like the Tiffany I once knew and who I

suspected it might have been. "Sharon, reiterate to her that not even my parents are allowed back unless they give their names and identification."

"Yes, sir."

I heard her do this and she screamed like a banshee. Sharon asked me if I heard it. Everyone in the city probably heard it. I told her to have security escort her out and to make sure the police were there as well. The woman was off her rocker. I turned on the video feed in my office and connected it to all the security cameras. Then I watched my security team drag her out of there. I would have a talk with them because she never should've been able to get to this floor in the first place. Her face didn't look remotely familiar. What in the hell did she want with me? She must've been just another crazy person who had seen my picture in the media.

My phone rang and it was Carl from security.

"I was just getting ready to call you. How did she get to the executive floor?"

"She must've been watching when a group of employees came through. She came through the main entrance and there were several people at the front desk inquiring about appointments, and she walked through behind the group of employees with badges."

"Who was on assignment at the front door?"

"No one, sir."

"No one?" I began to seethe. This was one of the things I had stressed to the team repeatedly. "And why was that?"

"Our usual doorman had to leave for a moment to use the restroom."

"So the guard had to take a piss and you couldn't get anyone to cover for him? Did I get it right?"

"Yes, sir."

"Carl, would you and Joe come up to my office, please?"

"Yes, sir."

My body twitched from head to toe. I was angry. Whoever

was running ground floor security had fucked up. I punched my desk, in order the relieve my frustration and anger, and ended up bruising the shit out of my knuckles. As I was massaging the pain out of them, Haley came in and asked if I was ready.

"Bring them in," I said. A muscle ticked in my jaw as I prepared for the upcoming confrontation.

The two men, who were much bulkier than I was, and that was saying a lot because I was no small guy by any means, walked in. "Take a seat." My tone was not inviting.

They sat on the couch I'd indicated while I paced for a moment. I drew in a sharp breath to control the rage that swept over me.

"My first question to the two of you is this. What if she'd been a terrorist wearing a vest loaded with C-4?"

They mumbled some gibberish, but I answered for them. "I'll tell you what. We don't know how many deaths would be on your heads because you didn't have a better hand on your team downstairs. Who's in charge down there?"

"That would be—"

"You are, Carl. I hired you because of your past experience. You are the head of security. Everything they do falls under your umbrella. If one of them screws up, it's your fault. Now I want whoever's in charge down there in my office immediately."

"Yes, sir." Carl pulled out his phone and made a call. "He's on his way, sir."

"When this mess is resolved, you are to immediately conduct a meeting with your team, followed up by a memo, reminding them that if at any time they need to leave their posts, they must find a replacement. From now on I want two people at the door. I want line markers at the desk so if more than two people show up at once, they form a line and don't confuse the guards. Am I clear?"

"Yes, sir."

Haley came in and said Aaron Blankenship was here. I looked at Carl and he nodded. "Send him in."

He walked in and was told to take a seat. Then I busted his balls too.

"Aaron, what is going on down there? Did the circus come to town and no one informed me?"

"No, sir."

"I'm only going to say this once. If one of your guards has to use the restroom, get a replacement for him or her. Is that so difficult?"

He glanced at Carl. "Aaron, Carl didn't ask you the question, I did."

"Yes, sir, it is because we're shorthanded."

"And why is that?"

"Because two replacement guards haven't been hired yet."

"I see. Carl, how many entry points does this building have?"

"Eight, sir."

"And how many guards are on the other seven."

"None."

"How long have we been shorthanded, Carl?"

He squirmed. "Two weeks, sir."

I wanted to chew nails.

I directed my question to Aaron. "Are you telling me that you've been shorthanded all that time?"

"Yes, sir."

"Thank you, Aaron. You can leave."

He walked out, leaving Carl and Joe. I told Joe, "You can leave too. Carl, you stay."

Joe left and I sat down across from Carl. "What the hell is going on and don't beat around the bush."

He sighed. "I guess I haven't been paying as close attention as I should've been."

"You guess."

Suddenly, he seemed deflated, as though the air went completely out of him. He put his head in his hand as he sat there.

"What is it, Carl? This isn't like you."

"I should've come to you earlier, but I didn't want to mix work with my personal life."

Carl had always been a straight shooter, so I was baffled by this behavior. "What do you mean?"

"My wife left me a few weeks ago. It's messed with me in a bad way. I'm sorry. I should step down because I can't focus like I should. Like Aaron said, there are issues that I've let go and things have fallen through the cracks. I'm sorry."

"I'm sorry too, Carl. Do you need to talk to someone? You know the company offers assistance with that."

"Maybe. I don't know what I need right now. But if you want my opinion, Joe should take over for now."

"Okay. Why don't we do this? Why don't you take a medical leave of absence to get your head straight? When you feel better, come back and a job will be waiting for you."

"Yeah, I think that's best."

"Have Haley call HR for you and they'll guide you through the proper steps."

"Thanks, Mr. Thomas. This will be a big help." He left the office and then I realized I had to get Joe back in here and let him know he would be acting head of security until Carl returned.

When he came back, I didn't divulge any of Carl's information, but we got to work on the meetings he would have to run with his team and then the hiring of new guards. I made sure he understood the importance of having two people at the front entrance at all times and that I wanted security detail at all entrances from now on.

Joe was onboard and eager to please. He would implement these things immediately.

I checked the clock and it was only ten. What a morning so far. At noon, I called Cole.

"Hey, you busy for lunch?"

"No, s...Evan."

"Let's grab a bite somewhere."

"Sure."

We met in the lobby and walked across the street to this great little deli. While we ate, I picked his brain for Christmas presents for Sylvie.

"So, you two are still together?"

"Yeah, we actually are. I think she's ready for the jewelry gift."

He grinned. "Wow. You work fast."

"Not really. It's because I'm so old and know what I want."

"Uh huh." He chomped on his sandwich. "Still, that's fast, but I'll go with it. What are her favorite things?"

"You mean in jewelry?"

"Yeah. Does she like bracelets, earrings, rings?"

"She wears them all."

"Okay. How fancy do you want to get?"

"What do you mean, fancy?"

"Let me rephrase that. How much do you want to spend and don't give me a dollar amount? Just say money is no object or I'd like for it to be modest."

I swallowed my bite before answering. "Money's no object." It never would be where Sylvie was concerned."

"Go to Tiffany's. Every woman's dream is to have something from Tiffany's or that's what my wife says."

"You think so?"

"Uh huh. Or if you know any of her friends, ask them."

A crew from the office walked in and waved. I smiled and waved back. "Why didn't I think of that?"

"My wife always says, men only think with the brain in their pants and not with the one in their heads."

I nearly choked on my water. Not at the statement, but because it came from Cole. He looked so straight-laced and geeky, who would've thought he married someone like that?

He pounded me on the back. "Jeez, I didn't know that would choke you up."

"It's okay. I'm going to have to meet your wife. She sounds absolutely brilliant."

Cole chuckled. "She is. She married me, didn't she?"

I glanced at him and he wore a goofy expression on his face that was only matched by his goofy bow tie and glasses. There was no way I was going to hold back the laughter. If his wife was attractive, the man must have something going on between the sheets.

TWENTY-NINE
EVAN

I HIT ROSE UP THAT AFTERNOON FOR CHRISTMAS PRESENTS. She didn't agree with the Tiffany idea.

"Sylvie is a one of a kind girl. I'd go to one of those boutique jewelers and get her something there. Tiffany's is cool, but that's not her style."

"You're right. She doesn't really wear traditional jewelry now that I think of it. Thanks for the heads up."

Robert called and said he was on his way to pick up Sylvie and wanted to know if I had any desire to go. I would've loved to, but I wasn't quite ready yet. "I'll have to meet her at home."

I finished up at the office around six and took a taxi home. When I got upstairs. Whatever Rita was cooking had the place smelling amazing. I had all intentions of sneaking into the kitchen and peaking, only she was still in there.

"Dammit."

"What's wrong, Mr. Evan?"

"I was going to taste whatever you had cooking in here. But you're still here."

"All you have to do is ask." She opened the lid to a pot of bolognaise that looked scrumptious. "What time will your new roommate be here?" she asked with a twinkle in her eye.

"Anytime now. Robert is picking her up."

"Ooh. I can't wait to meet her."

"Don't you spoil her worse than me. I might get jealous."

She laughed. "I'll spoil you two equally."

I heard voices then. "They must be here." I hurried to the foyer in case she had a lot of bags.

"Hey," I said, wrapping her in my arms. Then I kissed her. "I've missed you."

"Me too."

"Your bags?"

"Here's the first load. Robert is getting the second."

"Is there more?"

"Nope. This was all I brought. I figured I could get more later. But I do want to unpack some of this, so it doesn't look completely crushed."

"Come on." We went to the master bedroom and I showed her to her own closet.

"I thought I would share with you. I had no idea there were two."

"Yes, ma'am. So you can buy more shoes if you want."

"I'm pretty well set, thanks."

She rolled her suitcase in and set it on the floor where she opened it and began to take her clothes out. I had more than enough hangers in there for her, so I asked if she needed help.

"I'm good, but you might want to help Robert. I feel sorry for him. The next one is huge."

"On it."

Robert was struggling to get the thing out of the elevator. "How in the world did you get that thing out of the car?"

"Well, sir, it wasn't nearly as bad as getting it in. I didn't know they made suitcases this large. Ms. West could fit in here, I believe."

"She probably could. Let me take it from here. Thank you, Robert. We'll see you in the morning around seven thirty."

"Yes, sir. Enjoy the evening."

By the time I got to the closet, the other bag was empty.

"Your big boy is here."

"Aww, I'm so glad because you are a sight for sore eyes."

"I was talking about this gigantic suitcase. Were you planning on killing someone and stuffing their body in here afterward?"

She just eyed me. "No! A girl needs stuff when she travels."

"Seriously. If we go anywhere longer than a week, are you going to take that?"

"Sure am."

I'd definitely have to add some major back exercises to my workout regimen.

"Meet me in the kitchen when you're finished. I want you to meet Rita. She's dying to meet you."

Sylvie stopped what she was doing, hopped to her feet, and said, "I'll come right now."

We stepped into the kitchen and Rita exclaimed, "Oh, Ms. Sylvie, it's so nice to meet you. I knew you would be beautiful and perfect for Mr. Evan." Sylvie beamed as Rita hugged her. "I told Mr. Evan I couldn't wait to spoil you. All you have to do is tell me what your favorite things are and I'll get them for you. And I love to cook, too, so please let me know what you like."

"Thank you. Evan tells me wonderful things about you. It's so good to finally meet you too."

It was easy to see Rita already loved her by her huge smile. I knew Sylvie would be spoiled, just like I was.

"How soon will you be ready to eat so I can prepare the pasta? Everything else is done," Rita said.

Sylvie looked to me for an answer.

"I'm ready whenever. Sylvie?"

"Same with me."

"Great. How about twenty minutes then?"

"That's perfect. That will give me enough time to finish unpacking."

After we finished, and I said we because I helped, we headed to the kitchen to eat. Rita had our places set at the island. Sylvie dove into her food and said it was the best bolognaise she'd ever eaten. It was fantastic. Rita left before we ate, but Sylvie would let her know tomorrow.

"Do you want dessert now or later," I asked.

"If I keep eating like this, I'm going to be as huge as the Goodyear blimp."

"Shut up. You won't be able to resist her dessert."

"What is it?"

"Chocolate creme pie."

"Oh, no. I love chocolate creme pie." She crossed her hands over her chest and sighed.

"Let's have some later."

We cleaned up and went to watch TV. I had other things on my mind, but before long, Sylvie was sound asleep. She looked so adorable I didn't dare wake her. I carried her to the bed, took her pants off, then her shirt. She mumbled in her sleep, but never woke up. Damn, she was really out, and it was only nine thirty.

That chocolate pie was calling my name, as I went and grabbed a piece, and watched some more TV. I hit the sack around eleven. At six in the morning, I heard Sylvie groaning. Reaching for her, the bed was empty. Where the hell was she and was she hurt?

"Sylvie? What's wrong?" Following the sound of her voice, I found her sitting on the bathroom floor. It surprised me that I even heard her, but the reason was she hadn't shut the door. "Hey, are you okay?"

"I think I have the stomach flu. I got up to go to the bathroom and nausea hit me like bam. I feel awful."

I put my palm on her forehead to see if she was warm. "You don't seem to have a fever. Do you have any body aches or a headache?"

She had her knees pulled to her chest and her chin was resting on them. "No. But I know I'm gonna hurl again at any minute."

"Let me get you a cool cloth."

I did and came back to put it on the back of her neck.

"Thank you. Maybe I have food poisoning."

"Yeah, but I'd have it too. It may be a virus or something. Just sit for a while and maybe it'll pass."

"Ugh, I hope so. I never get this stuff."

I sat there with her, but soon she was throwing up as I held her hair. When she was done, she asked me to leave.

"Why would I leave?"

"It's gross." She got up and brushed her teeth.

"You can't help being sick."

She shrugged and walked to the bed.

"Feel better?"

"Yeah, I do. I may take a shower in a minute."

"You're not going to work, are you?"

"Why not?"

"Because you just threw up. You probably have a virus."

"What if it's gone?"

I sat next to her and took her hand. "Babe, stay home. You'll feel better tomorrow."

"Promise?"

"I promise."

I kissed her on the cheek and headed to the workout room. I hoped whatever she had wasn't contagious because I'd rather have anything over a stomach bug.

When I came back to the room, she was sleeping, so I showered, dressed and left her a note on the bedside table. I told her to call me when she woke up.

Work was stacked up today because of all the fiascos yesterday. I jumped right in and was up to my elbows when Sylvie called.

"How's my girl feeling?"

"Actually, I'm feeling pretty good. Just worn out. I've decided to go into work."

"You sure that's a good idea?"

"Yeah. If I start to feel awful, I'll go to the townhouse. I'll have Robert drop me off there so I'll have my car, just in case."

"Great idea. Keep me posted, babe."

"I will."

"Hey, I love you."

"Love you too."

I hated the thought of sleeping without her, but it would have to do. I wouldn't put pressure on her if she didn't feel well. And who knows, I might be under the weather by tonight.

THIRTY

SYLVIE

GOING TO WORK MIGHT NOT HAVE BEEN THE BEST IDEA, BUT staying home wasn't either. Off and on I'd get nauseous, but then it would pass, and I'd feel fine. Maybe it was some weird virus, like Evan said. I washed my hands a lot and used hand sanitizer so I wouldn't spread whatever I had.

Around lunch, Rose came in and wanted to know if I wanted to go eat. We went to the cafeteria and I only grabbed a few items for lunch. She eyed me because she knew I usually had a big appetite.

"What's up with you today. Are you on another one day diet?"

"Ha ha, funny. Actually, I didn't feel well when I woke up, as in I threw up."

"Ick. Was it something you ate?"

We walked to a table and sat. "I don't think so, because Evan didn't get it and we ate the same thing."

"Hmm. A virus?"

"That's what I'm thinking."

Her eyes dug into mine. "It sure was short-lived."

"For sure, and I'm glad. I don't usually get those things."

"Seriously, Sylvie. Viruses usually last longer."

"What's your point?" By now, I had taken a few small test bites and my stomach felt somewhat better with food in it.

"Never mind."

"Rose, tell me. I'm your best friend."

Her eyes penetrated mine. "Do you think you might be pregnant?"

"Preg...what?"

"Well?"

"No! I'm on the pill."

"Um, hello." She pointed to herself. "I got pregnant with Montana on the pill."

"You did?"

"Yes. And then Greg nearly beat me to death for it. But you know that story. It was because of the antibiotics I'd taken. No one warned me about them."

My brain scrambled around in search of whether or not I'd been on any recently when Rose asked, "Weren't you on antibiotics for a sinus infection right before the wedding?"

Suddenly, the room spun, and everything blanked out except for that one indecent, lust-filled night that I couldn't even remember. "Shit, shit, shit."

"Shh, keep your voice down. And don't panic. It may be something else like you said."

"Ugh, I don't think so. My pants have gotten a bit snug and I've been so damn tired this past week."

She patted my hand and said, "Why don't you go to the store and get a pregnancy test. Then you'll know for sure."

"Will you do it? I just...can't. I don't want anyone seeing me buy it. If my mom finds out, I'm toast."

"Sure. I'll leave early today and run to the store and pick up a couple. I'll meet you at your place afterward. Oh, wait. Will you be going back there?"

"Yeah, I'd planned to spend the night here tonight. Hey, can you pick up a few groceries while you're there?" I made a pitiful face. It wasn't that hard because I was feeling worse than pitiful.

"Sure, make me a list before I leave, but don't give me a week's worth."

"What would I do without you?"

How I ever got through the rest of the day, I don't know. I was a mess. I wanted to cry whenever I thought about it because I knew Evan would die if I was because of what that skanky ex-girlfriend of his did to him. Fuck me upside down. What was I going to do?

When five o'clock hit, I ran for the door, barely telling anyone goodbye. My wheels actually squealed as I left the parking lot. I probably lost a year's worth of wear on them. All I wanted was a glass of wine to calm my nerves, but if I was pregnant, that was a no go.

Rose knocked on the door a few minutes later and my stomach instantly cramped. Her hands were laden with bags, so I helped her in and after I put up the groceries, I stared at the pregnancy tests.

"I bought two different brands so you could compare results. I figured if they both say positive, then you're pregnant."

My stomach dropped like I was riding a rollercoaster.

"Will you hold my hand?"

"Not while you're peeing, but after I will."

"Okay." I went to the bathroom with the kits and peed. Then I cleaned up and brought both sticks out to the living room as we waited.

"This is worse than when I took my boards," I said. My hands were practically dripping with sweat and my heart was jumping out of my chest. "I can't look. You tell me, Rose. I'm not even sure if I want to know."

It seemed like she was quiet forever. "Time's up," she finally said.

"And?"

"According to both tests, it appears you're going to have a baby." Then she hugged me as I was frozen in my seat. What in the hell was I going to do now?

I broke down into one sobbing heap. Everything in my mind centered around what Evan had told me about his past relationship and the fake pregnancy. Would he think I had done this on purpose just to trap him? The mere idea of that made me wail even more.

Rose hugged me and said, "Hey, it's going to be fine. You and Evan adore each other and will make amazing parents. Look at how awesome you are with Montana."

Her words which were meant to bring me comfort only set off another loud crying jag. "He's going to hate me," I managed to eke out between wails.

"Hate you? Why on earth would he hate you? That's ridiculous."

I couldn't tell her the whole story. Or could I? Would that be betraying his trust? I sniffed my tears back and only said, "It has to do with his past. And I promise you he'll hate me, Rose."

"You're different from anyone in his past. The reason I say this is because Pearson told me. He talks to Evan, you know."

"Even so, I know it will cut him deeply. And then there's my mom."

"Your mom? What about her. She loves Evan, doesn't she?"

"Not enough for me to be pregnant without the benefit of marriage. When she finds out, she'll try to put me in a convent."

Rose gave me an eye roll, which was out of character for her. "Come on, Sylvie, you're thirty years old."

"You think I'm joking? She dragged me to church not too long ago because I mistook her for Evan on the phone and answered in a sexy voice."

Then she busted out in a belly laugh. I smacked her arm. "This is not funny. I'm going to have a baby and you're laughing."

"I'm laughing at you answering the phone like that and your mom being on the other end. Oh, God, I wish I could've seen her face."

"No, you don't. When she got here, it was like Joan of Arc sweeping in. The only thing missing were her soldiers. You don't know how intimidating my mom can be when she wants to."

"You're forgetting something."

"What's that?" I asked.

"You have a weapon named Evan. Wasn't she gaga over him?"

"Yeah, but when it comes to this, I'm not sure that'll work. And then there's my dad. And what will Pearson say?"

"He'll be pissed at Evan if Evan doesn't treat you right. I do know that."

Tears dribbled down my cheeks again. "Why me? And why now when things were going so well?"

"Maybe it was meant to be. When I got pregnant with Montana, I was in denial because I knew what would happen. I eventually had to tell Greg and he ended up beating the shit out of me because I told him I wouldn't get rid of her. Now look at us. I have no idea what I would do without that precious darling in my life. Look on the bright side of things, Sylvie. Put your amazing counseling skills at work on yourself."

She was right. This baby might've been created out of one indecent night of drunken lust, but look what that had brought into my—into our lives. I was in love and if what Evan had told me was true, so was he. If he didn't want any part of this baby, then so be it. I would handle things like an adult, a mother, and carry on.

"Thank you, Rose. I need to pull up my bootstraps and deal with this. The creation of life is a miracle and I need to start acting like it and stop wallowing in my self-pity." That was convincing. I only had to believe it myself.

"That's right. And you know I have your back. Your sisters and family will too, just wait and see."

"Promise?" I said, my voice about to crack into another waterfall of tears.

"Get over here, you big dork."

I walked into her open arms where she patted my back.

"I know this seems like a mountain right now, but I promise

when you hold your baby for the first time, you'll wonder how in the world you could ever have doubted this."

Rose left and a few minutes later Evan called. He knew something was up.

"Are you still feeling bad?"

"No, I'm better, just tired."

"Do you think you should go to the doctor?"

Oh, yeah, but not for what you think.

"Maybe. I'll see how I feel tomorrow. I miss you."

"Babe, if only you knew."

Please, God, don't let him run from me.

I held back a sob as I said, "I'm planning on coming back tomorrow night."

"I was hoping you'd say that. Are you all right?"

"Yeah, I was just about to sneeze."

"Okay. For a minute there, it sounded like you'd been crying."

Thank God he couldn't see me. My eyes were probably red and swollen by now.

"Nope, I'm fine, other than sore eyes from reading charts today." That much was true.

"I'll let you go so you can get your rest. I don't want you to get any worse. I love you, sweets."

"I love you back and will see you tomorrow."

"Can't wait."

I prayed when I got there, he wouldn't absolutely lose it when I told him the news. I stared at the stick with the two pink lines on it, indicating I was pregnant. Should I save it to show him, or maybe take a picture of it. There were two other tests in the box Rose had bought so if he didn't believe me, I could retake the test.

My doorbell rang, which was strange. Who would be visiting me now?

I looked out the peephole and panicked. It was Evan. Shit. What was he doing here? I shoved the stick in my pocket and opened the door with a smile. There would be no way to hide my eyes now. I would have to tell him the truth.

"Hey," I said, opening the door. "What a great surprise." He walked in with a smile.

"I was almost here when I called, but I wanted to surprise you." He took my chin and lifted it up as his smile disappeared. "I'm glad I did now. What's going on. I knew you'd been crying."

The dam broke again as he put his arms around me. Sobs shook my body as I bawled my stupid eyes out again.

"Sylvie, please tell me what's wrong so I can help."

I hiccupped a few times and stammered, "Please... tell me... you won't...hate me."

"Hate you? How could I possibly hate you?"

"When I tell...you what's wrong...you might."

"Sylvie, then you don't know me very well. Babe, just tell me so I can help."

I gripped his white crisp shirt he still had on from the office, which was now tear-stained, and decided to just spill it. "Evan, I don't have a virus. I'm pregnant."

THIRTY-ONE

EVAN

THE WORDS PIERCED MY BRAIN. PREGNANT? HOW COULD SHE be pregnant?

"I don't understand," I said. "You said you were on the pill."

"I am. Or was. It doesn't matter now."

"How could you be pregnant if you're on the pill?

Digging into her pocket, she pulled out a little stick and handed it to me.

"Is this what I think it is?"

"The results of a pregnancy test I took a little while ago. They're supposed to be very accurate. Two lines mean pregnant." Tears bubbled out of her eyes, but at this moment I couldn't think straight. My mind went straight to the past, and that wasn't working out so well.

I rubbed my face, trying to get a grip on my emotions, which were all over the place. Anger was winning out, which I didn't want. Taking two giant steps backward, I closed my eyes before I unleashed what was on my mind. Accusations flowed through me, but were they really valid? The logical part of me was at war with the emotional side.

"Can I say something?"

"Why the hell not?" I snapped. She jerked as though I'd

slapped her. Didn't that just make me feel terrific? I shut my eyes once more and blew out a lungful of frustration. "Look, I'm sorry."

"You should be. That was uncalled for. I didn't ask for this."

"Neither did I."

"I want to explain. You said I told you I was on the pill that first night."

"Yes, you clearly did. Twice, in fact." My tone was clipped. Reining in my fucking anger wasn't possible right now.

"I was, dammit. But I'd also been on antibiotics the week prior."

"So? What does that have to do with anything?" I asked.

"Since I was under the influence of tequila, I'm sure it never entered my mind to mention that, but antibiotics can reduce the potency of birth control pills."

I wasn't sure I heard correctly. "Can you repeat that?"

She did. "You've never heard that before?"

"No. Why would I?"

"You're a very intelligent man. I would think during your past relationships, somewhere along the way one of your girlfriends might have mentioned it."

This clearly wasn't her fault. "I should never have taken the word of a drunk woman."

"I did tell the truth. This drunk woman just forgot about the antibiotics. The truth is, I forgot until I took the pregnancy test. And when it turned up positive, I couldn't figure out how in the world it could've happened because I never missed a pill. So I thought back and that's when it hit me."

My response was, "I honestly didn't know about the antibiotic effect, seeing as I never got involved with women long enough to find that out after my *ordeal*. Not only that, I usually wore condoms, except for that one night. Jesus, why did I have to miss that one damn night? So I suppose this was my fault for being so fucking stupid."

"Are you saying you regret all of this?"

"How could you possibly read that into what I just said?"

"Your tone of voice and the fact that you said you were stupid. To me that just reiterates your regrets of getting involved with me."

My mouth snapped shut. That's not what I meant, but she was upset and so was I. We needed to talk this out, but I wasn't sure how to go about it. I was angry and she was misinterpreting what I said.

"You know my past and what happened with Tiffany."

"Yes, and I'm trying to make this as easy as possible, but there doesn't seem to be a way to do that."

"Yes, there is. I'm trying to figure out how to say this."

"And you're putting me on her level after all."

"That's not what I said. You keep putting words into my mouth. A baby wasn't quite what I expected from you."

"And you think it's what I expected from you?"

"This isn't the first time I've been around this block."

"There you go again, comparing me to your ex."

"I am not. Why do you keep saying that?"

"Because you keep acting that way. What am I supposed to think? I knew you'd be angry and wouldn't want this baby. But don't worry, Evan. That's fine by me. I won't expect a single thing from you. Unlike Tiffany, I don't plan on using this baby as a means to get your money. I've always been honest about that. But just be clear. I will have this baby and do not intend to get rid of it." Her nostrils flared as her eyes sparked. Even though her eyes still dripped tears, I had touched her maternal nerve and her fists were up, ready to fight it out.

"Calm down, Sylvie."

She squinted at me and then her pointer finger took aim at my chest. "Calm down? You know something? You just hit my nuclear reactive button, cowboy. The way I see it is this. I'm taking responsibility for my actions, but you're not. You're putting all the blame on me, and if you haven't figured this out yet, it takes two to make a baby. I was drunk off my ass on tequila. Yes, I told you I was on the pill. What man in their right mind would take the word of a drunk woman? You should've worn a condom anyway. So this pregnancy is entirely your fault, pill or no pill. You told me you loved me. If that were remotely true, you wouldn't be acting like a pouty little teenager who isn't getting his way. I think you should leave."

"Leave?"

"As in go back to the city."

"Are you serious?"

She stood there with her arms crossed. If she could blow smoke out of her nose, she probably would.

"Of course I'm serious. Have you even been listening to me?"

"I can't go home. Robert is gone and I don't have a ride."

"Oh, my. Poor man. Haven't you ever heard of Uber?" Sarcasm oozed out of every one of her pores. This was a side of her I'd never seen. She could definitely dish it out.

"Of course I have."

"Order one. They're great. They may not serve champagne and caviar, but they'll get you home just fine."

"That's not fair."

"Neither is comparing me to Tammie Lou."

I gritted my teeth. "Tiffany."

"Whatever."

"You really want me to leave?"

"Do you really think I want someone in my home who puts me on the level of an old girlfriend who was a lying, cheating scoundrel? How would you feel? It certainly doesn't seem anywhere close to love by my standards."

My brows pinched together. She was right and it was probably best we had time away from each other. I had to think. I needed to wrap my head around this. She'd made some valid points and I hadn't connected all the dots. I did the only thing I knew. I punched in Pearson's number.

"Hey, man. What's up?"

"You busy?"

"Nah. You need something?"

"Can you pick me up? I'm at Sylvie's. I'll explain when you get here."

"Yeah, but where do you want to go?"

"Anywhere. Hell, if you can get me there."

"I'm on the way."

Sylvie's stare singed through my coat. Shame coiled within me at the way things turned out. I should've handled this better. And I would. I just needed a few hours to figure out how.

Turning around, I said, "You probably hate me right now, but I honestly do love you. With everything I have. I just have to process this."

She didn't budge an inch or respond. I had to wonder if she even heard me. I dipped my head and walked out the door. It about broke me to leave her like that, but there wasn't anything else I could do at the moment. I knew one thing. I would figure something out to get back into her life and to put that beautiful smile back on her face.

THIRTY-TWO

EVAN

I WAITED IN THE PARKING LOT. PEARSON PULLED UP A FEW minutes later and I got in his car. He sat there and didn't drive off.

"Wanna tell me what this is all about?" he asked.

"Man, I fucked up in the worst way." I groaned. "What the fuck am I gonna do?"

"Can we backtrack a bit? What exactly happened?"

I rubbed my face, and my scruff scraped my hands. "I don't even know where to begin."

"Try the beginning."

"Promise you won't hate me?" Now I sounded exactly like Sylvie had. Only with me, it made me sound like a fucking pussy.

"What the fuck did you do?"

"Sylvie's pregnant."

"Jesus. I think I know where this is headed. Please tell me she knew about Tiff."

"She did. But that doesn't make this any better. I knee-jerked and you can pretty much put two and two together."

"You asshole," he swore.

"Oh, yeah. I didn't exactly act like her knight in shining armor." I leaned my head against the headrest, but I knew he wouldn't let me off easy, especially since it was Sylvie we were discussing.

"I want the details, man. You promised you wouldn't hurt her."

"And I had no intention of doing so. Swear to God."

"Oaths like that mean shit if you don't keep them, Evan." My hands plowed through my hair, nearly yanking it out.

"This is what happened. It took me completely by surprise. She was sick, nausea, throwing up, and we both thought it was a bug. But no, it's a baby instead."

I explained everything from the way I found out to how she misinterpreted everything I said. "The thing is, she was right. I could see why and everything that came out of my damn mouth sounded fucked up. I was pissed and lost control. Then when she got pissed—which I don't blame her at all for—everything went downhill. She kicked me out, man. Got very sarcastic with me. I'd never seen that side of her, but she unleashed on me and gave me a tongue-lashing I won't soon forget."

"You've just been treated to the West family temper, my friend. And she has inherited a healthy dose of it. So what do you want me to do?"

"I need your advice."

"My first inclination is to tell you to go back in there and get on your hands and knees and beg. But knowing Sylvie, she's going to have to cool off. Do you want to go home? Come to our place? What?"

"Do you mind calling me an Uber? I don't know how."

Laughter exploded out of him.

"Shut the fuck up."

"Mr. Rich Boy doesn't know how to call an Uber."

I wanted to kick Pearson's ass right now. "And how do you know about this magical car ride?"

"Dude, I was so fucked up most of the time, I lived in Ubers."

"Sorry."

"No apologies necessary. But I'll be happy to get you one." I watched him closely as he tapped an app on his phone and with a couple more taps, he said, "It'll be here in about four minutes."

"That's it?"

"Yep."

"No wonder everyone raves about them."

"Getting to the city will be pricey. You'll owe me."

"No worries. How much?" I pulled out my wallet.

He shook his head. "I don't want money. I just want you to fix what's between you and Sylvie. You made me a promise and you'd better damn well keep it. Can I let you in on something?"

"Please."

"Other than Rose, she's super tight with her sister, Piper. I mean she's close to Reynolds too, but Piper is the one I'd place my money on that she's going to call because her mom is going to shit over this."

"And?"

"Call Piper and ask for her help."

"I don't know, man. She doesn't really know me."

"Take it from me. Aunt Cindy is over the top for you, and Piper thinks it's hilarious. Call her because she's on Team Evan. If anyone can help, it's Pipe."

A car pulled up behind us and Pearson said, "Your ride's here. Keep me posted on what happens."

"Yeah and thanks. Text me Piper's number please and I'll call her tonight."

He nodded as I got out. The ride into the city wasn't bad but the damn driver wouldn't keep his mouth shut. He was a big talker and yammered all the way home. All I wanted to do was lay my head back because it was about to explode. By the time I got out of the car, I was sure it had leveled up to migraine status, even though I'd never had a true migraine before. A large stiff drink was in order and then maybe I'd have the balls to call Piper. I wondered if Sylvie had called her yet, because I didn't want to tell her the news before Sylvie had a chance.

There was a note from Rita on the island with instructions for dinner, but I was not even close to being hungry. I guzzled three fingers of my favorite scotch and made that call to Piper. It went to her voicemail, which didn't surprise me. I didn't answer a lot of calls from numbers I didn't recognize.

About an hour later, after my second drink, the phone rang. I answered it because it was Piper.

"Piper?"

"Yeah, hi Evan. I suppose you're calling about Sylvie."

"Well, yeah, I hope you listened to my message."

"I'm outside her place, getting ready to go in."

"Is she okay?"

"When she called, I thought her place had burned down. I could barely understand her she was crying so hard."

"Shit."

"You can say that again. She's about as dandy as a pregnant lady who's pissed off at her boyfriend."

"Yeah, about that. I need your help."

"My help? How?"

"You see, I totally fucked up. And I need to make it up to her. She really took me by surprise and my reaction was the worst. I love her, Piper, and would never want her to be alone or have this baby alone. I'm not sure what she thinks right now. Other than she probably hates me."

"Yeah, you're not high on her list at the moment."

"Didn't think so. This is where you come in."

"If you give me some ideas, I'll try, but I'm not sure she'll listen. All she cares about right now is the baby."

"What is she going to tell your parents?"

"Nothing yet. But I'll find out more when I see her."

"Can you call me later?"

"Tomorrow, because I'm spending the night."

"Good. I'm happy knowing she won't be alone."

"I can tell you one thing. You're really going to have to grovel after this."

A.M. HARGROVE

"I'll do whatever it takes. I swear. I can't stand the thought of her being alone through this?"

"Hey, what am I? I'll be there, you know."

"You know what I mean."

"Yeah, I'm just tightening that chain around your neck."

"Thanks. I'll be waiting for your call, but in the meantime, I'll try calling her too. Try and talk her into answering, will you?"

"Oh, brother, do you have a lot to learn where my sister's concerned."

"I'm just figuring that out. And Piper? Thanks."

There was a hollow feeling in my gut. At the time, I hadn't thought what I'd done was too damn awful, but for me to put her on the level of Tiffany, spelled distrust and that was terrible. I can't even imagine what my reaction would've been had the shoe been on the other foot. I'm sure I would've gone ballistic.

Even if it took all year, I'd fix this. I'd use every trick up my sleeve if I had to.

THIRTY-THREE
SYLVIE

PIPER CAME THROUGH THE DOOR AND HUGGED ME. "THIS WILL be fine soon. You'll wonder why you cried this hard."

"How can you say that? My heart has just been completely crushed."

"It can't be that bad."

"Not only that, when Mom finds out, she's going to send me to a nunnery somewhere." I sniffed.

"Are you getting snot in my hair and on my jacket? If you are, I'm going to kill you, even if you are desperate right now."

I stepped away from her with my lower lip poked out and trembling. "I can't believe you. I'm broken and pregnant and may end up on the streets and you're more concerned about your hair."

She was taking her coat off, inspecting it, when she stopped and gave me a once-over, right before a most ungodly sound came out of her. At first, I thought she'd passed gas. But then when she put her hand over her mouth, slapped her knee, and stumbled to the couch, I knew she was making fun of me in my time of dire need.

"I don't believe you. Here I am in mortal distress and you're laughing."

One hand flew up in the air, waved around and she rolled on the couch, yelling, "Stop, you're killing me."

Killing her? What the hell was I doing?

I growled at her and stomped into the kitchen to do what? I couldn't get a glass of wine or even a shot of liquor for that matter. Being pregnant sucked balls. And this was day one. What the fuck was I going to do for the next thirty plus weeks?

Footsteps clicked on the floor behind me. "I'm sorry, Syllie."

"Don't call me that in my time of need."

"Okay. Sorry." She squeaked those two words out, so I knew she was on the edge of laughing again.

"What is so fucking funny, Pipe?"

"Oh, gawwwd. First, when you said you'd be on the streets." Her tone hit that high pitched level that a voice sometimes did when one was trying not to laugh.

"Yeah, what about it?"

"Why would you even think that? You're gainfully employed, have a family who loves and cares about you, friends who adore you, and you also have a baby daddy."

"Don't you dare go there." My finger was dangerously close to her nose.

"Sylvie, put your finger down, hon. I value my eyes and nose. Another thing, you're thirty years old. Stop letting Mom push you around. A nunnery. Sister Mary Sylvie." She actually snorted at that.

"How dare you steal my snorts. You never snort."

She looked as surprised as I was.

"Oh, God. I hope that was a temporary miscalculation of my soft palate." She massaged her throat.

"Was that it? Anything else make you laugh at me in my delicate condition?"

She snickered then she scanned me. "You don't look any different from the last time I saw you and you weren't delicate then."

"Well, I am now. Try being this upset and not being able to drink a glass of wine or down a shot of liquor or two."

"Okay, I'll give you that one."

Before I could make a snarky comeback, my phone buzzed. I checked it out and gasped. "Shit, it's Evan."

"Answer it."

"I can't."

"Why not?"

"I don't want to talk to him just yet."

Piper shrugged. "You're gonna have to do it sooner or later."

My phone dinged this time with a text: **Sylvie, please talk to me. I know I screwed up. Give me a chance to make it right. I love you.**

"What did he say?" Piper wanted to know, reaching for my phone. "It sounds like he wants to apologize.

"I'm not ready for that."

"Why don't you at least give him a chance and talk to him?"

"I just can't right now." I broke into a sob on the last word. This crying was ridiculous. I was sick and tired of it and didn't think it would ever stop.

All of a sudden, I found my head being squished between Piper's ample breasts as she hugged me. Piper was taller than me and much more endowed. No one could figure out where she'd gotten her large Ds from, but they were spectacular, except now they were suffocating me.

"Pipe, I can't breathe," I mumbled into her chest.

"Oh, sorry." She released me and asked, "Are you ever going to give me the full story?"

"Yeah, but not today. I'm so raw inside, I just can't deal."

"Can you at least tell me what happened at the wedding?"

We sat down and I spilled my guts.

"I can't believe you kept that to yourself. After the reception too. Of all things, Sylvie. I saw you two together and you were hilarious the way you were—"

"Please stop, Pipe. I can't deal with anything that has to do with him right now."

She put her arms around me again, but gently this time. "What are you going to tell Mom and Dad? Christmas is coming up and the family will be there. Will you tell everyone then?"

I practically yelled, "Are you out of your mind? What do you suggest? Just as everyone is getting ready to take a bite of turkey I announce I'm going to have a baby? Can you imagine the havoc it would create?"

Instead of looking appalled as I expected, Piper cracked up. "Oh my God. That would be awesome. Mom's face would crash right into her mashed potatoes."

"Pipe! You have to be on the crazy train to hell. That would be Armageddon."

"You're right. Maybe you should wait until the apple pie is served. She'd look way more funny with ice cream on her face."

"Would you stop?" But then I broke into a smile.

"See, you agree. You can't hide that grin."

"God, that would be funny. 'Hey Mom. Guess what. You're finally getting your wish. You're going to be a grandmother. I'm preggies! Whoohoooo!' Then you could all hop out of your chairs and dance."

"I liked it better before you added the dance part."

"You're killing my fun," I said with a pout.

"We could tell Dad ahead of time. You know he'd have your back."

I grabbed her hand. "Piper, this isn't a joke. Do you really think he will?"

"Dad will always have your back, no matter what. Remember what he used to tell us when we were growing up? 'No matter what happens, I'll always love you. No matter how terrible you think something is, it's never that bad. As long as you still have breath in your body, you're always my daughter, and you'll always have my love.'"

I gazed at her in amazement. "How did you ever remember that?"

"How could you forget it? That was the most profound thing he ever told us."

As I reflected upon it, she was right. Dad had said many things to us over the years, but that was the most significant. How could I have forgotten?

"You're right. I'll tell him first. Maybe he can advise me about Mom."

"Seriously? He's the one who always needs advice about her." Piper laughed.

"True. I guess I can't worry about that now."

Piper gazed at me thoughtfully for a long minute.

"What?" I asked.

"Have you discussed this with Pearson?"

"You mean about being pregnant?"

"Yeah."

"No, but I assume he knows because Rose does."

"Can he talk to Evan?"

My hands gestured wildly. "Absolutely not. This is between Evan and me and that's where it stays."

"Things must have been pretty good between the two of you before this happened?"

It took me a while before I responded. I wanted to say they weren't. But then I remembered everything with clarity and a warm glow filled me. It had been much better than great.

"It must've been pretty damn awesome with a secretive smile like that," Piper said.

"I wasn't smiling."

"The hell you weren't."

"Okay, I admit it. Things were pretty great." I told her almost everything, leaving the out the sordid details. My belly clenched at some of the things I talked about. The emotions it conjured up were all over the place and those damn tears started flowing again. "I hate pregnancy hormones," I wailed.

"Seems to me you're a fool. You should talk to him and give him a chance to apologize again. You're only hurting yourself. Besides, do you honestly want to go through having a baby alone?"

"You mean, you won't be here with me?"

"Um, yeah, about that. I'm leaving in late June."

"Where the hell are you going?" My voice squeaked out a soprano note. She was full of surprises today.

"As soon as the school year ends, I'm heading to Europe. I've applied for a master's program in the U.K. and in all likelihood, I'll get accepted."

"You're going to give up your teaching position here?"

"Yes. I want my master's in English Literature and what better place than Cambridge?"

"You'll miss the birth of my little nubbin."

"I know, and I'm really sorry. But I applied for this way before I knew about nubbin."

My heart ached with this news and I cried even more. I needed to stop wearing eye makeup. It ended up under my eyes in dark circles, irritating them. What would I do without Piper? A profound sadness filled me. I flopped back on the couch with my face buried in a pillow and sobbed like a baby.

"Good lord, Sylvie, you're going to wear yourself out like that."

"I can't help it."

She patted my back.

"I'll be here until you're near the end."

"Why can't you just stay until nubbin pops her head out?"

"What if nubbin's a boy?"

I sat straight up and ogled her. "She can't be. I don't know a single thing about boys." I sniffed.

Piper laughed. "You'll be a quick learner. Besides, you have two cousins named Grey and Hudson, who have boys. I daresay they'd be willing to help."

"Daresay? Have you been reading Jane Austen again?"

"Guilty as charged. *Pride and Prejudice*."

"Don't you have that blasted book memorized by now?" I asked.

"Maybe, but quit changing the subject."

"You're right. Grey's wife, Marin, and Hudson's wife, Millie, would love to help. I know that. But it would also be nice to know myself."

"And you have Aunt Paige," Piper said with a wink.

"Don't say that. Mom would die. I wish they were close like they used to be."

Piper said, "Hey, at least they're speaking again since Pearson and Rose's wedding."

I nodded. About that time my phone rang. When I checked the caller ID, I saw it was Evan again. My belly lurched to the floor.

"Who is it?" Piper asked.

"No one."

She grabbed my phone. Then her expression changed, and I knew what she was going to do. I tried to get the phone back, but she jumped up and moved out of reach.

"Hi Evan. This is Piper, Sylvie's sister. I'm so happy you called. My sister is right here and would love to speak to you."

She extended her arm with the phone in it. I gritted my teeth, because I was pissed at her. I didn't know what to do or say. She'd really put me in a shitty position. Her brows shot up as she tapped her toe.

I finally took the phone and said, "Hi Evan."

THIRTY-FOUR

EVAN

HER TONE INDICATED SHE WASN'T EXACTLY OVERJOYED TO BE on the phone.

I hesitated before I asked. "Sylvie, how are you?"

"I've been better." Sarcasm oozed from her. I didn't like it and wanted to chase it away.

Calmly, I said, "The same can be said for me. I...that is can we talk? I want to apologize for my awful behavior."

"There's no need."

"But, there is. Please, give me that chance."

"Give me one good reason why."

This was it and I had to make everything right. "Because I believe in us, in that what we have between us is a once in a life-time thing. Please, give me a chance, Sylvie.

I heard muffled sounds in the background, as in maybe her sister was telling her something and she had her hand smashed against the phone. I wanted to tell her just to mute it, but I didn't.

She finally came back with, "You have one chance, Evan. But that's it."

"I can be at your place tomorrow any time after work. Will that work for you?"

"What time?"

"Six?"

"Fine. I'll see you then." The call ended.

I exhaled the breath I'd been holding. Piper must've said something because I couldn't imagine her letting me come over otherwise. Now to get through the rest of tonight and tomorrow. It was amazing how one woman brought me to my knees. I'd faced a boardroom full of executives who were ready to cut my head off and never flinched. But with Sylvie, I was so afraid of what she might do. Tomorrow could spell the end of my life as I wanted it or the beginning of our lives together as they could be.

The alarm went off forty-five minutes early to allow me to get in a difficult workout. After my shower, I packed an overnight bag. I was feeling hopeful, just in case.

Work was insane, but I told Haley, I had to be out of the office by four forty-five. I didn't want to be one minute late getting to Sylvie's.

My phone rang right before noon. It was Piper.

"I was worried you weren't going to call."

"Yeah, well, I did my best in putting a good word in for you. You're on your own now."

"I owe you big. Anything you want."

"Don't worry. I'll think of something."

"How is she?" I was afraid of her response.

"To be honest, I told her she was being a big baby about this. I think her hormones are whacky because I've never seen her cry so much."

"Great. Just what I need on top of yesterday."

"After you called, she sat there with a stupefied look on her face."

"What do you mean?"

"I mean she looked like she'd been hit on the head with a sledgehammer. She didn't wear it very well. Anyway, that's so unlike my sister. She needs to see a doctor. I'm telling you, those hormones are out of control."

I sighed. "I'm the last person who's going to suggest that to her."

"Somebody needs to."

"You should. You're her sister."

"Yeah, but doing it last night would've been too much. Well, good luck tonight. Team Piper is pulling for you."

"Thanks." Her comedic side had me chuckling for a second, until I thought about what I faced ahead.

The afternoon flew by since I was swamped with work. I checked the time to see it was already almost four thirty. I wrapped up the project I was on, closed my computer, and grabbed the small overnight bag I'd brought in. Telling Haley goodbye, I took the rear exit.

Robert was waiting outside by the time I walked out of the building. I'd be able to get the rest of my work done on the ride over. Traffic wasn't horrific, and we arrived at Sylvie's a little before six.

"Do you mind waiting? I don't know how long I'll be."

"No, sir. I'll be right out here."

"Thank you."

I knocked, and her door opened. But it wasn't Sylvie. It was Piper.

"Hi, I'm Piper. We met at Pearson and Rose's wedding." She winked. What was going on? Then she mouthed, "She called me to come over."

"Yes, I remember. I'm Evan."

"We met over the years at Pearson's. But I was much younger."

"In pigtails, if I remember."

"Hey, I loved those pigtails."

I chuckled at her. "Well, you've changed quite a bit."

She laughed and it was a great laugh that reminded me of Sylvie's, minus the snort. "I hope so. I've sprouted, you might say."

She was tall, maybe five feet ten. Her hair was dark, like

Sylvie's, but her eyes were bright blue and sparkled mischievously. Piper was also beautiful, but in a different way than Sylvie.

"Is Sylvie here? I was supposed to come over tonight."

She said, "She's here." Then mouthed, "She's acting pouty again."

I mouthed my thanks right as Sylvie made her entrance. And she looked awful. Red and swollen eyes highlighted her face. Other than that, she was paler than I'd ever seen her. It gut-punched me because this was my fault.

"Hey," I said. The thing I wanted most right now was to pull her against me, hold her, and tell her everything would be fine. Only I knew she wouldn't accept that.

"Hi."

"How are you?" I asked.

"Not so good." She aimed her thumb at her face. "Can't you tell?"

"You always look gorgeous to me." I noticed Piper had slipped out of the room. "Can we sit?" I asked, motioning toward the couch.

"Sure." We both took a seat, she on the opposite end from me, which was awkward.

It took everything I had not to pull her into my lap. My fists clenched by my legs.

"So, what is it you wanted to say?"

Putting my hands in the prayer pose, I pressed them to my lips before I spoke. "I'm more than sorry about last night. You said some things that made complete and total sense, but at the end of the day, when I got home and thought about everything, I realized something. Well, that's not exactly correct. I realized a lot of things. First off, my reaction was awful, over the top. It was knee jerk, which was uncalled for and I don't even know why I did or said those things. But I can't take them back. And I'm very sorry about that. But here's the other thing. You were right. I should never have taken your word the night of the reception.

But I did. And as I thought more and more about it, I'm glad I did because I'm actually thrilled you're pregnant."

"What?" she cried out.

She gawked at me. Pushing to my feet, I paced for a second, then spun around, facing her again.

"Yep. You heard me. I'll repeat it too. I'm ecstatic you're going to have a baby. My baby. *Our baby*. There. I know it's not what you want to hear."

"You're damn right it's not." Indignation was etched all over her. Her angry face reappeared.

"That's fine. But the reason I'm happy is because I adore you, Sylvie West, and there isn't anyone else on this earth I'd want to have a baby with. You'll be the greatest, most loving mother in the world, and I'll be with you every step of the way. That is if you'll have me. I'd marry you tomorrow if you'd say yes. We are great together, you and me. Yes, I made a mistake and fucked up, pretty badly too. But I'm not above apologizing when I do. And you know what? That's not the only mistake I'll make in our relationship. But what we have is much bigger and better than throwing it away because of one, two, hell, a dozen mistakes. One thing I can promise you is I'll always be true to you and you'll always be able to count on me to have your back and be by your side. Love is more than four letters. Sometimes it can slay you, crush you, destroy you. But it's also showing, doing, caring, overcoming our mistakes, and creating something monumental between us that no one can tear apart. I'll prove this to you if you only give me the chance.

My gut was on fire the entire time I spoke.

"Evan, come here."

I did as she asked, waiting for her to tell me it was over.

"No, come here." She pointed to where she sat, but between her legs.

"I don't understand."

"Do I have to spell it out for you?" She grabbed my wrist and pulled me close so she could kiss me. I'd heard the phrase *my heart soared* before, but I'd always thought it was a ridiculous one. Now I knew it was real because mine was flying around the room, bumping the ceiling right now.

"I love you too, and you're right. I'll also make lots of mistakes."

"Are you crying?"

She wiped her eyes. "I seem to be doing a lot of that these days. I think I'm super hormonal. And to think I have another eight months of this."

"Just come to me, babe and I'll brush those tears away."

THIRTY-FIVE

SYLVIE

EVAN AND I DECIDED TO TELL DAD THE DAY BEFORE Christmas Eve. We invited him over before dinner on the ruse that I needed help with something in the townhouse. We'd talked it over the night before and Evan thought it best that he spoke with Dad without a big crowd and he also wanted to talk with him alone. He wouldn't share what he wanted to say, even though I'd wheedled him to death.

"Sylvie, you won't get it out of me. This is something I need to do, man-to-man. That's the only thing I'll tell you and it may be difficult for you to understand, but I'm sorry."

"Actually, I admire you for this. I'm a little scared to tell Dad, but not anywhere close to the way I feel about telling Mom. With her, I feel like a twelve-year-old again."

There was a knock on the door, indicating Dad's arrival.

"Hey Sylls, how's my girl?" He gave me one of his famous bear hugs as he called them. Dad always smelled like a blend of peppermint gum and Old Spice aftershave. Mom had tried to get him to use expensive colognes, but he'd have nothing to do with them. He'd said, "My grandfather used Old Spice, my dad used it, and by George, so will I." My sisters and I loved it, but now I understood why Mom wanted him to change. Although smelling him today was so nostalgic, I didn't want his hug to end.

"Everything okay, Sylls?"

"Um, yeah. Come on in." I held his hand as we walked inside to where Evan was.

"Evan, how are you?"

"Fine, sir, and you?"

"I'm well, thanks. So Sylls, what's broken?"

Evan and I shared a brief glance. "Dad, take a seat." I walked him to the couch. "I sort of fibbed. Nothing is broken today, so you lucked out."

"I don't understand." Dad and I had the same eyes. They'd been dubbed the West eyes—gray and penetrating. I was feeling the full brunt of their power now. When I was a teenager, those same eyes made it impossible not to tell the truth. They'd have me squirming in no time, exactly like I'm about to do.

"Dad, Evan and I want to tell you something and we wanted to tell you privately, without an audience. We thought you had that right. And we would've invited Mom, but she's been acting a bit strange lately."

"I see. So, what's this news?"

"You may not be happy about this right now, but you're going to be a grandfather." I grinned stupidly.

He didn't look at me at all. Those West eyes went directly to Evan. "I expect you'll take care of this in the proper way?"

I wasn't sure what he meant by that. Before I had a chance to say anything, Evan stepped in.

"Yes, sir. Sylvie and the baby will never want for anything."

Dad clenched his jaw and said, "That's not what I meant."

"What *do* you mean, Dad?"

"Sylls, your generation is much different than mine."

"That's right. If you're implying what I think you are, then no, marriage is not in the picture yet."

"Sylvie Lenore West. What are you thinking?"

Evan tried to interrupt, but my hand flew up as I rose to my feet. This was my battle and I intended to fight it.

"Dad, this is the twenty-first century. Women are not at the mercy of men to marry them. We are perfectly capable of taking care of ourselves."

Dad followed me and stood. "That's not what I was talking about. The baby should be raised with a father."

"He or she will be. Evan will be present all the time."

Now he was really angry. His eyes nailed me again and it took everything in my body not to shrivel and run. I stood my ground and stared back in defiance. "We can't possibly get married yet. We're not ready. We need to get to know each other better first." Oh, shit. Why did I say that?

"Then what the hell are you doing sleeping with him?"

"John, if I may—" Evan began.

Dad pointed to him and said, "You keep out of this."

"I'm afraid that's impossible since it's my baby she's carrying."

"Wait a minute. How far along are you?"

"About six weeks."

He was silent for a moment as his jaw ticked. "This happened at your cousin's wedding, when you were so drunk you could barely walk, didn't it?"

My face instantly blazed. Why would he even ask me that?

He unleashed his fury on Evan. "You knew how inebriated she was, yet you took advantage of her. What kind of a man are you?"

I would've expected Evan to raise his voice, argue, or something. But he didn't. He stood there and when my dad was finished with his tirade, he finally replied in a calm voice.

"John, I can't blame you for being upset. But Sylvie and I can't take back what happened. We can only move forward. And she's right. Getting married right now doesn't make sense since this relationship is relatively new to both of us. Did we make a mistake? Most certainly. But I can tell you this. I love your daughter. She's a very special woman and I do plan on marrying her. I was going to have this conversation with you in private, but neither of us anticipated this kind of reaction from you. We're sorry things turned out the way they did, but I am *not* sorry one bit I'm going to be a father and that she's the mother of our child."

Oh, this man just made my heart swell. If it got any larger there wouldn't be room for anything else in my body. I went up to him, put my hands on his cheeks, and said, "You're the best." Then I kissed him.

"Dad, Evan is right. We can't unmake our nubbin. But we're going to do our best to be great parents. We're not asking you to like us, we only want you to love your grandchild."

He slumped down on the couch, hanging his head in his hands. His reaction surprised me. Mom acting this way would've been the norm, but Dad, no.

I sat next to him and asked, "Other than this, is there something going on?"

He released a long sigh. "I probably should've mentioned this to you and your sisters before, but I think your mom may have early onset of dementia."

"What are you saying? She's only fifty-five. How is that even possible?" My thoughts pinged all over the place, searching for some solid ground to settle upon.

Dad lifted his head, and his eyes were filled with anguish. Dad had always been there for me, when I'd fallen off my bike and skinned both knees, or when the neighborhood girls had acted cliquey, like girls often did. All I needed to do was come running to him and he'd soothe away my hurt, bandage me up, or wipe my tears, and tell me I was better than those other girls, and my happy would return. He used to tell me he carried around sugar to sprinkle over me every day to make each day sweet, and I'd believed him. Now it was my turn to sprinkle his life with sugar and carry some of the burden for him.

Grabbing both of his hands in mine, I asked, "I want to help,

Dad. What can I do? Are there tests?"

"I'm taking her next week, but she doesn't know. She covers things up. She went to the store yesterday and was gone for so long, I kept calling her. I finally got the truth. She got lost coming home. Sylls, how many times has she gone to the same store over the years?"

"Oh, Dad." I leaned my head on his shoulder.

"There are so many things, I can't begin to recount."

"I knew she hasn't been herself lately."

Evan stood by and let us talk. There really wasn't much for him to say.

"I told Mom I'd make a few things for Christmas dinner, but do you want me to come early to supervise?"

"No, because we ordered the turkey. I told her in no uncertain terms was she cooking. It's too much for her. Piper and Reynolds are handling the side dishes that you aren't and I ordered everything else, including dessert. Pretend you don't know. I told her we'd put everything in the oven and act like we did it. If you come earlier, you'll blow it for us."

"That's a great idea." I patted his hands. "Do you want me to go to the doctor with you?"

"I wish I could say yes, Sylls, but then she'd suspect something."

I threw my arms around him and cried. I cried for him and my mom. I couldn't imagine Mom going through this. She was such a proud woman.

"Dad, do you want us to keep quiet about the baby? We could tell Piper and Reynolds another time."

"That may be best. I'm worried what this will do to your mother."

Under the circumstances, so was I. Evan took a seat in the chair near me. He said, "We don't need to mention a word to anyone until they guess by Sylvie's appearance. We'll do whatever you want, John."

"I appreciate that. But I still wish you two would get

married." His eyes pleaded with us.

I figured it was best not to respond. He was going through so much and another argument was too much for one day.

"I'd better get going. I hate leaving her alone for too long. I worry she'll get into something and a disaster will ensue."

I cringed thinking how his life must've changed.

"We'll see you on Christmas then, Dad."

After he left, I couldn't stop worrying about him and Mom, which of course, led to more tears. That was the last thing I'd expected. Evan was sweet to try and comfort me, but I didn't think there was much he could do.

"I had no idea this was going on." Guilt clawed at me for the way I'd been feeling about my mom when all this time she may have some serious illness.

"I know, babe. It's written all over you. But I did want to say something. What I told your dad was true. I do want us to get married and live as a family. I don't mean tomorrow or next month, or even before the baby's born. But I love you and want to be in your life as well as the baby's. I never thought I'd say those words to any woman, so I'm not just doing this because you're pregnant."

I was nearly dizzy with everything going on. "Evan—"

"Sylvie, I didn't tell you this so you could give me some sort of answer. I only wanted to share my feelings and let you know the things I told your dad were the truth."

I probably would've had a better reaction if he'd told me a bomb exploded outside. This was not the time for me to be thinking about something like this with my parents front and center on my mind.

"Evan, I appreciate what you're doing, I really do. I don't mean this to sound the way it's going to, but with worrying about Mom, and how Dad is going to deal with her, I just can't think about us right now."

He pulled me close and held me. "That's why I'm here. This is what love is all about."

THIRTY-SIX
EVAN

"ARE YOU OKAY, MR. THOMAS? YOU'RE LOOKING A BIT PEAKED today," Haley said.

I passed her saying, "Just a lot on my mind."

After last night, Sylvie and I knew we had to keep the news about her pregnancy to ourselves. John, Piper, Pearson, and Rose were the only ones in our inner circle, and it had to stay that way for now. Sylvie also wanted to bring her sister, Reynolds, in too. As I told her, I was afraid if too many people knew other than her mom, her mom may be angry we held back from telling her. Sylvie said everyone would have to pretend they hadn't known, but she couldn't keep it from Reynolds when Piper knew. I finally agreed, so she was going to call her tonight. Even though the timing was bad, considering Cindy's issues, this pregnancy excited me more than I ever thought possible. As I pondered this, the realization of how I felt about Sylvie was the reason. I knew we'd have our ups and downs and no, this was not the best way to start out a relationship, but if I was going to have a baby with anyone, it would be her. What she didn't know and what I hadn't told her was I would marry her even if she hadn't been pregnant. She was mine and had been since that very first night, only she hadn't known.

"It must be this week, with Christmas being so close. So much to do," Haley said.

"Yeah," I answered absently.

"There are some papers for you to sign on your desk, sir. There are also some reports that need your approval."

"Fine. I'll get on that. Don't forget, we're doubling up this week so we have everything in order for next week's vacation."

"Yes, sir. It's on your calendar."

"Thanks, Haley."

True to her word, there was a fair amount of work piled on my desk so I got right to it. I didn't want to leave anything hanging when I left at the end of the week. Of course, there would always be things I needed to check, but that could be done anywhere.

At one, Haley poked her head in and said, "I'm going to lunch, sir, and I thought I'd see if you wanted anything since you were still here."

"Thanks, Haley, but I'm elbows deep. I'll see you when you get back."

"Yes, sir."

I never ended up eating as I worked straight through lunch. In fact, the whole week ended up like that. I was working double time in order to have a free week off. I'd be taking off from Christmas Eve until the second of January. Initially, Sylvie and I had talked about going out west, but now with her mother, we postponed everything.

Sylvie moved back to the city and was going back and forth to work every day, but it was easy to see it took its toll on her. Every day she fell asleep in the car on the way home from work, Robert informed me. She claimed it was an enjoyable luxury nap she wouldn't have otherwise. But that spurred me into motion. I hired a realtor to find a place in between the city and where she worked to shorten the commute time.

We were staying at her place for the holidays since we're having Christmas Eve dinner with my parents out at one of the local restaurants, and then having Christmas dinner with Sylvie's family.

The night before Christmas Eve, we were driving back to the townhouse. The realtor had called and said she'd found three properties that met my criteria. I asked if we could see them the following day. She agreed to meet us at one o'clock.

Sylvie had gone to work this morning, with her suitcase packed for the week.

"I thought you still had things at your townhouse?" I had said.

"I do, but I still have my favorites here, plus my makeup and stuff. I'm going to have to get some more stretchy pants. My jeans are getting too tight already."

"Get whatever you need. I'll give you a credit card. And you don't need any makeup. I've seen you with and without and you're gorgeous both ways."

Her radiant smile had been everything to me then.

My phone buzzed, bringing me back to the present. The corners of my mouth tilted up as I read her text.

Thinking about you. Can't wait to see you.

My fingers tripped over the keys and I shot her one back. **I miss you and can't wait to see you too. I want to do wicked things to you.**

I saw the three dots moving and they stopped. Then a picture appeared of her face. It was hilarious. Her eyes were bugged out and her mouth circled. She was making a shocked face, but I responded with something she wouldn't expect.

Hmm. Looks like you're practicing for tonight, with your mouth like that. And I added a laughing emoji.

It didn't take her long to send me her response.

One track mind.

Oh, yeah. See you in a bit, babe. I hope you're wearing sexy undies!

This time she did shock me. She sent me a pick of what was

under her skirt. Now it was my turn to send her the shocked face picture.

She laughed so hard, in fact, she sent me the video. I was happy I could do that to her. But that picture, it was priceless. I stared at it a little too long because I was squirming by the time Robert pulled into the garage.

"Here we are, sir."

"Thanks, Robert. I hope you have a wonderful holiday and I'll see you on the morning of the second."

"Yes, sir and the same for you. Merry Christmas, sir."

I wouldn't be needing his services since I'd be driving up myself.

My bags were packed, and I had everything ready to go, but I had one stop to make before I left. It was at the jewelry store where I needed to pick up Sylvie's gift.

I hurried over there and checked out my purchase. It was perfect so I had them wrap it up and then went back home. I was on my way out of Manhattan and to Flower Power to pick her up. There was a gorgeous lake near her home where I wanted to take her to give her the necklace. Luckily, I made it there around four. The receptionist checked me out and then escorted me to Sylvie's office. When she knocked to announce me, she told Sylvie she approved.

"I take it that's a good thing?" I asked.

Sylvie only rolled her eyes. "That was Starr and she can be a bit over the top at times."

"If she approves of me, then I'm Team Starr."

"I thought you were Team Sylvie."

"Oh, I'm one hundred percent Team Sylvie."

"Did I hear something about Team Sylvie?" Rose asked, entering the office.

"Well, hello there, stranger." I hugged her. "How's my best friend doing?"

"He's just perfect." Her cheeks flushed a bit when she answered.

"By that look, I can tell he is."

"The two lovebirds are over-the-top, Evan."

"I think it's great."

"Wait until you spend some time around them," Sylvie said.

"Sylvie, wait until they spend some time around us." And I made that shocked face. She cracked up.

"Am I missing something?" Rose asked.

"Nothing except your friend can be quite naughty when she wants."

"I see." Rose eyed us both with a grin. "Are you two going to Paige and Rick's on Christmas?" she asked.

"Yeah, later on after dinner. You and Pearson will be there, right?" Sylvie asked.

"Of course we'll be there. We'd love for you to drop by." Rose looked so excited. "I can't wait to tell everyone about..." She circled a finger, indicating Sylvie's stomach.

Sylvie's smile turned downward. "Rose, you can't."

"I can't?"

"No, because we're not telling Mom. She's been having some health issues, so we're going to wait a bit."

"Oh, Sylvie, I didn't know." Rose hugged her.

"I know. I haven't told anyone because we don't know for sure, but Dad thinks she may have dementia."

"Oh, shit."

Sylvie's eyes watered, but she held her tears back. "You can say that again."

"I don't blame you. It's wise to wait. But still come."

"Okay, I'll call Pearson, as long as it's not too late," I said.

"Evan, you know it won't be. We'll be there until eight or so."

"I'll still call first, just to make sure." I never wanted to wear out my welcome.

"I understand." Then she hugged Sylvie saying she had to go. "I'll see you guys. Merry Christmas."

Sylvie seemed awfully quiet. "Hey, are you all right?"

All of a sudden, she was crying. "I hate this crying crap."

"Come on. Let's get out of here."

She sniffed and snorted her tears away, and then we left. "Where's your car?"

"Over there."

"I helped her into the passenger's seat and off we went. She thought we were going to her place, but when I didn't turn on the road she usually took, she asked where I was headed.

"It's a surprise."

"What kind of surprise?"

"A good one, I hope."

We got to the lake and she said, "Oh, I love this place and haven't been in ages."

"Then I'm glad I brought you here. I thought it might cheer you up. Button up your coat and wrap your scarf around you. I don't want you catching a chill."

"Yes, sir."

Those words brought back a memory of that novel she'd been reading, so I asked, "Did you ever finish that dirty duke book you were reading."

She snorted a laugh. "It's the Raunchy Duke." A couple of snorts later, I finally had the answer. "And yes, I finished. It was very raunchy and very dirty."

"Hmm. Did you learn anything?"

"Why do you ask?"

"Curious, I guess."

"Then maybe you should read it."

"Maybe I should." I got out of the car and held out my hand for her. We walked arm-in-arm to the lake and found a bench to sit on. The sun was about to set over the other side and the views were outstanding.

"Look how pretty."

I stared at her profile and said, "I agree. She's absolutely stunning."

Sylvie turned to face me and said, "You're too kind."

"No, just honest. Sylvie, you should accept my compliments

because I mean them with all sincerity. Her eyes zeroed on mine, digging for the truth. Her eyes didn't see, they analyzed. And the truth was there because I would never lie about that. She was perfect in every way and I hoped she saw it blazing through.

Her hands cupped my cheeks as she pressed her lips to mine. "Thank you, Evan."

Reaching into my pocket, I pulled out the gift. "This is for you. Happy Baby, my love. You're going to be an awesome mom."

Tears dripped from her eyes, but it wasn't all out sobbing like she often did. "It wasn't supposed to make you cry. Please open it. It's intended to make you happy."

Her fingers slid under the wrapping paper as she carefully took it off. When she got to the velvet box, she said, "Oh, Evan. You didn't."

"Didn't what?"

"Get me jewelry."

"You'll have to open it to see."

She lifted the lid to see the beautiful necklace. Hanging from it was a gold pendant and in the middle sat a perfectly cut diamond. Its cut and brilliance sparkled and caught the light perfectly. It wasn't fancy, but it was elegant, with gold filigree around the pendant. On the back I'd had her initials and mine engraved at the top, leaving spaces for more to be added.

"The stone reminded me of the way your eyes sparkle," I told her.

"It's dazzling. I love it, everything about it." She leaned over for a kiss. "I want to put it on, but I'll wait to get home so I don't have to bother with this scarf and coat."

"There's something else. Turn it over."

She did and saw the initials. Then I explained how our child's could be added.

One hand covered her heart. "I've never had anything so lovely or meaningful before. Thank you for such a beautiful and thoughtful gift." She kissed me again.

"Let's go home. I want to see how it looks around your lovely neck."

"How do you always know the right thing to say?"

"I only say what comes to mind."

"You won't be saying those things for long."

"What do you mean?"

"I'm going to look like I swallowed a watermelon in a few months."

"Didn't you know?"

"Know what?"

"Watermelon is my favorite fruit."

THIRTY-SEVEN
EVAN

SYLVIE WOKE UP UPSET AND THINKING ABOUT HER MOM. IT was Christmas Eve and I wanted this to be a great day, not a terrible one. We had that appointment with the realtor at one, so I was going to do my best to cheer her up.

Her hands latched onto me and she asked, "What will I do? My Dad has always been so strong. He's the one I've always depended on."

I stroked her hair and said, "First, now you have me to lean on. And second, it's time for us to be strong for him. You're not in this alone. If there's anything he needs, I can help. I have a lot of connections and don't forget Grey. He does too."

"Maybe I should call Grey."

"Sylvie, don't you think you should let that be your dad's decision? Maybe we're jumping the gun a bit."

"What do you mean?"

"Think about it. You're a psychologist. The brain is complex, right?"

"Yeah. Oh, my God! How could I have been so blind? What if she's deeply depressed?"

"That's what I was thinking."

"And combined with menopause, it can do super weird things to your body and mind."

"Exactly. Think about the strange things your body is going through right now with your pregnancy."

All of a sudden, her arms were around my neck and she was snuggling me.

She pulled back and said, "Thank you. I've been so emotional, it never entered my mind that could be it."

Her smoky gray eyes that were clouded with pain cleared and it eased me somewhat. I hoped I hadn't given her any false illusions though.

"Why don't we get out of here?" I suggested.

"Where do you want to go?"

"I don't care. Brunch?"

"Okay. I could go with something light."

Since it was a gorgeous day for December, I suggested something different. "I have an idea. Why don't we pick something up and have a picnic somewhere?"

Her eyes lit up as she grinned. "That sounds wonderful. Can we go back to the lake?"

"Anywhere you'd like."

We dressed and drove to a great deli to pick up some carryout food. I had her stay in the car while I ran inside and purchased an array of things I hoped would tempt her. They packaged it up in a box with everything we needed.

It wasn't five minutes later, and my phone rang. I answered it on blue tooth. Pearson's voice echoed through the car.

"Hey man, Rose told me about Aunt Cindy."

"Yeah, we're not sure what's going on, but Pearson, don't breathe a word of this to anyone, not even Grey. Sylvie's dad doesn't want anyone to know until they're certain what it is."

"I get that. And no worries. I won't say a thing. Tell Sylvie we're thinking of her."

"She can hear you. We're in the car."

"Hey, Sylvie. I'm so sorry about this, especially with—well, you know."

"Thanks, Pearson."

"Hopefully, we'll see you two at my parents' tomorrow."

"Talk later."

Sylvie's hand landed on my thigh. "That was sweet of him to call."

"I've noticed ever since he went through rehab and got with Rose, he's much more considerate. More like the Pearson I used to know before he went with that huge law firm."

"They sure did a whammy on him."

"You know, we've talked about it and I'm not so sure it was the firm as much as it was that one partner that badgered him. Pearson is so damn competitive, he let him get way too far under his skin."

"He's a much better man now, even though he went through hell and back to get there."

"Jesus, Sylvie, every time I think about when Grey called and told me the news of what happened, I get serious chills. I'll never forget that day. It was brutal."

"I remember. And poor Rose blamed herself."

"She shouldn't have, but thank God, it turned out okay for them."

We pulled into the parking lot and thankfully, the place was empty. Touching her cheek, I said, "Looks like we have the lake to ourselves."

"I guess everyone is getting ready for Christmas."

Unloading the trunk, we set up our picnic site and took seats on the blanket. It was brisk but not too bad. I'd grabbed an extra blanket for Sylvie in case she got cold.

"What's in the box?" she asked.

"Aren't you eager?"

"Yeah. That's a big box."

I unpacked it and when I kept taking things out, she asked, "Who else is coming?"

"No one. Why?"

"You have enough food in there for an army."

Shrugging, I said, "I wanted you to like what I got. I didn't know how your stomach would react."

"That was thoughtful of you."

Picking up each container, she opened them up and made little murmurs of joy that drove me slightly insane. "By the sound of things, I take it you like?"

Grabbing a fork, she slipped it out of the plastic wrap and started to sample what was in each container.

After a few minutes of her moaning, I said, "Jesus, Sylvie, you sound like you're having an orgasm."

The fork was in her mouth and she stopped what she was doing. Then she slid it out and with her mouth full, she asked, "I do?"

"Yes. And it's making me...well, you can guess." My eyes flicked downward and then back up. Hers must've followed because she focused on my dick.

She swallowed her bite of food and said, "I did that?"

"You always do that. Can you promise me something?"

"What?"

"No, you have to promise me first."

"But what if it's something I can't do?"

"You can do this."

"How do you know?" she asked, her eyes full of questions.

"Trust me, I know."

"Okay."

"Can we jump on the bed naked sometime, like we did the night you can't remember. I've never laughed so hard in my life."

"Shit, Evan. I can't believe I did that."

"You *made* me do it."

Her playful side emerged, and she laughed. "That's so weird. I never jump on the bed."

I clicked my fingers. "The day after Christmas, we're going back to my place so we can jump on the bed."

"You're a big kid at heart, you know that?" She pointed her fork in my direction.

"And so are you, which is why we are going to have the best time parenting," I said.

She dipped her head and gave me one of her serious gazes. "Evan, parenting isn't all about fun. What about the stinky diapers and middle of the night feedings?"

"I'll do it."

"You don't have the boobs to do it."

"Can't we do that pump thing into a bottle so I can help?" I really wanted to and when she mentioned the boob issue, it saddened me.

"I'll have to ask Marin or Milly. They both had twins, so they must've done something different."

"It would've really been exciting to have twins."

Her lower jaw slackened. "Are you serious? They definitely run in the West family. Dad and Uncle Rick have them on their mom's side, I think. Do you have them in your family? But no way do I want them."

"My grandfather was a twin. Maybe next time."

"What would we do, Evan? What if we have twins at some point?"

"Then we'd get two cribs, two times the amount of diapers, twice as many of everything. And we'd love them with all our hearts. That's what we'd do."

Instead of a smile, I got sobs. What was I going to do with my girl until these emotions passed? I needed to talk to someone about this on how to cheer her up. Because right now I was as helpless as a guppy without water.

THIRTY-EIGHT

SYLVIE

POOR EVAN. ALL HE'D BEEN EXPOSED TO WERE MY TEARS AND family's bad news.

"I have an idea," he said. "Let's take a walk by the lake."

"Okay," I said, sniffing. He handed me a tissue first. Then we went for a walk.

As we walked, he told me some of his boyhood stories about Pearson and him. They got into lots of trouble. Not bad things, but kid stuff like broken windows, borrowing things from the neighbor's garage, and then forgetting to put it back. One time, one of their neighbors went out of town and they decided to have a pool party at their house. They invited all the kids over, not realizing the neighbors were coming home that day. There were about twenty or more kids in their pool when they came home. Evan had climbed the fence and unlocked it for all the other kids.

"I was in deep trouble for that one. My dad told me I couldn't go outside for two whole weeks, but I ended up driving my mom so crazy, we secretly made a deal. I would go out and then be back inside by the time Dad got home from work."

"You were awful."

"Not really. I was just rambunctious. I ran a lemonade stand one summer in the entrance to the neighborhood but didn't make any money because I tried to charge a dollar per glass. No one would buy any because it was too expensive. I figured why sell it for so cheap when I'm working my ass off out there in the sun?"

He was so serious when he told me that story. "That's how you became such a shrewd businessman."

"Maybe, I don't know. But it was true. I squeezed fresh lemons and all. And those assholes were too cheap to buy my fresh lemonade. So I put up a sign that said I would donate some of my profits to charity."

I stopped walking and grabbed his hand. "How awesome. How much did you end up donating?"

"Hardly anything because they still wouldn't buy. So I moved my stand right outside of the entrance to the pool and bam. My sales soared. I took off the donation to charity sign because I figured I didn't need it anymore. It was impossible to keep up with the demand, so I had to stop selling the fresh and switch to the powdered kind. My mom made me drop my price too. But I still made a good bit of money."

"I'm envious. I had to babysit for my little sisters. I would much rather have sold lemonade."

We kept walking with leaves crunching underfoot, and I took in the beautiful scenery. The winter sky was bright blue painted with white streaks. A gentle breeze blew as a hint of snow was in the air. The sun winked off the surface of the lake, reminding me of bright silver coins.

I inhaled the fresh air and said, "I love this place. "It's so peaceful."

"I knew you loved it. I'm glad you wanted to come back here. It's one of my favorite places too."

"Mom used to bring us here when we were little to feed the ducks. Reynolds was afraid of them and would scream and cry. They'd chase her while Piper and I would laugh."

"Shit."

"What's wrong?"

He turned and said, "We left our food out. I forgot about the damn ducks." He took off running.

I didn't think we'd gone far, but he ran much faster than me. By the time I caught up with him at our blanket, it looked like an army of vultures had descended.

"Holy crap. The ducks did that?"

"Look at the blanket." He waved his arms in exasperation.

There were muddy duck prints all over it and our boxes of food were destroyed. It struck me as hilarious and I completely lost it. At first, he just stared at me as though I was cuckoo. But then he joined in. It was amusing. We'd lost our extravagant brunch to nothing but a bunch of voracious ducks.

"I hope they don't get sick from all this fabulous food," I eventually said when I could talk.

"Not me. I hope they throw up. That's what they get for stealing our food. And I had barely tasted it."

"Then maybe I need to treat you to lunch somewhere else."

He waggled his brows. "Oh yeah. What did you have in mind?"

"There's an amazing place not far from here."

His eyes filled with disappointment.

"What, you wanted something else?" I asked innocently.

A smile tugged at the corner of his mouth as he took one large step towards me. His hands cupped my cheeks as his mouth possessed mine. His kiss wasn't gentle, nor was it brief. It was demanding and awakened an ache deep within me. Desire flamed to life as I gripped his jacket to hold on. I did not want this kiss to end, but it did, abruptly. My breath dragged through my lungs harshly and all I wanted was more.

But Evan was a tease. He stepped out of my reach and began to clean up our picnic.

"What are you doing?" I asked.

"What does it look like?" That grin returned, and with it, full-blown lust.

"Hurry up." I helped him pile everything into the box so we could throw it away.

"Why?"

"Let's go home."

"What are we going to do there?"

"What else? Have lunch, of course."

Evan picked up the box and found a trash can to deposit it in. Then he stuffed the blankets in his trunk, and we got into his car.

"Sylvie, if you think I'm going to wait until we get to your place, you're mistaken."

"What do you mean?"

"Take your pants off."

I gaped at him. "You mean we're going to do it here? In the parking lot?"

"I don't see why not. There's no one around, unless you count those pesky ducks."

"What if someone comes."

"That's my plan." He quirked a brow.

I slapped his arm. "Be serious for a minute."

"I am being serious. Take off your pants. Now."

Call me crazy, but I did. The last time I'd had car sex was in college and it wasn't great. He pushed his seat all the way back and reclined it.

"Climb on over. Are you wet?"

"I've been wet since that kiss."

The words barely left my mouth when he crushed his lips to mine. His hand went between my thighs and found my clit. I was wet all right. When he slid inside of me, I gave no resistance, except for the fact that he was large and stretched me wide. Thrusting deep, I moaned my pleasure as the swell of him surged against me, while his thumb worked my nub.

Our mouths separated and he said, "You're so hot, Sylvie. How does this feel?"

"Perfect."

He thrust faster and I caught his rhythm as he continued to plunge into me. The first tingles of my climax hit, and then grew stronger until my muscles flexed around him and I called out his name. He groaned and came right after me.

"I needed that," I said.

"So did I."

Someone pulled up next to us.

"Oh, fuck."

"Don't worry, sweets. Just slide on over and put your pants back on. These windows are tinted pretty dark."

I did as he told me, but there was no way they couldn't see inside. My hands trembled as I pulled my jeans on.

"Of all the places to park, why'd they park right next to us?"

"No idea."

"Thank God they didn't come a few minutes earlier. At least we were fast."

"True."

Then we heard a knock on the window.

"Evan, I can't look at them. You have to handle this."

He rolled his window down and I heard a familiar voice.

"Dude, what are you doing here? Your windows are awfully steamy." He laughed.

"Pearson, what are you doing here?"

"What does it look like?"

I turned to check. He was in running clothes with his friend, Petey. Shit. I'd never hear the end of this. Then he stuck his head in the window and sniffed. "Yeah, I know what you guys have been up to."

"No, you don't. We came for lunch, but the ducks attacked our food."

He laughed but didn't believe us. "Yeah, right."

"Seriously, man. Check out that trash can over there."

"Okay. But then why were your windows steamed up?"

"We were talking."

"Uh huh. What I can't figure out is why here and not at home?"

"Go run." Evan rolled up the window to a chuckling Pearson.

Of all the luck. I grabbed his hand and said, "I think it's time to go and get the real lunch now."

"We'll have to do a grab and go because we have an appointment."

"An appointment?"

"Yep."

"With who?"

"You'll see." He flashed a secretive smile. What was he up to?

We went through the drive-through of a fast food chain and ate in the car. Then we drove for about twenty minutes, until we pulled into a long drive. It ended at a huge home, where a car waited. I was super curious now.

"Come on."

He got out and walked around to help me out. Then an older woman got out of the other car. As we approached her, I felt utterly ridiculous.

Evan said, "Hi Marti, this is Sylvie West. Sylvie, meet Marti. She'll be our realtor. Let's go look at this house she wants to show us."

He gave my hand a gentle squeeze as I gawked at him. House? What the hell was going on?

THIRTY-NINE
EVAN

"Sylvie, it's wonderful to meet you. Evan has told me some of the things you both want in a home. Let me know what you love or hate about this place because I'm making a list, okay?"

Sylvie had the craziest expression on her face. It reminded me of what Piper had said—like she'd been hit on the head with a hammer. I nearly chuckled.

I leaned down and whispered, "It's going to be okay, babe. I wanted a house in between Flower Power and the city. We needed to start looking."

The only thing she did was nod like an automaton. Poor thing was shocked. We followed Marti up the three steps to the front door. It opened to a large foyer and a grand staircase, yet it wasn't overly formal, which was what I liked.

"Wow," Sylvie said.

On either side of the foyer was a formal living room and a dining room. Both were huge and perfectly decorated. The paint was in neutral shades and the light fixtures weren't fancy. I liked that too. So far, so good.

"These rooms are huge," Sylvie said.

"They look larger because there isn't any furniture in them,"

Marti said. "The owners were transferred and had to move quickly."

The living room opened into a huge den which then opened into an enormous kitchen.

"Oh, my God. This is a dream kitchen!" Sylvie ran directly to the kitchen and inspected it.

It had Carrara marble countertops, a huge island, white cabinetry, state of the art appliances, and reminded me a lot of my kitchen.

As those thoughts hit me, Sylvie said, "This kitchen reminds me of the one in the city."

"I was thinking the same thing."

"I love it."

"Say the word and it's yours."

Marti said, "Don't you want to see the upstairs and outside first?"

We continued the tour and the master suite was fabulous. It was better than mine, if that was even possible.

"Evan, I can't believe this." It had a sitting room off of it, which could be a temporary nursery.

"Are you thinking what I'm thinking?"

"Yes!" Her eyes were filled with excitement. I already imagined a tiny crib in there and a rocking chair too.

As I was daydreaming, Sylvie had wandered into the bathroom. She called out, "Evan get in here."

When I did, she said, "This shower is like yours."

I was surprised and happy to see it was. The bathroom was perfectly designed to be a his and hers. It had two of everything, including commodes, except it only had one gigantic tub. The shower itself was in one enclosure, but there were two of everything inside of it.

"No, babe, it's double of mine. Let's check out the closet."

"Look, we don't need any furniture."

The closets had everything you needed in them. They were fantastic.

The other bedrooms, all five of them, were all ensuite, and all had big closets and fabulous bathrooms too, but not anything like the master.

A large laundry completed the upstairs, along with a cozy library.

On the lower level, there was a huge workout room, complete with all the exercise equipment one could desire. Marti said the owners didn't want to take it because it was too cumbersome to move. I liked that. There was also a pool table as well. It was an excellent man cave.

"Oh, Evan, this house is unreal." Sylvie beamed.

Marti said, "We know what you like, Sylvie. How about looking at the outside now?"

The back yard was private, our closest neighbor was not in sight and would never be. A large screened in porch led to a covered porch which had an outside cook area, a bar, and fireplace. There was a pool too.

I was sure Sylvie loved the inside, but I was in love with the entire place. I was ready to buy it now.

Marti asked, "Are you ready to look at the other two?"

"Can you show us the specs on them?"

She pulled out her folder and handed them to me. We looked them over, but neither of them had what this house had.

"Marti, excuse us for a moment, will you?"

"Sure."

Sylvie and I wandered off. "This place has everything that the others don't. Do you like it?"

"I love it, but isn't it expensive?"

"Don't worry about the price, just answer me."

"Yes, I love it."

"The location is perfect. It should only take you about what, twenty-five minutes to get to work? I know that's a lot longer than you're used to, but it's better than driving in from Manhattan."

"Twenty-five would be an easy drive."

A.M. HARGROVE

"I need to ask you something. Will you be able to stay here by yourself if I'm traveling?"

"Sure, I'm okay with that."

"This place will have a new security system like none other and it will be fenced and gated, but still, with a baby, I want you to feel safe here."

"I will. Plus, I have a gun."

"Say what?"

"Yeah, Dad taught us all to shoot, so I have a gun."

"Sylvie, when our child gets older, that gun will be under lock and key. But that's a conversation for another day. I'll hire a security guard to stay with you if need be."

"I'll be fine, Evan," she assured me.

"So you're good with this house, or did you want to look at the others?"

"I love this one. The others didn't have the master suite or the kitchen this one had. Or at least the pictures and plans didn't show it."

"Let's talk to Marti then."

We told Marti, and she agreed about the other houses.

"Let's put a contract on this one then. If everything comes back fine, as in the inspections, I want it."

"That's excellent. I'm thrilled for you. Have you done a pre-approval for your mortgage."

"There'll be no mortgage. I'll be paying cash."

Both Marti and Sylvie's eyes circled like golf balls.

"Did I hear you say cash?" Marti asked.

"That's correct. Let's get this done ASAP. How soon can we get everyone on this?"

"Right after Christmas. Shouldn't take long at all."

"Great. Call me." Marti agreed to get everything moving. "Let's go, babe." I grabbed Sylvie's hand and we walked back to the car.

Her Christmas gift should be sitting in her parking lot by now. I hoped she liked it.

246

"Let's time the trip between here and Flower Power."

"O-Okay. I can't believe you're paying cash. That house was in the millions."

"Yeah. Are you timing us?" I didn't want to dwell on the money issue. It wasn't a big deal to me. I earned it the hard way, invested it, was earning more, and it was growing daily. I had more than I would ever spend in this life and then some.

"Um, yeah. That house though. It's amazing."

I glanced at her and she was fingering the necklace I'd given her. My mouth curved into a smile. About twenty minutes later, we arrived at Flower Power.

"Here we are."

"Yeah, twenty-one minutes. But then again, not much traffic."

"Is there a lot of traffic in the morning?"

"I'm not sure on these roads. But it can't be that bad."

"Sylvie, I'll hire another driver for you."

"No. I'd prefer to have a car at work. Besides, I like to drive. And then there'll be daycare. I'll need a car if the baby gets sick or something."

"Daycare? You wouldn't want a nanny?"

"I hadn't thought of that."

"It would be much easier. I don't want you to have to worry if the baby gets sick. If we have a nanny, you wouldn't."

"I'll always worry. I did want the baby to go to preschool though, so she's not behind when she starts real school."

"She, huh?"

"Yeah, I secretly think of nubbin as a she. I don't know much about little boys."

"I do. That's where the daddy comes in." I reached for her hand. We were just about to pull into her parking lot, and I wanted her Christmas present to be a surprise. I said, "Babe, I'll do anything you want. But we can still have a nanny when she goes to preschool too."

We parked next to the brand new shiny white Mercedes SUV with the big red bow on top.

"Look, Evan, someone's getting a new car for Christmas."

"They are indeed." I reached into my pocket and pulled out the key fob. "Merry Christmas, love."

FORTY

SYLVIE

WHAT? A CAR? HE COULDN'T GIVE ME A CAR.

"Evan, are you nuts? You can't give me that."

"Too late, babe. It's a done deal. Let's go have a look."

We got out and he opened the door. It was one of those magical openers like his where you only needed to be close to the door with the key fob and it automatically unlocked. I checked out the interior and it was gorgeous. It had that new car smell and I'd never owned a brand new car. Sure, my parents did okay, but I'd worked for everything I had. I wasn't spoiled or considered rich by any means.

"This is gorgeous, but it's too much."

"Nothing is too much for you. Did you check out the back seat?"

"I haven't finished looking at that fancy console. There's a TV on it."

He shook his head. "It's a computer like mine. Now look in the back."

I did as he asked. "Evan, you bought a baby seat!" I squealed.

"I thought you'd never look!"

I opened the back door and the seat had a handle so it doubled as a carrier. "This is really cool." I hadn't even started investigating these things yet. I was impressed that he was way ahead of me. Jumping into his arms, I thanked him with kisses.

"The reason I bought this was not just for you to have a new car but because it would make it a lot easier on you with the baby. Your car is entirely too small. I checked out the back and getting in and out with the carrier would be too hard. So I figured you'd need an SUV."

He was right, but he could've bought me a less expensive one. I wasn't going to argue that point with him though.

"Thank you for being so thoughtful."

"You're welcome. Let's take it for a drive so I can teach you everything about it."

"I'd love that."

After about a half hour of parking lot instructions, we headed out. The computer had so many features on it, I doubted I'd ever use them all. The thing I loved best was the Bluetooth phone where I added all my contacts. I also loved the voice activation so I could just tell it what to do. I was the boss of my car, haha.

The ride was awesome. Evan told me how it would handle the snow in the all-wheel drive. It had an automatic traction control so it would be safer to cart the baby in.

"I'm wondering if you're concerned for me or is it just for the baby?"

Suddenly he was kissing me. "Don't ever forget this. You're the most important person in the world to me. Yes, I'm concerned about our child, but you come first, Sylvie."

Wow. He'd never used that tone with me before. I nodded and swallowed. "Okay."

When we got back home, he said, "The title will arrive here. The car's in your name."

"You're being way too generous. I don't know what to say."

"Just tell me you love me."

"I love you so much, and not just for the car. It's hard to remember what my life was life BE."

"BE?" He looked confused and it was comical because Evan rarely was in that state.

"Before Evan. You've made me forget as in wiped those memories away. Maybe because life was so boring, and I never knew love like this."

A smile that radiated love appeared on him. "Are you ready to go inside and show me some more appreciation?" he asked, boyishly.

"I am. And I have an idea of what I'd like to do to you too."

We went inside, but I ran back to the car to pull off the giant red bow. "I drove all over town with this thing on."

"I know. I was with you."

Giggling, I said, "I wonder what everyone thought."

"They envied you. They wanted to look like that smokin' hot dark haired beauty driving the brand new SUV."

"Sweet talker."

When we got inside, I showed him how much I appreciated my gift by walking him to the couch and giving my best Dyson-lollipop combo imitation ever. When I was finished, his lazy grin told me mission accomplished.

His glistening cock lay exposed on his lap, and it was still semi-hard. It made me a bit jealous to realize I'd lost out on having it thrusting inside of me.

"Come here." He pointed to his lap. I straddled him and he kissed me. "You're the best at that."

"Thanks. I practice daily on a banana."

"You can't be serious?"

"Yep. Every day before I eat one for breakfast."

"Why don't I ever see this phenomenon?"

Shrugging, I said, "It's a private matter, kind of like masturbation."

"Masturbation's not private. I totally want to watch you do that. I bet you look so sexy with your thighs spread and your hand working your pussy. Are you noisy?"

"No!"

"Show me."

"I can't."

"Yes, you can. I've seen all of you. Surely you can do it. You've rubbed your clit when you're on top before."

"That's different. Getting myself off is for me alone."

"Why?"

"Because." There was no way I could do that with him watching.

"What about this? Why don't you slide off those pants and start things off and I'll finish them for you?"

"You won't make me do it too long, will you?"

"Not if you show me what you do to get yourself off when you're alone."

"Okay. But it's nothing special."

"Everything you do is special."

I was naked from the waist down and he said, "Everything off."

"But..."

"Please."

I stripped bare. "Can we go to the bedroom?"

"Sure."

I climbed onto the bed and spread my legs while he watched. This was completely awkward. "Do you mind looking the other way?"

Affection glowed from his eyes as a corner of his mouth turned up. "Babe, how am I supposed to watch if I do that?"

My tongue poked the inside of my cheek. "All right. Can you close one eye?"

He only chuckled.

The only way to do this was with my eyes closed. There was no putting it off, so I began and fantasized that it was Evan's fingers and not mine. My breathing sped up and when I felt his tongue on me, I stopped, but he grabbed my hand and put it back.

"Keep on going."

I kept up the motion, but wanted his cock, not my fingers, deep inside of me on the place that would get me off. I let his tongue be my master, as my desire mounted, and sought after my orgasm. He teased my clit until he coaxed me to climax. My nipples longed for his touch and my pussy begged for his cock.

"I need you, Evan. Now. Inside."

He gripped himself and pumped it a few times, which was a total turn on, then slowly pushed inside me.

"Ahh, I needed this." I wrapped my legs around him, crossing them at the ankles, and rocked against his pelvis. He was bearing the weight on his elbows as we continued this rhythm. Every time he pulled out, he would inch back in and I'd grind myself against him. This was different than our usual frantic, explosive sex we engaged in.

Under half-lidded eyes, he watched me as I did him. Our gazes were locked, and I noticed a sheen of perspiration on his forehead. It was an overwhelming sensation, watching this man I adored, making love to me like this. Sensuality oozed from him and I wished this could last forever, but I was too close to coming for that. His mouth dropped to mine and we breathed together as my inner muscles first fluttered, then contracted around him, bringing him over with me.

His hot breath was on my shoulder and then he was kissing me there. "I love you, Sylvie. 'They slipped briskly into an intimacy from which they never recovered.'"

"That's so beautiful."

"I've always thought so. It's F. Scott Fitzgerald from *This Side of Paradise*."

"I've never read it."

He ran a finger across my lower lip. "You'd probably find it a bit different from your dirty duke." He smirked.

I poked his ribs. "The Raunchy Duke."

"Yeah. I need you to read it to me."

"Never." I kissed him. "I love you too, Evan."

"You think you're distracting me, don't you?"

"Maybe."

"Where is it?"

"What?" I asked innocently.

"Your dirty duke."

"He's resting comfortably in my e-reader."

"Let me meet him. You won't have to read it to me. I just want to read the best chapter if you'll show it to me."

I thought about it for a minute. This could actually lead to more amazing sex. I reached for my e-reader on the nightstand and opened it to one of my bookmarks. "Here you go." Then I waited. His eyes glowed and he grinned. Then I learned something. Evan was a speed reader. He was flying through the pages like crazy.

"Are you done?" I asked.

"With six chapters. Your duke is a total kink hound." He rolled on his side. "Is that what you're in to?"

"Not BDSM, no."

"But the other stuff?" A smile tugged at his lips as his brows arched. He was waiting for my answer.

"Yeah, I'm game for some of it. To be honest, when I read it, it turned me on."

"Nice. Passionate, sensuous, and curious about things. I love that. I'd love exploring this, if you're interested."

"Yeah, I would. As long as it doesn't get too kinky."

"We've already done the flogging. I think a few more toys might be in order."

A few more toys? I wondered what he had in mind.

"What kind?" I asked.

"Just leave that to me, my kinky duchess. You won't be sorry," he said, leaning down to suck my nipple. With that as an entry, I knew he was right.

FORTY-ONE

EVAN

On Christmas Day, we expected the worst and got more. Sylvie woke up early and fixed the food she'd promised to take. She made some sweet potato concoction that was delicious, fresh green beans, and mashed potatoes. She put those in a crock pot to keep them warm. Then she made a special dessert. It was called fake pumpkin cheesecake that she didn't have to bake. I helped her peel the potatoes, both sweet and regular, and prepare the green beans for cooking.

We loaded everything up and drove to her parents. Her sisters were already there, and the only thing we had to do was pop the sweet potatoes in the oven for thirty minutes and bake. Her mom became unreasonably upset over that.

"Sylvie, you knew my oven would be full."

"But I asked you yesterday, Mom, and you said it'd be fine. I'll run them back home and bake them."

Piper ran interference by suggesting she microwave them.

"The dish won't fit," Sylvie said.

"Can you put them in a different one?"

They rummaged through Cindy's things and found one. Problem solved. Fifteen minutes later, we were ready to eat. It was very strange because her mom acted like the food Nazi, wanting to serve dinner immediately. There was no casual talk or banter. We all took seats at the table and John said the blessing.

We'd been eating for about twenty minutes when Cindy stared at me and asked, "Well, who are you, young man?"

Sylvie nudged my leg with hers, as we were sitting next to each other. "Mom, this is Evan Thomas. You remember him from Pearson's wedding? I brought him here before Thanksgiving to meet you and Dad."

"Pearson got married?"

Sylvie just went along with it. "Yeah, in the islands at the beginning of the month. Evan was in the wedding."

Then it seemed like she wanted to cover up her faux pas, so she said, "Of course. And how are you, Ervin?"

Reynolds sputtered out a laugh. "Gee, Mom, his name is Evan."

Cindy scowled. "That's what I said. And mind your manners. You're not supposed to disrespect your elders."

Reynolds' brows knitted as she stared at her mom. She glanced at Sylvie as Sylvie shook her head slightly.

"Anyone want some turkey?" John asked.

"I do," Piper said.

"I second that," Sylvie answered.

"It smells delicious," I added. "And thank you for inviting me. This all looks wonderful."

"Thank you for coming, Evan," John said. Cindy looked at me in confusion but said nothing.

I thought I'd add something nice, so I said, "You have a lovely home, Cindy."

"It can be if I can just get the girls to tidy up their rooms. Never a day goes by that I'm not making up their beds. You know how teenagers are."

Clearly, that had been the wrong thing to say. Everyone looked up. John grimaced, Piper was embarrassed and started to say something, but Sylvie ran a finger across her throat, telling her to cut it.

"Is there any gravy?" Reynolds asked.

Cindy's eyes lasered in on Sylvie. "Didn't you bring it, Sylvie?"

"Oh, I forgot." Sylvie squeezed my thigh this time. She never mentioned making gravy, so I was sure she didn't forget it.

"Can't I rely on you for anything? What is going on over in that devil's den of yours? You're not getting enough church in your life." Cindy's face contorted in anger.

"Now Cindy, let's not ruin our delicious dinner," John said gently, trying to calm her down.

"And how am I doing that? I only speak the truth. You know how I told you your daughter is talking like a hussy on the phone. That's why she didn't make the gravy. How could she, spending all her time whoring about town?"

Sylvie's jaw tightened as her cheeks flushed. She turned toward her father, so I couldn't see their interchange. Piper and Reynolds looked as if they'd been struck by lightning.

"You know, I think there may be some gravy in the kitchen after all. Let me check," John said, getting out of his chair.

"And how would it have gotten there? By magic?" Cindy asked.

Reynolds laughed awkwardly and said, "I do have a magic unicorn."

"Young lady, that's not funny." Cindy pointed her fork at Reynolds.

"But Mom, don't you remember that stuffed unicorn I loved when I was a kid? You told me it could do all kinds of magic."

Cindy stared at her with a puzzled expression, and then her hands rubbed her temples as she shoved her chair away from the table. How could she be angry with Reynolds for saying something like that?

She stood but didn't get very far because about two feet from the table she collapsed on the floor in a heap.

"Oh my God, Mom. Are you okay?" Sylvie ran to her and picked up her hand. "Dad! Mom fainted."

John hurried into the dining room and checked her pulse to see if she was breathing, which she was. Then Cindy's eyelids fluttered open.

"What's going on?" She came to and didn't remember fainting.

Sylvie said, "Should we call 911?"

"What for?" Cindy asked.

"Mom, you passed out and don't remember. Something's not right," Sylvie told her.

John was holding her hand and said, "She's right, Cindy. We should get you checked out."

"Nonsense. I just got out of the chair too fast."

"Fine, if that's all it is, I'll be happy. But I'm not comfortable with letting it go. It could be your heart and I don't want to take a chance, dear."

All the girls were on his side. Reynolds said, "You don't have a choice. We're making you go, Mom."

"But what about all this food?"

Sylvie volunteered, "I'll put everything away and we'll meet you there."

She grunted her objection but finally agreed. John hustled her out to the car, with Reynolds and Piper on their heels, before she could change her mind. Sylvie and I stayed behind to fulfill the food duties. Then we were on the way to the hospital.

"Call Grey," I said.

"I don't want to interrupt his Christmas. They may be in the middle of gift opening with the kids."

"I doubt it. Those kids probably woke up at the crack of dawn and they don't eat until later. It would be nice to have his input. If you don't do it, I will."

"Okay." She made the call and he immediately said he was on his way.

When we got there, John, Piper, and Reynolds were in the

waiting room, trying to persuade Cindy to stay. A few minutes later, Grey and Pearson walked in.

"Aunt Cindy, tell me what happened." He took her hand and his professionalism got through to her.

"My goodness, they're making a big fuss over nothing."

"Don't you think you need to let the doctors decide that?" Grey smiled warmly at her.

"Well, I only had a slight fainting spell."

"Hang on a second," Grey said, patting her hand. He walked to the desk, exchanged a few words with the receptionist, and came back. "Uncle John, Aunt Cindy, follow me."

The three of them went through the *Do Not Enter* door marked for employees. Grey had his key card that allowed them entry. No doubt, he was using his clout to push her through the red tape faster. I was also sure he would see to it she didn't have any heart issues either.

I walked Pearson to the side when he said, "Grey's worried about her heart."

"I was just thinking that. But then there's the dementia issue. Did you mention it to Grey?"

"No, because I wasn't sure if you wanted me to."

"I'm sure John will. After what I witnessed in the short time I was with her, there's definitely something going on."

Sylvie joined us then. I explained how Grey was concerned about her heart. "I figured he would be with her fainting like that. But she's totally confused too. I'm not sure how Dad's been coping, to be honest. Do you mind if we sit with my sisters? I need to tell them too."

When she told Piper and Reynolds, they weren't at all surprised, given the way their mother had acted during dinner.

"I guess now we find out if what happened today was related. I hope Dad tells Grey about it," Sylvie said.

"I'm sure he will," I said.

We sat and waited, and that was the most difficult thing in

the world. Grey came out about an hour later to give us an update.

"It's not her heart."

"Grey, did Dad tell you about how she's been lately?"

"Yeah, he did, Sylvie, and that's what I was going to tell you. She's going to have a CT scan, an MRI and an MRA. I wanted to make sure her heart was fine first, with the way she just passed out. It could've been an arrhythmia and I wanted to rule that out before we moved on. She's in line for the CT scan now."

"What's an MRA?" Piper asked.

"The same as an MRI but they look at the arteries in the brain to make sure she's not having mild strokes, or TIA's—transient ischemic attacks. They are usually the precursor to the big one."

"I see," I said. "And then what?"

"If those come back normal, the neurologist will test her for dementia. And honestly, that's out of my ballpark. I called in a friend and he's examining her now."

Sylvie touched his arm and said, "Thanks, Grey. I hated to disrupt your Christmas with the kids and all."

"Don't be silly. You're family. If you hadn't called, I'd have been pissed. Let me go back in and I'll give you an update as soon as I'm able."

Everyone called out their thanks as he left. The next hour and a half dragged by. We talked ourselves out with funny stories from when we were kids, trying to cheer each other up. The waiting room kept getting more and more crowded as the afternoon wore on. Pearson called Rose to keep his family up to date as well.

I let my own parents know what was going on. They were expecting us soon, but it looked like we may not make it there after all. They were fine, considering the situation with Sylvie's mom, not to mention we'd had dinner with them last night.

Grey finally returned, but the haunted look in his eyes told me the news was grim. Our group moved to an unoccupied corner.

"I told Uncle John I was going to tell you the same thing that the neurologist just told him. The results of the MRA were fine, but the results of the CT scan and MRI weren't. I'm sorry to be the one to tell you, but it appears Aunt Cindy has a brain tumor."

FORTY-TWO

SYLVIE

THE WORDS *BRAIN TUMOR* TUMBLED AROUND IN MY HEAD before I could latch onto them.

Reynolds was the one who said, "A brain tumor. Is she going to die?"

Us girls all huddled together, with Evan on my right and Pearson on Piper's left, which left Reynolds in the middle. Grey crouched down in front of us and took Reynolds' hands.

"We don't know anything conclusive yet. She's going in for another CT scan in a few minutes, so we can determine if there are any metastases to the lungs."

My hands covered my mouth as I inhaled a sharp breath. This was so unexpected I couldn't accept it. "Lungs? The brain? If both are involved, what kind of chance does she have?"

"Again, this is out of my league, so it's best that we wait for the test results to come in. But, and I've already told Uncle John this. I would highly recommend her going to the city for treatment if it does come back a malignant tumor."

Piper grabbed Grey's hand. "You mean there's a possibility it may be benign?"

"Yes, but due to the size and location, Ben thinks it's most likely malignant. I don't want to give you any false hopes."

"Ben?" Pearson asked.

"Sorry. Ben Abrams. He's the neurologist I called in."

"Would surgery be an option?" I asked.

"Again, it's too soon to tell."

"Does Mom know?" Reynolds asked.

"Not yet."

"Oh, my God. Poor Dad. All this time he's been thinking it was dementia and it was a brain tumor. Shit. I can't imagine what he's going through."

"You ladies will need to do your best to support him because he's very upset right now—not just with this news, but with what you said, Sylvie."

Evan took my hand and said, "Grey, if you need anything, call me. And you know what I mean."

I wasn't sure what he was implying, but Grey nodded. I would ask him later.

"Oh, and one other thing. We'll be admitting Aunt Cindy, so if one of you could pack a bag for her and bring it to the hospital, I'm sure your dad would appreciate it."

I immediately volunteered to do it. "Evan, you can take me to my place, and I'll get my car. That way you can go to your parents, for a while. There's no sense in you hanging around here."

He laced his fingers with mine and said, "Let's discuss this on the way."

We told everyone goodbye and headed to his car.

"Babe, I'm not leaving you for a second."

"I love that you want to be with me and offer your support. It means more than I can say. But there isn't much for you to do and your parents deserve some of you too."

Right before we got into his car, he pulled me up against the broad expanse of his chest and said, "Mom and Dad are already aware of what's going on. I don't want to leave you alone. You have enough to shoulder already."

My arms had already wound around his waist and I loved his

warmth. Hating to let him go, but knowing we needed to get a move on, I said, "It'll only be for an hour, two at the most. I think we can manage that. Don't you?"

He studied me with his leaf green eyes and his gaze reached into my heart. It was strange, but I knew this was bringing us closer together.

"You win. I'll go, but I won't stay longer than two hours. You have my word."

"It will be better this way too because Piper and Reynolds need a car. They came with Dad and I imagine he'll stay longer, or even spend the night. I may as well bring him a change of clothes too."

Evan helped me into the car and off we drove. I had him take me home so I could get my car.

"You're sure about this?"

"Yes. Don't worry, I'll be fine." I kissed him as I got out of his car.

"Don't do that. It's my job to assist you."

"You mean get out of a car? Jeez, Evan, I've been doing that my whole life."

"True, but that was before you had me around."

"Okay, but I'm fully capable of getting out of a car. Now go. And tell your parents I'm really sorry."

"Seriously, Sylvie. Be careful, okay?"

"I will. See you in a little bit. I love you."

"Love you too."

I climbed into my brand new SUV and went back to Mom and Dad's. When I got to their room, I figured it would only take a few minutes to pack bags for them. It did for Dad. Mom was another story. Her drawers were a mess. Nothing made sense to what was in them. I found shoes in her underwear drawer, makeup stashed in her sock drawer, and things stuffed in places I couldn't believe. She'd always been so neat and tidy, at first it shocked me and then I got super upset.

It made me wonder how Dad had missed all this. Hadn't he

checked in here when he'd put the laundry away or had he left all that to her? And if so, how had she even managed to accomplish that task? And then there was the matter of her closet. I could see how he'd missed that since they each had their own, but I found everything but the kitchen sink stashed in there.

"Mom, I should've known something bad was going on when you started acting so nutty. Now I feel horrible about all this," I said through sobs. Between this and my pregnancy, I was going to have a red clown-like nose forever.

It took me ages to find her pajamas. My phone rang while I was hunting them down. It was Piper.

"Where are you?"

"Pipe, you wouldn't believe this place. Her room's a wreck. I can't find a thing in here."

"How did she ever get dressed?"

"I've no idea."

"Okay, we were just worried. Give us a call when you leave."

"I will."

After I hung up, I began my search, and it was then I noticed her clues. There were sticky notes with arrows on them. But she'd put them in places where Dad wouldn't see. She knew something was up and was trying to hide it. But why? Maybe she suspected dementia as well and it frightened her.

I found the first one in the drawer by her toothbrush. I followed it and it took me to her face wash and creams. The next was in that drawer pointed to the cabinet below it. It was there she had all her nightgowns and pajamas stacked. There was another sticky note in there pointing to the cabinet next to it. Yes, I found her underwear! Beneath that pile, I saw another sticky. There was no arrow this time, only the word, *shelf*. That narrowed it down. There were only a dozen or so shelves in here. Their bathroom was huge, so I started with the floor to ceiling cabinets on the opposite wall. When I went through all of those and didn't find anything but sheets, towels, and other things, I moved back to her closet. It too was huge. Might as well start at one end and work my way down.

I should have done it in reverse because when I got to the end, I found the next items. They were her jeans and casual clothing. The jeans were neatly stacked, along with her yoga pants. Underneath them was a note with an arrow, pointing to the opposite wall. I think she was indicating the tops that were hanging up. I took a couple pair of yoga pants and two soft shirts. I found a duffle bag of Dad's, so I put her pajamas, underwear, clothes, and all her toiletries inside. Then I grabbed some slippers I'd seen plus a couple of pairs of socks. What should've taken me minutes took me over an hour and a half.

Right before I drove off, I texted my sisters, telling them I was on the way. My phone rang as I was driving. Thinking it was them, I answered, "Didn't you get my text?"

"No, I just pulled into the hospital parking lot and didn't see your car. Are you okay?"

It was Evan and he made it back before me.

FORTY-THREE
EVAN

My parents could not have been more understanding.

"How about taking some food over to the girls?" Mom asked.

"That's kind of you, Mom. But I'm not sure any of them can eat with the way things are going."

"I understand. How awful for them."

We were eating dinner, and as wonderful as I'm sure it was, it all tasted like sawdust to me. The only thing on my mind was Sylvie.

"You seem to be very taken with this girl, Evan." Mom smiled.

"The truth is I'm in love with her. You probably noticed that last night."

Mom smiled. "I did but didn't want to say anything in front of her. The way you doted on her was a giveaway. I'd never seen you like that with anyone before."

"She's perfect for me and I hope you like her."

"Evan, we like anyone who makes you happy."

Dad asked, "When will they find out what kind of tumor it is?"

"I don't know. Grey couldn't say because that's not his area.

But they're running more tests and hope they can figure it out soon."

"Well, I hope it's the good kind." Mom patted my hand.

"Same here, Mom."

After we ate, Dad and I spent some time talking about my business. He was very interested in it as he'd worked on Wall Street before his retirement a couple of years ago. I suggested an early one because I wanted him and Mom to enjoy their time together vacationing and doing the things they loved. They would never have to be concerned about money because Dad invested well and if they ever needed anything, I would help. I also sent them anywhere they wanted to go. All they had to do was tell me, and the trip was set.

When I arrived back at the hospital, Sylvie's car wasn't anywhere around. I wondered what went wrong, so I called her, but she was just pulling in.

I was at her door as she shut the engine off. When she opened the door, I said, "Let me get the bags for you."

She popped the hatch, and I grabbed them.

"Evan, you wouldn't believe my mom's room." When she told me how long it took her and why, it was hard to believe her dad hadn't found this upsetting.

"That's what I thought, but then again, after I had time to think it over, he probably thought she was covering up her confusion of the dementia. And that makes total sense. If you could see all the clues she left herself, you'd get it. If he found those, he was probably convinced she had it."

"Sylvie, I feel for him right now."

"My heart is breaking for him. I want to do something, but I don't know what. We haven't even seen him yet."

Putting both bags in one hand, I put my other arm around her, hugging her tightly against me. "Let's go and see if he's come out yet."

The girls were waiting for us when we walked in. "Any news from Dad yet?"

"Nothing. We sent Pearson and Grey home. Grey said there's nothing more he can do until the CT of her chest is done and read."

"When will that be?"

"Later today," Piper said.

We sat together and moments later, John came out. We all jumped up and ran to him. He put his arms around all three of the girls as they hugged each other.

He was the first one to speak. "Come on. Let's sit. I need a break."

We took him to our corner, the one we'd been occupying for most of the day, and he spilled his guts to us, amid tears.

"I feel just terrible thinking she was hiding memory loss from dementia. I thought she had early Alzheimer's. A brain tumor never entered my mind."

His eyes were red and swollen and he looked as bad as we all felt.

"Dad, it's not your fault. We all should've picked up on those clues. I thought she might be depressed. Evan and I even talked about it," Sylvie said.

Piper joined in saying, "I thought she was going through some sort of mid-life crisis, Daddy. Don't blame yourself. That's not fair."

"Yes, you're not to blame. If anything, us girls should've noticed. You see her every day. We don't. We're the ones who should've stepped in and done something." Reynolds added. She was right. When you're with someone every day, you don't notice those things as they occur. It's when you're not that they seem more drastic.

I finally stepped in. "If I may, the important thing is now you *do* know and maybe it's not the worst news and there may be help for her."

"He's right, Dad. Let's focus on the positives for now. In the meantime, I brought both of you some clothes. I didn't know if you wanted to stay with her or go home." Sylvie pointed to the duffle bag and I carried it.

"It's best if I stay because of her confused state. They've sedated her so she's resting, finally."

It was going on seven thirty when Grey, Pearson, Rose, Paige, and Rick came in. They were carrying boxes of food for everyone.

Paige said, "We brought you something to eat, since none of you got a chance to do that."

Rick and John hugged, while Paige gave all of the girls one. "If you girls need anything from me, I'm only a phone call away."

She took plates, forks, and napkins out of the boxes and then started passing around plastic containers filled with traditional holiday food. I declined since I'd eaten at my parents. Everyone else was grateful because they were hungrier than they thought.

Grey went back in to check on Cindy and to see if she'd had the CT scan yet. When he came back, he told us the news was good and that her lungs were clear.

"That's encouraging, right?" I asked.

"Yes. But we won't know the type of tumor until a biopsy is performed."

"I can't imagine someone going into my brain for a biopsy," John said.

Grey explained about a procedure called stereotaxis and that it was performed when the surgeon used a CT scanner to assist him. According to Grey, it wasn't that bad. They would have results in a few days, if that's what they decided to do.

"How long will she be here?" Piper asked.

"If they do the biopsy tomorrow, then until the day after. They may decide to wait. In that case, she may go home tomorrow."

While Grey spoke, I thought how not knowing was almost worse than knowing. But then, what would we do if the news was terrible? How would we think then?

"I'm sorry this has ruined your holiday. But let's think positively," Grey said.

"In all honesty, Grey, what did your friend really think," Sylvie asked.

His eyes bored into hers. "Sylvie, doctors don't like to speculate."

That was pure bullshit. They dealt with survival rates and speculated all the time and by not giving her an answer, he basically had. His friend pretty much thought the worst.

She stared back at him and gave him a slight nod. And he knew she'd figured it out. Maybe it was best they'd deal with each other straight up. Sylvie didn't seem the type to dance around an issue. But dealing with her mother's tumor may be an entirely different matter.

FORTY-FOUR

EVAN

THE BIOPSY WAS SCHEDULED FOR TOMORROW. FROM THERE, A
treatment plan would be set.

"How do you feel about things today?" I asked Sylvie. We
were lying in bed, having just woken up.

"Like my mom has a brain tumor and my dad is dealing with
a crazy person who can't comprehend what's going on."

"Yeah, that scene yesterday was awful."

When the sedative had worn off, Cindy had demanded an
explanation and then insisted nothing was wrong. John explained
about the brain tumor, to which she had said it was complete
nonsense. We called Grey in, hoping that would help. She didn't
believe him either and said we were conspiring against her to
lock her away in an insane asylum.

Sylvie asked the doctor if this was normal. He said it was
normal for personality changes, but this was highly unusual,
which made him believe her tumor should be removed as quickly
as possible.

The doctor kept her on a mild sedative because that
controlled her crazy—as bad as that term sounded—symptoms.
Once he was satisfied it worked, he released her to return the
next day.

"At least the medication is working until they can get some answers with the biopsy," I said.

"Evan, it freaks me out about that. What if she won't be around to see our little nubbin?"

"Hey, hey, hey." I pulled her on top of me. "Don't even think that way. We're going to make sure that doesn't happen."

"How? I'm so scared."

"I know, baby, I know. So am I, but I don't care if we have to take her somewhere else, we're going to find the best doctor in the world for whatever it is she has and get her the best treatment available."

"My dad has financial resources, but not those kind."

"Maybe not, but I do."

"He'd never let you do anything like that."

"He won't have a choice, and neither will you. This is your mother's life we're talking about."

She'd been playing with the hair around my neck, but when I uttered those words, she shuddered and buried her face against my shoulder. I abhorred saying them but needed to get it across to her that there wasn't time to waste.

"I'm sorry, babe, but she needs the best care possible. With Grey's input, I think we can find it. And money is not an issue. Now I want you to do something for me."

"What is it?"

"Nothing bad. Just stand up."

She got out of bed, so I walked around to her side. Then I got up on the bed and extended my hand to her.

"What are you doing?" she asked suspiciously.

"Come on. Get up here."

She offered me a crooked grin. "Is this what I think it is?"

"That depends. Now get up here with me."

She climbed up on the bed and I took both her hands in mine. "Now jump!"

I hopped up and down until she joined in. At first, she didn't have quite the response I'd hoped for. But then all of a sudden, a huge guffaw burst out of her and she went nuts. We jumped and jumped, until we were out of breath.

"Look, Sylvie. My head almost touches the ceiling."

"I can touch it with my hand."

"I can touch with both."

"Show off."

We had these little contests going when suddenly, a huge crack sent us both to our asses as the bed frame broke.

She gawked at me for a second and said, "Oh, my God! We broke the bed." Then she howled again. "I hope this can be fixed. It was my grandma's bed and Mom will be furious if she finds out."

"Let's see how bad it is."

We got off and one of the side rails had completely splintered apart.

"Holy shit, Evan. Look what we did." She covered her mouth and tried not to laugh.

"Pretty damn impressive if I say so myself."

"Do you think it can be fixed?" A giggle eked out of her.

"Hell, yeah. Anything can be fixed for the right price. "I'll make some calls and get someone on it."

"Really?"

"Yeah. I'm sure my mom knows of someone. She loves antiques."

"This isn't really an antique. It's just an old family thing."

"I think it's a gorgeous bed. I can see our daughter having this in her room one day."

Sylvie flew into my arms and kissed me. "Can you really?"

"Can't you? Was this your bed growing up?"

"No, not until my grandma and gramps moved into an apartment and I was lucky enough to inherit it. I always told her when I was little that I loved her big bed. I used to spend the night with her and my gramps, and I'd make gramps sleep in a different bed so I could sleep with her. She'd read me all sorts of stories about handsome princes and knights in shining armor on big white horses. She'd make some up too. Those were always my favorites. Since I loved her bed so much, I think that's why I was the one she gave it to. I was a teenager by then."

"Sounds like you were her favorite."

"I was the first and was five before Piper came along so yeah, I was definitely spoiled. I'll never forget the day Mom told me she passed. I was getting my master's and it nearly killed me. Gramps died a year before and I think she died of a broken heart. Her last year was so hard on her, she was never the same after he was gone. Our phone calls were sad because she was so devastated. I tried to cheer her up and would visit when I could, but I think her soul had already moved on, you know? It was like she was nothing but an empty shell."

"I can understand that. She didn't have anything to live for."

"Yes! I would tell her to live for us because we loved her so much, but she said I wouldn't understand until I found my special one. Now I know exactly how she felt. I don't know how I'd do it without you."

Sylvie stared at me with softened eyes. I felt like her grandma. I don't know what I would do if something happened to Sylvie. Having her in my life had opened my heart up and had shown me things I'd never thought I'd see or feel. It was impossible to think of life any other way.

"Jesus, Sylvie. I know how your grandmother felt. I have no idea what I'd do without you either. In some ways, your dad is feeling that now." I lifted her chin and drowned in her beautiful eyes. They reminded me of the foggy gray mist that rolled off the mountains in the morning. I sunk my fingers into her silky hair and brought my lips to hers. This wasn't about sex, this was about the closeness we shared. I wanted to be sure she understood I would always be her person, like her grandfather was to her grandmother. We were already there and would stay that way forever. My lips touched hers for a moment before pulling her against me. If there was one thing I could do, it was hold and comfort her.

FORTY-FIVE

SYLVIE

THE NEXT MORNING, EVAN AND I MET MY TWO SISTERS AND my parents at the hospital. Grey was there too, along with Uncle Rick and Aunt Paige. Mom was holding Dad's hand and squeezing it so tight her knuckles were white. I sat next to her and hugged her. She lifted her head, but when her eyes met mine, they were glazed.

"Hey Mom. I'm here with you."

"Hi, Sylvie. Dad said I'd be staying here tonight."

I'd assumed she would, so I said, "I figured you would. I'll be holding your hand when you wake up."

"Am I going to sleep?"

Shit. I had no clue what Dad told her, so I shrugged and said, "Well, at some point, I imagine you'll get tired."

"I guess so." Then she leaned close to my ear and whispered, "Why are Paige and Rick here?"

"I don't know. Did you ask them?"

"No, I didn't want to be rude."

Damn, those tranquilizers were doing their job.

"I can pull them aside and ask nicely if you want."

"No, that's okay."

About that time, a nurse opened the door and called mom's name. Dad stood and helped her to her feet.

"Do you know what they want?" she asked.

"Honey, why don't we go and find out." Dad was handling this fine, but the lines around his eyes along with the purple half-moons beneath them told the truth. He was extremely worried. I pushed my fist to my mouth to prevent the sob that threatened to burst forth.

Aunt Paige started to say something, but I quickly grabbed her arm and shook my head. After they were gone, I explained.

"She had no idea why you were here."

"Sylvie, this is just terrible."

"I know. Dad is the one who's really getting hit. Mom is so difficult to deal with if she's not on those tranquilizers."

"That's what Gray said. Hopefully they can get some good news on the biopsy."

"Waiting will be awful." I couldn't imagine how Dad would feel.

"Gray said two days."

"Yeah, that's what the doctor told Dad too."

Evan had been talking with Gray but I noticed he slipped away and went back to where they had taken Mom. Evan came over to me and put his arm around me.

"How're you holding up?" he asked.

"I'm fine. This will be a long two days, but I'm mostly worried about my dad." He'd always been our rock to lean on. I was so thankful for Evan.

Aunt Paige touched my arm. "If you girls need anything, even if it's a home cooked meal, come over. You know I cook every night. I could make extra plates for your parents too."

"We may take you up on that," I answered.

"Hey everybody," Evan began. "I'm going to round us up some decent coffee. Text me or Sylvie what you want, and we'll get it for you."

A round of thanks went up as our phones beeped.

"I'll go with you," I said.

"I was planning on it." He took my hand and off we went.

"This is nice of you."

He shrugged as though it was nothing. "It was selfish. I needed coffee and that hospital crap won't do."

"I'm glad you wanted to go because I already need a break. Plus I'm such a coffee whore too and I agree with you on hospital coffee. I've had to limit myself to only a few cups a day since the pregnancy. And decaf is just bleh." I made a nasty face.

"I didn't realize you're such a coffee fanatic."

I cast him a sidelong glance. "Seriously? Well, I suppose we haven't spent enough time together for you to notice I'm a fully charged girl."

His penetrating gaze sent serious shivers racing across my skin, leaving a path of goosebumps behind. "You don't think I've noticed that? I know exactly how charged you get, Sylvie."

"I was talking about coffee, Evan." I playfully smacked his arm.

"My mistake." His expression told me he didn't make any mistake at all. He knew exactly what he was doing.

"You're incorrigible."

"Me? You're the one who jumped on my back at your best friend's wedding reception and yelled giddy-up." His laugh echoed throughout the car.

"Okay, cowboy, I get it."

"You sure did. That night anyway. Begged for it as I recall."

Jesus, I wanted to bury my face in the seat, only it wasn't possible because there was a gigantic console in the center.

And he didn't stop. "That reminds me. I distinctly remember you bringing up something highly unusual."

He was not going to go there, was he?

"Please don't."

"Don't what?"

"You know exactly what." My face most likely was burning as bright as a Christmas light.

"The clit flogging?" He laughed.

"Yes."

"I'm very curious about something. Did your dirty duke do that to his duchess?"

"No, and you should know because you read the dirtiest part."

"Then where did you come up with that?"

"From the Mischievous Marquis."

His jaw dropped open. "How many of those books like that are there?"

"There's an entire series of about twelve of them."

"Well, damn. Are they all BDSM?"

"Yep." My eyes danced with humor.

"Hmm. Set the stage for me."

"You really want me to do this? We're pulling into the coffee shop."

He put the car in park and leaned over. "I would love to hear it. Tell me."

I wondered if he planned to use this on me and if so, I was all in. Evan tying me up and doing some of those dirty things to me had me clenching my thighs together.

"They're very similar to what you already read."

"I don't care. Set the scene up, please."

"Sure. Usually the woman is a virgin, innocent and unsuspecting. The man is experienced and likes things a bit rough. So he binds her wrists and ankles to the bedposts and then blindfolds her. She's obviously frightened because this is her first time, but he tells her he's not going to hurt her. He teases her until she's moaning and begging for more. Then he releases her ties and has her get on her hands and knees. When he first spanks her, she cries, but soon she's into it. It's super hot because each time he spanks her, it comes with something special."

"Something special? What do you mean?"

"I mean his fingers do things to her too."

"Ahh, I get it."

"Oh, and her bright pink ass totally fires him up."

"I can see why." Evan's voice was strained.

"I'm sure you can."

"Your pink ass hiked up in the air is a killer. Don't tell me anymore. Let's go get the coffee."

"That's it? You don't want to hear what else he does?"

"Not now. Later."

He jumped out of the car like his ass was the one that got spanked. I giggled to myself. By the time he got around to opening my door, the bulge in his pants was obvious.

"Um, Evan, you ... you're a little..." My finger wagged up and down, pointing to his bulge.

"I know. Why do you think I couldn't listen to anymore?"

I snorted. "Maybe you should pull your T-shirt out."

"Good idea." He tugged it out of his pants, and it helped. Too bad his jacket wasn't just a bit longer.

"That's better."

We went in, placed the order, and it took a while because everyone wanted something different. That was fine because it was worth it in the end. An extra-large latte was much better than plain old coffee any day.

When we made it back to the hospital, Piper told us Dad had been out.

"What did he say?" I asked in a panic.

"Only that Mom would be going into surgery in about thirty minutes. As soon as she was through, he or Gray would let us know."

"Isn't Dad going to sit with us?"

Aunt Paige answered. "No, apparently Gray is taking him to the doctor's lounge and they're going to wait in there. Your father is extremely upset and Gray thought it best that way."

"Oh." I was disappointed that Dad didn't want to wait it out with us, but I also understood. He was the kind of man who wouldn't want to burden anyone.

It turned out to be the longest wait I could remember. Mom

came through the procedure fine, and they did frozen sections of the biopsy, confirming it was malignant, but they weren't certain of the type. We would find out in forty-eight to seventy-two hours. Mom would be moved to a room and she was currently in recovery.

"Can we see her?" We all wanted to know.

"It's best to wait until they move her to a room because she's heavily sedated," her doctor answered.

"How long will that be?" I asked him.

"At least three hours. Why don't you all go home and take a break? Come back this afternoon around two."

It sounded great, so we left the hospital with plans to get something to eat. Aunt Paige invited us to lunch at their place, but we declined.

"Why don't you join us?"

We all went to a local eatery and had just ordered when my phone rang. It was Dad. "Hey Dad. We're all at a restaurant. Do you want us to bring you something?"

"Sylvie. They had to take your mother back to surgery because she started bleeding in her brain. I'm not sure what's happening."

"We're on the way."

FORTY-SIX
EVAN

AFTER SYLVIE RELAYED THE TERRIBLE NEWS, WE RUSHED BACK to the hospital to be with her dad, who was waiting for us. As it turned out, the bleeding wasn't serious. It was only where they had taken the tissue samples, thank God.

The surgeon relayed the news as John fell back onto the chair with relief.

"She's back in recovery and doing well," the surgeon said.

"What are the chances this will happen again?" Sylvie asked.

"I can't say. But it's not uncommon. That's why we monitor the patient very closely. If she goes the next twelve hours without, she'll probably be okay. The next twenty-four, she'll be good to go home."

"Thank you," John said.

That meant twelve hours of pure paranoia. I remembered them mentioning that before the surgery but I didn't really think it would be an issue. Guess I was wrong.

"Doctor, do you have our cell numbers?" Sylvie asked.

"I have Mr. West's and of course I have Grey's."

"Good. We're going to get my dad out of here for an hour or two," she said.

"That's probably the best thing you can do right now."

John was still sitting, and Sylvie took one arm while Rick took the other. "Come on, Dad, let's get out of here."

"I can't."

"You don't have a choice." Sylvie tugged on him.

He grimaced.

"Really, John, it'll do you some good. You look like shit." Rick was right. He looked horrible.

"Sorry, Dad, Uncle Rick's right," Piper said, then hugged him. "You won't be any good to Mom if you don't take care of yourself."

Reynolds added, "Yeah, Dad, and we don't want to have to take care of both of you."

John held up both hands. "Okay. You win."

They escorted him out and we went back to the restaurant we'd abandoned.

Lunch was great. The restaurant gave us the same table, adding a seat. They were very accommodating. John even managed to eat. Once he started, he gobbled up everything. We were only gone an hour, but it worked wonders for him. He seemed re-energized.

Cindy was fine and they transferred her to a room, where Sylvie's dad had a recliner he could sleep in. She was released the next day.

Sylvie and I didn't go to the hospital because her dad said it might confuse Cindy and he could handle her. He would call us when he had her settled. We still had the issue of telling everyone about the pregnancy.

We were sipping coffee, watching TV, aka the financial channel, when my phone rang. I quickly jotted down on a piece of paper that it was Marti, the realtor. After a few minutes, I hung up.

"She has the inspection set for today. Actually in about an hour. She said it should be ready by tomorrow. She also wanted to know if we want a home warranty. I said yes, even though the house is only three years old."

"With the way things are made today, you never know."

"That's what I was thinking. The house has a lot of high-end appliances, and that roof is enormous. If it gets a leak or something, we're covered."

Sylvie chewed on her lip.

"What's wrong?"

"Are you sure about this? It's such an expensive house." She twisted her hands.

"Is that all you're concerned about?"

"Mostly."

"What else?"

"You saw the house I grew up in. It wasn't small. But that place is gigantic. I'm worried I'll never be able to keep it up."

I wanted to laugh but didn't want to hurt her. Instead I took her hands in mine.

"Sylvie, honey, we're going to hire a housekeeper and someone to cook for us. I would never put that on you. That house is way too enormous for you to handle, plus a full-time job, and a baby. You'll have a nanny at your disposal too. What other concerns do you have?"

"What if I can't find you in that monstrosity?"

Now I did laugh. "You can text me?" She pulled a hand out of my grasp and punched me. "Ow, why'd you do that?"

"First, that didn't really hurt. I've seen your hunky muscles. Second, I don't want to have to text my husband to find him in our own home."

"Your husband?" I glowed inside.

"Did I say that?" The crests of her cheeks grew pink.

I cupped her cheeks and kissed her. "Yes, you called me your husband."

"That was a huge slip."

"And I have hunky muscles, huh?"

"Shut up, or I'll punch you again."

"I love you."

"I love you too, you big goofball." She grinned at me.

"Marry me."

"Of course I'll marry you, but not right now."

"Fine, as long as I know you'll be Mrs. Evan Thomas one day, I'm happy." I kissed her again.

"Evan, if this stuff with Mom wasn't happening, things would be perfect." A stress line formed on her brow.

"Babe, I'm sorry and I wish I could make it disappear."

She caved into my chest. In a muffled voice, she said, "Me too."

"Why don't we get out of here? Do something fun. You have the next couple of days off, we should go shopping or to a movie."

"Maybe."

"Nope. Let's shower and go."

That's what we did. We drove into the city and I took her shopping. We had an assistant help us, bringing in all sorts of items that she'd be able to wear well into her pregnancy and after the baby came. Then we had an early dinner and drove back home.

Her dad called with the news that Cindy's release went well and she was home and settled in. He didn't want any visitors because she was resting comfortably.

"That's a relief," Sylvie said.

"I'm glad it went well."

"Agreed."

She was excited about her new clothes too. "I love everything you bought me. The pull up jeans in particular. It's weird how tight mine are since I'm not quite eight weeks yet."

"Maybe it's because this is your first. Anytime you need a thing, just ask. And by the way, how much do you owe on your mortgage? I want to pay it off."

Her mouth tightened into a stubborn line. I had seen that angry look before and I'd just fucked up and crossed the line. I was in the land of pissed off Sylvie.

"Absolutely not."

FORTY-SEVEN
SYLVIE

PAY OFF MY MORTGAGE? WHAT THE HELL! "EVAN, I AM NOT A charity case."

"I have no intentions of treating you like one."

Anger choked me. "Then why are you doing it?"

His hands flew in the air wildly. "Christ, I thought I was doing something nice."

"Nice is taking me shopping. Paying off my mortgage is telling me I'm not capable of it and need you to do it, hence, charity."

"Jesus, Sylvie, you took it the wrong way. All I wanted to do was make you debt free."

Now I quivered with indignation. The fact he thought I couldn't do that on my own sent me into the land of downright-pissed-off. "And why can't I pay my own mortgage off?"

"You can. You're fully able to. I just thought—"

"Let me stop you right there. Before you say these kinds of things, please run them by me first. What about—Hey, Sylvie, would you like for me to pay off your mortgage?"

He aimed his gaze at me rubbing his chin. Then his shoulders slumped. "Yeah, I didn't ask, did I?"

"No, you did not."

"Shit, I apologize. It's my take charge demeanor coming through."

Annoyance still hovered on the tip of my tongue, but I swallowed it down. I thought about what I wanted to say before I spoke. "Evan, I get that you run an enormous business. My mind can't even comprehend what you do. I don't understand what managing a hedge fund really means. I realize you have a lot of employees and own multiple companies, which makes you naturally dominant, but you have to drop that behavior with me."

He took my hands in his. "You're absolutely right. I'm controlling, but we're a team and as a team, we work together. This is a learning process for me. When it comes to money, it's my nature to go into overdrive. I'll do my best, Sylvie, even though I'll make mistakes. It's the money man in me."

"Okay, money man. I'm going to pay off my own mortgage unless I say otherwise. Got it?"

"Yes, ma'am."

"Thank you for understanding."

We ended up watching a movie and then going to bed. I was still tired from this pregnancy, that I fell asleep quickly.

The next day turned into an amalgamation of highs and lows. I woke up to the smell of bacon cooking and a happy face. When I shuffled into the kitchen wearing my favorite bunny slippers and cozy robe, Evan handed me a mug of coffee.

"I took the liberty of putting in some sugar and cream for you." He topped it off with a kiss.

"Mmm. That's better than any coffee I've ever had. Thanks for cooking breakfast. The bacon smells scrumptious."

"Want a piece? It's done. Oh, and how many eggs?"

"Two, please."

He popped some bread into the toaster and scrambled the eggs as I reached for a piece of bacon.

"Yum. Crisp, just the way I like it. I didn't even hear you get up."

"Yeah, you were snoring like an old hound."

The piece of bacon stopped about six inches from my mouth. "Say what?"

"You were adorable, though."

"An old hound?"

"Sawing logs, babe. What can I say?"

"I don't snore." No way did I snore. Nope. Not me.

"Okay, whatever you say." He took the toast out of the toaster, buttered it, plated it along with the eggs and set everything on the table. "Let's eat. I'm starving."

We both sat and scarfed down breakfast. "This was delicious. I didn't know you could cook."

"I'm pretty good at breakfast but suck at everything else."

"Can you make pancakes?"

"Yeah, why?"

"I'm giving you a heads up then. They're my favorite and I'll be ordering them a lot during this pregnancy, which, by the way, I think that nausea thing has passed."

"So soon? I thought it was supposed to last for twelve weeks or so." He rose and collected the dirty dishes.

"Me too, but maybe I'm lucky." I got up to help.

"I hope so."

We were cleaning up the kitchen when his phone went off. He dried his hands and answered it.

"Hi, Marti." Pause. "That's great. Okay, we'll see you there."

"Babe, that was the realtor. The inspection's back already. She wants to meet us at her office to go through it. She said there was nothing outstanding."

"That's really good, right?"

"Yeah. I told her we could meet in an hour. Is that okay?"

"Yeah. I need to shower and so do you."

We got ready and headed over to her office. She had the inspection in hand with a smile.

"The only things he found were very minor. The air filters on the HVAC units needed changing and the dryer vent needed cleaning. Whoever did their laundry wasn't good at cleaning the lint filter, apparently."

"What else?" Evan asked.

"That's it. The owners accepted your offer, so basically the house is yours if you still want it."

Evan asked, "Sylvie, are you in?"

"I am if you are."

"It's a yes, Marti. We need to go to closing then, and my bank will need all of the owners' bank information for the wire transfer."

"Excellent. I'll set it up and get back to you ASAP."

I left in a daze while Evan was excited. He was used to large monetary transactions, while I, on the other hand, was not.

"Hey, you with me or on another planet?"

"Huh?"

Laughing, he said, "I've been talking to you and getting no response."

"Oh, sorry. I'm a little overwhelmed. I can't believe we just did that."

He stopped walking and turned me to face him. "Listen, I'm looking at it as another investment. And if we absolutely hate it, we sell. That's it."

"I need an attitude adjustment. So what were you asking me?"

"What decorator do you want to hire?"

Oh shit. He's going all decorator on me now.

"I don't know any."

"I don't up here, but I'm sure Mom does. You have to tell me what you like, Sylvie."

"Comfort not stiff. I love how your place in the city is done. It has that lived-in feel. I don't want ultra-modern."

"I agree. I'm pretty sure we're on the same page then."

We decided to furniture hunt for the hell of it because if we rented out my townhouse or even kept it if I wanted to spend the night there, we'd still need it furnished. It was hilarious testing out the beds, but then Evan said he wanted a bed like the one he had in Manhattan.

"Oh, my God, yes. That's the best bed in the world. It's so comfy."

"Great, then that's off the list. I'll order those for each of the guest rooms, and we'll leave the baby's room for later. I assume you'll want to use that small room off the master for a while."

"Yes. After the first few weeks. At first, I want nubbin to be next to me by the bed, so I don't freak out."

He held my hand as we walked through the store. "I understand. I don't want to freak out either, plus, it'll be easier with the feedings. But we'll have video surveillance for the baby."

"You mean a video monitor."

"Nope. I want the entire house equipped with video surveillance so we can see that baby at all times with the nanny. I'm not taking any chances."

Damn, this was steroid safety protocol. I touched my belly and said, "It's hard to believe there's a baby inside me."

"I know. I can't wait for the next doctor's appointment to see how much he's grown."

"You mean she."

My phone buzzed. It was in my coat pocket, so I dug it out. "It's Dad. I hope it's a good report."

"Hey Dad."

"Syll, I'm following the ambulance to the hospital. Your Mom had a seizure and then another one immediately after. I'm not sure..."

"Dad, we're on the way." My heart ripped through my chest at his words. I wasn't sure how much more of this I could take.

FORTY-EIGHT

EVAN

WE RUSHED TO THE HOSPITAL, WHERE JOHN AND SYLVIE'S sisters waited.

"What's happening?" Sylvie asked.

"They're talking about transferring her to the hospital in Manhattan."

"So soon? They don't even know what she has yet."

Grey came out. He'd probably been here anyway. "Hey. Sorry this is happening. I talked to her doctor as soon as she got here. The tumor's causing the seizures, which is why they want to transfer her. Uncle John, I'm assuming you told them?"

"Yes."

"Usually when someone has a seizure, they have a latent period afterward, but she's not. These aren't the usual seizures you think of either, with convulsions. She's having temporal lobe seizures, which is where the tumor is located. She presents like she's having a stroke in a way. Our concern is that they aren't really stopping, so her neurologist wants to get her in to the doctor that's going to treat her."

John asked, "You mean surgery?"

"Hopefully, if they can. If not, radiation."

Sylvie latched onto my hand. "But Grey, do they even know what it is?"

"At this point, they need to stop the seizures and they know she has a mass on her temporal lobe in the brain. Even if it's a non-aggressive form of cancer, something needs to be done." Grey scratched his head. "The conclusive pathology reports aren't back yet, which they should any time now, but we know the frozen sections indicated a malignancy."

Then we noticed the neurologist walking toward us. "Hello everyone. I know Grey's filling you in, but I wanted to update you. We have her transfer approved and the hospital in the city is ready with a room. Her new doctor will be Dr. Bernard Casey. He's one of the best neurosurgeons around. We also got the results of her biopsy. I'm afraid it's a glioblastoma."

John said flatly, "That's the worst possible kind."

Sylvie asked, "How do you know, Dad?"

"I've been reading up on the different types."

Grey patted him on the back. "Uncle John, I'm sorry. But if anyone can help, Dr. Casey can."

I stepped forward. "If any of you want to stay at my place, I have plenty of room. There's no need to get a hotel. I also have an extra apartment, if you want privacy. Neither of them are far from the hospital."

"That's very kind, Evan," John said.

Grey looked at us. "Go home and pack a bag, everyone. You'll be there for several days at least. Don't forget, Hudson and Milly are there too if you want a place to hang out with screaming kids and barking dogs."

It was meant to be humorous, but we only nodded. We were too somber to think humor right now.

Pulling Grey to the side, I asked, "Look, I know legally you're not allowed to tell me anything, but do we need to look outside the area for help on this, as in a better doctor?"

"I honestly don't think there is one."

"How long?"

"I can't really say, but if I had to guess, less than a year."

"Fuck."

"I did not tell you that. Understand?"

"Perfectly."

"And Evan. Again, this is not my area of expertise and doctors have been known to be wrong all the time so ..." He held his hands up.

"I got it."

Sylvie and I went back to her place to gather our things.

"Evan, Mom has to make it another thirty-eight weeks. She has to live to see her first grandchild."

"Babe, let's think positive. This guy, Casey, is supposed to be the best. And if he's not, we'll find the best. Are you doing okay?"

"Fuck, no! What kind of a question is that? I want this tumor to disappear. I want rainbows and flowers and I want Reynolds to make her unicorn to wield some magic right now."

I let her vent until she was out of words. "So do I, babe." I held out my arms and she walked right into them. "Of all the things I can do for you, taking this away isn't one of them. But I promise to be here and do whatever I can for you and your family."

"Thank you. I'm grateful you're here. Sorry I snapped at you."

"That's what I'm here for."

Her phone buzzed and I asked her if she wanted to get that.

"Not really. I do need to call Leeanne at work. She needs to be aware that I may be missing more than the next couple of days."

"Will that be a problem?"

"It might be because they don't have extra counselors on hand."

"Hopefully your mom will fly through this and you won't need to worry about it."

"Evan, I pray to God she does. I can't imagine life without

her. All those times I complained about her are coming back to haunt me. I feel terrible now, knowing she was really sick."

I rubbed her back but didn't know how to respond. It was a heavy burden their family carried. "How could you have known? How could any of you? She didn't complain of the usual symptoms except for her strange behavior. Even the doctor said it was unusual. I know it must be a terrible thing to bear, but sweetheart, even in retrospect, you probably wouldn't have done anything different." I kissed the top of her head and just held her.

"Thank you for those words. It'll be a while before I allow myself to believe them. I know cognitively they're true, but my heart aches something fierce with the knowledge of what's going on..." She only shook her head.

"It's okay. Well, not really, but maybe it will be. Now let's get moving so we can be there at the hospital when she arrives."

We gathered our things and left. On the way out to the car, I said, "Sylvie, you're the most important person in the world to me. If there's anything you or your family needs, please let me know. I can help however you want."

I called Robert on the way and filled him in. Then I asked him to meet us at the garage. It would be easier to have him drop us off as opposed to taking a cab. After the call, I said, "Robert extends his hopes that your mother has a speedy recovery."

"He's always been kind to me."

"Yes, I'm fortunate to have him."

Robert was there, waiting for us when we arrived.

"Hello, sir. I'm sorry to say it's good to see you."

"Thank you, Robert."

"Ms. West, may I say the same for you?"

"Thank you, Robert." Sylvie began crying again. Robert said, "Ah, now, Ms. West, you must be positive. Doctors don't know everything."

Sylvie went up to him and hugged him. "Robert, her situation is bleak. The tumor is the worst kind and even if she makes it through the surgery, I'm not even sure how long she has."

"Ms. West, only God knows the answers to that so go and be by her side because she needs you now."

Good advice. "We'll take our things upstairs and be right back down."

Robert stopped me. "Sir, I'll take care of that after I drop you off."

"Thank you. I guess we can go."

We got into the limo and rode to the hospital. When we were close, Robert wanted to know at which entrance we wanted to be dropped off.

"Let's go to the main entrance and start there." I relayed this to Robert.

There was a large information desk when we walked in so that's where we went and gave Cindy's name. They, in turn, asked us for identification.

I had never been to this hospital, but it was certainly secure, which was a good thing. We pulled out our driver's licenses, and then the guard gave us badges with our names on them. "Stop here every day when you come in and pick one of these up as they're only good for twenty-four hours."

"Thanks," I told him.

There was an escalator straight ahead, and at the top sat a huge bank of elevators. She was on the eleventh floor, which was for surgery patients, according to the guide. When we stepped off, we easily located her room.

We were the first ones to arrive. Two nurses were with her when we got there.

"Mom." Sylvie rushed to her side. She was out of it and barely opened her eyes.

One of the nurses said, "She's heavily sedated to keep her calm. They medicated her before transporting to keep the seizures at bay and we just gave her another dose. I'm Marilyn and this is Dena. We'll be here until eleven when the shift changes. Dr. Casey should be in any time, but if you need anything, we're right out there. When she goes to surgery, she'll be transferred to the SICU, of course, so we'll see you back here when she's well enough to leave there." She had kind eyes and a warmth about her. I supposed working in this environment would make you sort of special that way.

"Thank you, Marilyn. I'm her daughter, Sylvie, and this is my fiancé, Evan. The rest of the family should be here any time now."

As she finished speaking, the other family members walked in. John went directly to the bed, while Piper and Reynolds hung back. Marilyn gave them the same speech she'd given us before the two nurses left the room.

Piper said, "You two made it here fast."

"Our things were mostly packed," I explained.

"Right." She looked like she'd been crying.

"Hey, where do you want to stay? Honestly, there's room in my place. It has four bedrooms, so each of you could have your own room. I also have a cook, so you'd have great food at your disposal, and a driver as well. But if you'd rather stay in the apartment, that's fine too."

"My dad doesn't want to put you out and is talking about a hotel," she said.

"That's ridiculous when I have much better options."

"What does Sylvie think?"

I glanced over to where she was, next to her dad, and said, "We haven't discussed it, but I think she'd say my place. It's plenty big. I'd hardly know you were there. There's even a garage for you to park in and come and go as you please. It would save you from all those expenses."

"We don't want to impose."

I huffed out a breath. "If it were an imposition, I wouldn't have offered."

"Then I'll make the decision and go with your place. That

way we'll all be in one spot and it'll be easier going back and forth."

"You have chosen wisely."

She bowed and said, "Thank you, old knight."

"Are you an Indiana Jones fan?" I asked.

"Oh, yeah. And from that line, I know you are."

"I have the entire collection. We can watch it if..."

"Yeah, if..." she said.

It was an awkward moment until Sylvie joined us. "Hey, at least Mom is comfortable."

"Good. Evan and I took the bull by the horns and made the decision of where we'd be staying," Piper said.

"Oh?"

"They're staying with us," I said.

"I'm glad. There's plenty of room and you'll be more comfortable."

Dr. Casey walked in with his iPad and introduced himself. "Can we talk outside? There's a private room right across the hall." We followed him and everyone took a seat. "Normally, I like to try a few things before surgery, such as radiation, but your wife, Mr. West, isn't getting any better. I've had the opportunity to review all her scans and with the seizures she keeps having, I believe we need to see if we can remove the tumor, or at least part of it. I'll be honest. I don't want to fill you with false hopes. I'm not happy with the location of it, or the size. I'm not sure how much you know about glioblastomas, but they're not our friends. They're aggressive, and as I like to say, they have a rootlike consistency to the way they spread, which makes removing them complicated. The other difficulty is the location. The temporal lobe controls many functions of the brain such as, memory, sleep, hearing, not to mention it also contains the hypothalamus which controls many of the bodily functions. So removal is always a risk. But, my opinion is at this point, we have no other option unless you want to keep her sedated, as she is now."

Shit. I didn't think it was this bad. Sylvie slumped and pressed a fist against her chest. I took her free hand, though it didn't do much good. It was lifeless as I held it. I felt as useless as the pad of paper sitting on the table in front of me. And the worst thing? There wasn't a damn thing I could do to make it any better.

FORTY-NINE

SYLVIE

DEAR GOD, PLEASE LET MOM GO PEACEFULLY. IF YOUR PLAN ISN'T for her to be here much longer, I beg you not to let her suffer.

I repeated those words over and over in my head. The thought of life without her was unbearable, but life with her in pain, was even worse. I'd heard stories of people with brain tumors and they weren't pleasant. It was something I wouldn't wish on my worst enemy, but my mom? I would take the tumor and put it in my own head if I could.

Dad's vacant stare had me worried the most. He and Mom were peas and carrots. They had barely spent any time apart. What would he do without her?

"Babe," Evan whispered in my ear.

"Yeah." My voice sounded dead, even to me.

"Let's take a walk."

I allowed him to lead me away from the room of doom. That poor doctor. How did they do it? How did they tell patients terrible news like that and then go home and deal? I could never. Then I thought about my cousin, Grey, who had to deliver news like that. I'd never thought about it before.

"How do you think Grey handles it?"

"Handles what?"

"Telling patients their loved ones are about to die or have died."

Evan stopped and faced me. "Oh, Sylvie. I hate this with everything in my heart. I don't know what to say to you other than I'm so very sorry, my love."

"I know. And you don't have to say it."

"As for Grey, I never gave it much thought, which is totally insensitive of me."

"Same here. I thought about what Dr. Casey told us and I don't know how they do it."

"You amaze me." He reached out and touched my cheek. "You've just received terrible news and yet you're thinking about the doctor instead of yourself. How selfless can you be?"

I placed my hand over his. "It's not selfless. It's the analytic counselor in me."

"Hey, don't pull yourself off the pedestal I've placed you on."

"Stop it, you goofball." Happy that he brought a smile to me for the first time in I didn't know how long, I kissed him. It was supposed to be a quickie, but I folded myself around him and deepened the kiss. There was no way I was stopping this moment. Eventually, someone cleared a throat behind us and said, "Get a room." We broke apart to see Piper and Reynolds.

Piper said, "For a second there, I thought I might have to throw a bucket of water on you two."

"Jealous?" I asked, grinning.

"Hell yeah, I'm jealous. I haven't seen that kind of action in months."

"Okay, ladies, I don't think I want to be a part of this conversation." Evan held up his hands.

"You'd better get used to it, slick, if you want to be a part of this family," Reynolds said. "This is us. We do it all the time. And details. Oh, God. Every tiny one."

"All right. What did Sylvie say about me?"

My sisters stared at each other blankly for a couple of

seconds and then Reynolds said, "Nothing. Now that you mention it, that's really weird."

Evan's green gaze captured mine as his grin widened. "Either you were secretive because you hated me, or you loved the fact that we were together. Which was it?"

"I think you know the answer to that." It was the latter, only at the time, I stubbornly refused to admit the truth.

"Other than swallowing each other's tongues, what were you guys up to? We couldn't find you, so we decided to look for you," Piper asked.

"Why? What happened?"

"Nothing, so calm down. We didn't know where you went."

"Oh." I instantly relaxed. "We just went for a little walk to get rid of some tension."

"Uh huh. And how did that *walk* work for you?" Reynolds asked.

"Better than just sitting there. I'm on edge so I'm not rising to your bait. Anyway, the news Dr. Casey gave us wasn't promising, so I had to do something."

The mood grew somber again. "Yeah, it's pretty bleak," Piper agreed. "How do you think Dad will hold up?"

"Dad's strong, but this is going to be really difficult on him," I said.

"Hey, you guys are acting like Mom doesn't have any chance at all," Reynolds said. "That's not what the doctor said. Yes, the surgery is risky, but what if it goes well and she can get treatment?"

I knew those particular tumors were bad, but Reynolds had a valid point. "You're right. We need to start thinking more positively. I tend to hope for the best but expect the worst. That way if the worst does happen, it doesn't take me by surprise. But one thing we all need to do is pray. Not only for Mom, but for Dad too."

Piper said, "I don't think he'll be leaving the hospital until she does."

A thought struck me then. "Dad's always been here for us, through thick and thin. This is our time to repay him. If he won't leave her side, then we'll take turns for him. One of us will be with her so he can at least get some sleep."

Piper eyed me. "But what about you? And does anyone even know?"

"Know what?" Reynolds asked.

Since it was just the four of us, I decided to tell her. I was supposed to call her before Christmas but she didn't answer that night and news like mine wasn't something you left as a message. I took Evan's hand and gave it a little squeeze. "Reynolds, Evan and I are expecting a baby."

"What?"

"Yeah, I'm pregnant."

Her hand went to her mouth. Then she said, "Oh, my God! I'm going to be an aunt."

"You sure are."

"Does Mom—?"

"No. Dad does and we wanted to tell her, but he asked us to hold off. That's when he thought she had dementia and wanted to take her to the doctor first. Then the shit hit the fan and well, here we are."

"Am I the last to know?"

"No, the only ones that know are Piper and Dad. Oh, and Rose, because she forced me to take the pregnancy test."

Reynolds hugged me then. "I'm so excited for you two."

"We're pretty excited too. Except for this."

"I brought my magic unicorn and I'll ask it to make it all okay," she said.

I chuckled. "Thanks."

Then Reynolds broke into tears. "What are we going to do if Mom dies."

"Hey, it's okay." I held her. "If she dies, we'll all be together as a family and be strong for each other, like we always are." I didn't want to avoid the possibility of her death or ignore it either. "We'll have each other to get us through this."

"It won't be the same."

"I know it won't. But we won't have a choice, will we?"

"No."

"And we wouldn't want Mom to suffer, would we?"

"No."

"Then the best we can do now is pray for her and be here for her and Dad."

"Okay. Why are you so good with this stuff?" Reynolds asked.

"It's what I do."

She wiped her eyes and I handed her a tissue to blow her nose. "Thanks, Syll."

"Anytime. I'm always here for you."

We headed down the hall, as a team, to Mom's room. Dad was there, holding her hand when we got there.

"Hey. Her surgery is scheduled for eight in the morning. The doctor said he would keep her sedated until then so she'd be comfortable and not have any seizures. Tomorrow morning, she'll be awake to talk to us, before they take her down."

"What time?" Piper asked.

"They'll come for her at seven thirty so come at seven."

"Are you staying the night here?" I asked.

"Yeah. I don't want to be away from her."

"One of us will stay with you," I said.

"No. I want to be alone with her."

I wasn't sure that was a good idea, so I said, "Dad, I don't think—"

"Sylvie, I know you're trying to help, but I've been married to this woman for thirty-three years and dated her for two years before that. I've loved her for over half my life. What she's going through right now is more than I can bear and I want—no need— to have this time alone with her. I know she's your mother and you love her dearly, but she's part of me. Can you understand that?"

"Yeah, Dad, I can. You know how to reach us if you need us and we're only a cab ride away. Can we get you some dinner before we leave?"

"That would be nice, and I would be grateful for it."

Evan pulled me aside and said he would have something better than the hospital cafeteria food sent over.

After we hugged and kissed Dad, we left for Evan's place. It was a sobering moment for all of us.

FIFTY

EVAN

EARLIER, I HAD CALLED RITA AND ASKED HER TO MAKE EXTRA food for dinner that we could eat later that night. I had her wrap up a plate and had someone take it to the hospital for John. When we arrived home, the place smelled of her cooking.

"Wow. This place is awesome," Reynolds said.

Sylvie showed them around while I went to the kitchen. Rita left a note explaining where everything was. She'd made Greek chicken and potatoes, a huge salad, and a large chocolate cake. There were also a variety of cookies too. There was a freshly baked coffeecake for breakfast, along with some other bakery items. She'd thought of everything for us.

The girls wandered in and I told them about dinner. None of them seemed overly enthusiastic about eating, but my bet was when it was out in front of them, they'd change their minds. I was right. After a few bites, they polished their plates and even went for dessert.

Sylvie patted her stomach. "If I keep eating like this, I'll have fifty pounds to lose after nubbin is born."

"Nubbin?" Reynolds asked.

"We don't know if it's a boy or girl yet, so that's what we're calling it."

I cleared my throat, drawing their attention. "That's what she named it before she told me. I call it baby."

She poked me in the chest. "No you don't. You call *me* baby."

"True, but when we're not together or I'm thinking about it in my head, that's what I call it."

"Nubbin's weird," Reynolds said.

"It is not," Sylvie huffed.

"Yeah, it is. It sounds like you're talking about someone's nose. Hey, look at that nubbin on that dude's face."

Piper busted out a laugh. Sylvie tried not to, but couldn't help it. Piper said, "It does sound dorky, but I wasn't going to tell you."

They all turned to me and no way was I getting in the middle. "Don't you dare do this to me."

"Evan, come on."

"Nope, not gonna do it."

"Why don't you call it peanut?" Reynolds asked.

"Because that's what everyone calls their baby," Sylvie replied.

Piper jumped up, yelling, "I know. Call it button!"

"I really like that. I think we should have that as a family thing," Reynolds said.

"I like it too. Evan?" Sylvie asked.

"I love it." It was so much better than nubbin, but I didn't tell Sylvie that. There were so many times I caught myself starting to call it nubbie, or the nub. I was glad she was changing it to button. I also didn't tell her it reminded me of nipple or clit. That would've gone over like a bomb.

We watched TV for a while then went to bed. Sylvie had already shown her sisters to their rooms earlier, so we said good-night after we made plans to leave for the hospital at seven.

"There are plenty of breakfast items in the kitchen and there will also be coffee. I have large take-out cups for us so we can even eat in the car if you want to sleep as late as possible. If you forgot anything, just look in the bathrooms. I have them pretty well stocked."

"Thank you, Evan. You've been more than helpful," Piper said. Reynolds came up and hugged me. This was sure a huggy family.

Sylvie and I were in the bathroom brushing our teeth and getting ready for bed.

"Evan, what about the house?"

"What about it?"

"Don't we have to do some things over there?"

"It can wait. This takes precedence. The inspection went well. All we need is to close, and she was going to set that up, remember?"

She slid the back of her hand across her forehead.

"Come on, let's get in bed. You look exhausted."

"I am."

I pulled the covers back for her and helped her get in. Then I went to the other side.

"Evan, will you hold me?"

"You don't have to ask." I pulled her against my chest and brushed her hair off her face.

"Tomorrow is going to be so hard."

"Just lean on me. I have a strong back and it's there for you all the time."

"I wonder if it'll be strong enough to get me through the day."

"What are you talking about?"

"It's just that...I don't know."

"Babe, I know you're expecting the worst, but please don't lose hope.

"HOPE IS the thing with feathers
That perches in the soul
And sings the tune without the words
And never stops at all."

. . .

"THAT'S BEAUTIFUL."

"It's Emily Dickinson. But you have to believe and have hope. Don't give up yet, babe."

She softly touched her lips to mine. "You're right. I've thanked God for you every day, Evan. I have no idea what I would do without you."

I kissed her this time and answered, "I love you, Sylvie. Every part of you. In good times and bad. That's what love is. It's not about the beautiful and wonderful times. It's about hardships and dealing with difficulties. Ask me how I know, I can't tell you, but I know I'd do anything for you. And facing adversity is a part of life, unfortunately. But as a team, we can weather any storm."

"One plus one equals four."

Chuckling, I said, "In our case, it certainly equals three with button in there."

She snuggled deeper against me and said, "Yeah. Our little button. I can't wait to see what she looks like."

"You mean he."

Soon, her soft snores came to me, and I fell asleep right afterward.

My phone's alarm woke us both up. We groaned and I was pleasantly surprised she slept the whole night.

"We'd better get moving," I said.

She slipped out of bed and made it to the bathroom before I even moved. I let her have some privacy before I joined her. By the time I got there, she was already in the shower.

"You're quick today."

She called from rinsing her hair, "I know. I need to get this mass of frizz tamed before we leave."

"I love it curly. Why don't you ever wear it that way?"

"You really like it like that?"

"If I didn't, I wouldn't say so. It's gorgeous and not frizzy."

She turned off the water and opened the shower door. Damn, I wished I'd been looking the other way. Sylvie, wet and slick was something I didn't need right now. My dick, which popped its head right up, didn't need it either.

"You're serious about my hair?"

"Huh?" I was staring at her luscious tits.

"My hair." Then she caught me staring and noticed my erection and said, "Apparently you like what you see."

"Oh, yeah." I fisted my cock as I headed to the shower. I'd have to take care of things before we left.

"What are you doing?"

"What does it look like? Taking a shower."

"That's not what I meant, and you know it."

"If you must know, I was taking things into my own hand."

She shoved me and followed me in.

"Sylvie, what are you doing?"

"What does it look like? Turn the water on, Evan."

How could I refuse my lady? I did as she requested and watched her drop to her knees. She licked my most sensitive parts and then went down to the base and back to the tip. Her hot tongue circled it a few times, before she put it into her mouth. I stared at her hollowed cheeks as she sucked me off. Fuck, it was unreal. Slowly, she slid her mouth up and down and tongued my tip. My arms braced myself against the cool tiles as the water rushed over us. This was amazing, watching my love give me a blow job like this.

"Fuck, Sylvie, just like that." She ran her tongue around my balls and then back up my cock. When she sucked me again, she took me deep, deeper than I thought she'd be able to. Each time I hit the back of her throat, she'd swallow, and I'd almost shoot off.

"Babe, I'm gonna come."

She didn't let me go, so I told her again. "I can't hold back." She looked up at me and blinked. That was it. I let it go and she swallowed every drop, licking and sucking me bone dry. I pulled her up and kissed her, hard.

"Christ, Sylvie, you trying to kill me?"

"No, just trying to make you come."

"Mission accomplished." Now it was payback.

I dropped to my knees, put one of her legs over my shoulders, and ran my tongue from one end of her slit to the other. I wasn't wasting any time on this. I delved into her pussy, then zeroed in on her clit. After some intense licking, I sucked her until I kissed an orgasm out of her. I wasn't finished. My finger tunneled inside of her and found her G-spot. Massaging it while she quivered, my tongue repeated the actions on her clit. Her breathing and cries told me she was getting close again. When she tumbled over the edge, her leg gave out and I caught her in my lap as we sat on the floor. Our mouths crashed onto each other's and we made out like teenagers.

We broke apart with loopy grins on our faces. "I hate to break this to you, but I still need to shower, and you need to get dressed."

"Yeah. But that was awfully fun."

"It was. Tomorrow, same place, same time?"

"It's a date." I helped her stand and she wiggled her ass on the way out.

"Tease," I called out to her.

"You ain't seen nothing yet."

I laughed as I finished, glad I was able to put a smile on her face. I'd do my best any way I could.

FIFTY-ONE
SYLVIE

We arrived at the hospital, each of us carrying our breakfasts and I had a bag for Dad, knowing he wouldn't have taken the time to eat. As we walked into Mom's room, she looked at us and her eyes sort of lit up.

"Look, it's the girls, John. What are they doing here?"

"Honey, I told you they were coming to visit."

Confusion clouded her eyes. Dad shook his head as he stood behind her. "Hey Mom," we all said as we came up to the bed.

"Goodness, I need to get up and make you girls lunch. You must be starving. Are those the Christmas presents? You can put them under the tree."

Shit. She thought she was at home and had no idea she was in the hospital. I glanced over at Dad and he shrugged. He'd probably been dealing with this ever since she woke up. He would leave her range of vision and make gestures, indicating we should go along with her.

"Okay, and Mom, we're not starving. Lunch can wait," I said.

"Well, that's a relief. I'm so tired for some reason. Must've had a terrible night's sleep." She suddenly went blank and stared at the corner of the room.

Dad said, "She's having a seizure again. When she comes out of it, she'll not remember you coming in."

"Should we leave?"

"No. It won't matter."

It took several minutes, but Mom blinked and then was back. "John, what are all these people doing here?"

"Hi, Mom." Piper went up to her.

"Piper, why are you here?"

"I wanted to see you."

"Where are your sisters?"

"We're here, Mom," Reynolds said.

It was painful, seeing her like this. She began to get agitated.

"John, what's going on. I need to get dressed and go shopping today."

"Oh, honey, we have plenty of food. I went to the store yesterday."

"Did you buy the turkey?"

"I sure did. Everything's ready."

"Oh, thank you."

The nurse came in and hooked up the IV in her hand to a line for fluids.

"What are you doing?"

"Mrs. West, that's your liquid nourishment for the time being, so you don't get thirsty."

"Now why would I need that when I'm perfectly capable of drinking water?"

The nurse patted her hand and said, "Of course you are, but this is just in case."

"In case of what?"

"In case you get extra thirsty and there isn't anyone to bring you water."

"My John will always bring me water, won't you, dear?"

"Of course I will." Dad was concerned about how to handle this because he kept glancing at all of us and I didn't know what to do. Telling her would only make it worse because she was completely confused.

Another nurse came in and told us the doctor was on the way.

Mom said, "Doctor? What doctor?"

The nurse quickly answered, "It's Dr. Casey, Mrs. West, and you're going to love him."

"But why do I need a doctor when I have all this cooking to do?"

The nurse waved her hand. "Let your daughters do the cooking. Isn't that right, ladies?"

"Yes. Mom, we'll cook so you can relax," Reynolds said.

"I can't even rely on you girls to clean your rooms. You don't know how to cook a turkey. You'll burn it. You know how your father detests dry turkey. Besides, I don't like to leave my girls by the stove alone. They're too young." Then she blanked out again, and to be honest, it was a relief.

God, please help Mom get through this surgery.

The nurse said, "I'm giving her a mild sedative. Dr. Casey requested it as part of her pre-op."

"That's so weird. She thinks we're eight or something," Reynolds said.

Dad said, "She's been like this all morning."

"Dad, I'm sorry." I walked around the bed to hold his hand.

"Me too, Sylls, me too."

We stood there, watching Mom when Dr. Casey breezed in. "Good morning, everyone. I'm on my way to the surgery suite and wanted to stop by to see if you had any other questions."

"No. She's been in and out of it, but she doesn't know what's going on," Dad explained.

"I didn't expect her to. I wanted you to know that this will be a long procedure—six hours at the minimum. I'll send a nurse out periodically to give you updates. If it takes longer than that, don't be alarmed. These cases can vary from one patient to another. You already know she'll go from recovery to the ICU and their visitation policy is restricted to ten minutes every hour with two visitors at a time. If you want to leave, now would be the time. They'll be taking her from here to pre-op, where she'll stay until the OR is fully prepared and I finish getting scrubbed in. Then we go to work. You won't be able to see her until she's in recovery, and that's after she's out of anesthesia and almost ready to be transferred to the unit. Any questions?"

I had one. "Dr. Casey, what are her chances of making it through the surgery?"

"We have really good outcomes data here. My bigger concern is getting to the part of the tumor that's causing all her issues."

"What are the chances of you being able to remove it all?" I asked.

"I won't know until I get in there."

"Thank you."

"I'll be seeing you after the procedure. The waiting room is on the sixth floor, where the surgical suites are, and there is also a canteen there where you can get snacks and coffee. If I were you guys, I'd get out of here for a couple of hours and come back at ten. I have your cell number, Mr. West, if I need you for anything."

Dad nodded and said, "Thank you."

We all walked around Mom's bed and kissed her on the cheek, and then left Dad to do the same by himself. He joined us in the hall a few minutes later, where we stayed until they wheeled her down.

"How about going back to Evan's instead of going to a restaurant? He's close and has everything we need," I suggested.

Everyone agreed, so Evan called Robert to pick us up. When we arrived, Rita was already at work. She made several pots of coffee and tried to get food into Dad, but he claimed he wasn't hungry.

"Mr. West, you need a solid meal. You're no good to anyone if you don't eat. Now eat this coffeecake. If you can't get past the first bite, I'll drop it."

He accepted the piece graciously, as my dad would do, but after the first bite, he was hooked. Rita watched with her hands on her hips and beamed.

"This is the best coffeecake I've ever had," Dad said.

"Good. Have another piece. And you haven't even tried my chocolate cake yet."

"Dad, the chocolate cake is amazing. Rita's the best," I told him.

"Don't tempt me, honey. This is delicious."

Rita refilled his cup as he gobbled up his second slice.

"Now, Mr. West, can I offer you something a bit more healthy like some fruit or yogurt?"

"I'll have some fruit."

She dished up a medley of pineapple, grapes, different melons, and strawberries. It looked so colorful and delicious, I asked for some too.

He and I sat at the island together and ate our fruit.

"Dad, this reminds me of when I was little, and you used to take me to that old fashioned soda fountain for lunch."

"Yeah, I remember. They closed down about the time Piper came along, but that place had been around forever." He eyed me for a second and said, "I can't believe you remember. You were just a little tyke then."

"How could I forget those hot fudge sundaes and how Mom would get mad at you because I'd have a stomach ache when I came home."

We laughed and then became serious.

"Sylvie, what will I do without her? Even if they get the tumor, she's not going to beat this thing. It's a bad motherfucker."

In all the years I'd known my father, I'd never heard him use a bad word. The fact he just did, made me understand how much research he'd done on this type of tumor.

I leaned my head on his shoulder and said, "I don't know, Dad. Team West will band together and deal somehow. I haven't been with Evan very long, but I love him with everything I have, so I kind of understand what you feel. I haven't the years you and Mom do, but if something happened to him, it would be like losing the other half of me."

"That's exactly right. I know I'll go on, but right now, I don't know how."

"I love you, Dad."

"I love you too, Sylls."

As it was nearing the golden hour of ten, we had Robert drive us back to the hospital. He hugged me when we got out of the car. "Thanks again, Robert. You're so kind."

Dad leaned close and said, "That's quite a ride your man has."

"I know. At first all of his, um, wealth was a little intimidating. But I'm warming up to it."

"Sylls, exactly how wealthy is he?"

"I'm not really sure, but his business must be something. You know that's not my thing."

"That never did impress you much."

We made it to the sixth floor and located the waiting room, our hangout for the next however many hours. It was huge with at least a couple of dozen people in there. Rita had packed us several large goodie bags so we wouldn't have to eat vending machine food.

Evan brought his computer, at my suggestion, so he could get some work done. There was actually a table with some chairs, and he was sitting there typing away. His offices were closed for the week, but that didn't stop his work from piling up.

The doctor's word had been good, and a nurse would show up to give us updates that everything was going as expected.

Noon came and went, and we all dug into the goodie bags as none of us wanted to leave. I ate two chocolate chip cookies and an apple, just so I could say I was eating healthy. I did find some milk in the vending machine, since I was supposed to be drinking it every day.

It was just after two-thirty when the doctor came out. That

made it six and a half hours, which was about right. He corralled us into a small room right off the waiting room and told us to have a seat.

"The tumor was large," he began. "I found the area that was causing the seizures and got that taken care of. Then, as I told you how these tumors are, it was deeply rooted in her brain. I was removing as much as I could to give her the best chance with radiation, but what we didn't know, what the scans didn't show, it had already spread into her hypothalamus. Her body temperature shot up and we couldn't get it under control. We tried everything we possibly could. I am terribly sorry to tell you, but she didn't make it."

FIFTY-TWO

SYLVIE

WHAT WAS HE SAYING? "SHE DIDN'T MAKE IT? AS IN THE surgery?" I asked incredulously.

"That's right. When her temperature rose, we tried everything we could to bring it down, but everything we tried failed."

"I don't understand." And I didn't. What did one thing have to do with the other?

"The hypothalamus controls many of the body's functions, such as temperature, and the tumor had infiltrated it. As we were removing one of the roots as I described, something must have triggered the section of the tumor in the hypothalamus and that's what we speculate made it rise." He rubbed his face and then neck, as though he was as baffled by this as we were.

"Are you saying she died?" Piper asked, her voice rising.

"I am so sorry, but yes."

Everyone was stone-faced. My heart fell to my gut as I held a hand to my chest. Everything went instantly numb for a second, and my head swam. I'd had bad premonitions about it, but not this way. I thought if she'd died, it would be days later.

Evan held my hand and asked, "Sylvie, are you feeling all right?"

I huffed out a breath, but it didn't help. "Can't breathe."

"Inhale slowly," Evan said. "Now exhale."

Logically, I understood this, but my heart was tripping in my chest and I was beginning to black out.

I heard a chair scraping and then a second later, an oxygen mask was covering my face. "Breathe normally." Dr. Casey's voice came to me.

It wasn't helping. I was hyperventilating. The oxygen was only making it worse. Now my fingers tingled too. I pulled the mask off and said, "Paper bag."

I heard Evan say, "She's hyperventilating."

A paper bag materialized over my mouth and I breathed into it. After several long slow breaths, things eventually evened out. Then I burst into tears. Loud ugly ones.

My mom, the one I used to tell everything to, was forever gone from this world. I would never see or talk to her again. Or share laughs with, or hold her hand. And she would miss the birth of her first grandchild and never see Evan and me get married. Everyone huddled around me as my heart and soul ruptured. I had to pull it together for Dad. This was his time to mourn, not mine. I sought Evan's hand and tightened my grip on it. Somehow, I drew from his strength.

When I was able to speak, I apologized to the doctor, who was still with us.

"Don't be sorry. She was your mother." Then Dr. Casey asked, "Do you want to see her?"

"Yes," I immediately blurted out.

Reynolds asked quietly, "How does she look?"

He gently said, "She has a large bandage on her head, but otherwise, very peaceful."

"Is she bloody?" Piper wanted to know.

"Not at all."

"Okay then." Piper's voice shook.

"Dad?" I asked.

"Yes, of course."

"Where is she?" I wanted to know.

Dr. Casey said, "She's still in the surgical suite. I can take you there now."

We followed him over and when we walked in through the physician's entrance, everyone sort of bowed their heads to us. He took us into the room where she was. There were all kinds of equipment scattered about, but everything had been cleaned up and she had nothing attached to her, no wires or IVs. She only had the large bandage wrapped around her head as he'd indicated. She looked very peaceful lying there. No stress lines on her forehead, none around her eyes or mouth for that matter.

"I'll leave you now and please, stay as long as you'd like. There are nurses outside if you need anything and, Mr. West, you'll have to fill out paperwork for the hospital."

"Thank you, Dr. Casey." I shook his hand because Dad seemed to be incapable of anything.

He went to Mom, wrapped his arms around her, and laid his head on her chest. I couldn't watch, because it broke my heart all over again to see it. Evan held me as my sisters sobbed. I held out one arm and they came to us. We stood in a circle and clung to each other. I was completely lost and didn't know what to do. The moment was endless as we stood together. Time passed, only none of us seemed to be aware of it.

A nurse peeked her head in and caught our attention. By our, I mean my sisters and me.

"I'm sorry to disturb you, but may I have a word with you?"

We walked out and she said, "I hated to interrupt, but these are the forms Dr. Casey may have mentioned. The hospital will need to get these filled out before you leave. I can go through them with you, if you'd like. We can fill them out together and then have your father sign, to make it easier on him."

"That sounds best. Piper, Reynolds, why don't you stay with him and I'll take care of this."

They did and the nurse, Evan, and I went to a lounge where we sat and went through them. It was simple enough and we filled them out in no time. There was the question of an autopsy, and I opted out of it since we knew how she died. I also knew which funeral home Dad preferred because there was only one near us, so I put that on the form. The hospital would take care of calling them.

We were walking out when Dr. Casey came in. "How's your father?"

"He's still in there. I'm not sure how I'm going to get him to leave."

"Shall I have a word with him?"

"That's very kind of you, but I'll handle it."

"Ms. West, can I say something?"

"Sure."

"Your mother didn't suffer. Her tumor was large and in the worst possible location, and I don't mean this to sound harsh, but the way this ended may have possibly been a blessing. I know it's not what you wanted and it's such a shock, but maybe it will help you and your family cope with your loss."

"Thanks, but I won't tell my dad that for a while."

"I understand."

I sank against Evan when we were alone. "I feel slightly relieved, even though I hate she's gone. It sounds terrible but to see her suffer everyday...I'm not sure how Dad would've handled that."

"Dr. Casey was right. Had it been me, I would've wanted to go like your mom."

When I checked the clock, I couldn't believe it was after five. "We should probably get Dad out of there."

We walked back in and he was now standing, holding Mom's hand.

"Dad? How are you?" I asked.

"It'll be a long time before I'm okay."

We circled around him and put our hands over his. "I filled out the hospital forms, so all you need to do is sign them."

"Thank you, honey. What would I do without you girls?"

"You don't have to worry about that Dad, because we're here," Piper said, putting an arm around him.

"I have an idea. Instead of going home tonight, why don't we all go back to Evan's and have one of Rita's good home-cooked meals? Then we can get a good night's sleep and head home in the morning." I glanced at everyone, waiting for their responses.

Piper and Reynolds were in. Dad, not so much.

"I don't know, Syll. I think I want to go home."

"Come on, Dad. When was the last time you hung out with us?" Reynolds asked.

"Christmas," he said, "and it wasn't very good."

"Right. Mom would want us to be together now. You know in your heart I'm right," Reynolds said.

"Yeah, Dad," Piper added.

"I agree," I said.

"Okay. You girls win. But I want to say goodbye one last time to my wife."

We said our goodbyes amidst an ocean of tears and left Dad alone. He joined us a few minutes later, signed the forms, and we headed to Evan's.

FIFTY-THREE
EVAN

Rita didn't have much warning, but she'd anticipated we were coming. She had plenty of things prepared for us. There was lasagna, salad, meatballs, another huge cake, and of course cookies. She'd made up a charcuterie platter as well.

"I need a Rita in my life," Piper said.

"Right? She's amazing," Sylvie said.

"I confess. She spoils me to death," I said, stuffing my mouth with cheese. "John, may I get you something to drink? Wine, beer, something stronger?"

"Stronger, please."

We went to the bar and I let him choose what he wanted, which ended up being a nice bourbon, and I poured him three fingers, straight.

"Thanks." He took a long sip and said, "This is excellent."

"Glad you like it. Help yourself to anything in here."

Then he glanced around and said, "Nice place you have here."

"Thanks again. Make yourself at home and take a look around if you want." I wanted him to feel welcome. "I believe Sylvie put your things in one of the guest rooms yesterday."

"Thank you, Evan. I really appreciate everything you've done."

"John, I love your daughter. And because of that, her family is my family. I'd do anything for you."

He rubbed his face, swallowed several times and it appeared he was trying not to cry.

"How about I show you around?" I offered, hoping to change the subject.

He nodded so off we went. I ended the tour with his room, showing him where everything was in the bathroom. "If you want a shower or anything, feel free. I know one thing Sylvie will insist on and that's you eat something. So before you decide to hide out in here, if that's what you want, you'd probably better get a bite first."

"You're right. She can be pretty adamant about things when she sets her mind to them."

"Yes, sir, I've already figured that out."

He sized me up and down, then asked, "I know you can take care of her financially, but I'm not concerned about that. The only thing I want for my daughters is they find the kind of love I had for their mother. If you can provide that, I'll be a happy man."

"I love Sylvie with all my heart. I'd walk on broken glass for her. Or a bed of nails, or hot coals..."

"Okay, you don't have to go that far." He half-chuckled. "I just don't want this marriage ending in divorce. The rich and famous have a way of tossing their wives aside for a younger, newer version of the old one."

"I understand why you feel that way, but can I say I don't come from that kind of background? My family is like yours. My parents have been married for almost forty years and I want the exact kind of marriage they have, or that you had. And so does Sylvie."

"I appreciate that. Can you do me a favor? Can you two please get married before that baby arrives?"

"John, I would gladly marry Sylvie, but she wants to wait a little."

"I'm going to kill her. That baby needs a father. Her mother will die—" He crumbled at his own words. "Jesus, it's so hard to believe."

"Please, sit." I motioned toward the bed and we both sat. "Can I tell you something and I may be stepping over the line?"

"Yeah, what is it?"

"If I had been the one with that tumor, I would've wanted to go the way Cindy did. I know it was unexpected, but the suffering would've been...well, let's say going under anesthesia would've been my preference."

"I hadn't really thought of that. I mean I had, because she just fell asleep and didn't wake up, and she's in a much better place now, but the suffering, yeah, it would've been awful. I read so much about brain tumors, I prayed every night for her not to have that particular one."

"I don't even know much about them and I'm not sure I want to."

"No, son, you don't."

Sylvie walked in just then and said, "Hey you two. I wondered where you went."

"I gave him the tour and showed him his room."

"Dad, you're not trying to sneak off without dinner, are you?"

"I told you," I said.

Sylvie crossed her arms and asked, "What did you tell him?"

"Only that you'd insist on him eating."

"That's right. Come on." She took his hand and off we went to chow down on Rita's food.

The group congregated in the living room after dinner and told stories about Cindy when the girls were growing up.

"Dad, you wouldn't believe how Mom covered for us, especially when it came to boys," Reynolds said.

"You think I didn't know? She always told me, but after the fact. That woman couldn't keep anything from me."

They laughed and cried about all sorts of things, but mostly how warm and loving their mother and wife was.

"Mom tried to act tough, and in the end, when her personality changed, I kept thinking back to how she used to be and couldn't figure out what was going on." Sylvie let out a sob. "I was so hoping she'd be here to see the baby when it comes."

"Oh, honey, that would've been her greatest moment too. You have to know that," John said.

"I do. Dad, you're going to have to be Gramms and Gramps all rolled into one."

"Sylls, you're forgetting something."

"What's that?"

"Your fiancé has two parents who, I imagine, will be thrilled when they discover they have a grandchild on the way."

She nodded, but I knew it was different for a woman. They usually had a special bond with their mothers, and it would be difficult for her.

Piper, who was looking rather awkward during this exchange, said, "I hate to change the subject, but what are we going to do about Mom's funeral?"

John instantly deflated. He looked exhausted, I wanted to tell him I'd handle things, but it wasn't my place.

"I'll call them in the morning. I want it to be at the church. Cindy became very involved there over the last several years."

"Have you called the priest, Dad?"

"Not yet. I'll do that in the morning as well."

Sylvie was sitting the closest to him, so she reached for his hand. "Do you think we should have the wake the evening before and the funeral the following morning?"

"That sounds fine. We can receive guests in the church hall afterward."

I made a suggestion. "Why don't I call Paige to see if she and Rick can handle the food and drinks."

"Evan, that's a great idea. They go to the same church and will know how many people to figure for." Sylvie mouthed a thank you to me.

"I feel so empty inside," John said.

Piper went over to him and sat on the floor by his legs. "Oh, Dad. So do I." She laid her head on his knee.

I was totally helpless and had no idea what to do. My phone rang, startling everyone.

"Sorry. I forgot to mute the darn thing." I checked it and said, "It's Pearson. Do you want me to say anything?"

"It's fine. Dad, you should call Uncle Rick," Sylvie said.

"You're right. I hadn't thought of it. I'll call him now."

I answered the phone while John went into the other room to call his brother. Then I relayed the terrible news. Pearson's reaction was what one could expect.

"Oh, man, I don't even know what to say. I wondered why we hadn't heard from anyone. I just figured you were wrapped up in everything that was going on, but certainly not this."

"Yeah, it's been really rough on everyone. We're all sort of in shock over it." I walked into the kitchen and continued talking, telling him what the doctor said about how bad the tumor had been.

"I'm really sorry. Maybe it was for the best, as bad as that sounds."

"I agree. It would've been hell on her had she made it."

"Can I talk to Sylvie?"

"Yeah, give me a sec." I took the phone to her and they spoke for a few minutes. When they were finished, she handed it back to me.

"Hey, I'll be in touch with funeral arrangements."

"Sure thing and if there's anything the family needs, let me know."

"Actually, I'm going to call your mom to see if she'd mind handling the food after the funeral. I'll handle the bill, of course. But they want it at the church hall after the service."

"I can talk to her, if you want."

"Fine, but I'll call her too."

"Sounds good. Talk to you tomorrow."

My next call was to my parents. Mom couldn't believe it. I

hadn't told her about the surgery because I expected to call her afterward.

"I can't imagine your poor Sylvie and her family. What can I do?"

"Mom, I'm lost. I've never been in this situation."

"Be there for her, son. That's about it. You can also handle some of the arrangements, to take the burden off the family."

"Paige will do the food. What else is there?"

"Flowers," Mom reminded me. "I can take care of that if you let me know what they want."

"Okay. I'll call you tomorrow after they visit the funeral home."

"Good. Talk to you then. I love you, Evan."

"Love you too, Mom."

In the morning, we left for Sylvie's place while her Dad went home and so did her sisters. We met everyone at the funeral home to set everything up. It was suggested we do a combination wake and funeral on the same day since tomorrow was New Year's Eve and the church would be occupied with services on the morning of New Year's Day. John decided that would be best instead of postponing it for afterward. We had been so wrapped up in everything, none of us had remembered about the holiday.

When we were driving home, I asked Sylvie, "There's something I'd like to do if you're okay with it. Would it be okay if we told my parents about the pregnancy?"

FIFTY-FOUR

SYLVIE

As soon as I heard those words, I started wailing. It was completely unreasonable, but all I could think of was Mom and that I never got the chance to tell her. The crushing pain of her loss was too much. Evan tried his best to calm me, and none of this was his fault. I wasn't angry. It was just that my guts had been ripped out because Mom had passed way before her time. It wasn't fair. Why did it have to be her? The world is full of evil people. Why couldn't it have been one of them who had a giant tumor in their brain?

We made it to my townhouse and Evan turned off the car. "Had I known this would upset you so much, I would never have brought it up."

"It's not that. I'm just so damn miserable over Mom and that we never were able to tell her." Only it didn't sound like that. It came out like a bunch of garbled words that he couldn't understand.

He carried me inside and waited until I was able to speak.

"She always talked about being a grandmother—the kind who would spoil the kids to pieces so when we came to pick them up, they'd be little stinkers. Only she never got that chance."

It reminded me of all the days and nights I spent with my grandmother and made me sad to think my button wouldn't have those special times. I hoped Evan's mom would be that same kind of grandmother...the kind that read stories, made cookies, took you to the zoo, and did all sorts of fun things.

"Babe, I'm so sorry, but I don't know what to say or do for you right now. I'm at a loss."

"There's nothing you can do."

"One thing though, our baby will give your father something to focus on. Maybe it'll help him deal with the loss of your mom."

I shrugged. "I hope so." I wiped my eyes and face for the umpteenth time. "God, Evan, do you think I'll ever stop crying? This is exhausting."

"You will, but you've just lost your mother. Grief is an ongoing process."

As a counselor, I realized that. Only it was different when you were the one who was experiencing it.

I rested my head on his shoulder. "True. I'm sorry for that reaction. It had nothing to do with your parents knowing about button. And of course we should tell them."

He smoothed my shirt, which had bunched up around me. "I didn't think it would be right for everyone in your family knowing and—"

I quickly cut him off. "You're exactly right. They absolutely should know. How do you think they'll react?"

He shrugged. "I'm not really sure."

"You don't think they'll see me as a gold digger who trapped you, do you?"

He tucked my hair behind my ear and smiled. "If they do, I'll tell them how you avoided me for days, wouldn't talk to me, and how I had to beg you for a date."

"Don't you dare! They'll hate me."

"Sylvie, don't worry. My parents have only wanted me to be happy. They'll be fine with this."

His eyes didn't betray his words, so I believed him.

"Let me splash some cold water on my face and get rid of my raccoon eyes. Then we can go."

"Only if you're sure."

"I'm sure."

Walking into the Thomas home was like walking into a warm blanket. First, Evan's mom wrapped her arms around me and just held me, while telling me how sorry she was. No surprise, I bawled again. When she released me, his dad did the same. Evan handed me a bunch of tissues. My nose was raw already. I wondered how it would hold up for another few days.

Evan's mom, Anna, said, "Darling, all the flowers have been ordered."

My head snapped to attention. Flowers! Shit, I'd totally forgotten. "Anna, you ordered flowers. I need to do that."

"No, I've taken care of it for everyone. Evan and I talked yesterday, and I told him I would. I hope you don't mind. The florist will call the funeral home to see where they should be sent."

The woman was a blessing. "How can I thank you? I don't know where my head was."

Evan put his arm over my shoulders. "Babe, you've been preoccupied with other things. Mom offered and I took her up on it. I forgot to tell you."

"You don't know how much I appreciate it. I need to call Dad, just in case." I quickly called him, and he'd forgotten too.

"Syll, can you ask her what she sent? Your mother loved roses so..."

"Hang on." I grabbed Anna's attention. "Anna, did you by any chance send roses from my dad."

"Yes, I called the funeral home and they said there would be no casket because you were doing cremation, so I ordered a lovely huge spray of red and white roses from him. I hope that's okay."

"Did you hear, Dad?"

"Thank her for me, will you?"

I ended the call, promising to do just that. "Dad was most appreciative."

Then I cried... again, dammit.

Evan explained to his parents about the funeral arrangements.

Then Greg asked, "Sylvie, can I get you a good stiff drink?"

Shit, here it goes. I glanced at Evan, and he reached for my hand.

"Dad, Mom, we have news."

"News? What news?" Anna asked with a furrowed brow.

"Sylvie and I are going to be parents." Evan pulled me to his side as he grinned.

"Parents?"

"I'm pregnant," I said. Then broke into tears. Jesus, I was so lame.

"Mom, Dad, she's crying because she never got a chance to tell her mom before...well you know."

"Oh, you poor dear." Anna came over and drew me to the couch to sit. "Now, now, things will work out just fine."

"Imagine that, a baby," Greg said, sounding like the average man. "Can I have a word, son?"

"Dad, anything you have to say can be said in front of Sylvie."

Greg eyed me and then Evan. He appeared reluctant at first, but then spoke. "Will you two be getting married?"

"Eventually," Evan said.

"Son, you know that's not the responsible thing to do." His tone carried a warning. He sounded like my dad.

"Dad, it's our decision."

It really wasn't. It was mine. Evan would marry me in a second if I'd consent.

"Greg, that's not your business," Anna said.

"And speaking of business, will you have her sign a prenup when you do get married?"

Evan's jaw snapped shut as his lips pressed into a thin line.

His posture stiffened like rebar. He was not pleased with that question, and I'd never given a prenup a thought. Yeah, I knew he was loaded, but as for how much, it was anyone's guess.

"Dad, you have crossed the line." Ooh, I'd never heard him use that tone around me.

"Have I?"

"Yes, you have. I built my businesses and wealth on my own and fully intend to disburse *my* money the way I want."

This was a battle of the wills, so I stepped in. "Greg, I'd like to say something. When Evan and I started dating, I didn't know who he was or what he did. To be honest, his money intimidated me and still does. I don't really have an interest in it."

"Sylvie, I'm sorry. You say that now, but when you start living the life, I'm pretty damn sure your mind will change."

"Dad!" Evan snapped.

I raised a hand to stop him. "Maybe it will, maybe it won't. But I fell in love with Evan, not his money. You can believe what you want. I didn't come here to argue that point. If Evan wants me to sign a prenup, I will. But all we wanted to do today was share with you our wonderful news, not argue about a wedding or money details. We are very excited about our baby and hoped you would be too. And Anna, now that our little button will only have one grandmother, we hope you will love her enough for two." I wiped the unending supply of tears from my face.

Greg looked as though I'd punched him in the gut and Evan only grinned. Score one for Sylvie...maybe.

FIFTY-FIVE
EVAN

Sylvie was bone-tired. Between the pregnancy, her mother's death, and the funeral today, I was praying she'd hold up. I didn't want to wake her, but time was running out. We had to be at the church at ten and she had to shower and eat.

"Babe." I nuzzled her neck.

"No. I'm not ready."

"I know. I didn't want to wake you, but it's already eight thirty."

"Can I skip today? I'm out of tears," she groaned.

"I wish you could, but you'd hate yourself."

She rolled over and rubbed her eyes. "These have been the worst days ever."

"Hey, I was thinking, since we won't get to celebrate New Year's, do you think your family would like to go to the house in Vail for a few days to get away? I have to work the first part of the week to catch up, but what about the end of the week? It would do everyone some good."

A slow smile appeared on her face. "That's very kind of you. We can make them go and yes, I think it would do everyone some good to get away. None of us are what you call great skiers, but what the heck."

Glad I was able to make her a tiny bit happy on this terrible day, I helped her out of bed and sent her off to shower, while I made coffee. I'd be sure she'd eat a big breakfast before we left for the church.

On the way, she surprised me with her statement.

"Evan, I was serious about what I said last night. I'll sign a prenup if you want, as long as there's a provision in it to take care of the baby. I don't care about your money for myself."

"Sylvie, you're not signing any prenup. You and I are forever, not just for a year, or even twenty. And I mean that."

"How do you know you won't find someone else when I get old and ugly?"

The fact she said that hurt. I took her hand in mine and kissed it. "One, you'll never be old and ugly to me. Two, when you get old, so will I. We're in this thing called life together. We're partners, remember?"

"Sure, but I'm going to get super fat with button, you know."

"It's not fat, it's button and I can't wait to see you that way."

"You're just saying that so I won't cry again."

"No, I'm not. Seeing you with your belly poked out and our baby in there excites me."

Her eyes burned into my cheek as I drove. I knew she didn't believe me, but it was true. I was thrilled with this pregnancy and couldn't wait to see our baby grow.

THE WAKE and funeral were exhausting, even for me, and I didn't know nearly the number of people Sylvie did. It seemed everyone in town came out to pay their respects. The service was lovely. The priest gave a short eulogy, but John was the one who brought everyone to their knees.

The girls tried to talk him out of it, but he insisted. "Cindy was my other half and this is my send off to her," he said.

They wouldn't have been able to stop him no matter what.

He'd made up his mind. When he eulogized his wife, love poured from the very depths of him. I could barely blink the entire time. I'd never thought of myself as a particularly emotional man, and yet as I listened to him speak of Cindy, tell how much he would miss her company every day, my face was as wet as Sylvie's.

From the time they'd met, he knew she was his. I felt so many similarities in my relationship with Sylvie, it was uncanny. He spoke about her love for her family, her strength, kindness of spirit, how she saw the good in everyone, and of her willingness to help others. Sylvie was like her mother and I wished I'd gotten to know her, the real Cindy.

His final words were, "The day you left me, Cindy, my heart cracked in two. One half will always be missing because it went to heaven to be with you."

Jesus, the man nearly broke me and poor Sylvie and her sisters. They sobbed like babies.

I ran out of tissues, but thankfully there was a box at the end of the pew we sat in. I handed her some more and then took some for myself. She passed the box down to her sisters. Her dad came and sat down with us and the priest concluded the service. We then proceeded to the church hall for the reception.

Paige and my mom were there, along with the caterer, having helped set it all up. I was hoping this didn't last long. But initially, the crush of people that flowed in had me worried. Sylvie looked like she was ready to collapse.

"Why don't you have a seat over there?" I suggested. "You look weary."

"It's not just that. I'm all cried out, Evan. I just want to stop shedding tears."

I hugged her and let her lean on me for a minute. Rose found us and asked her how she was holding up.

"Look at my eyes. I look like I have severe allergies," Sylvie answered.

"Leeanne is here. She mentioned something about you taking a couple of weeks off," Rose said.

About that time, a woman I hadn't met came charging up to Sylvie and pulled her into a fierce embrace. "My sweet, sweet Sylvie. I am so sorry for you." She kept her grip on her shoulders but shifted slightly and in a bit of a scolding tone said, "Where is your medallion? My darling, this is when you need your essential oils the most."

"Leeanne, I can barely remember to put my shoes on."

"And who is this charmer?" She directed her gaze at me.

"Leeanne, meet Evan, my significant other. You seem to keep missing him when he shows up at work."

"What a pleasure to meet you, Evan."

"Likewise." I shook her hand.

"You must make sure Sylvie wears her essential oil medallion. It will calm her and keep her on an even keel."

"Yes, ma'am, I certainly will." I'd do anything to help her emotional state.

Then she put an arm around my girl, and said, "Sylvie, I believe you should take two weeks leave. This has been an utterly difficult time for you. Rose has kept me up to date and I don't want you to get overly stressed, as though you aren't already. But the two weeks should help somewhat. We both know it will take a long time before your heart will begin to heal, but at least you won't have to counsel others while you need it yourself."

"That's very thoughtful of you. I appreciate it Leeanne."

"And Evan, will you please make sure she is well pampered?"

"I will do my best, ma'am." She was a take-charge woman. But I liked that she thought of Sylvie and not just of her business.

"Well, now that we have that settled, I'm going to find your father and give him my regards before I leave. Please call me if you need anything at all." She hugged Sylvie again and was off.

Rose took Sylvie's hand and said, "She's been so worried about you."

"That's very kind of her," Sylvie answered.

The two women chatted while I wandered off to look for Pearson. He was with Grey so we talked for a while. Then I found Mom and thanked her and Paige again for all their help. It was a good thing we put them in charge of the food because by the time everyone left, mostly everything was gone. Paige had called it right.

It was around three when we were able to leave, and a suggestion was made that we all go out to lunch. I was hungry and bet Sylvie was too. We hadn't eaten since breakfast because we talked the entire time during the reception. Everyone agreed, so Sylvie's family, my parents, along with Rick, Paige, and the entire West clan went to eat. There were fifteen of us, so we called around for a quick reservation and were lucky to get one at a nearby restaurant.

We'd driven Sylvie's SUV over to the church, so her family piled into our car and we drove over together.

I was driving when Piper said, "I love your car, Evan."

Sylvie half-smiled and said, "Thank you."

"This is yours?"

"It was my Christmas present from Evan."

Her dad whistled. "Nice gift."

"Isn't it, Dad?"

"It sure is."

"You'll have to test drive it."

"Gah, I wish I could find an Evan," Piper said.

"Too bad he doesn't have two brothers," Reynolds added.

"Guys, I'm right here," I reminded them.

They didn't care.

"We know. We'd still like it if you came from a bigger family." It was Reynolds who spoke.

"Tell that to my mom when we get to the restaurant."

"Nah, it's too late now."

We pulled in, they got out, and Reynolds said, "When we drove this car home from the hospital that night, we were talking about how much we liked it, but damn, Sylvie, we didn't know it was yours."

"Yeah. Had we known, we'd have kept it a few days," Piper said.

"All right, you two. Enough lusting over my car."

"What else can we lust over? Men are in short supply these days."

"You won't find one until you stop looking. That's your big sister's advice."

"Yeah, yeah, yeah." The two girls wandered ahead of us.

"Is that true?" I asked Sylvie.

"Sure is. I figured I'd never find anyone, until that night. Or should I say the morning I woke up with you, embarrassed out of my mind."

"Best night ever."

"Most indecent night ever."

"How would you know? You can't remember it."

"I sure felt the effects of it though."

Her grin got to me and had my cock trying to burst out of my pants. Good thing I had on a suit coat and an overcoat since it was cold outside.

What a woman she was.

FIFTY-SIX
SYLVIE

THE FOLLOWING FRIDAY EVENING, PIPER, REYNOLDS, DAD, Rose, Pearson, Evan, and I boarded his private jet and headed to Vail for our getaway. Once we stepped aboard, Piper and Reynolds went crazy. They started in again on how they wished Evan had two brothers.

"If you two keep going on about this the whole trip, we're leaving you here," Dad said. "You girls are too boy crazy. Your mother worried that Sylvie didn't care enough about them and I worry that you two are too fixated on them."

"Don't worry, Dad, they'll grow out of it. I did."

"It can't happen fast enough for me," he said.

Piper and Reynolds took their seats and pouted, both appropriately chastised. Rose and I chuckled behind their backs.

"Remember when we were like that a couple of years ago?"

"You mean you," Rose said. "After my ex, I was never man-crazy. In fact, I thought about women for a while, but then realized that would never happen. Thank God for Pearson. Too bad he had to be an addict for us to meet, though."

"God has strange ways sometimes. It actually brought Evan and me together."

Rose took my hand and said, "I'm so happy for you two. Even Pearson notices a huge difference in Evan."

"Really?"

"Yeah."

Then I told her about the way Evan's Dad reacted to the pregnancy and about the prenup.

"That isn't surprising. If he were my son, I'd do the same," she said.

"So would I and the money isn't what interested me in him anyway. I had no idea he even had any."

Rose laughed. "To think we'd be flying out to Vail in his plane, right?"

"I know. I can't wait to see his place. But I'm a little worried about my skiing."

"Hey, I'm there with you. We'll be bunny hopping."

Evan and Pearson took their seats across from us and Evan asked, "What are you two gossiping about?"

"Rose and I were just discussing the probability of us crashing on the slopes."

"You'd better not. No crashing for you or the button."

"Button?" Pearson asked.

"That's what we call the baby," Evan said.

Pearson gave him one of those man-to-man looks that said, *you are totally whipped, dude.*

"Hey, just wait until Rose gets pregnant," Evan said.

"Yeah, okay," Pearson said.

The pilot came out and introduced himself to us, greeted me again, and then told us all to buckle up for takeoff. Our flight attendant this time was Libby, who was maybe in her mid-forties. She'd already handed out drinks and said as soon as we were airborne, she'd serve our dinner.

It was a smooth flight and after we ate a delicious dinner of chicken or seafood fettuccine Alfredo, salad, bread, cheese, fruit, and dessert, we all crashed.

It was close to midnight when we landed, but we gained two

hours, so it was only ten o'clock. The nap helped. I'd actually went back to the bed to sleep, much to the jealousy of the others.

There was a large van waiting to pick us up and drive us to Evan's house, which was a forty-minute ride away. When we arrived, the housekeepers, a husband and wife team, were up and waiting for us. They welcomed us with a light snack and beverages, and Evan spoke to them awhile. They lived on the property in the caretaker's house, so they left shortly after.

Evan gave us a tour, and the house was amazing. In the center of it was a gigantic living area that had a large stone fireplace. There were four couches placed around it and a huge—I mean huge—flat screen above the fireplace. Off the living area was the kitchen and then down a hall was the master suite. It was unbelievable, with one wall being entirely glass. Evan explained that it overlooked the mountains, but you couldn't see now since it was dark.

The living room also had a glass wall, only it was broken up because it was made entirely of French doors that opened out onto a massive deck, with a round fireplace and a gigantic hot tub. Again, we'd be able to see it in the morning.

Upstairs were all the ensuite guest rooms, all eight of them. The house was awesome.

There was also a really cool room above the garage that had been transformed into a media room. It held a screen, and twenty-four recliner seats to watch your favorite movie on the big screen. There was even a genuine popcorn machine in there.

"I'm not sure I'll even want to ski," I said.

"Babe, you can do anything you want."

My dad just kept spinning around, staring at everything in awe. I was happy he was here.

"Guys, as much as I'd like to hang out, I'm hitting the sack. The button is still draining my energy and if I'm going to do any skiing tomorrow, I need my rest."

Evan walked me to our room and tucked me in after I brushed my teeth and washed my face.

"I'll be in as soon as everyone's settled."

"You don't have to. Enjoy your time with Pearson and my dad. This is your vacation too."

"I love you."

"Love you too."

I didn't even hear him come to bed, When I woke up, I was lying across his chest, and he was sound asleep. The sun was up, but I only knew because the room was a bit lighter. I had to use the bathroom, so I crept out of bed, but when I got back, Evan was awake.

"Good morning, sexy," he said.

I was naked and looked a mess. "Good morning to you. Can I look out the window? Will it bother you?"

"Of course not."

I rushed over to peek out and sucked in my breath at the view. Jagged mountains rose up before me and their majestic beauty nearly overwhelmed me.

"Oh, Evan! This is fantastic. Let's get married here."

"Now?"

I laughed. "No, not now. When the snow melts and we can do it on the deck."

He was behind me and said, "You surprise me."

"Why?"

"I thought you'd want to get married on the beach at Canouan."

"So did I, until I saw this. This magnificence can't be outdone. And I remember you said something about selling so let's do it before then."

"Sylvie, I'll keep this place forever if you love it this much."

I faced him, saying, "Your generosity, your kindness is extraordinary. But as much as I love this, I also want your place to be something you love too. Skiing is a passion of yours so you should have a place somewhere that you love. And you can get one with views that are like this, can't you?"

"I suppose. But your happiness means more than anything to me. I can always buy another place and if you're not happy, we'll keep both. I can rent this one in the winter, and we'll come here in the summer."

"You're crazy, but I love crazy."

We dressed and went to the kitchen to get the coffee on. Sam and Patty Garrett—the caretakers— would be in shortly. Patty would make breakfast for us before we headed for the slopes.

Everyone trickled into the kitchen for coffee and Patty was cooking up a storm. Sam had started a roaring fire and we'd opened the curtains to see a perfect blue sky day for the skiing.

The ski rental company had dropped everyone's skis and boots off the day before and our lift tickets had been purchased so all we had to do was show up.

The plan was to eat, get dressed, and go. Sam dropped us off near the bridge in Vail village, closest to the lifts with the most green runs for beginners. You couldn't drive in the actual village, so we'd have to do a bit of walking. Evan carried my skis. We would leave them in a locker tonight so we wouldn't have to carry them back and forth. Walking in the ski boots wasn't the greatest, but it wasn't that bad, either.

Piper and Reynolds were hilarious as they did dances on the street, and then Reynolds busted her ass. I had it on video.

"Don't you dare post that, Syll."

"Oh, it's going straight to Instagram. This is priceless."

"Pleeeasssse," she begged.

"Ok. I won't, under one condition. You stop talking about men."

"Yes, I promise."

Evan said, "Excellent move, wise one."

"Thanks."

We got to the gondola, which we rode and then transferred

to another lift. "Are you sure you're not taking me on a difficult run?"

"I would never do that to you. These are the runs the instructors use."

"Okay." I looked a bit leery, until I saw all the green run signs.

We skied down to signs and he let me choose which run to do. Then off we went with the others behind us. It was a blast. The skiing out here was so much better than where I had learned, that I was actually a much better skier than I'd thought.

We stopped at the bottom and Evan said, "You did great. I think a couple more on this and you could easily handle a blue."

"You think?"

"Sure. The groomed blues are great. We can try. If you're not comfortable, we can stay on the greens."

"Fine, but I want you to do whatever you want. You don't have to stay with me all day."

"Today, I'm yours. Tomorrow, Pearson and I will go off on our own."

The day ended for me around one. I was worn out. My muscles weren't used to this, so Evan was the one who suggested I call it a day, because he said that's when injuries occur. All the girls went in. Dad stayed and skied the blues, while Evan and Pearson did the expert runs.

Sam drove us home and I stared at the steam rising out of the hot tub. I gazed at it longingly, wanting to get in.

"Ma'am, you can get in. I've turned it on and it's ready." Patty must've noticed me eyeing the thing.

"Thank you, but I can't. I don't know if Evan has told you, but I'm pregnant and you're not supposed to use hot tubs during your early stages."

"Yes, he did, and I was unaware of that. I guess a hot shower will have to suffice. How about a nice cup of tea then?"

"That would be nice. Not the hot tub though." I snorted.

She looked at me, her eyes popping out. "No, I suppose not."

"Sorry, I snort when I laugh. It's kind of a family trait. I'm going to take that shower now." She probably thinks I'm a ding-a-ling.

When I got dressed and into the kitchen, a tray of cookies, cheese, crackers, and fruit were on the island, along with a large pot of tea, coffee, and everything to go along with it. I poured myself a mug of coffee and grabbed a cookie. The others joined me and we sat around the fire. I soon grew sleepy so I went to nap.

Evan woke me up when he came to shower. "What time is it?"

He said, "Five."

I'd slept about two hours. "Wow. I conked out."

"Good for you." He kissed me. "The afternoon was awesome. We did some terrific runs. I'm going to shower."

Dinner that night was nothing but Evan and Pearson telling their stories of their crashes and burns. They'd taken some tumbles that made me tremble, but Evan assured me all was well.

"It worries me. What if you break your neck?"

"It would be my leg or ACL, if anything."

"And that's supposed to make me feel better?"

"Well yeah. Those aren't life-threatening."

True, but still. The thought of him with any injuries was horrible.

"Babe, do you want to wrap me up in bubble wrap?" He bit his lips, doing his best not to laugh.

"Yes. But use the big bubbles, not the little ones."

"Okay. I'm not sure it'll fit under my ski clothes, but I'll try."

That did get a smile out of me. "Just be careful."

"I am. We push ourselves, but we aren't stupid about it. The falls are funny and if you were with us, you'd get it."

"Falling into a...what did you call it? Oh yeah, a tree well. That's pretty serious. What if you'd been alone?" A tree well was where the snow had built up around the tree but the base of the tree was still visible with no snow and they could sometimes be up to six to eight feet in depth.

"I'd have called ski patrol with my cell phone."

He got me there.

"It's fine. I promise. I never ski in unpopulated areas or out of bounds when I'm alone."

"Out of bounds?"

"Forget I said that. We'll talk about it later."

One thing was sure, he was an excellent skier. They'd taken one of those cameras with them and videoed each other. We watched some of it and he was amazing. I wished I could ski like that.

The next few days flew by and before we knew it, we were boarding the plane for our return home. As everyone got onboard, they kept telling Evan how wonderful the trip had been.

"We ought to go back in the summer. People think of Vail only in the winter. You should see it in the summer. It's fantastic."

Piper raised her hand. "I'm in."

"I thought you were going to do your master's in the UK," I said.

Everyone turned to her and stared. Dad had a bemused expression on his face. Oops. I'd let the cat out of the bag that I hadn't known was a secret. Piper glared at me.

"I'm sorry," I mouthed.

"What's this about the UK?" Dad asked.

"I was going to tell you and Mom right after Christmas, but everything got in the way. I applied at Cambridge to their master's program. I got accepted and I'll be studying British eighteenth-century and romantic literature. It's a nine-month program and then I may go on to either get a doctorate or another Master of English Lit and that's a two-year program. Either way, I start in June."

"Congratulations on your acceptance, Piper," Evan said.

"Yes, congratulations." Dad looked sad. "Your mother would've been very proud of you. She loved literature of all kinds. This would've been excellent news for her."

"I know, Dad." Piper hugged Dad.

I said, "Well, I'm going to miss you because you won't be around to see the button." I purposely stuck my lower lip out.

"That's okay. I'll be on diaper duty for you," Reynolds volunteered.

"That's what you say now, but when it happens, I wonder if you'll stick to it."

"I'm on board, Syll. You can count on it," Dad said.

I was hoping he would be. I needed him as much as he needed me. Since Mom wouldn't be there, he would have to fill two pairs of shoes when that time came.

FIFTY-SEVEN

EVAN

Sylvie's doctor's appointment was this week. I was meeting her there, eager to see the ultrasound and to ask her doctor a private question. When Sylvie mentioned about getting married in Vail, the wheels started spinning. The button was due in early August, so I was wondering if she'd be safe to fly in early June. I would take our families out for a small wedding. That is if she'd agree.

The doctor came in and asked a series of questions. Then it was Sylvie's turn. Yes, being tired was perfectly normal. Yes, it would go away soon. Yes, having to pee a lot was normal too. And my God, did she ever pee a lot. The doctor said that would improve, then worsen as the baby grew. I figured by then, she'd have to attach a toilet to her. That would save her so much time.

Then the ultrasound began. I was mesmerized by the images. But I wasn't by that wand they stuck up Sylvie's vagina. I'd always thought they rubbed goo on your belly and went to town. Apparently, I was off base there.

As she moved the wand around, I turned my attention to the screen.

"What can you see?" Sylvie asked.

"I have no idea."

The doctor made a few adjustments and the nurse pointed.

"Hmm."

"What?" I asked.

"Hang on." She moved her wand around and I still couldn't tell what I was looking at. It was all fuzz to me. Then something finally came into focus. Only it wasn't what I expected as I squinted at the image.

"Is that what I think it is?" I asked.

She chuckled slightly. "Yes. Let me see if we can get a different view." After a little more wand moving, a better image came up. The nurse hit the keyboard and the doctor said, "Here we have it. I want an abdominal view too."

"What are you looking at?" Sylvie asked.

I held her hand and laughed. "It's amazing."

"What is?" she hollered, trying to sit up.

The doctor placed a hand on her belly, saying, "Relax, Sylvie. I'm going to take another view."

Now came the jelly on the stomach part.

The nurse was typing something on the machine and up popped another image. It was gray until two distinct images of babies appeared. The doctor smiled.

"Oh yeah," I yelled.

"What?" Sylvie asked.

"Babe, you have two buttons in there."

"WHAT?" Sylvie almost bolted off the exam table.

"Sylvie, hang on a minute," the doctor said.

"NO! How can that be? Why wasn't it there last time?"

"It was. Sometimes one can be obscured behind the other when they're so small, and your first ultrasound was early. Hang on a sec."

"There they are," the doctor said.

The nurse turned the machine so Sylvie could see.

"Oh, shit. Oh, fuck, fuck, fuck. What are we going to do, Evan?" she asked. "Sorry about the language."

I held her hand and said calmly, "We're going to have two buttons, instead of one."

"Twins. Oh, my God!"

"Hey, it'll be fine. We'll have help and this will give your dad plenty to do."

"Oh, man, will it ever."

We left the doctor's office, Sylvie still completely dazed and me happy as hell.

"Of course you're happy. You're not the one who's going to birth the two of them."

She was right. "Maybe talking to Marin and Millie will help."

"You mean they can tell me how they managed not to murder their husbands?"

God, I loved this woman. "Yep. They'll tell you. One hundred percent they'll tell you." The only disappointing thing for me was my plans to get married would have to wait until after the birth. When I spoke to the doctor, she said travel would be up in the air, no pun intended, because twins were too unpredictable and early births often happened as did bed rest.

"I have an idea. Let's have a celebration dinner and invite everyone to attend where we can announce it."

By this time, we were pulling up to the new house.

"Why are we here?"

"Because. I have a surprise for you."

We got out and walked inside, where some of the workers were painting. We'd decided to change some of the colors in a few of the rooms.

"Surprise?"

"Yeah, come on."

We went upstairs and before we got to our bedroom, I picked her up and carried her over the threshold.

"What's going on?" she asked, laughing.

"Look."

The sitting area had been painted a soft green, since we didn't know the sex of the baby, and the decorator had already added a few little nursery touches, such as pictures and an off white rocker that also swiveled.

"Aww, Evan! I love it already."

I set her down and she walked the space with the biggest smile that only made me grin too.

"Sandy wants you to pick one of the fabrics she's chosen for the curtains and all the coordinating accents. But you like the color?"

"It's perfect. Thank you!" She threw her arms around my neck and jumped up, wrapping her legs around me.

"You're welcome. By that reaction, I can't wait until our bed arrives. Now hang on." I walked her into one of the other bedrooms.

"Oh, it's my bed. You had it fixed." I put her down so she could inspect it. "It's like new."

"Are you pleased? I thought it turned out really well."

She examined it very closely and said, "I can't tell where it was broken."

"I couldn't either."

She ran and nearly knocked me over. "Thank you. You're the most wonderful man alive, except for the twin thing."

"Babe, I hate to break it to you, but the woman is responsible for twins, not the man. You're the one with the eggs."

"You would have to get all scientific on me. The closing is still set for Monday, right?"

"Yep. At four. Nice segue, by the way."

"I thought so. When does the rest of the furniture get here?"

I laughed. "Sandy said you've been hard to work with because you're so particular about the price of things."

Sylvie scowled. "I don't see the point of spending ten thousand dollars on a sofa when we're going to have *twins* running around with dirty little hands getting them filthy. All I told her was I think we should get a couple of those slipcovered ones where you could wash the covers and put them back on. In my opinion, I don't think she liked my idea because it means less commission for her."

"That's an excellent idea about the couches. I'll pass it on."

"Evan, why does it have to come from you, though? If she's supposed to listen to me, why can't she accept my decisions?"

Sandy wasn't letting Sylvie make decisions and that pissed me off. "You're absolutely right. I'm going to call her and tell her she is to defer to you on everything from this point on. No more calling me. If I want something, I'll call her, but other than that, every decision about this house comes from you."

"Are you serious?"

"I am. We confer about most things and you make total sense about the couches. It would be nice to have washable covers. I wasn't aware they even made those."

She laughed. "Yeah, they do. Great for little kids, now that we'll have insta-family. So back to my original question. When do you think we'll be able to move in?"

"As soon as all the furniture gets in."

"You know what? Why don't you let me make that call to Sandy?"

"I think you're right. You handle it. Tell her if she has any issues with dealing with you, we'll find a new decorator."

THREE WEEKS LATER, the second week of February on a Saturday, we finally made the house our new home. Sandy and Sylvie made up and worked well together as a team on everything from the furniture to paint, to window treatments and all those other things decorators do to add that special touch to a home. I had to say they did an extraordinary job because after the movers left, and everything was in its place, the house was perfect.

"It's much better than I could've imagined," Sylvie said.

"Me too, babe. I am very pleased with your womanly touch."

"My womanly touch, huh? Seems to me you haven't felt my womanly touch in a couple of days with all this stuff going on. I've missed you since we haven't slept together in what?"

"One night," I quickly answered, picking her up and carrying her upstairs.

"One night? Are you sure?"

"Positive."

"It seems like a month."

"More like a year, but it's only been a night." I'd gotten to our room, which looked gorgeous in its soft tones of what Sylvie called spa blue and cream, and I tossed her gently on the bed. Then I kissed her, softly at first. But she quickly deepened the kiss, taking more from me than I was giving. I went along, sliding my hands up her shirt, freeing one of her breasts. I was just about to suck on one of her sensitive nipples when the door-bell rang.

"Aw, shit," she groaned.

"Let's ignore it."

"Okay."

My lips puckered around her nipple and I sucked as she moaned, and the doorbell chimed again, but this time, it didn't stop.

"Fuck, fuck, fuck. They're not going away," she said in frus-tration.

My dick was not happy at all, but it would have to wait. We got up and went downstairs to open the door.

On our porch stood Mom, Dad, John, Reynolds, Rose, Montana, and Pearson.

Montana yelled, "Welcome to your house!" She bounded inside while all the others came in behind her, carrying all kinds of food with them.

Mom said, "We figured with it being moving day, you wouldn't feel like cooking or going out, so we decided to surprise you with a huge home cooked meal."

"Wow! This is awesome," Sylvie said exuberantly.

"Yeah, it sure is." Not to sound ungrateful, but why in the hell couldn't they have waited just thirty more minutes?

FIFTY-EIGHT
SYLVIE—SIX MONTHS LATER

MILD SPORADIC CONTRACTIONS HAD BEEN HITTING ME throughout the day, but they had no consistency yet. When I spoke to the doctor this morning, she said to come to the hospital when they were five minutes apart and not to wait. I'd been lucky during this pregnancy. Although I was enormous, I had never experienced early labor so no bed rest, thank the Lord. Evan had been working from home a lot and it was Saturday, so he was here.

The babies had kicked me to smithereens and I couldn't wait for them to make their grand entrance into the world.

We'd decided to be surprised on the sex. I was hoping for one of each, but as long as they were healthy, it didn't matter to me.

Both of our dads were still upset we hadn't tied the knot, but I wanted to be un-pregnant when we did. They would have to get over it.

Evan and I were in the kitchen, making dinner, when the big one hit.

"Fuck!" I white-knuckled the countertop.

"A contraction?"

I nodded, but couldn't speak. He set the timer on his watch.

The countdown was on. When it passed, I wiped the sweat off my forehead.

"Fuuuuck. That was a monster."

"You should sit down."

"No. I'm walking this off." I made circles around the kitchen until I felt better. Then went back to help with dinner, although I knew there would be no eating for me. I'm not sure how much time had passed when the next one hit, but I was happy to be standing next to the island again. That countertop was a life saver.

Evan checked his watch and said, "Eight minutes. You should take a shower if you want one before we go."

"You're right."

He stopped dinner and came with me.

"What are you doing?"

"I'm coming with you. I'm your timer."

"Right."

It was a good thing because in the middle of my shower, another one hit. "Fuuuuck." I didn't have my counter to grip.

"You okay in there?"

"Fuuuuuck no. These are killers."

"You're at seven minutes. You'd better hurry."

Shit. At this rate, the babies would be born on their heads between here and the hospital. I hustled out of the shower and dressed.

Evan grabbed my packed bag, and we left. On the way, I had another one.

"Five minutes. You're really progressing fast."

"I know," I puffed between breaths. "Maybe this will be a fast labor."

Evan sped to the hospital and we got checked in quickly. They wanted to know why I waited.

"We didn't." Then Evan explained.

They took me directly to a room and contacted the doctor on call. Then I got super emotional. I wanted my own doctor, but he explained there wouldn't be time for her to get here. Then he gave me even worse news.

"I'm really sorry, but you're too far along to get an epidural."

"What?" I practically yelled.

"You're almost fully dilated and a hundred percent effaced. Your babies will be here soon."

"But it's going to hurt," I whined.

"I'm not going to lie. Yes, it will. But we'll make it as easy as we can."

"Evvvaaaaannnn," I cried out.

"I'm right here, babe. Hold my hand."

Another mighty contraction ripped through me then and I squeezed the hell out of his hand. He gave me his other one to hold too.

"You're doing fantastic, Sylvie. Keep it up and breathe."

I huffed and puffed, like the wolf in the Three Little Pigs.

"I'm never having another baby. Ever."

The doctor examined me and said, "Everything looks perfect."

I had all these things attached to me, including an IV. I hadn't noticed when they'd put it in, because I'd been in so much pain. Nice.

Another contraction hit and I yelled, "I have to push."

"No! Not yet. You can't push."

I kicked a foot out and almost connected with the doctor's head. Oops.

"But I need to," I protested.

"You're not quite there yet. I'll tell you when."

"UGGGGGH," I groaned and squeezed Evan's hands. His eyes were filled with worry, but at this point, I was filled with pain, so I didn't care. And then I started crying. My mom should be here with me.

Suddenly I yelled out like a baby, "I want my mom, Evan."

"Oh, babe, I'm sorry."

The doctor glanced up at us and I cried out, "She died."

"I'm sorry."

"She'll never get to see our little buttons." Then I cried even harder as the contractions continued on.

"Okay, Sylvie, it's time to push. Lean forward and give me everything you've got."

This was so not fun. It was like pushing a watermelon out of your vagina.

"Again, Sylvie."

"It's stuck," I yelled.

"No, everything is fine. Push again."

I pushed with all my might and the doctor said, "The head's crowning."

"Fuck that, I want the whole thing out." I gritted out.

Evan was behind me, and said, "Push some more, babe."

"Shut up, Evan. Why don't you push for a while?"

"Once more, Sylvie."

"UGGGGH." How do some women have so many babies?

"Here it comes. I need one more."

"That's what you said last time."

I pushed again. My head was throbbing.

"The head's out. One more."

The next push wasn't as hard. I guess the baby had a gargantuan head or something. I cried because I didn't want a baby with a humongous head.

"It's a beautiful boy! Congratulations!"

"Did you hear that, Evan? A beautiful boy!" They took the baby off for a minute, and the nurse called out a few things, but I was dazed by the whole ordeal.

I fell back on the bed and they handed the teeny thing to me. And God, he was teeny. How could pushing him out have hurt so much?

Then baby two wanted out. "Ayyy! Oh, no. The second one wants out."

"I was getting ready to tell you. But your body is already prepared so this one will be easier."

He was right. Two hard pushes and button number two popped out. Evan was holding baby number one, and the doctor said, "It's another boy!"

"Evannnnn, we have two boys!" I hollered. The entire hospital probably heard.

Evan chuckled. "Yeah, babe, I heard. Thank you for giving me such beautiful babies."

"But you haven't seen them yet."

The nurse handed me the second one. "Look how little he is."

"Don't worry, he'll grow. They weighed in at five ten and five eleven each, which are great sizes for twins." The doctor seemed pleased. "Now I need to ask if you're in any pain. We can give you something for that.

"I'm not sure. I'm sort of numb right now. And on a babies high."

"We need to deliver the placentas and then a nurse will come in to help with the breastfeeding."

"Someone's going to breastfeed for me?"

Someone laughed. The doctor said, "No, Sylvie, there's a lactation expert who will guide *you* through the process." Talk about feeling like a dumbass.

"Okay." I gazed at the baby I held and watched Evan hold the other one. It was amazing to see these miniature humans we'd created.

THE NEXT MORNING, I was double teaming the babies, as in feeding them, and they were voracious little eaters. I was going to be a pumping station for a while. Evan watched as they clung to me.

"That's going to wear you out."

"Maybe, but I'm going to give it my all, unless they don't thrive. And if that happens, then I'll supplement. I'll have to pump to have extra on hand too."

As I finished, the room was invaded with everyone, wanting to see the mighty mites.

"What are their names?" That was the unanimous question.

"Evan, will you do the honor?" I asked.

He grinned and said, "Number one is John Michael Thomas. And number two is Gregory Mills Thomas."

"We named them after their grandfathers," I proudly stated.

Both of their grandfathers had glistening eyes.

"Well, I'll be," Dad said. "What about that, Greg?"

"It's really something, isn't it?"

"An honor, for sure."

"Dad, do you want to hold your namesake?" I held John Thomas out.

Dad came up to me and took him eagerly. "Hey there, fella. Aren't you a cutie?"

"Greg? What about you?"

"It's been a long time since I held a baby, but I can't wait." I handed Gregory Mills off to him and his expression softened.

"You're going to be a strong little guy. I can see it already. And probably a troublemaker, like your Dad."

Evan chuckled. "Let's hope not. We'll have double trouble on our hands."

Suddenly the door burst open again and a panting Piper rushed in. "Where are they? Where are my nephews?"

"Piper? What are you doing here?" I asked.

"I couldn't miss this. I had to see them. I found a super cheap flight and took one day of classes off with permission from my instructors. I'm good. I have to go back on Tuesday."

She ran up to Dad and cried, "Oh, look at him. He's adorable. What'd you name them?"

Dad proudly said, "This one is John Michael."

Piper covered her mouth.

Greg announced, "And this one here is Gregory Mills."

"Oh, Sylvie, that's brilliant."

"Jeez, you haven't even been there a month and you're already talking like a Brit. Come give me a hug, sis."

She not only hugged me but gave me slobbery kisses on my cheek. She was like a huge puppy. "They couldn't be more perfect, Syll."

"I know. And I couldn't be happier."

Then she whispered in my cheek, "Evan looks like a peacock over there."

"He sort of does, doesn't he?" We both giggled. He was preening over Gregory Michael as his dad commented on how he already looked like his grandfather.

"He will be a very proud dad."

"Oh, yeah. Don't I know. Especially now that we have two boys. I'm going to be terrorized on a daily basis." She gazed at me with sad eyes. "Stop it. You'll find your Prince Charming when you least expect it. I promise."

"I miss you in England. But it's been good so far."

"Great. I'm happy for you."

"Any decisions on a wedding yet?"

"Now that the babies are born, maybe we'll do something. You'll be one of the first to know."

She hugged me again. I really missed her too, but I was reluctant to tell her because I didn't want her to be sad.

The babies were passed around like a bag of chips, which was fine. They had to get used to it because it would be like this for a few days. I was in my happy place and there wasn't anything that could ruin it.

FIFTY-NINE
EVAN

ALL THE PREPARATIONS WERE MADE. SYLVIE HAD AGREED TO marry me, she just didn't have any idea it was going to be this weekend. No one else did either. The entire clan was headed to Vail for Labor Day. We were leaving on Thursday for a long weekend getaway, or so she thought. She was excited to see the place with the aspens in their glorious fall colors. Even Piper was coming. She had finagled the trip, although I'd sent her the plane tickets, which I'd been happy to do.

We arrived at night. The babies did great, and we had many sitters with us. All the other kids stayed home with a variety of nannies, thank God. Baby twins were bad enough. All the supplies we had to bring along was ridiculous, but Sylvie was right. I'd initially wanted the Garretts to buy everything, but she said that was crazy when it was easy to bring it.

Carriers, port-a-cribs, and so on. The list was endless. Thank God the jet was big. We had to drive both of our cars to the airport though. Everyone laughed when we arrived.

Grey said, "Now you feel the pain we went through."

"Same here," Hudson said. "It gets better."

"I wouldn't change a thing," Sylvie said.

I beamed, proud dad that I was.

Now that we were here, my nerves were on edge. I pulled her rings out of the bag I'd placed them in. I hoped she loved them. If she didn't, we'd exchange them. Patty Garrett called the caterers and relayed all the information to me. The food would be set up for four o'clock on Saturday. That meant we had to be ready by then. I would tell everyone we were having a party on the deck that evening. The minister would arrive at four too. I had the marriage license. I had flown out here last week to do that. It took some wheeling and dealing, but I'd managed it.

Everything was set so Friday night we'd go out to dinner, leaving the babies here with the Garretts. They were excited about babysitting.

Dinner was fabulous at one of Vail's best restaurants and while we were there, I told everyone about the party.

"I had this harebrained idea to have a party out on the deck late tomorrow afternoon. The weather is supposed to be ideal and the Garretts helped arrange it. Actually, Patty arranged all the food through a caterer. We can relax and take it easy, but especially enjoy the views of the aspens."

"Ah, that sounds amazing. In the winter, you can't do that. Thanks for thinking about that." Sylvie leaned in and kissed my cheek.

"I thought you'd be pleased."

The following morning, I suggested a hike that day. Everyone was in. Patty packed us an amazing lunch and we all headed out around twelve. It was a three-mile loop, but we went slow and saw some great views, along with some wildlife. Sylvie snapped photos, and so did everyone else. The majestic Gore Range rose before us into the clouds, with its jagged snow-capped peaks, and we found a place to eat lunch around one thirty.

We returned home around two, and everyone went off to their rooms. Sylvie said she wanted to take a nap and a bath.

That would work out perfectly. I woke her up at three and she got into the tub, turning on the jets. Then when she was getting ready for the party, I brought out a dress I'd purchased for her. It wasn't fancy, but it was beautiful, and she would look perfect in it.

It was cream, off one shoulder, and straight, because she said her baby weight wouldn't leave—I said she was crazy because she looked great to me, but I wanted her to love the dress. It also showed off her sexy legs.

"I have a surprise for you." I held up the dress. "I thought you might want to wear this."

"It's gorgeous. Thank you." She put in on and as I suspected, asked, "Do I look too fat in it?"

"You look perfect. You are in no way fat, my love."

"My stomach still pooches out."

"Not to me."

I finished getting dressed and we walked out. The deck looked great. They'd even put flowers out.

"Evan, look. It's beautiful." She wandered around and looked at the flowers.

"I'm so happy you like it. Thank Patty for arranging it."

"Wow. It's really special."

Everyone began arriving and complimented me on how gorgeous it was.

"I love this place," Rose said.

"So do I," Marin agreed.

Patty came and asked for a word. "Sir, the minister has arrived."

"Thank you. Let me get Sylvie."

She tapped my arm and said, "Good luck."

I called out to my lady, and she came over. "Is there a problem?" I certainly hoped not.

"No, but can I have a word?"

"Sure."

We walked into the living area and I began. "Do you recall telling me how you'd love to get married out here sometime after the babies came, when it was warmer, and the views were fabulous?"

"Yeah. Oh, Evan, what have you done?"

I dropped to one knee and asked, "Sylvie West, will you be my wife, my forever person, and the mother of my children?" She gaped as I held out her ring.

"I'm already the mother of your children."

"Right, but I wanted to make it official."

"Holy shit!" She'd just noticed the ring. It was simple. A round diamond, flanked by two smaller ones.

"I wanted something to represent the boys. The one in the middle is for us and the two on either side is for them." I slid it on her finger as she gawked at the thing. "Babe, you can close your mouth now."

"This sucker is huge, Evan."

"It's only two carats."

"Like I said...it's huge!"

I hugged her and asked, "Well?"

"Yes, I'll marry you!"

"Today, as in now, because everything is set to go?"

"Holy crap. You mean someone is here to do it?"

"Yes! Come with me." We went to the kitchen and I introduced her to the minister. After about ten minutes worth of conversation, we were ready.

Patty handed Sylvie a gorgeous bouquet of white roses and I made sure I had the wedding rings. I called Rose and Pearson to the kitchen.

"Would you guys be our witnesses? We're getting married in a few minutes."

Pearson clapped me on the back, and I was positive I'd be wearing his handprint all day.

"It's about damn time, man."

Rose hugged Sylvie and the two were crying. Great. Now if we could pull them apart long enough to get everyone on the deck.

"Dude, I wondered why you had a sports coat on," Pearson said.

"Come on. let's go."

"Wait," Patty said, pinning a rose onto my lapel. "All set now."

The five of us walked outside and I made the announcement.

"I'm more than happy you all could join us for this trip, but especially so because Sylvie and I have decided to get married."

Both the dads were stunned. Mom was too. Everyone else clapped. The minister walked to the rail of the deck, and we followed.

He performed a simple ceremony. When it came time to exchange vows and rings, I pulled out Sylvie's, and her brows shot up. She was still shocked over the diamond ring I'd given her, but her wedding band was an eternity ring of diamonds.

As I slipped it on, I said, "This ring represents eternity. For the present, and the future. You're my forever love."

Her cheeks glistened with tears. She took the ring I handed to her and said the same words. I didn't expect any others. I'd already surprised her enough.

"You may kiss the bride."

I'd been waiting a long time to hear those words and I took advantage of them.

Soon, the clapping began, and we faced our guests. Rose handed Sylvie her bouquet back and she held it in the air and let out the biggest, "WHOOP!"

The dads came up to us then. John picked Sylvie up and twirled her around while my dad said, "Son, you make a father proud."

"Dad, I have a secret to share. I would've married her long ago, but she wanted to wait... to be sure we were truly meant for each other."

"Why didn't you tell me that?"

"It didn't matter. I knew it and that's all I cared about."

"I'm glad you found your other half. Life is so much better that way."

"Don't I know."

Dad went to find Mom, and Sylvie and I hugged and kissed all the family members here. Then it was time to celebrate. I could tell something was up though, so I asked, "What is it?"

"I wish Mom had been here."

"I'm pretty sure she was. I haven't seen your dad smile so much other than the day our kids were born."

"He told me that he was glad I found my other half in you."

"Seriously?"

"Yeah."

"That's the exact thing my dad told me."

"I guess we have great dads then."

"I know I have a great wife."

"And I have a great husband."

THE CELEBRATION WORE on while Sylvie and I watched the sun set over the mountains. There was a chill in the air, so she'd put on a sweater to keep warm.

"I couldn't imagine this if I hadn't seen it myself. This is really the perfect wedding spot. And thank you for having a photographer here."

"We couldn't possibly get married without one, could we?"

"Memories are the best. When we're old and gray one day, we'll show the kids how sexy their dad looked when we tied the knot."

"Not to mention they have the most beautiful mother in the world."

"I love you, my sweet talking husband."

"My words are the truth."

We snuck away from the reception as soon as it got dark and had our own party in our room. We celebrated the way the naughty duke would. I bought all sorts of wedding night toys for my bride. She loved every one of them, but kept reminding me it was the raunchy duke, not the naughty one. I reminded her she had a horny husband now so she could forget about that duke, whatever he was. I was going to start pulling all kinds of surprises on her.

She got a wicked gleam in her eye and it was game on. If she thought one indecent night was bad, wait until this one was over. She may even get that clit flogging after all.

EPILOGUE
PIPER

THE WHOLE CREW LEFT FOR THE AIRPORT TO GET ME THERE on time for my flight from Vail to Denver. My connection to London was leaving from there. Evan had been kind enough to fly me first class, so I'd have a bed on the way.

We said our goodbyes, but it was hard leaving again. Those cute little babies would look entirely different the next time I saw them.

I waved and went to check in. The flight to Denver was fine, other than I cried all the way. When I got to my connecting flight, I was told there was a problem. The plane had mechanical issues and they were rescheduling all passengers. Everyone was scrambling to get a seat. I was lucky enough to get re-ticketed on another flight, although it was in coach. That was my only option. At least I'd get back to London when I was supposed to.

I went to the next gate and waited to board. As luck would have it, I was in the very back of the plane, by the bathrooms and galley. So much for sleeping. Then I started crying again as I thought of everyone on Evan's fancy jet, on their way back to New York. I had the aisle seat, and was wiping my watering eyes, when this raspy voice said, "Scusami." He pointed to the seat right next to me. I was sure he spoke in either Italian or Portuguese, because it wasn't Spanish.

I stood so he could get to his seat and even then, I had to look up. He was tall, with blond to light brown hair, amazing hazel eyes, and wore glasses. There was something about men in glasses that I had always found hot. Sexiness oozed out of him. Even I noticed it in my depressed state of mind. I checked to see if he had a wedding ring on. He wore several rings, but I didn't know if they were the kind that indicated wedded bliss. I dropped my gaze down to his ass because it was right in front of me now, as he slid into his seat, and it was delicious. I'd been so focused on it, it wasn't until I heard him clear his throat that I snapped out of my ass-trance and sat down.

Sniffing back my tears, his gaze burned through me. I'm sure he was thinking his luck was rotten because he'd gotten stuck next to an emotional wreck of a woman.

Suddenly, some tissues appeared next to my hand. Turning my head, I noticed he was smiling.

"Thank you." I wiped my eyes, which I was sure looked like hell. My mascara must've been perched on my chin by now.

"You're welcome. I hope everything is okay?"

"I'm only being foolish," I answered, sucking back more tears. "I left my family behind. My sister just got married and has infant twins. My mother recently died, I'm on my way back to the U.K., and I was supposed to be on a different plane in first class, but it had mechanical problems, so here I am, crying my eyes out next to you. I'm sorry." I just told this poor guy my life story. What the hell was wrong with me?

"You too? I was supposed to be on that flight in first class. This was the only option, unless I wanted to wait two days, and I have to get back to the U.K. as well."

His beautiful accent made me smile.

"I guess we're in this together then."

"I'm sorry about your mother. I lost mine at a very early age."

I grabbed his hand, which surprised him, I think. "Oh no!

That must've been horrible. I can't imagine. I'm twenty-five, and it's killing me. Mine passed in January and I keep thinking it'll get better, but I find myself wanting to call or text her all the time, until I remember she's gone. I don't know how a young child could manage. I am so sorry for you."

"Yes, it was a terrible time for my father and me. He was very, very sad. I remember he cried very much, and I went to stay with my grandparents for a time. I didn't understand why my mother didn't come to get me. Children can't understand those things."

As he told me his story, I cried for the broken child he must've been.

"Ah, I did not mean to make you cry. It was a long time ago, and as you can see, my old heart has mended."

"I don't believe you. That's something you never get over. You only learn to cope with it."

"Perhaps you are correct. My father eventually stopped crying and I went back home. We grew close again and time passed."

"Did he ever remarry?"

"Sadly, no. He is still a single man, but a very busy one. I believe he is happy in his own way."

The flight attendant came through to check we were buckled up and they did the safety video. Soon after, we took off. Maybe with this handsome man next to me, the flight wouldn't be so bad after all.

When they announced we could use all devices, he pulled out a computer and began typing away. About a half hour later, he shut it down.

"Were you in Denver on business?"

"Yes, and it was my first time there," he said. "I would very much like to go back. And you were there as well?"

"No, my brother-in-law has a house in Vail. That's where we were."

"Do you ski?" he asked.

"Yes, do you?"

"Yes, I love to ski. I hear Vail is a wonderful place."

"It is. If you ever get the chance, you should go. By the way, I'm Piper."

He laughed. "Hello, Piper. I am Alessandro. I am very pleased to meet you." We shook hands and I didn't want to let his go. It was warm and *comforting*.

"Same here. And I take it you're Italian?"

"Yes. How could you tell?" he asked with a chuckle.

"Your British accent gave you away." We both laughed this time.

I added, "You speak English very beautifully."

"Thank you, so do you." I dipped my head as I chuckled.

We checked the movies and found we shared the same interests. We talked about books and discovered we both loved to read. He loved English and Italian literature and I shared with him my love for English literature too. We discussed how he both loved hiking and biking. I told him a funny story about how I was mountain biking once and crashed into a ravine. He didn't find it funny. In fact, he was concerned I could've been injured.

"That part was true. The funny part was when I showed up at work the next morning. I had to teach, and my face looked like I'd gone ten rounds with a prizefighter. My principal wanted to know who beat me up. She thought I'd gotten mugged."

"What did you look like?"

"I had a black eye and one entire side of my face was scraped. It was ugly. The students thought I was cool, though."

"You should be careful mountain biking."

"I am. That was a freak accident."

Sometime during the flight, I fell asleep. When I woke up, my head was on his shoulder and my arm was hugging him. Shit, what the hell.

I jerked straight up in my seat and he only chuckled. "I'm sorry. I didn't mean to do that."

"You were sleeping very soundly. I didn't mind a bit."

It was very awkward for me, because he stared at me as though he wanted something, something more. Or was that my imagination? And what more could he have. This flight would be over soon and then we'd go our separate ways. What good would it do? I didn't want to get involved with someone for a one and done. What the hell was I saying? A one and done? No way would I become a member of the mile high club with someone I just met.

How could I have known that after two vodka drinks, I'd be eating my words. It didn't happen in the bathroom. It happened in our seats. The lights were out, there was no one on either side of us, we had blankets covering us. His hand reached over to me, unzipped my pants as he watched me closely. His expert fingers soon had me heated and I worked his long thick cock as we each came as silently as possible. Technically, we hadn't *done* it, so I guess I wasn't truly a member, but still, I'd let this stranger bring me to a glorious orgasm as I bit my lips in ecstasy.

When he kissed me afterward and said, "Piper, you are a most sexy woman. I'd love to have you completely," I wanted to climb aboard that train and ride it forever.

Unfortunately, the flight landed too soon, and we walked to baggage claim. My heart was heavy once again as the thought of my lonely apartment waited for me.

We waited in line for our taxis, and when it was my turn, he kissed my hand and bid me farewell. I was disappointed he didn't ask for my number, but he did say he would only be here for six months. And wasn't that my plan as well?

THE FOLLOWING DAY, I dragged myself to class, still suffering from jet lag. I took my usual front row seat, but this time it would force me to stay awake. Only that wouldn't be necessary because in walked Alessandro. He headed straight for the podium, and said, "Good morning everyone. My name is

Professor Balotelli and I will be your visiting instructor for the next six months. His eyes scanned the room until they landed on me. They widened, and then his mouth curved up, as I broke into a sweat and automatically clenched my thighs. This was going to be an impossible six months.

The End

To be continued in ...

One Shameless Night

To sign up for a LIVE alert of **One Shameless Night**, click here: http://bit.ly/OSLALERT

If you enjoyed One Indecent Night, I would forever be grateful if you would leave a review.

Haven't read the other **West Brothers Novels** yet?

Find out more about Grey and Marin in **From Ashes to Flames** here: http://smarturl.it/FAtoF

She was the nanny. He was the boss. They both knew things would end badly.

Five minutes after walking through the door, I hated the sexy Greydon West.

I wondered why he'd ever had kids in the first place.

The broody, single father of two didn't know the meaning of the word fun.

The only things my regimented, hot-tempered boss seemed to care about we're his ridiculous spreadsheets.

But for some reason, his prickly, stiff-mannered disposition made me curious about what was hidden beneath that exterior.

Then, one day I stumbled upon the key that unlocked the mystery of Dr. West.

That was when the sexy dreams began ... the same ones that awakened me every night.

And that kiss we shared ... biggest mistake ever.

I knew nothing good would result from it.

But I couldn't seem to stay away because I was already in too deep.

I should've listened to those alarms in my head, but I ignored them.

Which was why I found my heart about to erupt in flames and there wasn't a damn thing I could do about it.

"A deliciously sexy slow-burn romance. I absolutely loved this book!!" Tia Louise, USA Today Bestselling Author

IN **FROM ICE To Flames** you can read about Hudson and Milly: http://smarturl.it/FITF

One Rule: No More Men.

Two years ago I walked away from a marriage I thought would last forever and all I got from it was Dick ...

And I don't mean the one between my stupid ex's legs.

I'm talking about the one hundred fifty pound furry dog said ex dropped off at my doorstep.

But I'd take Dick over any man, any day.

So why did I resemble my dog, panting and drooling, whenever I ran into Hudson West, my sexy new neighbor?

True, the gorgeous veterinarian was hotter than sin.

And my new roommate only made it impossible for me to avoid conversation with a man I didn't need.

Until tragedy struck and some jerk decided to run Dick down.

It was *hotter than sin* Hudson who came to his rescue.

Then it became impossible to ignore him.

It was only supposed to be a fling, a quickie, a one and done.

We both had reasons to keep it that way ... my one rule and his five-year-old son.

Except things didn't quite work out that way.

One turned into two, then three, annnnd you get the picture.

Before we knew it, he gave me a lot more than puppies and fairy tales.

And that stupid rule?

I should've stuck to it because now more than my heart was at risk.

This is a full-length, stand alone, single dad, contemporary romance.

In **FROM SMOKE TO FLAMES**, you can read about Pearson and Rose: https://smarturl.it/FSTF

"This story **engrossed me** from page one. I was **rooting for Pearson** long before I should have because he's so **complicatedly endearing.**" Jana Aston, NYT Bestselling Author

To put it bluntly, **Rose Wilson's** life sucks.

When she finally gets the courage to divorce her abusive husband, she never imagines his prick of an attorney could be so cold-hearted.

Needless to say, she loses everything, including her precious daughter.

Imagine her shock when said attorney ends up as one of her new patients at the substance abuse center where she works.

Rage sinks its claws into her as she throws his chart against the wall.

How can she remain an empathetic counselor to her worst enemy, bad boy **Pearson West**, who helped destroy her life?

Turns out, the cocky bastard, with his startling blue-gray eyes, way too sexy mouth, and tight jeans, soon has her lusting after him.

Can Rose rise above her hatred—and lust—and maintain her professionalism to help him?

Or will they both lose even more than they already have?

From Smoke To Flames (A West Brothers Novel, #3) features surprising plot twists, suspense, and a mix of lovable characters that will keep you turning the pages. If you like raw emotion, mystery, with a bit of humor, then start this series today.

FOLLOW ME

If you would like to hear more about what's going on in my world, please subscribe to my mailing list on my website at
http://bit.ly/AMNLWP
You can also join my private group—Hargrove's Hangout— on Facebook if you're up to some crazy shenanigans!
Please stalk me. I'll love you forever if you do. Seriously.

www.amhargrove.com
Twitter @amhargrove1
www.facebook.com/amhargroveauthor
www.facebook.com/anne.m.hargrove
www.goodreads.com/amhargrove1
Instagram: amhargroveauthor
Pinterest: amhargrove1
annie@amhargrove.com

For Other Books by A.M. Hargrove visit www.amhargrove.com

The West Sisters Novels:
One Indecent Night
One Shameless Night (TBD)

One Blissful Night (TBD)

The West Brothers Novels:
From Ashes to Flames
From Ice to Flames
From Smoke to Flames

For The Love of English
For The Love of My Sexy Geek (The Vault)
I'll Be Waiting (The Vault)

The Men of Crestview:
A Special Obsession
Chasing Vivi
Craving Midnight

Cruel and Beautiful
A Mess of a Man
One Wrong Choice
A Beautiful Sin

The Wilde Players Dirty Romance Series:
Sidelined
Fastball
Hooked

Worth Every Risk

The Edge Series:
Edge of Disaster
Shattered Edge
Kissing Fire

The Tragic Duet:
Tragically Flawed, Tragic 1

Tragic Desires, Tragic 2

The Hart Brothers Series:
Freeing Her, Book 1
Freeing Him, Book 2
Kestrel, Book 3
The Fall and Rise of Kade Hart

Sabin, A Seven Novel

The Guardians of Vesturon Series

ACKNOWLEDGMENTS

A<small>FTER</small> T<small>HE</small> W<small>EST</small> B<small>ROTHERS</small>, I <small>NEVER THOUGHT</small> I'<small>D DO A</small> spin-off series, but when Sylvie entered the picture, her voice spoke to me in volumes. Then the story unraveled in my head, and even though the beginning was much like many others where the couple wakes up in bed and one of them can't remember a single thing, this one unwinded in a completely different fashion. I hope you enjoyed their twist and especially how Evan turned out to be such an amazing shoulder for Sylvie to lean on. I just love these two!

And now dear readers, thank you so much for reading! You are the reason why all my books exists and why I get up in the morning and do what I love so much. My head explodes with so many story lines, I wish I could write them all faster.

There are many people who make my job as an author much richer but my book wifey, Terri E. Laine, and my bestie, Amy Jennings make every day, whether it's a good one or bad one, even better. Thank you my golden girls, and travel buddies. I love you to Europe and back! I'd say the moon but we haven't been there ... YET!

Thank you Angel Justice. You make me laugh so hard sometimes I can't stand it! Harloe Rae—we are seriously going to finally meet! Your kindness and generosity are a blessing. I adore you and thank you for everything you do! Nelle L'Amour, you are such a doll! I would be missing out on so much had I not met you in London. Thank you for your huge heart!

Thank you Candi Kane! Your messages kill me and so do your posts. But your tireless work amazes me. You rock, my friend!

Diane Plourde—thank you for being at my right hand whenever I need you. I don't know how you manage everything but you and your blog team are amazing!

Thank you, Maria, for your amazing cover. Oh, and our convos on FB. I seriously LMAO and I have to blame you sometimes for being behind on my books! #FloatieMan

Thank you, Nasha Lama, for handling my graphics and fixing what I break on my website. You are a genius. Hurry up and find a job, will you? JK!

Thank you, Ellie, Pet, and Rosa for the edits. You guys are the best on all my dumb errors.

And thank you, Hellions at Hargrove's Hangout! I love you guys—You are all awesome.

Thank you to all the bloggers and readers who promoted this book! I adore you all! I hope to God I haven't missed anyone and I'm sure I have. I apologize for the error if did.

ABOUT THE AUTHOR

ONE DAY, ON HER WAY HOME FROM WORK AS A SALES manager, USA Today bestselling author, A. M. Hargrove, realized her life was on fast forward and if she didn't do something soon, it would be too late to write that work of fiction she had been dreaming of her whole life. So she made a quick decision to quit her job and reinvented herself as a Naughty and Nice Romance Author.

Annie fancies herself all of the following: Reader, Writer, Dark Chocolate Lover, Ice Cream Worshipper, Coffee Drinker (swears the coffee, chocolate, and ice cream should be added as part of the USDA food groups), Lover of Grey Goose (and an extra dirty martini), #WalterThePuppy Lover, and if you're ever around her for more than five minutes, you'll find out she's a non-stop talker. Other than loving writing about romance, she loves hanging out with her family and binge watching TV series with her husband. You can find out more about her books www.amhargrove.com.

To keep up to date with my new releases subscribe to my newsletter here: http://bit.ly/AMNLWP